Rob Kinmonth

About the Author

CHRISTOPHER BRAM is the author of eight novels, including *Father of Frankenstein*, which became the Academy Award–winning movie *Gods and Monsters*, and *The Notorious Dr. August: His Real Life and Crimes*. He also writes book reviews, movie reviews, and screenplays. He was a 2001 Guggenheim Fellow and received the 2003 Bill Whitehead Lifetime Achievement Award. He lives in New York City.

LIVES OF THE CIRCUS ANIMALS

A Novel

CHRISTOPHER BRAM

Perennial

An Imprint of HarperCollins*Publishers*

Grateful acknowledgment is made for permission to reprint the following:

"Cotton Blossom," words and music by Jerome Kern, Oscar Hammerstein II, copyright © 1927 Universal-Polygram Int. Publ. Inc. on behalf of T. B. Harms Co. (ASCAP). International copyright secured. All rights reserved.

"Some Other Time," words and music by Leonard Bernstein, Betty Comden, Adolph Green, copyright © 1944. International copyright secured. All rights reserved.

"The Circus Animals' Desertion" reprinted with the permission of Scribner, an imprint of Simon & Schuster Adult Publishing Group, from *The Collected Works of W. B. Yeats, Volume 1: The Poems, Revised,* edited by Richard J. Finneran. Copyright © 1940 by Georgie Yeats; copyright © renewed 1968 by Bertha Georgie Yeats, Michael Butler Yeats, and Anne Yeats.

A hardcover edition of this book was published in 2003 by William Morrow, an imprint of HarperCollins Publishers.

HarperCollins books may be purchased for educational, business, or sales promotional use. For information please write: Special Markets Department, HarperCollins Publishers Inc., 10 East 53rd Street, New York, NY 10022.

FIRST PERENNIAL EDITION PUBLISHED 2004.

Designed by Renato Stanisic

The Library of Congress has catalogued the hardcover edition as follows:
Bram, Christopher.
Lives of the circus animals: a novel / Christopher Bram.—1st ed.
p. cm.
ISBN 0-06-054253-5
1. New York (N.Y.)—Fiction. 2. Friendship—Fiction. 3. Theater—Fiction.
I. Title.
PS3552.R2817L58 2003
813'.54—dc21 2002192195

ISBN 0-06-054254-3 (pbk.)

13 14 ❖/RRD 10 9 8 7 6 5 4 3

For all my friends who have worked
in and around the theater

The important point is not to feel a lot, but to feel accurately.

—BEING AN ACTOR

1

"You want strangers to love you?"

There was another long pause. "No," he said. "I just don't want them to hate me."

"And who do you think hates you, Kenneth?"

"Oh, everyone."

She laughed, much to his surprise. Her laughter was thin and professional, but not unfriendly.

"I'm joking, of course. Most people don't know me from the man in the moon. And it's not real hate. Not really. Even from people who *do* know me. It's fun hate. Faux hate. I'm the man-they-love-to-hate." He sighed. "Oh, all right. Yes. It does get to me. Sometimes."

"Of course," said Dr. Chin. "We'd all rather be loved."

She sat in an armchair, a mild, round-faced woman in a ruffled blouse, under a Georgia O'Keeffe painting of a skull in a desert.

Kenneth Prager sat on the sofa—the far end of the sofa—tall and lean in a charcoal gray suit. This was his first time in therapy, his second session. Forty-four years old, he had managed to avoid this rite of passage until now. He was not enjoying it. Not only did Chin expect him to do most of the talking, but she also refused to let him have the last word. His livelihood was built on having the last word.

He took a deep breath, smiled, and said, "They call me the Buzzard of Off-Broadway."

This time she didn't laugh but looked concerned, even hurt, for his sake. "And how does that make you feel?"

"Oh, I was flattered. At first. All right, somewhat miffed. A predecessor was called the Butcher of Broadway, so it's old material. When you get mocked, you want the jokes to be more original."

She wrote something on her notepad. He feared his flippancy revealed more than he knew.

"But that's not the cause of my depression," he said. "If it *is* depression. I don't feel guilty about my work. My caring what people think is just a symptom, not a cause."

Therapy was his wife's idea. Gretchen had grown tired of his glum spirits, his sour sorrow. He couldn't understand his unhappiness either. His life could not be better. He had a loving wife, a pretty daughter, a good job, even a dash of fame. He was only second critic at the *Times,* but strangers recognized his name if not his face. He should be happy. But he wasn't. This failure of happiness worried him. If the achievement of so much in life could not make one happy, then why bother living?

"I love my work," he insisted. "I've always loved theater. The immediacy of it. Real human presences. I enjoyed reviewing movies well enough, which I did for three years. But I was only third-stringer there and saw too much trash: horror-slasher-teen pics and such. So I was overjoyed when they moved me to drama. Where I'd always wanted to be. The unease didn't set in until after New Year's. I thought it'd pass, or I'd get used to the strangeness, but the strangeness only got stranger. Back in March, Bickle, the first reviewer, went into the hospital for heart surgery. So a few plums fell into my lap, including the big new Disney bomb, *Pollyanna.* Everyone panned it, not just me. We were all surprised when Disney pulled the plug. Nevertheless, I was the one who got congratulated for killing the beast. Which felt odd. Then there was a new play by the author of *Venus in Furs.* Everyone wanted it to be good. I know I did. But it wasn't. It was called *Chaos Theory* and was about madness and mathematics. I think it was really about AIDS—the author is gay—which I said in my review. But it was just so self-indulgent and preachy. It closed too. This time I got hate mail. Floods of it. From people calling me callous and homophobic. And I'm *not* homophobic. I'm in theater, for pete's sake. Well, not *in* it, but *of* it."

Chin was looking down at her notepad, without writing. Her pencil quivered. Had she read his review? Did she adore the play? She thought he *was* homophobic?

"So—" He hurried back to the real subject. "I was relieved when Bick returned and I was number two again. It took the pressure off.

But nothing's felt the same since. The strangeness returned. It felt worse than ever. Nothing has any savor anymore. Everything feels gray. I'm not sure what I want anymore."

She flipped through her notes, as if she'd lost her place. "You want to be number one again," she said idly, as if it were too obvious to mention.

He shifted uncomfortably on the sofa. "Yes, no, yes," he replied. "I should want Bick's job, shouldn't I?"

"You don't?"

"There's talk of retiring him. They need a replacement, which is why they moved me over to drama. As a test. And I wanted the job. Once. But I don't anymore. Only—I don't *not* want it either. I'm not sure *what* I want anymore."

She studied him with her round, smooth, full face. Kenneth couldn't tell if her stillness masked sympathy or disapproval. She seemed so cheerfully impersonal. In a less politically aware age, he could've thought of her as an inscrutable motherly Buddha.

"Like I said," she offered. "You want people to love you."

"Isn't that a silly thing for grown-ups to want? Especially someone in my line of work."

She shrugged—"silly" was irrelevant here. "Maybe if you praised more and criticized less?" she proposed. "Would you feel better about yourself then?"

He stared at her. "But I'm a critic. I'm paid to criticize."

"Aren't you also paid to praise?"

"Yes, but—" He shook his head. "I always feel what I say. And I say what I feel. I have nothing but my opinions to go on. If I'm untrue to those, I'm lost."

"So you let pride stand in the way of happiness?"

She was faintly smiling. Was she pulling his leg?

"Only pride in a job well done," he declared. "Otherwise I'm a hack. And I'm just as anxious praising as when I criticize. Because I can make success as well as failure. Because of where I work."

"The *Times*," she said.

"Yes. The *Times*." Had she forgotten? "That's what this love and hate are really about. People think I have all this power. But I don't feel powerful. I feel power*less*. I mean, I'm just another journalist on deadline.

I know, I know. It's not me that people hate. It's the *Times*. The *Times* has all the power. But people mistake me for the *Times*."

She gazed into him, calm and deep, as if hearing the running water of thought in his brain.

He followed his thoughts backward, upstream a few yards. "Are you saying that people *do* hate me, Dr. Chin?"

"Such a strong word, *hate*. I wonder why you keep using it. Do you hate them?"

"No. I don't hate anyone."

"There seemed to be an enormous amount of—not hate, but dislike in your remarks this morning about that Neil Simon play."

Kenneth froze.

"A harmless comedy," Chin continued in her gentlest tone. "People want to laugh. You seemed angry at them for enjoying a joke that you didn't get. I sensed a lot of rage in your word choices."

There was no safe haven in this city of newspaper readers, no refuge from his own prose. "That wasn't rage," he said. "That was wit. I was being funny. I want people to laugh. I just want them to laugh at fresh jokes, not stale TV one-liners. Do we really need to discuss a smart-ass review of an unnecessary revival of *Star-Spangled Girl*?"

"*You* call it smart-ass. Another interesting word choice. I'm no crude Freudian, Kenneth, but what does a child do with his ass?" Chin laughed, disowning the idea even as she delivered it. "You expressed your rage by *shitting*"—she laughed harder to get the word out—"on an audience who enjoyed a joke you didn't get. And maybe on a playwright who is more famous than you—or I—will ever be."

"Can't we talk about my dreams?" he said. "I've had some very interesting dreams this week."

"These questions disturb you? The critic hates to be criticized?" She laughed again, more amiably this time. "I'm just tossing out ideas, seeing what works as we get to know each other. But your reviews can be as revealing as dreams, Kenneth. They are dreams you dream with words. There was one phrase in particular I found revealing . . ."

Kenneth had trusted Chin when she was silent. As she talked more about his review, he lost all faith in her. He felt no rage toward Neil Simon or Simon's audience. Maybe he wanted to be loved, sure, but only by people who loved what he loved, which was good theater. Her suggestion that he be nicer in print proved that she didn't have a clue. Chin had been recommended as a therapist experienced in handling artists, which should have warned him. Any artist who'd spill his unhappiness to a shrink instead of pouring it back into his work was not someone to win Kenneth's respect.

He patiently heard her out. Finally, he took a deep breath and said, "I never took you for a Neil Simon fan, Dr. Chin."

"Oh I'm not. I don't know his work, only his reputation. I rarely get to the theater. In fact, I try to avoid it."

"You don't like theater?"

"My own little quirk," Chin admitted with a chuckle. "I feel embarrassed watching actors. All standing up there pretending to be people they aren't. Actors in movies or TV don't bother me. But seeing them live onstage makes me very anxious."

Kenneth couldn't believe his ears. She treated it as a comic tic, a matter of no importance. Physician, heal thyself, he thought. She's crazier than I am.

"But that's neither here nor there," she said and began to discuss the uses of self-forgiveness.

Good-bye, Dr. Chin, thought Kenneth. He needed to find another shrink. Her theater phobia was the last straw. Besides, she had no coherent program, no unified theory of psychology. She said so herself: she just tossed out ideas, seeing which ones stuck. And she laughed too much. It was impossible to take her seriously.

"You disagree?" she suddenly asked. "You think I'm talking through my hat?"

"No, not at all. I'm thinking it over," he claimed. "Digesting that idea"—even though he had no notion what the idea was.

He was not yet ready to tell Chin that they were over. He could do it on Monday, by mail. Kenneth Prager always expressed himself more forcefully on the page than he did in person.

2

He stepped outside to West Tenth Street, happy to return to the real world. Chin's office was in a burrow of therapists' offices on the ground floor of an old West Village town house. It was early evening, the middle of May. Sunlight glowed in the soft green trees and rust-red brickwork. Kenneth walked this street regularly—he and his family lived just a few blocks over on Charles Street—but he felt strange here today, oddly undressed after his talk with Chin, as if he were walking down the sidewalk in nothing but a bathrobe.

He hurried toward Sixth Avenue, passing one man in a suit, then another, relieved that he wasn't the only corporate type out in the open. Kenneth often regretted that they lived in the Village, where one occasionally saw actors—on the street, at the post office, in the supermarket. None ever spoke to him in these public places, yet they noticed him, as he noticed them, killer and prey off duty, cheetah and gazelle between meals.

But he did not feel guilty. No. He did not judge people, only their work. And he did not want people to *love* him, only that they respect *his* work. He wanted good theater, better plays, better audiences. He was an idealist—that's what he should have told Chin. The world fell short of his ideals, suffocated by the age's hunger for success at any cost. No wonder he was depressed.

He crossed Sixth Avenue in the shadow of the Jefferson Market Library, an enormous brick cuckoo clock with an absurd tower, and headed uptown, past the Soviet antique store and the good Chinese restaurant. He felt much too tall and conspicuous here—the sidewalk was very crowded. He turned left at the next corner, where a public school stood, P.S. 41, a big white box with a grid of windows and green panels in front, like an ugly office building from the 1950s. The first-story windows, however, were full of cheerful crayon pictures of stick-figure families. Live parents stood on the sidewalk under the sycamore trees, chatting to one another or on cell phones, a few sucking down cigarettes, one of the smokers Gretchen.

She'd come straight from the law office and wore her blue suit and plump running shoes. Kenneth was surprised by how glad he was to see her, his haven, his friend, his wife. He wanted to take her hand, but didn't. They pecked each other hello. See, I'm not such a bad guy, he told himself.

She ground out her cigarette. "You're stooping, dear."

Gretchen had noticed it first, how he often slouched now when he walked alone, as if to make himself less visible.

"So how did it go?" she asked. "Have a good session?"

"My last session," he declared. "The woman has no authority. No solid ideas. She talks like she just makes it up as she goes along."

"Which sounds reasonable to me."

"And she hates theater. Can you imagine? She's not someone who'll ever understand me."

Gretchen frowned. "Kenneth, you've barely started. There's always a period of adjustment. And it might be good for you to talk to some-one with a different religion."

Of course she'd say that, Gretchen, who hadn't accompanied him to a play in ages. He could not help taking it personally. Gretchen was tired of theater, tired of the *Times,* tired of him.

"Give her a month. Please? Just two more visits," she pleaded.

"Am I that difficult to live with?"

She didn't even hesitate. "Yes." She pointed at the doors and the people going in. "Speaking of religion, shall we join the congrega-tion?"

"This has nothing to do with that," he insisted. "Nothing at all."

"I'm glad to hear it. So let's go inside."

Tonight was the opening night of P.S. 41's seventh-grade produc-tion of *Show Boat.* Their daughter, Rosalind, was in the chorus.

Kenneth entered the school, and it was like stepping into child-hood, not his daughter's but his own. The front hall was all tiles and painted cinder block like the front hall of Birdville Elementary back in

Pittsburgh, with a harsh, timeless stink of pencil shavings and sour milk. Kenneth had hated being a child.

The auditorium was full of ancient echoes and bolted rows of old plywood seats without cushions. He and Gretchen took two seats on the aisle. He opened his program.

"*Show Boat,*" he murmured. "Not my idea of children's theater."

"Nobody asked you," grumbled Gretchen.

"You're right. Absolutely. I'll shut up."

No, this isn't about theater. It's about being a good parent, a loving father, a warm human being.

The rows slowly filled with other parents, a motley mix of ages, races, clothes, and classes. Nobody noticed Kenneth. They probably didn't know who the Buzzard was here. Or care. They'd come to watch their kids play make-believe.

There was no orchestra in the pit, only a piano, and not much pit either. The stage was small, with a shallow apron and shabby red curtain. A man popped out of the wings, presumably the director, a stocky fellow of indeterminate age and sexuality. His face was young, but he had a receding hairline. His plaid shirt was unbuttoned, the tail out, the sleeves rolled up. He came down to the pit and spoke to the piano player, a short, wiry, elderly black woman with a pearl necklace and busily articulate hands.

Finally, the principal got up onstage, a jolly lesbian in a tuxedo. Kenneth loved their neighborhood for such anomalies. See, he told himself, I'm not homophobic. She thanked the audience for coming, thanked the kids and their directors, Harriet Anderson and Frank Earp, for putting together such a fine show. Also the parents who raised money with bake sales. "Now sit back and enjoy: *Show Boat.*"

It was still light outside; no curtains hung over the high windows. Ms. Anderson clattered fiercely through the overture—her instrument needed tuning, but she didn't seem to notice. Then a flock of kids in black jeans and black T-shirts, Rosalind among them, shuffled out onstage with lowered gazes and nervous smiles.

Kenneth's heart swelled to see his daughter up there, blood of his blood, flesh of his flesh. She was taller than the others, a happy, long-legged colt, her panicky grin bound in braces. Lately she'd seemed distant. Or maybe Kenneth had less love for everyone these days—Gretchen too. But his love for his daughter gushed instantly when he saw her onstage.

Then the children burst into song:

Niggers all work on the Mississippi.
Niggers all work while the white folks play.

Kenneth was startled that they used the original Hammerstein lyric. The entire audience, in fact, lurched backward. The word stung even in a multicultural context—the chorus included white and Asian as well as black faces. But the kids looked tickled to be able to sing out a word that none were allowed to use at home.

The show then stumbled into the familiar songs and scenes, everything stripped to essentials. The text was cut, there was no scenery, the costumes were minimal. The entire cast was dressed in black, with only hats and coats to indicate their characters, prop costumes that were too big for the performers. They looked like kids who'd been rummaging in an attic. Kenneth assumed it was just a happy accident, giving the production a sweet innocence, a primitive charm. It was such a relief to see theater for theater's sake again, the joyful ritual of it, the raw pleasure.

Rosalind reappeared with a pack of girls carrying parasols for "Life Upon the Wicked Stage," sung by a tiny Hispanic girl. The father in Kenneth was indignant that Rosalind didn't get the solo, even as the *Times* critic recognized that her voice wasn't strong enough.

But none of the children were great singers, except for the Joe— "Old Man River" had a new kind of hurt when sung in a choirboy alto. No, it wasn't accidental. Someone involved in the production knew exactly what they were doing. At twelve and thirteen, the girls were already girls but the boys still had an unbaked childish androgyny, which gave a fresh twist to the book's multiple story lines of tough women suffering for their weakling men.

A pretty young mother sat directly behind Kenneth. He first noticed her laugh, a loud, sharp squeal over the smarter bits of business. Later, when he turned to Gretchen, he noticed out of the corner of his eye the woman scowling at him. He assumed she was a mother. Her auburn hair was cut lesbian short, but so many mothers nowadays had a butch, practical look.

Whoever she was, during the applause after "Can't Help Loving That Man of Mine" she suddenly leaned forward to whisper, in a plummy put-on accent, "When you write about this one day, and you will, be kind." And she sat back, happily cackling to herself.

3

Backstage in the wings, Frank Earp was all eyes and ears during the first act, as if the show were a mirage that would vanish if he even blinked. His entire body was engaged, a kinetic sympathy of muscles and nerves. When their Ravenal, as dumb and handsome as a Ravenal should be, jumped ahead several pages, he and Carmen, his student assistant—she stood at Frank's side with the open prompt book—hissed and whispered him back to his cue. The Magnolia was a pro, however, and didn't even flinch. Then Tony, their Joe, sang his reprise of "Old Man River" as sweetly as always. Frank quickly pulled the curtain closed, and the first act ended.

Instantly, Magnolia, Joe, and the rest turned back into children. They all went a little crazy, giggling and jumping around, scuffing up the dust backstage and spilling out into the hall.

"Guys!" cried Frank. "Chill! You did great, but we got one more act." He refused to play dictator-schoolteacher. That was Mrs. Anderson's job. She was a music teacher, while Frank wasn't any kind of teacher, only a ringer hired to help stage a school show. He'd never worked with kids before. They weren't so different from other actors, just shorter.

The show was going well, however. Nobody froze, no cues were flubbed beyond repair. The audience was nicely slapped by *niggers*. Frank had been surprised Mrs. Anderson wanted to use the lyric, but the old lady wasn't as old-fashioned as she liked to pretend. Tonight was opening night, tomorrow closing. It felt funny to work for six weeks on a show for just two performances, yet it gave the thing a kind of purity. Frank rode the same adrenaline roller coaster that had carried him through shows back when he was an actor himself.

"I'm only in it for the long green," he joked to friends. The P.T.A.

actually was paying him two thousand dollars. In his darker, hour-of-the-wolf moments, however, Frank feared a show like this was a dirty trick to play on kids, giving them a taste for something they could never get in real life.

Frank Earp had come to New York ten years ago, straight out of college in Tennessee, thinking he could have an acting career, a life in the theater. Well, he couldn't. After a decade of showcases, road shows, regional theater gigs, and temp work, last year he had taken a full-time job as office manager for an investor. It was good to have a steady income. It was a joy to say good-bye to acting. Yet the job left him with mental space and time for projects like this one. He was also directing a play for his former roommates uptown, a set of skits to be performed in their apartment on West 104th Street—Frank had his own place now, in Hoboken. It was wild to be doing two shows simultaneously, one with kids, the other with grown-ups, so-called, especially after his decision to say "Fuck theater." It never rained but it poured. This was only his hobby now, not his life. He preferred it that way. He had more time for life, meaning leisure, money, love.

He had spotted Jessie Doyle out front tonight. First he heard her laugh—single, sharp, birdlike notes of delight—then he recognized her goofy, lopsided grin out in the shadows. Frank was overjoyed that she'd come. He was distracted too, but it was a good distraction, like looking forward to the next movie in a double feature. When a song or scene went well and Frank could relax, he felt this show was not the only good thing that could happen tonight.

He stepped out into the hall to compare notes with Mrs. Anderson. He could call her Harriet to her face, but she radiated such old-lady authority that he still thought of her as Mrs. Anderson.

He found her at the drinking fountain. "So what do you think, Harriet? Will we get through this in one piece?"

She looked at him with her enormous, world-weary eyes. "Oh, they'll enjoy whatever their little darlings do," she said. "But I'm having a lovely time. Aren't you?"

He laughed. This was the smart approach to theater, the sane approach. Mrs. Anderson was well into her old-lady Zen years, and Frank was constantly learning things from her. "I'll have fun if you have fun," he promised. "See you later."

He found Carmen waiting for him backstage. "Guess who's here, Frank? You'll never guess. Not in a hundred years."

"Just tell me, sweetcakes. We got work to do."

Carmen, who was twelve, took on a chummy, big-sister air around Frank. He suspected she had a crush on him—a safe, make-believe crush. She was no Lolita, just a smart kid with bib overalls and pierced ears who was eager to be a grown-up.

"The *Times!*" Carmen announced.

"Yeah, right. Get out of here."

"No, really. Not Bickle, but the number two guy. Prager."

Leave it to Village kids to know the pecking order at the *Times*. "I should hope so. He's Rosalind's daddy." The girl had innocently dropped the fact early in rehearsals. "My daddy says that the problem with theater today is . . ." And who's your daddy? "Kenneth Prager of Arts and Leisure."

Carmen looked disappointed. Frank assumed that would be the end of it, but then the cast returned from the hall and toilets and he overheard Captain Andy and Magnolia whispering, "Did you hear? The *Times!*" Then Tony, his beautiful Joe with the church angel voice, came up and said, "Is it true, Mr. Earp? The *Times* is here tonight?"

"It's Rosalind's daddy, dammit!" He clapped his hands. "Come on, guys. Get your butts in the wings. Now!"

The second act began, and the kids performed differently, more deliberate and determined. They turned into little marionettes of self-consciousness, clumsy and coquettish—all for the sake of the *New York Times*. It broke Frank's heart. Damn Prager. He imagined him sitting out there like God, as if the show were solely for his benefit. Slowly, however, by the third number, the kids became themselves again, their self-consciousness turning back into I-can't-believe-I'm-doing-this ticklishness. They came back to life, gracefully awkward, awkwardly graceful. They were beautiful.

Frank loved children. He was in awe of them, touched and fascinated by their look and size and needs. He wanted one of his own. It was a recent development, the real reason he took this job, in fact. He hoped to cure himself. Just as walking a neighbor's collie two years ago had killed his desire to own a dog, he thought a school play would end his fantasies about fatherhood. And they were fantasies. He was thirty-one, a bachelor.

There were a couple of girlfriends in the past, but none he wanted to marry. He knew his desire to populate the world with half-shares of his chromosomes was solely about him, not his love of a particular woman. Some Russian author, not one of the giants but a later, forgotten figure— even Frank couldn't remember his name—once wrote that a man wants children only when he's given up on his own life. Frank pleaded guilty.

Nevertheless, his love for Jessie Doyle—and he was in love with her, in a hopeful, sketchy kind of way—did not include telling her "I want you to have my child." He might be getting primal but he was not Neanderthal. Besides, *Show Boat* had done its job. It had taken the romance out of children. Frank still liked them, as people, but he also understood that, like people, they could be real pains in the ass.

As the show approached its end, the players quickened their pace, like horses returning to the stable. Their eagerness gave their performances a new liveliness. Then the finale began, each performer taking one last turn. Frank held his breath. And suddenly, he could breathe again. It was over.

The applause started, the curtain calls began. Frank remained backstage, playing traffic cop for kids going out for bows. He had counted on curtain calls and rehearsed them, but he did not immediately appreciate the noise out front. It filled the auditorium: a sun shower of approval, a rainstorm of love. The kids stood out onstage openmouthed, delighted to find themselves adored. They began to wave at Frank to join them, first Magnolia, then the others, insisting he share this glory. Frank started out, then remembered Carmen and grabbed her hand. He hauled the startled girl with him into the shower that turned into a waterfall, a cataract. A few people even shouted, "Bravo!"

Frank was surprised by the old rush of joy. The auditorium was only two-thirds full, but the whoops and hollers and beating hands suggested an audience as big as the world.

Mrs. Anderson stood by her piano, applauding her cast, taking a few bows herself, then applauding Frank.

Frank and the kids applauded her. His tear ducts prickled and he told himself, Don't be a fool. It's just a school play. This is just the love of parents for their own.

Yet the high did not pass. He wished he could tell his stars, "Enjoy this now. Remember this. It will never be so pure again."

4

The kids snapped out of their trances and hurried offstage, jostling and steering Frank with them out to the hall. The tuxedoed principal pounced on him there, followed by a mob of parents. Everyone congratulated Frank, and he smiled and nodded and said what a joy it had been to work with Felix or Tiffany or Josh or Elektra while his eyes impatiently scanned the crowd.

And there she was. She stood against a wall in her khaki trench coat, a briefcase under her arm, grinning like a happy conspirator. She looked lovely and lovable, cool and smart, the source of tonight's most appreciative laughs. And Frank had seen her naked. That was two whole weeks ago, and they'd only talked on the phone since then, but here was Jessica in the flesh. Frank did not picture her naked now, but a memory of nudity seemed to illuminate her face—crooked smile, sharp cheekbones, short reddish hair—making it more real than any other face here.

When there was a lull in the storm of parents, Jessie came over, set her briefcase on the floor, and embraced him.

"God that was good!" she declared. "And *smart!*" She gave him a spearmint-scented kiss—on the jaw. "You didn't try to hide that these were children, but used it, made it part of the play. I was in heaven, watching those kiddos do theater."

He was tickled that Jessie understood what he'd done, even as his joy stumbled over the fear that she'd come for his play, not for him. He held her against his side. "I'm glad you liked it," he said and kissed the top of her head. "I'm even gladder you came. Thank you."

"I didn't just like it, I loved it. Everybody loved it." She pulled out from under his arm to face him. "Even Prager of the *Times.* Did you know the Buzzard was here?"

"Oh yeah. His daughter's in the show."

"He's got a kid? Poor thing. Still. Even *he* loved it. He was sitting right in front of me. I gave him a piece of my mind. Oh, not really. I was way too subtle. He's lucky I didn't stab him with my pen. When I think of what he did to Caleb's play." She laughed at herself. "But I'm telling Caleb about this show. One more night, right? He'd love it. It should bring him out of his funk."

Caleb was Jessie's brother, Caleb Doyle, the playwright, author of *Venus in Furs* and a new play, *Chaos Theory,* which had just tanked. Theater was in their blood. The Doyles were not a showbiz dynasty, however, but outer-borough New Yorkers, their background as blue-collar suburban as Frank's family, but Yankee, not southern. Jessie's love of theater was matched by her smarts, but she'd not yet found a vocation there. She tried different things—acting, writing, managing—a jill-of-all-trades. Right now she was personal assistant to Henry Lewse, the British actor, during his stay in New York.

"I don't care if Caleb sees this," said Frank. "I'm thrilled *you* came. Look, there's a cast party for the kids and I have to hang out. But then we can go grab something to eat and, uh, talk."

She made a face, an overdone look of sorrow and guilt. "I'm sorry, Frank. I know I said we could get together tonight. But I can't. I need to take care of something for Henry."

"It's almost nine o'clock. You on call twenty-four hours?"

"It's an emergency. I'm sorry. He's my job."

Frank was surprised at how angry he felt, angry and hurt.

"I'm meeting him uptown after his show," she explained. "I don't know how long it'll take. But it can't take too long. Hey. We could meet at Mona Lisa later. About eleven?"

"I remember the last time we did that. You never showed."

"That wasn't my fault. Henry needed to talk. I couldn't abandon him. Come on, Frank. I apologized for that already. Oh, all right," she conceded. "What if I come out to Hoboken when I finish with Henry?"

Which meant spending the night, which was what Frank had wanted all along. Except he hated the idea of making love to Jessie when her head was full of Henry Lewse.

"No," he said. "It'll be too late. We better not. I have an early rehearsal of Dwight and Allegra's play tomorrow anyway."

She studied him, timidly, skeptically. "You weren't going to ask me to spend the night?"

"I don't know. Maybe. If it wasn't too late." Of course he'd planned to ask her, but he couldn't now.

She frowned. "Jesus, Frank. Don't be this way. You don't have to be jealous about Henry. He's strictly business."

"I'm not jealous. Why should I be jealous?"

"He's gay," said Jessie.

"I know that." He also knew that Lewse was fifty-plus, but this was more complicated than sex or bodies. "I'm *not* jealous," he repeated. "I assume he barely ever notices you."

Jessie glared at him. "Oh no. He notices me. Believe me. He's helpless without me. He can do art, but he can't do life."

They said nothing for a moment, neither wanting to admit how angry they were.

"How about tomorrow afternoon?" she said.

"I told you. We're rehearsing this other show tomorrow. It opens next week." He feared he was being silly now and decided not to punish her further. "What about Sunday?"

"Sorry. Caleb and I are going to see our mom on Sunday." She curled her upper lip and rolled her eyes.

He rolled his eyes in sympathy. Mothers, they seemed to tell each other, and made their peace.

"But *see*?" she said. "It's not just my life that's full. Yours is too. We'll talk during the week. You're coming with me to Caleb's birthday on Friday, right?"

"I guess." He'd agreed to go but dreaded it. The party would be full of successful actors.

"But we'll talk before then," said Jessie. "Good night." She kissed his cheek again. "It was great, Frank. Really. You should direct more."

"I'm directing Dwight and Allegra's show."

"No, I mean big-time. For real."

"It's not like I'm turning down offers."

"But you're not pursuing them either."

He took a deep breath. He did not want to get into this discussion tonight.

Just then a tall man like a stooping scarecrow walked past. He called out, "Nice job!" before disappearing in the crowd.

"Oh my God," said Jessie. "Do you know who that was? That was Prager. The Buzzard!"

Frank looked and saw only the elevated back of a gray suit.

Jessie grabbed Frank's arm. "He said nice job! Can you believe it? Oh wow. You should feel so pleased!"

"Whoopee," went Frank. But he *was* pleased. He'd feel more pleased if the two crummy words had changed Jessie's mind about running after her boss tonight. Except he wanted to be loved for himself, not because he'd been patted on the head by the *New York* fucking *Times.* "Talk to you when we talk," he said and touched Jessie goodbye on the elbow. "I need to get backstage and make sure stuff's put away. Good night." He backed toward the auditorium and waved at her, pretending everything was cool.

She waved too, a light twist of her hand like Queen Elizabeth, then hoisted her briefcase under her arm and departed.

Frank slipped back into the auditorium. It was empty, the stage restfully deserted. As he feared, coats and hats were strewn all over. He felt like kicking the hats, but instead began to pick them up and set them on the prop table. It made him feel like a mom, ineffectual and sexless. He cursed himself for telling Jessie not to come by tonight. Why did he do that? He could at least have gotten laid. What kind of man says no to sex? Well, a man in love. Men were supposed to think of love as a way to get nookie, but Frank just said no to nookie out of love. Or was it only pride?

Maybe he wasn't in love with her. Maybe he only *wanted* to be in love. What was there to love? Jessie was nothing but trouble. She loved theater, and Frank loved that she loved theater, but Frank was giving up theater. And she loved theater not like Frank loved it, as a craft, but needily, therapeutically, with lots of personal strings. There was her brother, for one, a successful playwright. And now there was Henry Lewse. The great Henry Lewse, former star of the Royal Shakespeare Company, the Hamlet of his generation and all that crap, currently appearing on Broadway. Frank was unimpressed, but Jessie was infatuated. There was no other word for her devotion. Lewse *was* gay—famously so, a public homosexual—which meant Jessie's love would remain platonic. Only what the hell did she love then? His artistry? His fame? His success?

Her brother was gay too, but not half as successful, especially after his new play flopped. There was some kind of connection there, which Frank was reluctant to explore. He could call her a fag hag, except the name explained nothing. He knew so many gay men himself that his friend Dwight, who was gay, called *him* a fag hog. Frank had cast Caleb Doyle's new boyfriend in their uptown play in hopes of getting closer to Jessie. Toby was not half bad as an actor, although halfway through rehearsal he was suddenly an ex-boyfriend and Frank was still stuck with him.

Carmen appeared at the stage door. "Oh, Frank," she said. "I was going to do that. You should be outside talking to parents."

"They have their stars to talk to. Didn't your mom come?"

"Yeah, but she's talking to one of our neighbors, wanting the dirt on our landlord. Here. I'll help you."

"Thanks, sweetcakes."

She picked Captain Andy's coat off the floor and took it to the coat rack. "Actors are such pigs."

"Welcome to theater," he said. "Where there's the actors and the rest of us. Who clean up after the actors." He bumped his hip against Carmen's hip and she bumped back and they laughed.

5

Jessie sat in the fluorescent gloom of a rocking subway car, feeling guilty about ditching Frank—reluctantly, irritably guilty. She was attracted to Frank, kind of, just not in the way that Frank was attracted to her. Seeing his talent reflected in a pack of clever kids tonight made her feel warmer about him—for two hours anyway. So why didn't Frank use that talent? He could become a success if he set his mind to it. He called it purity, but Jessie called it waste.

She got off at Forty-second Street and rode the escalator up from her bad mood into the weird, white light of Times Square. Bright canvas billboards like full-page ads from *Variety* or *Vogue* hung overhead. Headlines raced around digital zippers two stories up. Digital images played in big monitors or over the curves of a black glass building.

Jessie always felt like a beetle in a website here, a cockroach in cyberspace. Worse, the electronic canyon was full of nice-smiling people, happy families grinning skyward. Everything was so damned boojhee nowadays. She missed the old Times Square, even though it had smelled like ass and been full of wackos. It'd been real, unlike this galactic shopping mall. Jessie herself felt quite real tonight, tough and businesslike, briefcase under her arm, trench coat snapping around her legs. She was a woman on a mission—and what a mission. She dug into the coat pocket and took out the smooth stone of her wireless, flipped it open, and poked in the new number.

"Hello? Skull? Jessie here. Digger's friend? I'm in Times Square. Where do you want to meet? Five minutes? Sure."

She clicked off, then checked the clock overhead, under the quarter-scale replica of the Concorde soaring on a roof. Perfect. She'd meet this guy at ten and have plenty of time to get to Henry in his dressing room at the Booth Theatre after the curtain.

Beautiful giants in their underwear, male and female, lounged behind the Concorde, continents of skin with sulky lips as big as sofas. Frank looked nothing like those men, but then Jessie looked nothing like the women. She was thirty-three but, depending on her dress and haircut, could pass for a twenty-five-year-old woman or a sixteen-year-old boy. Jessie was regularly cruised on the street by nearsighted chicken hawks.

She was suddenly sorry Frank had said no to a late-night visit. She'd offered it only as a consolation prize for breaking their date. Their one time in bed had been perfectly enjoyable, although it had clearly meant more to Frank than it had to her. Still, his refusal tonight made sex ticklishly attractive, itchily necessary. Surely Frank wanted to get laid. Maybe he hadn't understood that that's what she'd offered. He was a nice guy, sweet and considerate, but with nice guys you sometimes had to spell things out. If only he were ten pounds lighter. If only he were more serious about theater. If only he didn't love her more than she was ready to love anyone.

Jessie was marching west on Forty-second Street, past the Disney Store and Disney theaters, under Madame Tussaud's giant hand. Back when she was a kid, this street had been lined with third-run movie houses, old shells of the Great White Way showing kung fu flicks and soft-core porn. Now even the sad ranks of white marquees were gone. Broadway was a postmodern theme park, a virtual unreality. All the good theater work was being done downtown or in the shoe boxes on the far stretch of Forty-second Street beyond Port Authority. How pitiful that Henry Lewse had to work in this phony-baloney Las Vegas.

She went up Eighth Avenue, past the last surviving porno theater to the Milford Plaza Hotel. She entered a white marble hall like a deserted corner in an airline terminal. Muzak "Oklahoma" played in the lobby upstairs. She followed a sign down a passage to a coffee shop of fumed oak and red vinyl. The same Muzak played louder here. She glanced over the middle-aged couples in crayon-colored sweats before she spotted a twentyish guy sitting alone in a booth, in preppy glasses and sweater, not what one expected for a man named Skull. And he had a full head of hair. But a Mickey Mouse shopping bag lay on the table, the agreed-on signal.

"Skull?" she said softly. "I'm Jessie."

"Heeeeeey," he drawled. "Digger wasn't lying. You *are* pretty."

He was not stoned, yet grass gave him his style. "This your office?" she joked as she sat across from him. She wanted to seem like an old hand at this.

"I do a rotation. Here and there. I prefer the Edison. Old dude agents sitting around making deals? Nobody looks twice at a man on a cell phone. And I love their blintzes. Sooooo." He stretched out vowels like a Bob Dylan impersonator. "Bring the book?"

"Uh, I brought a play. I hope that's okay." She took a copy of *Chaos Theory* from her briefcase, the new Samuel French edition bound like a pamphlet in raspberry construction paper.

"Right. Yeah. Digger told me you're Caleb Doyle's sister. Bummer about his last show." He flipped through pages until he came to the swatch of new hundred-dollar bills. "Cooool." He patted the plastic Mickey Mouse bag. "You'll love this."

It seemed bad manners to peek but suspicious to onlookers if she didn't. Skull acted like they were being watched—illegality turned any act into theater. Jessie looked in the bag. A neatly rolled Baggie lay nestled between two wads of rolled-up newspaper.

"Oh thank you! I always wanted one of these." She folded the plastic bag and stuffed it in her briefcase.

Skull was looking through the play, like he actually intended to read it. "*Times* sure was mean to your brother," he said. "What's the word on when they're doing the movie of *Venus in Furs*?"

"No word. But hey. Hollywood." She was surprised a drug dealer knew so much about this. "Uh, are you an actor yourself? This is just your day job?"

"No way. Not me." He laughed. "But I read *Variety*. To keep up with my market base. And I deal tickets now and then. When that line's more profitable." He pointed at her briefcase. "For him?"

"Oh no. Uh-uh," she said quickly. "All for me."

"Heeeeey. None of my business. Most uncool to ask."

Jessie had brought the playscript tonight simply because she had a whole box of them at home. The publishers had jumped the gun on this one. But she enjoyed the idea of inadvertently starting a rumor that her brother was now a pothead.

When a waitress stopped by to ask for an order, Jessie used the interruption to say good night.

"Great seeing you again," she told Skull. "Until next time."

"Sure thing, doll. You know where to reach me." He mimed using a phone. "We're like all connected."

6

Jessie came out on Forty-fifth Street and turned right. Shows were letting out. The street was glossy orange with taxis picking up well-dressed old ladies and their hat-wearing husbands, old-school playgoers who'd come to Midtown for an expensive treat. They were smiling, most of them, but with relief rather than joy: they'd had their fun and could go home. The block was lined with unkillable, long-running dogs: *Jekyll and Hyde, Les Miz, Footloose,* and Jackie Mason. Only the McAuliffe Theater was dark, a sad hole in this gaudy carnival midway.

Chaos Theory had closed over a month ago, but the name still hung in the dead marquee. A poster remained in the gloom underneath. "An Important New Play by Caleb Doyle."

The producers had been idiots to open it on Broadway. Jessie liked the play—she *did*. A young woman marries a brilliant physicist, not for love but because she thinks he'll become famous. She wants to share his greatness. But the man's abstraction turns out to be a cover for schizophrenia. He gets crazier and crazier; the marriage is spent in police stations and mental hospitals. But she does not abandon him. Out of a love that is part guilt, part duty, she takes up the burden. Which was where the curtain fell. There was no cure, no happy ending—no tragic ending either. The playwright offered the audience nothing except damage control in the hell of mental illness.

All right, *Chaos Theory* was bleak stuff, pure spinach. And the production didn't help: actors standing like zombies on a bare stage covered in numbers. Jessie couldn't imagine many people wanting to sit through it, but the play might have succeeded Off-Broadway. Here it needed raves to survive. The producers pulled the plug the morning of Prager's pan.

There are few things sadder than a dark theater, but Jessie continued to loiter, enjoying this pocket of peace. Poor Caleb, she thought. Foolish, earnest, pigheaded Caleb.

Her pity was sincere. Failure made her brother human again. She'd never resented his success, although it sometimes made *her* feel like a failure. If he could succeed, why couldn't she? Jessie blamed herself for being too stupid, scattered, lazy, and flaky.

But Caleb had discipline. He had drive. He'd been writing constantly since high school: stories, poems, one-acts, even a novel. Jessie was seven years younger. Back when she was a kid, she loved it when her brother came home from college and she could hear the tap dance of the manual typewriter in the next room, a soothing sound like rain on a roof. He would call her in and read what he'd written, or better, when he began writing plays, they'd read it together. Jessie already loved theater, but Caleb fed that love, made it worse. Then he would send her away, shut the door, and the rain of words resumed. Later he disappeared behind the closed door of life with his boyfriend, Ben, just as Jessie disappeared behind the closed door of a marriage. Now they were both single again.

Caleb moved to Manhattan after college and began to write nothing but plays. One was produced at Playwrights' Workshop. Then another. Both got decent reviews, good enough to encourage him to write a third play. Nobody expected anything different from *Venus in Furs*. It wasn't an adaptation of the novel by Sacher-Masoch, but a chamber drama about Sacher-Masoch himself and his marriage to a woman who loved his novel and wanted to live it, a philosophical comedy about writers and readers, fantasy and reality, sex in the head and sex in life. A rave from the *Times* turned *Venus* into a surprise hit. The female lead became a star, the show moved to Broadway, and Fox bought the movie rights for a million bucks. My brother, the millionaire, Jessie had thought, which was hard to believe even after he moved from his dinky studio in Hell's Kitchen to a swank apartment overlooking Sheridan Square.

That was four years ago. The movie had never been made; a new play had come and gone. "The *Times* giveth and the *Times* taketh away." The joke was Caleb's.

Jessie resumed walking. Beyond the gloom of the McAuliffe, just down the street, was the bright oasis of the Booth. Up above, on the corner facing Broadway, art deco letters trimmed in white lights declared: *Tom and Gerry.* Canvas banners suspended below added "Gorgeous entertainment!" and "Smash Hit!" and "Five Tony Nominations!" On street level, under glass, Henry and the rest of the cast struck happy attitudes in the display cases, their nifty 1930s costumes promising glamour, wit, magic.

Jessie turned the corner into Shubert Alley and the stage door, behind the magic. It was like visiting the back of a fancy restaurant and seeing the trash cans. Which should have burned away the romance. But knowing the reality behind the illusion only added to the romance for Jessie. She felt deep inside the thing itself.

The doorman knew her and nodded her through. The white-brick hallway upstairs was deserted. The cast was all in the wings awaiting the curtain call. The play played in the PA system, miked backstage so actors could hear their cues. They were singing the elaborate closing quartet, celebrating the double marriage of Hackensacker and his sister, the Princess Centimillia, to Tom and Geraldine's identical twins. She caught Henry's voice declaring his love to his bride.

> I know not who you are, my dear,
> But my love is the best kind.
> Ignorance is bliss, I fear,
> And romance should be blind.

There is no justice, thought Jessie. Here was Henry Lewse, a genius whose real home was Shakespeare, Chekhov, Shaw, reduced to chattering bad rhymes on Broadway. *T & G* wasn't trash, especially compared with the current crop of techno-musicals. Based on the old Preston Sturges movie *The Palm Beach Story,* the book made up in cleverness for what the music lacked. Still, Jessie couldn't understand why Henry chose to do such piffle. He wasn't even the lead, but the Other Man, Hackensacker, an American millionaire of the 1930s, back when a million dollars was a million dollars. He couldn't sing, but he recited his songs, one a patter song, "How Awful to Be Rich," which was the hit of the show. Everyone assumed he'd win a Tony next month.

The loudspeakers filled with the crackly static of applause that grew into the usual standing ovation. Then the actors poured back-stage, led by a wedge of beagles. The dogs of the Ale and Quail Club strained on their leashes, snorting and drooling, poking ice-cold noses against Jessie's legs. She pressed herself to the wall. Human actors fol-lowed, a long sigh of performers who stank of sweat and makeup, a harsh smell like wet fertilizer. Henry came last, in top hat, tails, and pince-nez, grousing loudly to the Princess.

"What a ghastly audience! Who were those people on the right? They chattered even during the songs. I wanted to call out, 'Excuse me, are we disturbing you?'" He saw her. "Ah! Jessica, *mon amie.* So good of you to come. Please. Join me in my dressing room. Later, Marge," he told the Princess.

Jessie followed him inside and crowded herself into a corner.

Henry sat at his mirror. "What a night. What an audience. Half the laughs were missing. My timing was all over the place. I felt like an ele-phant on roller skates."

He didn't offer her a chair—there was no chair to offer. Like most actors, Henry understood the concept of Other People but forgot the physical consequences. Jessie didn't mind. To see Henry Lewse in an undershirt, his face buttered with cold cream, gave her the same roman-tic antiromance as her image of trash cans behind the fancy restaurant. She took the Mickey Mouse bag from her briefcase and set it on his table.

"You got the goods. Excellent. And what did it set you back?"

"Uh, five hundred dollars."

"Hmp. As bad as London. Yet we persist in calling it a nickel bag. Nostalgia, I suppose." Henry still carried traces of Hackensacker, the character's humorous humorlessness. "You sure you don't want a com-mission? As middle-woman? You spoil me. My wallet's in my trousers. Go ahead and— Oh drat. Nothing in there but a twenty. I know, because I stiffed the delicatessen delivery boy on his tip. The look he gave me. Do you mind terribly walking me to the cash machine? I do have the money in my account, don't I?"

"You got paid on Monday." Jessie deposited his paychecks, paid his bills, and managed his U.S. bank accounts. She also answered his mail, sent out his laundry, picked up his groceries, and arranged to have his apartment cleaned. And tonight she was his connection.

"So sorry, my dear. I am such a ditz when I work. Even this deep into the run, when I could do the show in my sleep. Only I can't sleep, which is why I need this." He patted Mickey Mouse.

There was a knock on the door. Miranda, the dresser, was here for his costume.

"Jessie, darling?" He stood up, holding out hands still covered with cold cream. "Could you?"

She stood behind him, reached around his waist, undid his buckle, and unzipped his zipper. For a moment, *she* was Henry Lewse, taking off his/her trousers. Jessie often forgot how short Henry was, only half a head taller than she.

"What did you think, Miranda?" he asked as he/she/they stepped from Hackensacker's pants. "Was the audience as bad tonight as I thought? These Friday-night people from New Jersey. They think they're still at home in front of the telly."

Henry was in his early fifties, or maybe later, but he had the muscular legs of a younger man, nicer legs, in fact, than Frank. Henry wore the same brand of boxer briefs as the model over Times Square, which disappointed Jessie. She wanted him to be more exotic.

She handed his trousers, shirt, and the rest to Miranda, then returned to her corner.

"Well, no good crying over spilt milk," he said as he sat back down and took out a handful of tissues. "I'll put this fucking night behind me and find my feet again over the weekend. Maybe that's why I was off tonight. The testicles know that we have to do this again tomorrow night and twice on Sunday."

That he could say "fucking" and "testicles" indicated he was shaking off Hackensacker. He wiped away the cold cream. The muddy beige mask gave way to a longish, solemn, masculine face. His strong features registered as handsome only from twenty feet away. This close, and on film, he looked his age, especially around the eyes.

He studied his face in the mirror, then scrambled the front wave of Hackensacker's dyed hair, attempting to fix his image.

"If you'll excuse me, my dear, I'll just hop in the shower. Only a minute. Meet you outside."

"Right. Sorry. Yes," said Jessie, blushing slightly, afraid that he thought she wanted to see him naked. One could never second-guess the modesty of actors. Not only had she just taken off his pants for him, but she'd already seen him naked, three years ago in London, making love to Vanessa Redgrave in *Antony and Cleopatra.*

Out in the corridor, she nodded at Tom, Gerry, the Princess, and the others as they hurried out and headed home. Henry had told her last week how the intensity of living "arse cheek to arse cheek" through rehearsals, previews, and opening night gave everyone cabin fever. They needed a break from one another, an escape from the hothouse of enforced familiarity. Later they might become friends again, maybe. Out of makeup and costume, these ordinary faces bore no trace of stardom, only a residue of extra thisness, as if they were just slightly more real than ordinary people.

Finally Henry came out, snugly buttoned into sky blue jeans and a jean jacket, dressed like he probably dressed back in his twenties when he was at RADA and then the Royal Shakespeare.

"Did you bring Mickey?" she asked.

He laughed and patted his jacket. "I did not forget Mickey."

Jessie was pleased to have made him laugh.

Although it was a Friday, only a handful of fans stood outside the stage door. There'd been dozens the week after opening night, but they dried up over the following month, and all that remained now were old-fashioned autograph hounds.

"Henry! Great show!" called out a fortyish man with a precisely trimmed, pencil-line mustache along his upper lip, a John Waters mustache without the irony. He was accompanied by an old lady in a blue-black wig, a long-necked boy with center-parted hair, and a plump young woman in a red velvet cape. They looked like refugees from other decades, but no contemporary person would wait to see live actors come out of a theater. It would be as primitive as hoping to see TV stars climb out from the back of your television set.

"Yes. Thank you. So nice of you to come. You're very kind," Henry muttered as he signed autograph books, a *Playbill,* and a poster. "Bye now. Thank you. Yes. Bye-bye." He raised his arm and twisted his hand at them like royalty.

It was a mingy kind of fame, but Jessie was sorry when she and Henry headed down the street. The farther they got from the theater, the less the chances were that anyone would recognize Henry Lewse.

She wanted people to spot him, know him, admire him—and wonder who *she* was, the mystery woman accompanying the Hamlet of his generation.

Alas, poor Yorick, he was soon anonymous. Even in the Citibank on the corner of Ninth and Forty-second, where there were always actors and acting students, nobody looked twice at the short, middle-aged fellow in denim who entered his code at a terminal and made pouty fish faces at the screen while he waited for his money.

7

Tsk, tsk, tsk went the machine as it counted out the money. Henry took the bills from the slot, a dry thickness of stiff, green paper. Two months in this country and it still felt like play money, the very stuff that he was here for.

"One, two, three . . . Oh dear, it's all hundreds. I hope you won't have trouble breaking these."

Jessie assured him that she'd be using it to pay her rent.

They stepped back out into the rumble and roar of Ninth Avenue. He wanted to tell her good night, but not yet. His motor was still running too fast. Only the grass would slow it down enough for him to be able to sleep.

"Friday night," Henry declared. "How I loathe Friday nights. Everyone else is having fun, but it's a school night for our profession. Have you eaten yet?"

She said she had. Sorry.

"Ah. I'm not terribly hungry myself. I'll just go home, fry up an egg, and partake of Mickey here. Which way were you walking?"

She offered to walk him home. They started up the block toward Fifty-fifth Street and his apartment.

"You don't have someplace else to run off to? It *is* Friday. Didn't you say you had some kind of boyfriend?"

"Some kind, yeah," she said with a snort.

Henry decided she didn't want to talk about her love life, which was fine by him. He didn't want to hear about it. Jessie was a nice girl and she did her job well—so well that he could forget about her entirely if only she didn't moon over him as if expecting pearls of theater wisdom, bird droppings of wit. Americans were such silly romantics, with none of the pride that enabled the English to keep their hero worship discreet.

"Ah, the city that never sleeps," he proclaimed as they strolled against the late-night crowd. "They say that travel, like love, makes you innocent again. *They* obviously never did a theater tour. I'm in a very strange state these days. The play is locked, my performance set. There's nothing for me to do each night except climb into my role and turn the ignition key. I'm committed by contract to stay on through this award thingy. The Tonys? If I win, heaven forbid, I'm obligated to spend the entire summer in this tedious show. It's a quandary, a lose-lose for Mr. Lewse." He laughed at himself. "Just listen to me. Ridiculous, ain't it? It's not like I have anything else lined up. And if I'm not working, I go bananas. I might fall in love, find religion, even try to find *myself,* heaven forbid."

Hearing his own giddy chatter, Henry realized he might be bananas already. He should say good night before he made a complete anus of himself.

They reached his apartment building, a concrete monstrosity back toward Broadway, a postmodern neo-something like a high-rise pigeon coop. He suddenly remembered there was something he needed to ask. "Oh, Jessie. You know that mail thing you set up on my computer?" Yes, she did. The e-mail. "I can't get into it. What do I click to open my mailbox?"

"It's easy. You just move the cursor over to . . ."

But he could make no sense of what she told him. "I'm sorry. You know what they say about actors. We remember our lines by forgetting everything else."

"If you like," she offered, "I can show you."

"Do you mind? If you'd show me just one more time, I'm sure I'd get it."

She looked pleased to be invited up: her eyes remained cool, but her mouth was fighting a smile. Henry feared this was a mistake. He might never be able to get rid of her.

"You spoil me, Jessica," he told her in the elevator. "I don't have much to offer guests. Well, you know my stock better than I do. But I could give you a cup of tea."

"I'll be fine," she said. "I'll just walk you through the process and then get out of your hair."

Henry had assumed a female assistant would be less complicating than a male one. There'd be no sexual undertones to muddy relations between management and labor. Jessie, however, was a closet Mrs. Danvers. Her worship was discreet, expressed in looks, not words. But it was definitely there, and completely unjustified. After all, she was intimate with the mess of his life, his unpaid bills, dirty underpants, and petty contradictions. Tonight, for example: he both wanted her company *and* wanted to be alone.

While Henry searched his pockets for his key, she took out her own key and unlocked the door.

"Ah, my home away from home," he sang as he entered and turned on lights. "A canny hole of me own to fart in." The producers had found this place for him just as they had found his batman, or rather batwoman. The flat wasn't too awful. Everything was in tasteful shades of gray—carpet, upholstery, walls—with a couple of chrome tables topped with glass. It was as restful as an empty brain. A Nautilus machine stood in the dining room. Henry now turned on the television with the sound off. He needed a silent flicker of life.

"You know where everything is, my dear. I'll let you to it. Call me when you're set up."

She promptly sat at his computer and turned it on. The machine was his, but only Jessie used it, for his correspondence, accounts, and money transfers. She was of that generation—their brains are wired differently—but he was still in awe of her ability.

"Are you sure I can't offer you some tea?" he called from the kitchen. "Or beer or wine?"

"No, I'm fine. Thank you."

Nothing in the refrigerator looked half as interesting as the bag of grass that he took from the Mouse sack. He poured himself a glass of wine, then rummaged in the drawer and found his rolling papers. Here was a manual task that he handled quite well. He crumpled a tangle of weed, sprinkled it into the fold of paper, licked the paper, and rolled it, slow and tight, producing a joint as neat as a toothpick.

He brought joint and wine out to the living room. Jessie was still messing at his computer.

"Something not right, my dear?"

"Oh, Henry," she said, sounding more like a mother than an employee. "You scrambled your files."

"Oh dear. This afternoon after you left, I tried again to get into my mail. The thingies kept disappearing."

"Files."

"I broke them?"

"No. You just put them into the wrong places. I have to shuffle them back to where they belong."

He stood behind her with his glass of wine and unlit joint and watched the various boxes expand and pop, contract and mate.

"Henry," she said. "Follow what I'm doing. Just take the mouse, slide it around until the cursor—"

"The what?"

"This arrow. See it on the screen."

"All righty."

"Slide it to the mail icon, then click twice. No. Here. You do it."

She stood up. He handed her his wine and joint and sat at the keyboard. He did as she told him. Instantly a new box appeared, an empty box labeled New Mail.

"What does that mean?" he asked.

"It means nobody's written to you."

"Oh dear. Nobody writes the colonel. My fucking so-called friends. Or did I give them the wrong address?"

"Maybe they can't imagine you plugged into the Net. You need to write a few notes to them."

"I suppose," he said with a sigh. "But tomorrow. This old dog is too fried tonight to do any new tricks." He noticed her mouth print on his glass—she had taken a sip. "So you *will* join me? Excellent."

She frowned at the wine. "Sorry. I took a swallow without thinking."

"Not at all. You deserve a reward for your very good deed. I'll pour myself a fresh glass. Did you care to share in Mickey?"

She didn't but told Henry to go ahead. She'd drink one glass of wine and go home.

While Henry curled up on the sofa, Jessie took the easy chair facing him. She picked a paperback book off the floor. " 'There is a new name for evil,' " she portentously declared. "Greville."

"I beg your pardon?"

"*Greville.* This novel. Big bestseller. About a psycho-killer genius with a yen for teenage girls. Like a trashy marriage between *Lolita* and *Silence of the Lambs.* Why're you reading it?"

"I'm not."

"Then why is it here?"

"I don't know." He took the book from her, a fat thing with a Tuscan landscape on the cover. "Maybe someone left it?"

"You've had visitors?"

"No. Alas." He flipped pages, remembered nothing, then tossed the book aside. He took up his joint. "Cheers," he said and lit up.

The tip caught fire like a fuse, with tiny crackles and hisses. The bitter smoke filled his lungs, promising peace, calm, silence. He held it down and held out the joint. "Yes?" he huskily grunted.

"No thank you." She leaned back in her chair; there was no disapproval in her gaze, only amusement, even pride.

It was fun to be the subject of a crush, so long as the crusher understood nothing could come of it. His batwoman knew he was gay. He never pretended otherwise, with her or anyone else. And she had a gay brother, that playwright fellow, so she must know. But just to be on the safe side, Henry thought he might reiterate the point.

He exhaled a gray gust and took a breath of clean air.

"What do you know about the Gaiety Theatre? Well, you wouldn't, would you? It's this old-fashioned queer club off Times Square. The costume designer took me there last month. I keep meaning to get back, but haven't. It had the most beautiful Puerto Rican boys, strutting their stuff in G-strings and less. Very hot." And he swallowed some wine, wondering what Jessie thought of that.

"Why haven't you been back? You afraid you'll be recognized?"

He burst out laughing. "You flatter me, my dear. Nobody knows me in this town. Oh, a few artsy theatergoers. But certainly no regulars at the Gaiety. No, in this country one isn't famous until one appears in a hit movie or is a regular on a television series. Not that that would stop me. The world knows which way my wand points. I do not need to slip among the soldiery, King Henry in mufti."

"You underestimate your fame," she said. "Anyone who cares about real theater art knows your work."

"Oh them." He took another sip of smoke, but spit it out—his throat had not recovered from the first blast. "Those few, those blessed few. That blessed band of brothers. A few critics and old farts. I've given my life to 'real theater art,' as you call it. And it's given me no satisfaction. Now that my youth has fled, I need to cash in on my so-called celebrity. Enough of this art shit. I want to make money. Bags of it. I want to sell out. If only I can find someone who'll buy. Does that shock you, my dear?"

She was smirking, not looking shocked, merely skeptical.

"Look at Vanessa," he said. "Or Hopkins or McKellen. Or Alan Rickman for chrissakes. Surely I have as much talent as those fakers. I'd make a lovely villain in a billion-dollar thriller. To die at the hands of Bruce Willis? The mere thought is enough to make me cream in my jeans."

"You don't really believe that."

"Oh, Mr. Willis doesn't get me hard. But the money does."

"That's what I meant. You're not serious about the money."

"Why not? What else is there to want from life?"

"But you were just complaining about being bored with *this* show. A big-budget movie would be even worse."

"You think? Maybe. I contradict myself? Very well. I contradict myself."

He smiled, hiding his irritation for being called on his conflicted desires. He took a deep drag on his toothpick of bliss, wanting to climb back into a soft chambered cloud. When she said nothing, when she just sat there, watching, her intelligence began to worry him.

He released his smoke. He took another gulp of wine. "I hope I didn't sound envious and bitter about those *other* actors, my dear."

She shook her head.

"You must understand. When I run down my peers, it's not out of hatred or envy, though those emotions may be present. It takes a faker to know a faker. No, we hate one another chiefly to get a change from hating ourselves."

He blinked at his own words—had he really said that? He let out a loud bark of laughter.

"Listen to me! What rubbish! What's in this stuff anyway?" He stared at the joint. "Is this what they call designer grass?"

Just then something beeped, like a signal from Jupiter. A second beep came from Jessie's chair.

Jessie dug into the cushion, fished out the cordless receiver, and passed it to Henry.

"Ah." He pressed the button. "Yes?"

"Henry? You're home? I thought I'd get only your machine. It's Rufus. In L.A. How *are* you?"

"Rufus! What a nice surprise. How good to hear your dulcet tones. And how's life in the world of sunshine, hot tubs, and penis?"

He was delighted to talk nonsense with a peer. His assistant's curiosity and this potent grass had made him much too serious. He licked his thumb and forefinger and pinched out the ember.

"What can I do for you, Roof?"

"I just called to say hello."

"Uh-huh. And whose number do you want? What dish on whose houseboy or boyfriend?" His teasing was jovial, harmless, brotherly.

"Hen? Are you partaking?"

Henry laughed. "We know each other too well, don't we?"

They had met fifteen years ago, in a *Vanya* at the RSC where Henry was Dr. Astrov and Rufus was the nameless workman with two lines in Act Four. It was Rufus's first baby step in the profession. They were lovers of a sort during the run, hygienic lust with a touch of play-acted romance. Rufus was a tall, beautiful, lazy fellow, but he'd achieved surprising success in Hollywood playing "the best friend" in romantic comedies. Or what passed for romantic comedies in these sorry times.

True to form, he did want a favor. He was coming to New York next month and needed to meet Christina Rizzo. "She's your new agent, right?"

"What? Where did you hear that?" Henry scowled. "All these damn little birds. Oh, all right. Yes. But it's not final yet. And it's not public. I haven't even told Dolly yet that I'm leaving her for CAA."

"My lips are sealed. But what's she like, this Rizzo?"

"An absolute cunt. But she promises to be *my* cunt."

"Lucky you. A good cunt beats a limp dick any day. And right now I'm being handled at ICM by a truly limp dick."

Henry laughed, tossing his head back. And he saw Jessie sitting across from him. He'd forgotten she was here. "Just a sec, Roof." He covered the receiver with his hand. "I'm sorry, my dear. I'm being terribly rude, aren't I?" But he was annoyed with *her,* especially since she'd heard him say *cunt,* a real no-no with Americans.

"That's okay. I should be getting home." She smiled at him as she stood up, a watery, hurt smile. So why the hell hadn't she left as soon as he started chatting on the phone?

"That's a dear," he told her. "I'll see you, what, Monday? Have a jolly weekend. Indulge yourself. Don't give me a single thought."

8

"Sorry," said Rufus. "I didn't know you had company."

Henry waited until he heard the door clatter shut. "Not at all. Only my personal assistant."

"Hmmmm."

"No, nothing like that. Female. Fiercely competent. But a bit of a nosey parker. Where were we?"

"I should let you get back to your chemicals." Rufus apparently had something or someone that he wanted to get back to.

"But you still enjoy life out there?" Henry asked. "You find the work satisfying?"

"The life makes up for the work. But I never was a real artist. Like you, Henry. I really should be going. But I'll see you next month. Take care of yourself."

"Yes. Of course. So good of you to call." His own tone turned curt, even icy.

"Good night, Hen."

"Good night." He punched a button and tossed the receiver onto the cushions.

A real artist, huh? What the hell was that supposed to mean?

But he was alone. At last. It was good to be alone. Ever since he arrived at the theater tonight, he'd looked forward to this moment, when he could stop being for other people and be simply for himself.

He gazed at the television. Silent men and women continued to come and go on the screen, as restful as an aquarium full of fish.

He was suddenly sorry that Jessie had left. Not only did he want company, but he also feared he'd been a horse's ass with her. He'd talked nothing but me-me-me-me. He should've asked how *she* was doing, about that boyfriend—who was he, what did he do, were they fucking? Not because he cared, but because it would give him something new to think about, someone beside himself. But Jessie might misunderstand and assume he did care about her, which was a dangerous thing to do to a crusher. No, being selfish was an act of kindness here.

One of the joys about being onstage is that you think only about the moment at hand, then the next moment and the next. Unlike the rest of life, where the mind is constantly looking back, hunting down bad deeds and missed opportunities.

Henry still had half a joint left, but he was afraid to light up again. He was stoned enough already. He decided to take a shower.

The clothes came off his body like dry husks. The warm needles of water ran like a brush through his fur. His chest hair and pubic hair felt as soft as mink—or silver fox; they were full of gray. The terry cloth towels felt equally complex and wonderful as he dried himself. Then he put on his robe and his mind went back to work.

Two months in New York and the novelty of a new life had already worn off. He was feeling restless again, discontent. The show was set, the reviews good. There was nothing for him to do now but ride out his contract and hope this would lead to a movie or even television work. In the meantime, he was bored out of his skull.

What to do on a Friday night? All over New York, people were doing what the whole human race does on Friday nights: they were getting laid.

The Gaiety Theatre was just down the street. There was also an intriguing bar called Stella's. But shopping for a hustler required getting dressed, and Henry was exhausted, horny but indolent, especially after this lovely grass. His itch was the sexual equivalent of the munchies. Thank God for Ma Bell.

He retrieved his cordless from the living room, sat on his bed, and took out the sheaf of bar magazines that he collected last month when Michael the costume designer showed him gay New York.

So many ads to choose from: beefcake with choirboy faces, hard men with chiseled chins, potbellied ponies in leather. Henry finally chose and dialed a number. A gruff, tough, recorded voice came on.

"Welcome to Paradise. You must be eighteen or older. You will be billed at your number. If you agree to the terms, press star now."

He pressed the button—he'd done this before—and heard a set of clicks like the tumblers of a combination lock falling into place. There was a moment of Muzak—it sounded like "Old Man River"—and another recorded voice clicked on: "Your request has been processed. Welcome to Paradise."

And his ear fell into a room of live voices:

"Me so horny." "Wall Street bottom looking for a top." "Any spankers here tonight?" "Hey, Wall Street. I got ten inches of raging manmeat hungry for your hole." "Where are you?" "Canarsie."

It was all actors out there, bad actors, the scripts stale, the roles flat and tired. A good actor can do wonders with third-rate material, but these guys were hopeless. There was one quiet, deadpan voice, however, that got Henry's attention.

"Anyone into words?" he said softly. "Just words. I'm staying in tonight. I'll get us off with talk."

"Hey, Word Man," said Henry in his butchest longshoreman voice. "You sound like just what I been looking for."

"All right. Why don't you give me your phone number?"

Henry gave it to him and hung up. Then he lay on his bed and waited, feeling a bit silly sprawled here in his bathrobe. The toenails of his left foot needed clipping. Finally the phone beeped.

"Is that you?" he said.

"It's me."

"So what do I call you?"

"Let's not use names."

"No skin off my dick," Henry muttered. "Whatcha into?"

"We're in church," said the man. "It's night. It's right after evening mass."

"Okay," said Henry uncertainly.

"We're with a half dozen women waiting to go to confession. We're the only men there. We notice each other. We wonder if we're both there to confess the same sin."

This was far more specific than anything Henry had yet to encounter in a chat line, but the guy was good. He knew how to set a scene. Catholic guilt was not on Henry's menu, though Catholics could make for very hot one-night stands. The fellow had a tenor voice with a nicely New York nasal burr. Did people still go to confession?

"All right," said Henry. "I go into the confessional first. Okay?"

"Sure."

"I'm in there a long time. When I come out, I look at you."

"And I look back. And we smile." He paused. "Then I get up to go in. I have a boner."

"Yeah, yeah. I can see it in your jeans."

"No. I'm not wearing jeans. We're both in coats and ties. We're dressed like working-class guys at a funeral. The kind of quiet guys who still live at home with their mothers."

The fellow certainly liked his details. "All right," said Henry. "You go into the confessional with a hard-on. What do you confess?"

"You don't need to know that."

"All right."

"But when I come out, I see you're still there, still on your knees praying. I don't pray. Instead I step over to the side door, the one that opens into the cemetery. I step out, looking at you over my shoulder. I close the door."

"I get up and step across the aisle and cross myself."

"No. You forget to cross yourself."

"Okay. I open the door to the cemetery. Where are you?"

"It's night, remember. I'm waiting for you in the shadow, away from the streetlight, sitting against a tombstone."

The base for the cordless phone sat on the night table by the bed. The little plastic matchbook with caller ID was parked beside it. Jessie had ordered caller ID for him, saying it would protect Henry from telemarketers. He never used it, forgot he even had it. He remembered it now, however, and took a quick peek, wanting a clue about the man's ethnicity, more meat for his imagination. The little calculator window read "Doyle, Caleb."

"You hesitate," said the voice. "You're nervous. But you're still excited."

"Oh yeah." This was Jessie's brother? It couldn't be. It was only the power of suggestion: Jessie was just here, she was still in his head. But he looked again and there it was: "Doyle, Caleb." Doyle was a common name, but how many gay *Caleb* Doyles were there in Manhattan? And the guy knew how to set a scene, like a playwright. Henry hadn't guessed that Jessie was Catholic, although the Irish name should have alerted him. Everyone in New York theater seemed to be either Catholic or Jewish.

"But you come up to me," the voice was saying. "You smell like Old Spice. And I grab your necktie and pull your face toward mine." "Oh baby, yeah," said Henry. "I'm stuffing my tongue into your mouth."

"Your warm tongue. Yeah, I feel it. And I can feel the cold stone through my trousers. And all around us the tombstones watch."

Henry hadn't met Caleb Doyle. He may have read *Venus in Furs* but could remember nothing about it except that the lead role wasn't right for him. He was sure he'd seen Doyle's picture but couldn't remember what he looked like. He imagined himself kissing the male twin of his assistant, a kinky but not unpleasant notion.

"I'm undoing your belt," said Henry. "I'm unzipping your fly. Oh my God. You're huge," he whispered.

"Uh-uh. It's no bigger than most. But the first sight of any hard cock is so exciting that it seems enormous."

Which was true, although Henry suspected most men would be put off by this kind of psychological realism.

"I'm crouching down," said Henry. "I'm pulling down your trousers and underdongers."

"My what?"

"Skivvies." Underdongers were Australian, not American.

"Oh yeah. I can feel the cold stone on my bare ass. I can feel your breath on my cock."

"That's not all you're feeling, buddy. I can't stop myself. I open my mouth, I got the head on my tongue. Then I take it in. All of it."

"Oh yeah. I can feel whiskers under your lower lip. God you know how to use your tongue."

"Hmmmm," went Henry, then made a thicker, full-mouth sound—"Mmghgh"—trying for verisimilitude.

"And your cock?" asked Doyle. "What're you doing with it?"

"I got it out. I'm working it." Which he was. His robe was wide open. He lay flat on his back on a warm bed in a bright room even as he knelt in a damp cemetery with a mouthful of dick. The mind was an infinitely elastic place.

"I've lifted my foot," said the playwright. "I'm rubbing it against your cock and balls."

"What kind of shoes?" said Henry.

"Loafers."

"No. They're dress shoes. With the little holes? What're they called? Wing tips. So I can feel the waxed laces against my testicles."

Doyle hesitated, and Henry thought he was going to argue, but then he said, "All right. Wing tips."

"I got my free hand under your shirt and jacket," said Henry. "I'm pinching your nipple."

"Oh yeah. I'm holding your head in both hands. I'm tracing your right ear with my thumb. Your hair's cut short. It smells like Old Spice. You use Old Spice because it's what your father used. Your father's dead."

"Uh-huh." This line of talk did nothing for Henry's cock. He brought them back to basics. "Your balls are tightening up. You're getting ready to blow."

"Yeah. Yeah. I am. You?"

"Getting there, buddy. Gimme a sec."

They said nothing for a moment, only hummed and sighed into the phone. Then the playwright announced in a rush, "I'm pressed behind you now, we're naked, we're on a beach, my cock is up your ass, your cock is in my hand!"

"Oh yeah, baby. I'm with you," said Henry, deciding not to fight the change of scene or break with realism.

"I'm going to make you come first, and then when I feel your sphincter clench my dick—"

Henry inhaled a groan, as if he were coming, but only to trigger his friend. There was nothing like a love cry to set off an orgasm.

"Ah!" the playwright cried. "Oh Toby! Yeah! Ah! *Ah!*"

It was beautiful to hear the man climax, but the sound did not finish Henry. He was more stoned than he'd thought. He arched his back and grunted—"Deeper, baby. Oh God. Keep it coming"—but none of his gifts as an actor could carry him across the mind-body divide. Nevertheless, he joined in a duet of moans and whimpers— words fail everyone at times like these—until all that remained was heavy breathing.

"Thank you," sighed Henry. "Wow. Thank you."

He looked at his cock, so stiff and stubborn and unmoved. Yet he felt some satisfaction, like he'd just moved an audience if not himself. "Your Toby certainly enjoyed getting his ashes hauled."

"Toby?" The playwright sounded alarmed.

"You called me Toby. Didn't you? Never mind." Henry decided not to pursue it. A man after orgasm can be testy and unpredictable, even when he was in another bed in another part of town. The breathing on the other end shifted from mouth to nostrils, satisfaction turning to a sound like remorse.

"Thank you," Henry repeated. "That was most satisfying. Uh, would you like to do this again sometime?"

"No. Sorry. I'm sure you're a nice man. But no. Those are my rules. Just once."

"Well. You got my number. If you change your mind." Henry could not resist adding, "You have quite an imagination, you know. You should be a writer."

"Good night."

"Sweet dreams," said Henry.

Click.

So *that* was his batwoman's brother? How interesting.

Henry lay on his bed, wondering why he should feel so tickled by this discovery. The world is full of secrets; other people's secrets are so much more interesting than one's own.

He closed his robe, tied the cord, got up, and went out to the living room. He vaguely remembered seeing something—and there it was, on top of a dozen books stacked on the sideboard, a play by Caleb Doyle, not *Venus in Furs,* but the new one, the bomb, *Chaos Theory.* Jessie must have left it here.

It was an acting edition in a mauve cover, with no picture of the author. Henry opened it and saw the dedication. Not to Toby but: "For Ben. A wiser, kinder man. In loving memory. 1952–1995."

The man died six years ago, which was a century in actor years, though maybe briefer in playwright time. Henry was relieved to learn that Doyle hadn't been fucking a ghost in his cemetery tonight.

So who was Toby? Who was Ben? More important, who was Caleb Doyle? This was yet another play about maths—what was it with dramatists and arithmetic nowadays?—but Henry began to read, hoping to get a clue or two about this odd, mysterious fellow with a fondness for tombstones and Old Spice.

9

He sat in the dark, an imperfect dark with a leak of street shine projected on his ceiling. Sheridan Square roared eight stories below. It sounded like a day at the beach out there with the buzz of people and surf of traffic.

Caleb did not turn on the light. He did not want to see himself sitting at his desk in nothing but a T-shirt, a bare-assed geek with a red dick like a piece of garden hose. A last drop hung there like a chilly tear. Ten minutes ago, he'd been depressed and horny. Now he was depressed and guilty. Horny was better.

He could not believe that he had just shared a very private moment with an anonymous spook. Where the hell did his unconscious dig up that cheesy Catholic fuck fantasy? He hadn't been to confession since high school. He hadn't been inside a church in years except for funerals. But jacking off was pure high school. His imagination had regressed to pubescent thrills of blasphemy, nostalgias of sin. Stupid stuff.

He bent down, picked his sweatpants off the floor, pulled them over his raw middle, and double-knotted the bow. Caleb Doyle didn't know it, but he was famous for his modesty. Friends joked that not even his lovers ever saw him naked.

Now it was safe to turn on a light. The fluorescent desk lamp fluttered on, his study appeared: wainscot, wallpaper, casement window, the bookcase stuffed full of books and manuscripts. More books were stacked on the floor, volumes of science and philosophy, newly purchased, but Caleb could read nothing anymore, not even the biographies that were his usual escape, tales of men and women, usually artists, with wonderfully awful lives: Billie Holiday, Scott and Zelda,

Caravaggio, Janis Joplin, T. E. Lawrence, and so on. The cordless phone lay on the desk, stranded like a turtle on its back beside the computer. The bulbous peach-colored Mac hadn't been turned on in weeks. The dark screen was a convex mirror where he now saw a pasty dweeb in a pink undershirt, black-framed glasses, and goatee sitting in an enlarged room like a college teacher's office.

The hip strip of beard looked ridiculous. The room looked much too serious. Here was the playwright at home, not a teenager who'd just beat his meat, but a grown man, a middle-aged writer who was turning forty-one next Friday.

He enjoyed rubbing his nose in the shit of his birthday. He was not letting the date pass in silence but marking it with a party. What a grand act of fuck-me masochism. Turning forty had been relatively painless; he thought forty-one would be easy. He'd decided to throw the bash in a defiant mood, during the brutal high of being trashed by the *Times*. He wanted to be proud that morons hated his play. The party had been intended as a "fuck you," not a "fuck me." But the high passed, exhilaration turned to grief, the failure of the play began to feel like the arrival of middle age. Celebrating the end of youth now seemed as perverse as inviting friends over to watch him blow his brains out.

Stupid thoughts. Three-o'clock-in-the-morning thoughts. But it *was* almost three in the morning—2:49 according to the digital clock on the sill. Caleb couldn't sleep. But a phoned-in orgasm did not induce sleep, it compounded self-pity. He wondered what Mr. 581— the number was doodled on the blotter—made of their little scene. The guy hadn't batted an eye at Caleb's program of evening mass and a blow job. Maybe because he really was a good Catholic who lived at home with his mother?

Caleb regretted using such tacky material. And he regretted blurting out a name when he popped: Toby. Of course he'd think of Toby. The boy was the last good sex he'd had—the last bad sex too. But his first memory was of the good sex, back when he believed that sex was love and love was happiness. His unconscious must miss the little oaf. Caleb hated his unconscious.

He hated his apartment too—he was gazing through the doorway at the soft shadows of the living room. The crash of lust hollowed him out, and he loathed everything now, even his home. The study was a mess—he needed mess for writing, except he wasn't writing—but the other rooms were so neat, so pretty. He didn't deserve this place. When he bought it four years ago, he'd been full of success and felt the world owed him. People called the apartment a penthouse, but it was more like a cottage, a little villa on the roof of an old office building over a bay of streets off Seventh Avenue. There was a terrace on two sides, oak floors within, English country furniture—purchased from the last owner—a tiny galley kitchen, and only two bedrooms, one of them now his study. His home was not as large as it seemed, yet he did not feel at home.

He got up and went out to the living room. Here is where, if this were a play or a novel, Caleb thought, he would pour himself a drink. But he didn't drink; he never had. He used to congratulate himself on failing to develop a taste for alcohol, but he found one could be just as miserable dry, a drunk of depression, a lush of melancholy.

He went to the double French doors and opened them. The city roared louder. He stepped out onto the terrace. The night air felt good through his shirt, the cold tiles nicely penitential on his bare feet. The genitals in his sweats drew up into a hard, safe bud.

High apartment buildings hung on the left and right of the terrace, walls full of dark windows with three, no, four bright squares of brotherly insomnia. Caleb strolled out to the far corner under the water tank on stilts; the angle plunged toward Seventh Avenue like the prow of a ship. The city below was still going strong at three in the morning. Stick figures gathered at the crosswalks in patchy shoals of light, then poured over, passing through identical masses streaming in the opposite direction. On the right, facing the wedge of leafy park around the corner, was The Monster, a cavernous gay bar that catered to the outer boroughs. Caleb never went there. Leaning on his parapet, however, and looking down at the pairs of men coming around the corner, some of them holding hands, he did not feel like Zeus on Olympus tonight but like a sorry ghost watching the spectacle of something he could no longer enjoy.

Caleb preferred looking down. But sooner or later, he would have to look up and see what stood on the far side of Seventh. Which he did now, gazing past a slate ridge of mansard roof at the two bright billboards over Village Cigars. The upper board featured a gaudy art deco cartoon of a woman in ermine and a man in a top hat, selling a new hit musical: *Tom and Gerry*.

The world was too cruel. It was not enough for you to fail, someone else must succeed.

Caleb hadn't seen the show, which Jessie claimed wasn't half bad, for a new musical. It gave her a job, as gofer for the great Henry Lewse, so Caleb couldn't despise the play completely. Nevertheless, he despised it. A reheated version of an old screwball comedy about life among the harmless rich, it was the perfect piece of gilded crap for this gilded age. This fucking age. It turned them all into whores, even Henry Lewse. Caleb was unimpressed by imported Brits, but he thought even less of Lewse after "the Hamlet of his generation" started peddling his butt on Broadway.

And the critics who hated Caleb's play kissed the ass of this one. Like that second-string hack, Prager. "Gorgeous entertainment," he called *Tom and Gerry*—his blurb and name now branded over the half-page newspaper ads. "A shapeless, talky, self-indulgent failure," he said of *Chaos Theory*—words now carved into Caleb's brain.

The billboard hung in the distance, praising one play while it secretly damned another, as fresh as a wound, as permanent as a house. It had gone up only two weeks ago. Caleb stared at it long and hard, telling himself that he'd stop seeing the sign in time.

You fail, but you go on. You think you've overcome failure. But it remains under your feet like the water of a frozen lake where you happily skate. But a sudden change in mood can drop you *through* the ice into the freezing water.

Failure spoiled everything. It even spoiled success. His new play was misunderstood—he knew that—but maybe success too was a misunderstanding. Except there he was misunderstood in his favor. Because the worst part, the cruelest thing about this great joke of a billboard across the street—one could almost hear it whispering, "The *Times* hates your play, the *Times* thinks you're stupid"—was Caleb's fear that Prager was right. *Chaos Theory* was bad, a pretentious, talky mess, its tenderness phony, its author a fraud.

"Fuck this!" said Caleb. "Fuck this stupid fucking mind-fucking shit about motherfucking—!"

He swung his fist against the brick parapet. The blow hurt, but not enough. He grabbed the fist in his free hand so he wouldn't swing again. He stepped back from the edge. He turned, then turned again and marched down the terrace to the door. He hurried inside and slammed the door, as if the billboard might be following him.

He began to pace the apartment, snapping on lights, then the television, anything to get him off this vicious train of thought.

Success was a lie, money was a lie, this apartment was a lie.

He shook his head, his arms and shoulders, trying to shake this craziness out of his body.

He should walk away from the lies and return to real life. Except he knew only lies and make-believe, nothing real.

No. Ben's illness had been real. And his death. And maybe, just maybe, his love.

Yet Ben's love had never seemed as real as his death. Love gained full reality only after it was lost.

He stopped in front of the television. He stared at it but saw no images, only a conflagration of colors and light. He turned it off and dropped into the soft leather chair. He drew himself into a ball.

Here was Ben again, in a cubicle of the ICU, a body so wasted it was nearly flush with the mattress, a man reduced to the beeping of a monitor, the clicking of numerals on the IV, an occasional breath fogging the clear plastic face mask.

This was only hospital porn, a code for sorrow as phony as a twelve-inch dick. The real experience was deeper, more difficult to describe: three years in and out of hospitals, months of hope lost, regained, then lost again. And not just Ben but others—so many others. And not just strangers but people they knew. Yet misery didn't love company, it hated it. And as Ben became less Ben-like, more alien, less lovable, his death grew more desirable. Until late one afternoon the monitor stopped beeping. His face changed color, the last tension of self relaxing into soft blue shadow. And he was gone. The body was taken out. And he became Ben again. Almost immediately. Because he could be remembered, not just as ill, but also as complicated and human, a large, affectionate, quiet man who had never needed Caleb's love as much as Caleb needed his.

That was six years ago. Before money, before success. Caleb

thought he'd worked through grief, but he'd merely crossed over it on a bridge of success. And now the bridge had fallen.

He lay on his side in the chair, closed his eyes, and clenched his teeth. He refused to play this game tonight. He would not use old grief to justify self-pity. That's all this was. One big pity party, as their mother would put it. He'd become an open wound of self-pity.

He took a deep breath—and laughed. He actually found a laugh inside his chest, a good, bitter bubble of noise.

No wonder Toby had left him. Caleb didn't want his own company either. He wished he could walk out on himself.

All right, he thought. While you're picking at scabs, why not dig at that one too?

"You don't love me. You love only my success. And now that I've lost that, you want to go."

"If I want to go, Caleb, it's because you're such a shit to be around. I don't know what you want anymore. If I didn't love you, I would've stopped seeing you weeks ago."

"That's not love. That's just feeling sorry for me."

"Caleb? Why are you trying to hurt me?"

"Because it hurts me to be with you. Someone who doesn't know me. Who doesn't know himself. Who's mistaken a few weeks of fun for love."

Or words to that effect. They hadn't said any of this so neatly, or all at once either. Caleb could not help rewriting and tightening up their scenes in his head. Toby was not very articulate—he had never even called Caleb "a shit."

But Toby was young. He was new to New York. He had escaped his family in Wisconsin. He wanted fun, good times, laughs, sex—he was just discovering the lewd joys of his body—as well as help with his acting career. So what if there was a streak of gold digger in him? He'd made Caleb happy for a few months. The fucker.

So Caleb forced the break. He'd needed to *make* Toby leave, before leaving could cause great pain to either of them. He was glad he'd never asked the boy to move in. He was happy it was over, for Toby's sake as well as his own. Or no, he was happy only for himself. It was too painful living in the presence of such a cheerful, hopeful, eager youth, someone who simply didn't get it. What did a twenty-four-year-old know of middle-aged doubt, grief, and failure?

So was *that* what was eating at him tonight? He was depressed over losing Toby? More than the failure of his play or turning forty-one or even the death of Ben? None of these causes seemed entirely right. He was only trying them out, like an actor trying out past experiences, looking for one that would give the deepest, most useful pain. Yes, the hurt was real, the pain, only he didn't know the exact cause. Here was another danger in being a writer. Everything in life seemed to be just an idea, merely a thought. And any thought can be rethought into something else.

10

A gang of birds whistled and shrieked in the maple tree outside the window on West 104th Street. The sun was bright, the hour early: ten o'clock. A half dozen half-awake actors sat on the pinewood floor or shabby sofa, wincing and blinking, sipping take-out coffee, their faces as rumpled as their clothes. They resembled a pack of nocturnal mammals stranded in daylight.

"I don't know," said Frank. "Can't we come up with something more interesting for Toby to do than brush his teeth?"

"What if he were taking a shower?" said Allegra.

"What if he was taking a dump?" said Dwight.

Frank groaned. "We want this real, but not *that* real."

Toby sat cross-legged on the floor, smiling, trying to be a good sport but looking as he often looked, like a large, uncertain deer.

The first public performance of this thing—play, skits, sketchbook, whatever one called it—was Friday, less than a week away. The show was titled *2B,* which really was the apartment number, a set of vignettes about roommate living in New York. It was supposed to be slice-of-life, but the script by Allegra's boyfriend, Boaz, was more slice-of-sitcom. Boaz had just moved here from Israel, and his brain was soaked in bad American television. Frank and the actors were reworking his words in Mike Leigh–style improvisations, hoping to find a few truths, or at least hide the worst clichés.

The bulk of the play took place in the living room, which faced the dining room, which could seat an audience of twenty. Frank had come up with the gimmick of breaking the play with an interval where the audience would be herded down the hall for a peek at the characters in their rooms. They passed the bathroom, so why not put someone there?

Toby was the only unaccounted body. They were brainstorming about what he could be doing.

"Take it from me," said Allegra. "I'm not the only one who'd like to see Toby's ass. And not on the pot either. I think he should be taking a shower."

"Or shaving," said Melissa. "I once had this boyfriend who always shaved in the nude. Made no sense to me. Doesn't it get cold when it hits the sink?"

A look of pain pinched Toby's eyes as he understood they weren't entirely joking.

Allegra, Melissa, and Dwight were all somewhat gaga over Toby. Frank didn't get it. All he saw was a tall blond pretty boy. Dwight once went into raptures with Frank over Toby's body, how it spread at the waist in "a true bottom's bottom," which meant nothing to Frank. He could understand the appeal of masculine men like Brad Pitt, intellectually anyway, but a faintly androgynous boy was too much like a failed girl, so why not hold out for the real thing?

He'd cast Toby partly because he was Jessie's brother's boyfriend—or was a month ago. Then they broke up, and Toby moved in here at West 104th Street. Dwight called Toby "Eve Harrington," but Toby seemed too dull for brownnosing, too earnest. Climbers have more charm. Even Frank in his self-absorbed acting days had known how to create a sociable, public persona. Toby was not a bad actor. Once he got something, he was clear and focused. But it took him forever to get it. In the meantime he was lumpy, sluggish, and, well, earnest.

"Ummmm," went Toby. "Naked? Do I have to? I mean, good grief. Will people take me seriously after they see my—ass?"

"Depends on your ass," said Dwight.

"I mean, I want people to see me as an actor. Not beefcake."

"But you're not beefcake, love," sang Chris, playing up her Jamaican accent. "You're cupcake."

Everyone laughed—all except Toby.

"And you're not the only one," said Allegra. "I'm naked in my bed scene."

"But you're in bed," argued Toby. "Covered by a sheet."

"And by me," said Dwight with a laugh.

"Please do not remind us," grumbled Boaz. A short dark man with a handsomely squashed face, Boaz looked chronically angry, not over Allegra but over what was being done to his play. He said almost nothing during rehearsals yet continued to attend.

"You all just hit on something," said Frank. "If people see Toby naked, it takes away the surprise of seeing Allegra and Dwight."

"Yeah!" said Toby. "Right! It's not like I'm shy. Good grief. It's just I don't want to spoil the ensemble."

"Yeah, yeah, sure, sure," said Allegra.

"Cheep, cheep, cheep," went Dwight.

"All right," said Frank. "Toby keeps his pants on. Why don't you just stare in the mirror," he told him. "For now. Your character *is* self-involved. Something else will come to us later." They'd wasted enough time on Toby's ass.

"Do you notice how Toby always says 'good grief'?" said Dwight. "I'll bet he had the title role in college in *You're a Good Man, Charlie Brown.*"

"Noooo!" said Toby indignantly. "I was Snoopy."

Frank slapped his hands together. "Guys! Come on. Let's try a run-through. Please!"

It was like herding cats. The insults might be smarter, but this crew was as unwieldy as the one down at P.S. 41. Frank wished he could bring Mrs. Anderson up here. She knew how to handle actors.

They ran through the scenes. They did not do them at full throttle, but it was more than just a read-through.

The apartment made a good performance space. A ramble of high-ceilinged rooms, once nice, now dingy, it was still owned by Allegra's aunt Alicia, who had moved to Miami. Allegra rented rooms to her theater buddies. Frank had lived here himself until six months ago, when he decided he was too old for this mattress-on-the-floor, six-people-one-bathroom kind of life. The circle of friends straddled thirty, but in the name of art they still lived like college students.

Which was the subject of *2B:* life in the lower depths of showbiz, or, rather, the bargain basement. The project was Allegra's brainchild, born when she learned her new boyfriend wanted to write plays. She needed an outlet for her frustrated talents and those of her friends.

Allegra Alvarez was Cuban, but her family had been in this country long enough, and possessed enough money, for their daughter to develop the bohemian ambition of a good, spoiled WASP.

The show was a trio of one-acts chopped up and shuffled together. In the first plot, Toby played a young actor who is rejected again and again at cattle calls and auditions—which was true for the real Toby too. It was true for them all. He delivers a series of whistling-in-the-dark monologues about how good his life is, addressed to Chris, who sits in front of a TV like a big, butch, Jamaican sphinx and says nothing.

"Had a great audition today. *And* an excellent job interview. I am so on top of things. You wouldn't believe how much they want me for the new Sondheim. And Salomon Brothers. I'm too multitalented for my own good. What would you do in my shoes? Business or theater? It's a hard choice . . ."

The monologues grow more absurd as Toby—or "Toby"—grows more desperate over rejection, failures the audience must figure out by reading between the lines. Toby had brought in these monologues himself, an ingenious acting exercise—Frank detected Caleb Doyle's hand here—but he couldn't make them work. Chris continued to steal their scenes with her deadpan silence.

In the next plot, Dwight played a smart-ass who has a safe, brotherly friendship with his roommate, Allegra. One night, when they're both in a panic over the mess of their lives, they jump on each other and end up in bed. This tale was fiction. Dwight *was* smart-ass, funny, and overweight—he tried to give his pear-shaped face a little definition with a fringe of beard—but thoroughly gay. No, it was Frank who had gone to bed with Allegra, two years ago. The sex had been unexpected, frantic, and so quick that neither was entirely naked by the time they finished. Weeks passed before they could overcome the mutual embarrassment of having stuffed their faces into each other's crotch. But they did, and they became friends again, laughed at what had happened, then forgot it.

So Frank was stunned when the situation appeared in Boaz's first draft. Allegra took Frank aside and confessed she'd told Boaz the story but changed the identities of the culprits. Frank wanted to drop this plot. Allegra insisted it was good comedy, which was true. They discussed and worked on the scene as if it were fiction. Curiously, after the first week, it *had* happened to two entirely different people.

In the third plot, Chris and Melissa were feuding roommates. "You are such a girl," Chris angrily spits, which was true. A feminine fluff-bunny from Texas, the real Melissa seemed entirely out of place here. She and Chris bicker over trivia: the phone bill, who used whose hair conditioner, toothpaste, toilet paper. Finally, a carton of spoiled milk ignites a screaming match. Their antagonism is revealed to be not over their being hot for the same guy, which was how Boaz first wrote it, but because they both auditioned for a dubbing job on a Japanese cartoon show. It was the weakest of the three stories, yet the show needed the fight in the kitchen, with dishes being thrown and trash getting flung. When the rest of the cast join to clean up the mess, Chris and Melissa begin to laugh, the fight is resolved, and the evening achieves a kind of home chord.

All right, it ain't *Long Day's Journey*, Frank told himself. But it was a good exercise, a smart way for actors to work on their craft and stay sane. He would've preferred something with less realism. This was beyond kitchen sink—it was bathroom sink. But seeing the pieces together today—they ran about an hour—Frank liked their liveliness, their occasional moments. It was not entirely hopeless.

When they finished, Toby cornered him. "My scene at the mirror, Frank? Should I be more upset? Or less? I was thinking thoughts about getting old, but I don't want it to be maudlin."

"It's fine, Toby. Just look at yourself. Let the audience read you, however. We need to work on your monologues. They're not there yet. They need more feeling. Panic, pain, something."

"I thought they were supposed to be funny?"

"Don't worry about the effect. Concentrate on the reality. You know what it's like to be rejected. Use that."

Toby looked horrified: his skin went gray, his eyes wide.

Did he think Frank was referring to Caleb Doyle? Frank didn't mean to bring up real pain; he wasn't that kind of director. He didn't know exactly what had happened between Toby and Caleb.

"You've just come back from a cattle call," he added quickly. "Or you got snubbed at a job interview for a job you don't even want—"

Toby's look grew colder, deader, like he hated having to think about any kind of rejection. Maybe that was the problem: he was feeling so rejected that he couldn't play it.

Then his eyes lit up. "I got it!" he said. "I'll use my panic attack from last week. When I thought I'd have to go back to Wisconsin."

"All right," said Frank uncertainly.

"Because I was feeling all desperate inside and thought that I'd have to explain to my folks . . ."

Frank heard him out, encouraging him with nods, even as he wished Toby would think these thoughts in silence. All actors worked like this, groping for connections. But the smart ones kept their mouths shut, for fear that they'd sound nuts.

They ran through it two more times and took a break. Half the cast stepped out on the fire escape for cigarettes—Allegra allowed no smoking here. She followed Frank to the kitchen and hung in the doorway while he poured a glass of water.

"Good good good," she said. "Going well, don't you think?"

"It's getting there," said Frank.

A black-leotarded foot appeared on the jamb beside her face. Allegra often did stretches when least expected. She barely noticed them herself. "So. How're things going with you and Jessie Doyle?"

"They're going." Frank was surprised that Allegra mentioned Jessie. He had decided to put Jessie out of his thoughts until the next time he saw her. A few words from Allegra, however, were all it took to open that door.

Her foot spread its toes inside the black fabric. "Good. I like Jessica. I do. She's so . . . eclectic. You two are a real good match."

Frank couldn't stop himself from smiling. It began in his chest, and he tried to keep it out of his mouth, but his lips pulled against his teeth.

"You know," said Allegra, "you might ask her to bring her brother when she comes to our show. Maybe we could get him to say something to put on our flyers."

Of course, thought Frank. This wasn't about Jessie, it was about Topic A. Allegra had absurdly high hopes for their pack of skits. She actually imagined some hotshot baby producer seeing it and taking it Off-Off-Broadway. She didn't even care that Toby was now Caleb's ex. Hope still sprang eternal for Allegra, while for Frank it had sprung a leak years ago.

"I don't know if Caleb Doyle is a money name right now."

"Then he should be flattered that we think otherwise."

"Real flattered, I'm sure. But okay. Why not? I'll ask Jessie and she can ask him. I can't promise anything." Actually, he dreaded asking Jessie. She'd think he was interested in her only for her brother. But then he could never be sure how Jessie wanted to be wanted. She might prefer being used as a means to an end rather than an end in herself.

"Ally, you're a woman." She was the wrong person to ask, but Frank needed to talk to someone. "I'm not sure how to read Jessie. If she wants to be pursued, or if I should take no to mean no."

The foot dropped to the floor. "Has she said no?"

"No. But she makes herself only semiavailable."

"But not totally unavailable?"

"Not totally, no."

"That's a good sign. I know *I* like being pursued. But only by guys who I want to pursue me. Only I don't know Doyle well enough to know if she's looking for anything serious."

"Do I look serious?" he asked worriedly.

"Duh? Mr. Sincerity?"

"Hey, I can be insincere."

"You slept with her yet?"

"Um, uh, yeah. Once."

"Oh." The single syllable did not sound promising. "But she's not *completely* avoiding you? That's good. Go ahead then. Keep pushing. Let her know *you're* available." She laughed. "At least until her brother sees our play."

No, Allegra was not objective here, but she could be humorous about her self-interest. Forget Jessie, he told himself. Concentrate. Work. Fix this stupid-ass play.

"Thanks, Ally," he said and went back to the living room to talk with Boaz about the music.

11

Hello, Jessica? Sorry to disturb you on your day off, but—oh, sorry. Henry here. I'm still a troglodyte on these things. But I just wanted to know if you took care of my quarterly payment on the tax stuff last week? That is due now, isn't it? Or do I not need to worry about it till year's end? Now that I've said all this, I see it's nothing that can't wait until Monday. Oh, also, did I understand you right, your brother is Caleb Doyle, the playwright? One of my colleagues was praising his work the other day. What can you tell me about him? He's into maths, right? I was wondering: could you ask him for an explanation of algorithms? It's something I've never understood, but he sounds like the kind of man who could explain it to a bear of little brain like myself. Is there any possibility that you could introduce us? This message does not entirely make sense, does it? Sorry. No need to get back to me today. We can take care of all this Monday. But you know me. I might forget everything by then."

SUNDAY

12

The Hudson River raced outside their window, a soft mirror of quicksilver on a bright, windless morning. The high steel gate of the Tappan Zee Bridge swung forward on the left, slowly at first, then more quickly. Then the span of girders shot overhead and the train plunged into greenery: clouds and sprays of fresh new foliage. They had left the sanctuary of the city for the wilderness of suburbs.

"Sometimes he talks to me like I'm his only friend in the world," said Jessie. "Other times he forgets I'm even there. He takes me for granted. Which is a kind of compliment. I guess." She laughed. "He's such a mess. He makes *me* feel practical."

It was Sunday morning, and she and Caleb had a Metro-North car almost entirely to themselves. They were going home for Caleb's birthday. His party was Friday, but their mother refused to come to the city. So they went up to Beacon for the day.

Caleb sat by the window with several sections of the *Times* in his lap. Jessie didn't understand how he could still read the paper that had made his life so miserable. The Sunday edition was the worst. He didn't read the *Times* now but listened to her with a mild, patient, vague expression.

"And spoiled?" she said. "Jesus. Before the show opened, he was sure it would be a turkey. Gloom and doom, gloom and doom. Then the rave reviews came, but did they make him feel better? No way. Now he complains about how obvious it all was."

Jessie was telling her latest Henry stories. She had begun back at Grand Central with the declaration, "You'll never guess what Henry wanted me to do the other night. Buy him a little pot. And I don't mean ceramics." Which was a pretty good joke, she thought, although Caleb gave it only a faint smile.

"He can't do life, only art. But he's narrow even there. It didn't hit me until the other day: he doesn't do anything *except* act. He doesn't direct. He doesn't write. He doesn't even teach. It's a wonder he's no crazier than he is. A spacey, spoiled, self-absorbed mess. His life in New York would be a total disaster without me to look after him. Seriously. And not just doing his accounts or buying him dope."

"Are you bragging or complaining?"

Caleb's tone was dry and neutral, but she felt scolded.

"A little of both," she admitted. "But it *is* interesting. A chore and a privilege—to work so close to a real genius. See what makes it tick. Clay feet and all."

Caleb frowned.

"I don't mean that you're not one, Cal. A genius."

"Who said I was?" He lowered his face, crushing his tuft of beard into his neck. "*Genius* is such a crock word. There's no such thing, especially in theater."

She hated his new beard. It was supposed to be cool, but the little strip looked forced and artificial. The style was already five years old, if not older. But Caleb was even less of their age than she was. With his goony black-framed glasses, a goatee only made him look like a goat in a library.

"Acting *is* a kind of genius," she argued. "A freakish ability to think with your whole body. Instantly. Not in slow motion the way that writers or painters do."

His eyes lost focus, turned distant and preoccupied.

Jessie charged on. "I've come to the conclusion that actors, the best actors anyway, are idiot savants. From one minute to the next with Henry, I never know if I'll get the idiot or the savant."

She often did all the talking with her brother. Sometimes she blamed him—he was so miserly with his thoughts, so anal retentive— but other times she blamed herself, fearing she chattered away only to prove to herself that she really existed.

"Actors have this magic thoughtlessness," she said. "I don't. Which was my problem as an actor, both back in college and the classes I took at HB. I'm not saying I'm too smart to be an actor. I'm just too conscious. Too rational."

She was asking for it now, but Caleb still said nothing. He remained deep inside his head.

"Working out a new scene?" she said irritably. "Lost in your next big project?"

He produced a heavy sigh. "I told you. There is no next project."

"All right. We don't have to talk about it."

"Nothing to talk about. I haven't written a word in months. I can't imagine why." His sarcasm wasn't bitter but cold and smug; Caleb could be so damned righteous in his suffering.

"You will again. Just give it time."

"Hm." And he turned away and looked out the window.

All right, she thought, he's not writing and can't talk about it. She understood that. But she was determined to get his attention. So she played a dangerous card.

"Frank says Toby's really good in this play they're doing."

He didn't even blink. "Good for Toby."

"You're coming, aren't you? To see it?"

"Not this weekend. Next weekend. Maybe. I have my wonderful party this weekend, remember."

She sniffed. "I get Toby a part in a play, and you don't want to even see it? Because *he's* in it?"

"I'm not afraid of seeing Toby." He knotted up a corner of his mouth. "And you didn't get him the part. Frank cast him."

"Yeah, but Frank met him through me."

"How *is* old Frank these days?"

He was only changing the subject, but Jessie hated the condescension in his tone. "I thought you liked Frank?"

"What's not to like?"—implying that there was nothing to dislike either.

"You should've gone to his show, Cal. It was good. Last night was the last night, so you missed it. But Frank's a smart director. It was wonderful watching those kids do theater. And *Show Boat* is really interesting, more complex than I ever gave it credit for . . ."

Caleb zoned out again.

She angrily dug her wireless from her pocket and beeped it on.

Caleb winced. "Who you calling?"

"Just need to see if there's anything from Henry." She did it solely for effect. Henry had called yesterday, but that was a rare event. She'd brought the phone today for effect as well, a prop to remind herself that she was indispensable to *someone*.

There were no messages, of course, not even one from Frank. She turned off the phone and shoved it back into her coat.

"Henry left the weirdest message yesterday," she said. "Asking about you."

"Me?"

She'd forgotten about it until now, it made so little sense. "He wanted to know if you were Doyle the playwright."

"Probably wants me to write a play. With a fat part for him."

"Actually, he wanted to know if you could explain algorithms."

"Huh?"

She laughed. "That's what he said. I don't get it either."

"Jesus. You use a couple of half-assed math metaphors, and people suddenly think you're Einstein. What does Henry Lewse want to know about algorithms for?"

"Beats me. Maybe he just likes the word. Or maybe it's his way of saying hello. You've never met, right?"

"No."

"You should. I think you'd like each other."

He drew another heavy sigh. "I have nothing to say to Henry Lewse. I'm so tired of actors. All actors."

"Henry's not like other actors. He's different. He has a brain. He has soul. He's a serious artist. I think you'd find you have a lot in common. What if I brought him to your party on Friday?"

Caleb stared at her. "Haven't you heard yourself go on and on for the past half hour? Bitching and moaning about your crazy boss. Selfish and self-absorbed? The idiot savant? The pothead?"

"He's *not* a pothead. He just needs grass to help him sleep."

"A lot in common, huh? Yeah. Right. The pathetic failure and the happy sellout."

"Henry didn't sell out."

"What else do you call it? The man sold his soul for a Broadway fucking musical. What's next? A sitcom? *Hollywood Squares*? He's kissed his artistic ass good-bye. He just doesn't know it yet. Or maybe he does and that's why he needs to get stoned to get any sleep."

Jessie glared at her brother. Henry Lewse was hers. Only she had the right to trash Henry.

"No," she said. "You have *tons* in common. Yeah, Henry's spoiled. But no worse than you. And no more self-absorbed. I'm sorry your play tanked, I'm sorry you're so unhappy. But that doesn't give you the right to be so righteous and pissy about everything."

"I'm not pissy. I'm depressed."

"You . . . *geniuses*." It wasn't the right word but no other word came to mind. "No matter how much success you get, you want more. You and Henry both. If you're not bitching about failure, you're bitching about success."

"I haven't had any success to bitch about lately."

"No. Your play cratered. And it was a good play. *I* liked it. But you'll write others. You call yourself a failure, but us *peons* would kill to have the kind of success that you call failure."

He was silent. He gave her an apologetic look, but didn't apologize. "You don't understand. Success doesn't make everything all right. It makes you vulnerable. You wonder why you wanted to do any of it in the first place. It doesn't take away our right to complain. I have plenty to complain about. Look at me. I've got no boyfriend, no job, no work in progress, nothing."

"You have a million bucks."

"Not anymore." He looked angry that she mentioned his money, then embarrassed. He nervously glanced around to see if anyone could hear. "It was never a million," he whispered. "Not after all the commissions and taxes. Since then it's just dribbled away."

"Your penthouse hasn't gone up in value?"

He opened his mouth, then closed it. "But what's money? Work is what counts. But you need success to keep working. I don't know if I'll ever get another play produced. Which makes it impossible to write a new one. I don't know what to do with my life now. The only thing I can count on is that I'll get an obituary in the *Times*."

"Which I won't!" cried Jessie. "And I'd kill for a *Times* obit."

He stared at her. And he laughed. It was a mirthless, dry laugh, but justified. She had to laugh with him.

"Listen to us," said Caleb. "How the hell did we get here?"

"You started it. Trashing Henry." Even after laughter, however, she remained angry. She felt protective toward Henry, hurt that Caleb didn't take her seriously, and, despite herself, resentful that her name never *would* appear on a *Times* obituary page—probably.

"You're hardly a peon," said Caleb. "You're smart and talented and hardworking. Henry Lewse is damned lucky to have you."

But he did not look at her as he spoke, as if embarrassed to say such things to his own sister.

13

The jazzy rhythm of wheels quickened, grew louder, then died away, leaving only suburban sounds, birdsong and lawn mowers. They stood on the platform in Beacon. There was a smell of cut grass, sickly sweet like marzipan. The smell worried Caleb, as if he'd forgotten to mow the yard, a chore that he hadn't done in years.

He was relieved that Mom wasn't waiting for them in the parking lot. He hadn't told her what train they were taking, insisting they'd catch a cab. Being driven by his mother would've made him feel like a kid again, helpless and dependent.

"What a dump," grumbled Jessie during the cab ride. "Welcome to Loserville. Next door to the capital of the world, but people carry on like they're out in Bumfuck, Iowa."

The homely old landscape flowed by: service stations, minimalls, their old high school—a brick box with smokestacks like a factory. Jessie became more animated, repeating cracks that she'd said a million times before. Caleb had recognized long ago that his sister often spoke in order to stop herself from thinking.

They turned a corner onto a shady street of stout houses on short lawns, an old working-class neighborhood where nothing seemed to change except the makes of automobiles in the driveways. The cab ground to a stop in front of a white house with a glassed-in porch and heavily banked tulip beds. The grass was already cut—Mom did it herself now. She took care of the garden too. The tulips were in full bloom, segregated zones of scarlet, yellow, and mauve.

"I'll get this," said Caleb when Jessie opened her purse. "Out of my millions."

The cab drove off, and they stood side by side, brother and sister facing a house that looked as wholesome as milk, as pretty as a funeral. They started up the driveway.

The louvered door opened. And there she stood, in a work shirt, designer jeans, and big smile. She wore no lipstick today but must've been to the hairdresser recently. Her hair was waved, the gray washed away in a uniform shade of beige.

"Hello, dears," she called out softly, for fear of disturbing the neighbors. "Did you have a good ride up?"

Caleb got to the door first.

She touched his shoulder gently and kissed his cheek. "Happy birthday, Cal."

"And a happy unbirthday to you."

She rolled her eyes, as if this old joke were too original for her. "I can't say I like this, dear." She fingered her own chin. "Makes you look like a billy goat."

"Just being fashionable."

She waved him through, then kissed her daughter on the cheek. "Jessica. You look good, dear. You've lost weight?"

"Not an ounce!"

They could never make other people understand why this quietly composed, seemingly harmless woman drove them nuts. But then Molly Doyle wasn't other people's mother.

The house was furnished in Ethan Allen from three decades back. The family room bookcases were stuffed with old paperbacks, the mysteries their mother read as obsessively as she once smoked Salems—she had quit smoking five years ago. Hanging on the walls were shelves crowded with knickknacks: ceramic thimbles, dainty animals, blue-eyed Hummels, the tchotchkes that first appeared when Jessie went off to college, then metastasized after their father's death. They had been a shock after Mom's years of blunt practicality, an eruption of preciousness. Jessie once made a crack about this mob of fragile doodads, and Mom blithely replied, "Well, I don't have to worry about grandchildren breaking them, do I?"

She was very subtle. Calm and reserved, reasonable and civil, she hated the theatrics of confrontation. Caleb often wondered what would've happened if they'd had a more dramatic mother, a good loud Italian, say. Would he and Jessie have avoided theater?

All that remained of their father was a single photo on the mantel, a handsome, hawk-faced man in a knit sports shirt. He'd been a cop in New York City before they were born, then a cop up here in Beacon. Mom displayed no pictures of him in uniform. He left law enforcement when they were kids to manage the local golf course. Bobby Doyle had been a friendly, noisy, sociable guy, a man's man who preferred the company of men. He could be a doting, sentimental daddy when Caleb and Jessie were little, but he hadn't known what to make of them as teenagers. Caleb remembered him as sometimes irritable, often well-meaning, always baffled.

The dining room table was prettily set, but there was no aroma of food from the kitchen, only the house's peppery smell of old flowers. The last traces of cigarette smoke and Old Spice aftershave had faded years ago. Mom must have picked up something ready-to-serve at ShopRite.

"Come on into the kitchen, kiddos. You can tell me what you've been up to while I get things started in the microwave."

He and Jessie each took a diet soda from the refrigerator and sat at the Formica-topped table. Caleb liked the kitchen. It was the room where he felt most at home. These were his roots, he told himself, a faintly shabby lower-middle-class kitchen with floral curtains and a mint green refrigerator from the 1960s.

"Old-fashioned midday Sunday dinner," said Mom without a speck of irony as she popped open plastic containers. "Usually I just have a soup and sandwich alone. So. Tell me. What have you two been up to?"

Jessie looked at Caleb with her eyebrows skewed together, daring him to go first.

"Oh, the usual," he said. "Writing. Errands. Meetings. Nothing special." But he couldn't be completely dishonest. "I got to say, writing is very hard now. After the last play did so badly."

"But you got paid, didn't you?"

"Yeah. But not nearly as much as everyone hoped."

"You'll do better next time. I just know it. And Jessica? How are things with you?"

She didn't understand; she didn't have a clue. She thought playwriting was just another job where you worked for a fee and sometimes got a bonus. But theater was a foreign world to their mother. She had never even seen one of Caleb's plays.

Molly Doyle hated the city. She grew up in Queens but left when she got married. She knew New York chiefly through the eyes of her cop husband: a city of criminals. She had learned to tolerate her kids' living there but refused to visit, not even for a performance of her son's work. Caleb had come to accept this, treating it as eccentric, even amusing. His therapist insisted he must resent his mother. But he didn't. Part of him, in fact, was relieved that she never saw his plays. He feared she wouldn't understand. Or worse, that she would.

Jessie was telling a story about working with Henry, in a boastful manner, with none of the resentful notes that Caleb had heard on the train.

"Nice, I'm sure," said Mom. The name Henry Lewse meant nothing to her. "I forget. I know you told me, but is he married?"

"No. But I'm safe around him. He's a famous homo."

"Hmp." The noise was meant to sound calm and worldly but came out as a judgmental squeak. "Are you seeing anyone?"

Jessie shrugged. "Not at the moment."

"Now don't cut off your nose to spite your face. Men *are* hopeless," Mom admitted. "But good company now and then. And you don't *have* to marry them. Not anymore. Just because you-know-who turned out to be a stinker . . ."

The microwave began to beep.

"Here we go. Get your plates. Let's move to the dining room."

Jessie angrily cut her eyes at Caleb as they got up. He could almost hear her thinking: do you fucking believe this? But he was most struck by her refusal to mention Frank. As if she were protecting him. Once Mom started asking about Frank, it would poison the poor guy for good. Caleb liked Frank. He did. He suspected Frank didn't like him, but that was fine with Caleb. In fact, he admired Frank for not liking him.

Mom never asked Caleb if *he* were seeing anyone, but that was fine with him too.

They all sat at the table. Molly poured wine for herself and Jessie, then asked Caleb if he'd like some. "It is your birthday."

"Why not?"

They did not say grace. Their mother still went to mass, but talking to God at the table, even in the privacy of her family, must strike her as too public and melodramatic to be completely sincere.

"So cheers," she said, raising her glass. "Again, dear. Happy birthday." She took a deep swig. She enjoyed the glass or two that she allowed herself each day.

There was the click-click-click of utensils as they ate.

"It's nice to have both my kiddos home today," Mom declared. "Especially when one is turning—how old?"

Caleb frowned. "Do we have to keep track? Forty-one," he confessed. "Doesn't that make *you* feel old?"

"But I like getting old," she claimed. "I have a good life now. A nice life. I enjoy the peace and quiet."

Caleb wanted to scoff. Except she did seem content. She appeared perfectly happy with her gardening, her mysteries, and her solitude. A weirdly self-sufficient mother, she was satisfied with a visit from them every month or so. She refused to take money from Caleb. Social Security and her two pensions gave her everything she required, thank you very much.

Yet anyone who was truly content would be more open to life. Wouldn't she? She would acknowledge the past now and then. Molly Doyle never talked about her childhood in Queens, which Caleb knew had been hard. She never discussed her years as a cop's wife. She didn't talk about their father at all. She avoided all mention of the dead. She never alluded to Ben either. And she had liked Ben, she liked him a lot, much to Caleb's surprise. He used to bring Ben up here and they would flirt, his mother and his boyfriend. Big and husky and masculine— more masculine than Caleb, anyway—Ben enjoyed talking to women. He brought out a side in Molly that her children rarely saw, friendly, flippant, smart-ass. And she liked the fact that Ben was a teacher—he taught math in a private high school—a more grown-up career in her eyes than playwriting.

She was sorry when she heard Ben was sick. She was stunned when she heard he died. She almost came to town for the memorial service. She called at the last minute to say she'd decided against it. It wasn't her world, she said. She'd feel like an intruder.

Caleb was annoyed to find himself using Ben again. It was a

strange memory to direct against his mother, although it didn't feel entirely like an accusation. He shifted his wineglass over to the left of his plate so that he'd drink more slowly.

He noticed Jessie scowling while she chewed, still fuming over the mild jab about her divorce. It was up to Caleb to get a conversation going or they'd pass the meal in silence.

"How about you, Mom? What are you up to these days? The yard looks good. The tulips are coming up nicely."

"They are now. No thanks to Mrs. Gagliano's dumb pony of a dog. Her Great Dane, Percy. He thought my flower bed made a very pretty bathroom. I kept having to chase him off as the bulbs began to sprout. I had words with Mrs. Gag." She chuckled. "I told her, in no uncertain terms, that if she didn't keep him on a leash, her Great Dane was going to be great danish."

No, their mother was not without spirit. She had humor and wit, a sharp Irish tongue directed at others, usually the neighbors but sometimes at her own. One of the reasons that Caleb and Jessie visited home together was to avoid jokes at the expense of the absent party.

"Meanwhile, Mrs. Gag keeps going back for face-lifts. I think she's on her third, but who's counting?" Mom smiled and cut off another piece of chicken. "Her eyes get any bigger, they're going to pop right out of her face."

14

Mom cleared the table, then brought out the cake, a chocolate cake from ShopRite with no words written on top, just six candles. The tiny flames were invisible in daylight.

There is nothing sadder, thought Caleb, than sitting in front of a store-bought cake while two people in delicate moods sing "Happy Birthday" at you. He blew out the candles without making a wish.

"Oh. Almost forgot," said Mom. She left the room again. She returned with a gift-wrapped item shaped like a book. "Just a token."

Caleb undid the paper. It *was* a book, one he'd seen in stores, an anthology titled *Stupid Reviews,* a collection of bad notices given to great novels and famous plays.

"I thought you'd get a kick out of it," said Mom. "See? You're in good company."

"Thank you. Thank you very much." He was stunned—not over the book but by the thinking behind the book, the awareness. He was surprised she had noticed. She could seem so oblivious, so lost in her own world. Then, in a gesture or question or gift, she'd reveal that she really did understand. In her fashion.

"I saw that awful man in the *Times* yesterday," she said.

"What man?"

"The critic. The one who attacked your play."

His mother never saw *Chaos Theory,* but she read the review.

"He's there almost every day, Mom. He's a regular."

She clicked her tongue and bared her teeth. "Makes me angry just to see his name. What gives him the right to say such things? So high and mighty."

"He's a critic, Mom. It's his job."

"How do you know he wasn't right?" said Jessie. "You never saw the play."

She stared at her daughter. "I know your brother. He doesn't write bad plays." She studied Jessie, suspecting a trap. She shook her head. "Pffft. You two. You take everything I say so seriously. I should never have brought up that man. Why're you defending him?"

"I'm not defending him," said Jessie. "He's an idiot. But I know that because I saw Cal's play."

Mom took another breath. "Jessica. You just want to contradict me. Let's change the subject."

They ate their cake: Click-click-click went the forks.

The trouble with their mother, thought Caleb, is she has no performing self, no social skin to put between herself and the world.

"I guess you're looking forward to your party on Friday," she said, starting over again. "That'll be your real birthday."

Caleb clenched his teeth. "This is just as real," he muttered. He could use a thicker social skin himself.

"Will there be lots of people?"

"Tons," said Jessie. "And famous people too."

"Like who?"

"Oh, Cherry Jones. Kathy Chalfant. Victor Garber. Who else, Caleb?"

He knew this was futile. "Claire Wade said she might come."

"Sorry. I don't know any of these names."

"Claire Wade!" cried Jessie. "She's a movie star! She was in Cal's play. *Venus in Furs* made her famous. Her name's everywhere!"

"If they're not on *Rosie O'Donnell,* how do you expect me to know them?" She looked both sheepish and annoyed. "But *that* name sounds familiar. If I saw her face, I'm sure I'd recognize it."

"So come to the party," said Caleb. "You can meet her and see if you recognize her. You can meet all these people."

She became flustered. "Thank you, dear. But I can't. I'll feel out of place with so many famous people who I've never heard of."

"Come to my party," Caleb commanded. "I want you to. *Please.* Why can't you?" He turned the invitation into a challenge, a dare. He was suddenly angry with his mother. He couldn't understand why.

There were so many reasons to be angry with her—but why now, why today? He tried to stuff his temper back in.

Jessie was staring at him. "Caleb. She hates the city. Remember? She won't come to town. New York scares her."

"It doesn't *scare* me," Mom declared. "I'm just not comfortable there. It's big and noisy and—I don't like the element it attracts. But I'm not scared of it."

"Forget it," said Caleb. "I just thought you might like to meet my friends. And see where I live." She'd never even been to his Sheridan Square apartment.

He wolfed down his cake, cursing himself for giving in to her, just as he'd cursed himself a moment earlier for losing his temper.

"Do you still have Dad's old revolver?" he suddenly asked.

"What? What's your father have to do with this?"

"Not him. His revolver. His gun. A snub-nosed .38? You used to have it in the drawer by your bed." That was another absurdity here: this timid woman owned a gun.

She quizzically tilted her head, wondering what he meant. Jessie was staring at him as if he'd gone nuts. Did she think he wanted to use it on himself?

"If you're so afraid of the city," he said, "you can visit us armed. It should fit in your purse. Or bring Mace. Or some pepper spray."

"I get it. You're being funny." And she laughed lightly, without conviction. "I never understand your sense of humor. You're being silly. But I'm not afraid of New York. It's a young person's town. I'm not young anymore. Since I don't have any reason to go, I don't."

"I'm giving you a reason. Come to my party."

"Jesus, Mom," grumbled Jessie. "You're so scared of the city that you've never even seen one of Caleb's plays."

"That's not why. The timing just never worked out. I meant to go but didn't want to go alone. My friends were always busy, and then the play was gone."

"*Venus* ran for two years," said Jessie. "Your friends were busy all that time?" Caleb and Jessie wondered how many friends their mother actually had.

She was flustered now, confused and angry. "Back off! Both of you! I can't think with you ganging up on me." She tapped two fingers against her mouth, like a memory of cigarettes. "Let me think about it. Can't I think about it? Before I make any promises. Is that fair? Maybe I'll come early, while it's still light. Just for a little while. I *would* like to see Cal's new apartment."

"It's not new anymore. He's had it four years."

Caleb jumped in before Jessie made things worse. "Yes, Mom. Do. Think about it. I want you to come. I'd love to see you there."

He wanted to be kind now. He was ashamed of himself for opening up such a can of ugly worms. We all have our phobias. Hers was the city. He should not take it personally. He should let her enjoy what peace she had.

"I appreciate the invitation, dear. I do. I'll think about it. More cake? Both of you. There's plenty. I'm wrapping up what you don't eat and you can take it with you. I don't need cake around the house."

15

Passive-aggressive be thy middle name," said Jessie. "What's she fighting anyway?"

The light over the river was fading from orange to gold. The train was packed. The other passengers appeared rested and content after their weekends in the country, but Jessie felt totally fried.

"We can't do anything right. Even if I got remarried tomorrow, and started making grandkids, she still wouldn't take me seriously. She doesn't take even *you* seriously. She feels no pride in being mother of a successful playwright."

"Formerly successful," said Caleb. "But she doesn't know that either." He did not sound bitter, only tired, resigned, sad. "We should look at things from her point of view," he added. "She has this nice, quiet, suburban life. And we come barreling up there, like two creatures from Mars, wanting her total attention. We need her more than she needs us."

"I need her like a hole in the head. Why're you defending her?"

"I don't defend her."

"You indulge her. You play along in all her little games."

"She doesn't know they're games."

Caleb didn't get it, but Mom didn't get under his skin like she got under Jessie's. Sons are tone-deaf to mothers.

"Mom doesn't take your work seriously, you know."

"Thank God for that," he claimed. "It keeps my shit in perspective."

"She won't come to your party."

"I know that too." He shrugged. "Inviting her was just my way of fighting back."

"Do you really want her there?"

The corner of his mouth pinched itself into a smile. "No*oo*o."

Jessie smiled too and shook her head. "She is *so* repressed."

"And *we're* what she's repressing."

Jessie burst out laughing. Perfect! She didn't know if it were true, but it gave a nice twist to their mother's stony chill, and an important role that she could share with her brother.

She felt very close to Caleb now. They understood each other better than most sisters and brothers. Feeling good about him made her feel good about herself. The edges were gone, the frayed ends burned clean. No, there was nothing like a day with their mother to bond them together.

They could be quiet now, they could stop talking. Then Caleb said, "You're right about my apartment. It's probably worth an arm and a leg now."

She made a face, a "say huh?" look.

"What we were discussing this morning?" he explained. "My lost million? I could sell my place and use the money to do something real with my life. Law school. Grad school. Peace Corps. Something."

She'd heard him talk this way before and was never sure how to take it. "Peace Corps," she said. "You could teach Chekhov on the Amazon. *Uncle Vanya* in mud and war paint. Or better, you could start a new religion there. Where Kenneth Prager is Satan."

"That's funny," he said. "I like that." But he didn't smile. "No, I wish there were something I could do. Or wanted to do."

"Give yourself time. You'll start another play and get lost in that and won't do anything else."

"No. I probably won't," he said sadly.

Poor Caleb, she thought. He'd achieved what he wanted in life and felt trapped in it. She'd achieved nothing and felt trapped in that. It was hard for her to feel sympathy. She tried, but she couldn't make sympathy flow.

"Excuse me," she said and took out her phone.

Caleb did not look annoyed. In fact, he seemed relieved that she didn't pursue their topic. "Checking for a Henry message?"

"Screw Henry. He's already at the theater. I want to see if Frank's free." She turned toward the aisle, her back to Caleb, and entered numbers. This was a sudden impulse, a surprising idea—she didn't know where it came from—but it was as if a space had just opened in her head and she wanted to put Frank in it.

"Frank Earp here. I cannot take your call. But if you'll leave your name and number, I promise to get back to you."

There was no smart-ass message or clever recorded music, the thirty-second shows that most of their friends put on their machines, only a plain message and a beep. Which was so Frank.

"Hey, Earp. Jessie here. Just did the Mom thing. Was wondering if you're free for dinner."

She waited for him to pick up. He didn't.

"But I guess you're off rehearsing tonight. Sorry. Forgot. But I hope it's going well. Talk to you later. Bye."

She was quick and dry and matter-of-fact, even though she was surprised by how disappointed she felt.

"Not in," she told Caleb as she put away her phone. "I forgot about his rehearsal."

He was watching her, studying her. "I noticed you didn't mention him to Mom."

Jessie frowned. "He's none of her business. Or yours either."

"True."

She said nothing for a moment, then, "I like Frank. I do."

"He must like you."

"Like a ton of bricks. I don't deserve to be liked the way he likes me." But she did not want to talk about Frank. "You must've felt something similar with Toby."

Caleb twisted his mouth at her, then surrendered to the topic. "Uh-uh. Frank's smarter than Toby. He's got better judgment. He likes you for you. Toby liked me for other reasons."

She shook her head. "Frank can't be all that smart if he likes me for me. I don't see what he sees there."

Jessie waited for Caleb to contradict her, or better yet, point out lovable traits that she forgot. Instead he was quiet, disappearing back into his own thoughts, dwelling on Toby or *Chaos Theory* or the Amazon, she couldn't guess.

16

Thinking white thoughts, blank thoughts, null thoughts, Henry stared at the figure in flannel pajamas and pince-nez specs in his dressing room mirror. The orchestra began the reprise of the Ale and Quail Club song, his cue. And his innards became a tangle of snakes. It was ridiculous. He'd already done the show once today, yet his stomach still went bonkers, his hands turned ice cold.

He made his way through the submarinelike hallway lined with intestinal pipes to the high, dark factory space directly behind the stage. A stagehand wearing a headset helped him into the lower berth of the sleeping compartment that would be rolled out so he could meet Gerry, the runaway wife. It was like getting into a coffin.

What a ridiculous life. You do nothing all day, then your mind rages like a burning house for three hours, leaving you exhausted, useless, stupid. He was getting too old for this. Thank God he had tomorrow off. Tonight he should do something, go somewhere, visit bars, meet people, something.

The machinery whirred, the coffin moved, the music changed. He squeezed his dick for luck.

Gerry's foot kicked the curtain.

Henry stuck his head through the cloth—into the blinding light. He remained stone-faced while the darkness beyond the glare recognized and applauded him. There had been no instant applause until the *Times* told the world that he was the best thing in the show.

He turned his head so that Gerry could plant her foot on his face. And the play took over. He responded to Gerry's foot, the audience's laughter, the illusion of crushed specs in his eyes, the audience again. All the gears of the world engaged: his mind with his body, his body with the world. And he did it instantly, without time for thought. He could stop thinking. Or no, he thought *without* thinking, swinging from line to line, gesture to gesture, laugh to laugh. Like Tarzan flying through the trees, carried along on waves of fear that were indistinguishable from joy.

It was heaven.

17

❦

"I am not nothing. I am not nothing. I am not nothing."

Toby Vogler sat alone in the locker room during his break, studying his monologues from *2B* before he went back to work. His lines were written in pencil on one heavily creased sheet of paper.

"I *am*. Not nothing. I am *not*. Nothing."

Frank had told him at rehearsal today that this single sentence was the key to his role. He delivered it only once, but he decided to use it as a kind of mantra, planting it deep in his subconscious where it would secretly color everything his character said or did.

"Not. Not. Not," he went. "Nothing. Nothing. Nothing."

It was almost midnight and he'd changed his clothes again—for the third time tonight—and was back in sailor whites: baggy blouse, loose black kerchief, bell-bottoms. He wore a white cap on his head and red flip-flops on white sock feet. Out front he could hear the spastic zap of hip-hop, Raoul's music. He came after Raoul. He should be getting out there.

As soon as he stood up, his hands turned cold, his stomach filled with icy flutters. It was stupid to suffer stage fright here, but he did. Toby shook out his arms, trying to shake away his jitters.

There was no mirror backstage. There was not even a real back-stage at the Gaiety Theatre, just a locker room like a walk-in closet. Toby went down the narrow hall littered with cigarette butts to a cor-ner by the curtain where Tubes, the sumo-fat emcee, sat on a stool, just out of sight of the audience.

Raoul's number ended in a light smatter of applause. Hands here were usually too busy doing other things.

.

Toby passed his home-burned CD to Tubes; he carried his music with him for fear that Tubes would lose it. Raoul came through, a boilersuit and jockstrap bundled in his hands, as indifferently nude as a horse. "All yours, schoolboy. It's one big wrinkle room tonight." Tubes took his microphone. "Wasn't that nice? Yes. Pride *is* a deeper love." He spoke in a sleepy velvet monotone. "And with a tool like that, Raoul can love even deeper. But now, for something real nice, let's take a sentimental journey with our boy in uniform, *Bud*."

The music started, "Sentimental Journey," a Big Band number from the 1940s. Completely different from the other music, the song always got the audience's attention, which meant only that the quiet grew quieter. Nobody here ever talked much anyway.

Toby eased out onstage, strolling into the bright light. He didn't look at the men, but he could feel their stares. It was like a roomful of laser pointers and his body was covered in a chicken pox of dots.

He was a drunk young sailor, full of beer and testosterone, all alone in the big city. He smiled, he turned, he wagged his butt. He shifted from foot to foot like a man who needs to relieve his bladder. With his back to the audience, he unbuttoned the thirteen-button fly, rocked on the balls of his feet, and pretended to take a leak.

He'd first done his sailor strip to "Sing, Sing, Sing." He loved the music's energy but could do that number only once a night. This slow routine could be repeated again and again.

Toby did not do this strictly for the money. He needed money, but the dancers here got only fifty dollars a dance. They made their real bucks out in the Apollo Room, the theater lounge, where they might pick up another fifty by stepping into a cubicle with a customer, or a few hundred by going home with one. Toby had gone whole hog only once. Sex with a stranger was just ticklish and annoying, like going to the doctor, and creepy afterward when the guy took out his wallet and showed photos of the wife and kids. No, Toby came to the Gaiety chiefly to dance. Dancing made him feel good about himself, cool and tough, handsome and wanted. He did it only once a week—he had a day job at Kinko's—but once a week was enough. I am not nothing, I am not nothing, I am not nothing.

He faced the audience with his fly half buttoned. "Make them laugh, make them cry, and make them wait," Mrs. West had told their drama class in Milwaukee. Now and then some young fag would shout out, "Fuck the tease, man. Show us your dick!" But not tonight.

He mimed entering a hotel and going upstairs to a bare closet like his room at the Y when he first came to New York. Real images, the teachers at HB Studio said, strong sensory memories. He wanted a bed or chair here, but Tubes said, "No props, kid. This ain't Lincoln Center." He undid the kerchief, he lifted the blouse up.

He wore no undershirt. The song did not last long enough for an undershirt. He wore flip-flops because shoes were too awkward to untie onstage. He would've looked good in boots, but he didn't own any. He wore white socks so there'd be a place to put his tips. Flip-flops looked silly with socks, but the floors here were filthy.

He stroked his pecs and rubbed his abdominals, pulling the skin taut to show their definition.

Guys told him he had a nice body, but Toby wished it had more muscle, extra meat to hide his kidness. Yet he loved feeling the static electricity of eyes brushing over his skin. There were only a dozen pairs of eyes tonight, the late show on a Sunday. Nevertheless, these eyes too wanted his body, ached for it. And they couldn't have it, no matter how badly they begged or how much money they offered. It almost made up for all the times *they* refused him—at cattle calls, auditions, and tryouts. "You're too old for the part. You're too young. You're too tall, too short, too blond, too bad, thank you." Nobody ever gave him a second look. He dreamed that one day, one night, one of those directors or casting assistants would come to the Gaiety and hit on him in the lounge. And he could look them up and down and say, "You're too old, too fat, too ugly. Sorry."

I am not nothing, I am not nothing, I am not nothing.

He fumbled at his belt like a drunk; the slide buckle popped undone. He let gravity do the rest. The bell-bottoms fell to the floor, bringing the boxer shorts down an inch before they caught on his hipbone. He stumbled out of the white puddle. He stretched, he scratched, he sniffed his armpit. He picked his blouse off the stage and flung it over his shoulder like a towel—Tubes wouldn't even toss him a prop towel for his act. He ambled down the runway, as if heading down the hall to the showers, walking into the stares.

The vocal part of the song kicked in, a woman singing wistfully about leaving for heaven at seven.

He already felt naked, swinging and thickening inside his shorts. He wore boxers only here—elsewhere he wore briefs—so the novelty of their looseness was like a secret, extra nudity.

Only now did he glance down at the audience, idly checking out the upturned faces. A few crumpled dollar bills were set on the runway by men who hoped "Bud" would stop and perform just for them. Toby kept going. He'd collect the money on the way back.

Suddenly, despite himself, he wondered if he'd see Caleb here. Which was stupid. Caleb didn't know about his hobby. Toby had given it up after they met and didn't resume it until after Caleb dumped him. Of course there was no Caleb by the runway tonight, just gray heads and bald heads, beady eyes, shiny glasses, and one big grin. Not a cruel grin, but a careless, friendly grin—as out of place here as a grin in church.

He came to the end of the runway. He mimed turning on a faucet, testing the water. He let the tension build. He could feel the stares harden from a ticklish cloud into something wiry like cat whiskers. He tossed the towel/blouse on the floor. He stuck his thumbs into the waistband of his shorts—there was a soft growl at his feet. But "Bud" remembered that he still wore his cap. He stopped, pulled off his cap, drunkenly smiled at it, and shook his head. And all at once, still clutching the cap, he bent forward, pulled down his shorts, and stepped into the "shower."

He was naked so quickly that the whole room went "Huh?" A mix of sighs and murmurs followed, and the audible creak of erections— no, only chairs. He slowly turned, "soaping" himself, luxuriating in imaginary water and real stares, a warm bath of cat whiskers. It got him harder; he helped it with his hand. His dick felt as big as a two-by-four. He could hide behind it. The song was almost over. He stroked himself, he flexed his ass—once, twice—and waited for the blackout.

And waited. And the song ended. And the lights stayed on.

Good grief. Tubes had missed his damn cue again.

Toby tried to stay in character, but silence wrecked it. Everything disappeared: shower, hotel, drunk sailor. There was no fiction to hide in anymore. Toby stood absolutely naked in front of a pack of old men, a gawky, bony kid with a boner. He counted to ten, but the lights still did not go out. Without music, the fourth wall vanished too. "Hey, Bud?" someone cried out. "You need help finishing that?"

But his erection was dying. He didn't even have his dick to hide in anymore. Toby had no choice but to become Toby again.

He declared his act over by releasing his dick. He stood there a moment, hands at his sides, his right foot tapping. Then he leaned over and grabbed his clothes.

He stomped up the runway with his red flip-flops snapping at the crowd. He did not forget to pick up the dollar bills left wadded on the runway like candy wrappers. When he reached the stage, he kicked his trousers up into his hand and plunged through the curtain.

Tubes stood beside the CD console, all three hundred pounds of him quaking with wheezy, stifled laughter.

"You jerk!" said Toby. "You did that on purpose. Why? What did I ever do to you?"

"Sorry, *Bud*. I couldn't resist. You take this shit so seriously. And you're cute when you're naked. Not just make-believe naked, but naked naked."

18

Toby angrily stuffed his uniform into his locker and pulled on his real clothes. He was done for the night, he couldn't wait to be out of here, but he had to visit the Apollo Room one more time to get paid. Dancers were not required to trick with customers, but Mr. D., the owner, insisted they mix. Toby slung his backpack over his shoulder and headed down the hall, hoping nobody would recognize him in street clothes.

The Apollo Room looked like a basement rec room back home, with paneled walls and shag carpeting. Along the rear was a carpeted platform where dancers lounged like house cats with cigarettes, pretending not to notice the men who noticed them. The other dancers weren't a bad bunch, Toby had discovered. They were bitchy at times but too laid-back to be vicious. Their one vice was laziness.

Toby made a quick circuit of the room. He'd learned to stop seeing men once they were eye level. Then he hunted down Mr. D. and found him at the wet bar by a large bowl of stale potato chips.

"And you performed twice?" Mr. D. asked as he took a fat roll of bills from his pocket.

"No. Three times. Ask Tubes if you don't believe me."

"I believe you, Bud. Three times, sure." He always tried to take advantage of the fact his dancers were often too stoned to count. He paid Toby with three fifties. "Hey, if you want to pick up another hundred, there's an ex-Marine putting together a little party for himself."

"No, thanks. Got to go. Class in the morning."

"Uh-huh."

Toby claimed to be in college, which nobody believed at first—

they all told their johns they were NYU students—but his arrogance and all-around priggery convinced people it might be true.

"Oh, I can't work next Sunday. I'm in a play. It opens Friday." Mr. D. was not impressed. "You're not quitting again, are ya, Bud? Nobody likes a quitter." But dancers quit here all the time, of course, what with drugs and jail and love.

"No, just next weekend. I'll be around after that. Good night."

He was almost out the door when a voice spoke at his shoulder. "Excuse me. Bud? I caught your act. And I must tell you: it was utterly delightful."

Toby reluctantly turned toward what sounded like a fruity old queen. He would smile and nod—there was no point in being rude. But the man's face was not the usual middle-aged blob; it had sharpness, good looks, distinction.

"And hot. Very hot," he added in a convincing English accent.

"Uh, thanks." Toby studied him. And he understood. The face was distinct not because it was handsome but because it was famous. He'd seen it in magazines, the *Times,* and under glass outside a nearby theater.

"Excuse me." Toby lowered his voice to a whisper. "But aren't you Henry Lewse?"

The man looked startled. "Who? Oh no." He laughed. "Good God. Not me. No. Never."

He laughed louder and turned away. But he kept turning until he faced Toby again, smiling.

"I suppose I am," he admitted with a chuckle. "My apologies. I didn't expect to be recognized *here.* You flatter me. I never guessed that I was so well known in this country."

"I'm an actor myself, you see," Toby explained.

The face hardened, the smile faded. "Good for you."

Toby held out his hand. "Toby Vogler."

Henry Lewse took and shook the hand. He was shorter than Toby, and dressed all in blue, jeans and a jean jacket.

"Toby? Short for Tobias?" The name seemed to puzzle him.

"Yes. And everybody here thinks 'Vogler' is Jewish, but it's a Swedish-German name in Wisconsin."

Henry Lewse appeared to think about that, then lost interest in his name. "I should have guessed you were an actor. Your number was so much more polished than the others."

"It's supposed to end with a blackout. It got mangled tonight."

"Technicians," said Henry Lewse sadly. "They do muck up the magic." He pointed at Toby's backpack. "I'm sorry to see you're leaving. I would've enjoyed a chance to chat."

"I don't have to be anywhere," Toby confessed. "I just wanted to get out of here."

"A reasonable want. Do you mind if I walk out with you? I should be heading home myself."

And Toby finally saw it: there was sex in Henry Lewse's eyes. He wasn't shocked. No. But he was disappointed that a genius of the stage and screen could look at him with the same creepy lust of everyone else who visited the Gaiety.

"I should tell you, Mr. Lewse. I'm not like the other dancers. I just dance. I don't hustle."

"Oh? Oh. I wasn't thinking *that*." He laughed. "Besides, it's a point of pride for me that I never pay for it."

"Sorry to insult you. I just didn't want to lead you on."

"No apology necessary. A natural assumption given the nature of this place. Let's drop the mister. Friends call me Henry. Could I invite you, friend to friend—actor to actor—to join me for a drink?"

"What? Me? Sure!" said Toby. "Or hot chocolate. I don't drink."

"Terrific. And so much safer too. Shall we?"

Toby couldn't believe his luck. This was Henry Lewse. And Toby had him all to himself. He noticed Raoul watch them leave, looking more amused than envious. But Raoul probably didn't even know who Henry Lewse was.

Toby grew more excited as he trotted behind him down the long flight of stairs to the street. He'd heard about this great actor and openly gay artist for years, seen his picture in magazines, read scores of interviews and profiles. If this homosexual could succeed in the theater without telling lies, maybe Toby could too. He had never seen Henry Lewse onstage. He was sure he'd seen him in a movie, but couldn't remember any titles. What would Henry Lewse think if he asked for Toby's favorite role and Toby couldn't name one? He'd think Toby was a fraud. Then Toby remembered seeing his *Hamlet* on video back in college. Thank God. There was solid ground under his feet. He hadn't liked it much—he didn't *get* Shakespeare—but it was good to know that they could always talk about *Hamlet.*

Whatever happened, he was not going to go home with Henry Lewse. He'd gone home with Caleb the night that *they* met, but that was different. That was love at first sight. And Henry Lewse was an important British artist, Toby told himself, much too serious to want a one-night stand with an American nobody. Besides, the man was old enough to be his father.

.

19

Henry led his pretty American down the stairs to the street. They came out between *Beauty and the Beast* and Howard Johnson's. Straight couples sat in the restaurant windows, drinking and eating, betraying no awareness of the Sodom directly over their heads. The Gaiety Theatre had been a wonderful surprise tonight, a sanctuary of live sleaze in this wholesome electronic Eden. And look at what he'd found there. Bud or Toby, whatever the big blond's name, loped worshipfully beside him.

"The city that never sleeps," Henry declared as they walked through Times Square. "The city that never stops eating. Unlike London. Where one is hard put to get a drink after eleven."

The sidewalks were less crowded now, their chief occupants giddy packs of high schoolers. Lights still glowed and shimmered at two in the morning, like the pretty aura of a migraine.

"I know a good place where we can go for a natter," said Henry. "I can get a drink and *you* can get your hot chocolate."

The twenty-four-hour coffee shop in the Milford Plaza stood halfway between the Gaiety and Henry's bedroom. Maybe the boy was sincere when he said he didn't hustle; Henry was sincere when he said he never paid for it—well, almost never. A long, friendly chat should undo any reservations Toby might have. That the boy would be drinking hot chocolate only added to the challenge.

"Again, I liked your act," said Henry. "Very smart, very sexy. Good music too."

"Yeah, that old swing stuff is great," said Toby. "And I want to remind the men in the audience of their good old days."

"My boy. We're not so old as that." He laughed. "No, what you put us in mind of is our fathers." It never ceased to amaze Henry how often actors hit upon the right effect for the wrong reasons.

"We studied your *Hamlet* in college," Toby confessed. "We watched it on tape. Over and over. Wow."

Yes, the boy *was* an actor. Alas. He had looked so hot onstage, dumb with sex, drowsy with lust, lazily swaying to the music and losing his clothes. He hadn't seemed to give a damn about the audience. Pale and lanky, but with heavy haunches, he had looked utterly naked, not dressed in muscle like the cast-iron ox who preceded him. His cock stuck out like a finger peeking from a hand puppet. He'd been such an antiperformer that Henry hadn't guessed he was an actor, not even when the music stopped and the boy awoke, as if from a dream, and clomped off like an insulted ostrich.

"You were like a punk Hamlet, a pomo Hamlet," Toby was saying, and all the other slogans about that ancient performance.

No, he was no rough-trade beauty. He was an actor, merely an actor. Which explained the Marcel Marceau touches during his strip. Henry had wanted to go home with Bud but was getting Toby instead. Which *might* be interesting—he couldn't tell yet.

"You're the Hamlet of your generation," Toby concluded, a phrase that still made Henry cringe. "You brought Shakespeare to life for me. You made me want to be an actor."

Henry smelled the warm, sweet bullshit of flattery and was not entirely pleased. Up ahead was the ten-story billboard of a beefy fellow in briefs. "But why want to be an actor?" he asked and pointed at the figure. "When we could want *that*."

Toby gazed up. "You mean, go to bed with him?"

"That'd be nice. Or maybe *be* him. A shameless, brainless beauty. Without a thought in his head."

Toby looked suspicious, unsure. "Not my type," he said.

"Oh? And what *is* your type?"

"I don't have a type. Except right now I'm in love. With a playwright. Maybe you know him. Caleb Doyle?"

Henry blinked, then blinked again. "Can't say that I do."

How curious. And *Toby*? He knew he'd heard the name before. This was *the* Toby?

"Didn't he write *Something Chaos*?"

"Chaos Theory," Toby said eagerly. "And other plays too. That one just closed. But it was a good play. I think it's his best."

Curioser and curioser. Henry already knew Doyle, aurally but intimately. He had wanted to meet him in the flesh but was meeting his fleshy boyfriend instead. New York was a small town, but this felt like an improbable trick of fate. Henry was full of actorly superstitions: the Scottish play, a fear of purple, the need for rain on opening night. He couldn't guess what this linked pair of encounters might mean. Lust became more complicated—and more interesting. He still wanted to bed Toby. After all, he'd already bedded Toby's boyfriend, in a manner of speaking. But he did not feel as impatient as before. He was willing to take his time.

They came to the coffee shop at the Milford Plaza and sat in a red upholstered booth by the window.

"It's called the Celebrity Deli," said Toby, looking at the menu.

"Alas," said Henry. "I see no celebrities tonight."

"Except for you."

Henry smiled. "You're too kind."

He could look at Toby head-on now, across the table: clear skin, soft nose, wavy sand-colored hair, a sweet suggestion of bags under his eyes. He looked even sexier in clothes than he had onstage, in the same way that Henry often found the dressed boys on the covers of skin magazines more alluring than the meat pies inside.

The waiter returned. Henry ordered a Manhattan. Toby actually ordered hot chocolate.

"So. Toby. You're an actor." Henry had learned to avoid certain subjects with Americans, but the boy looked so good that he decided to risk it. "Who have you studied with?"

It opened the inevitable floodgate: college classes, HB Studio— "Herbert Berghof," Toby explained—the Method, of course, and a book praised by that great butch boor, David Mamet. Henry looked for a place to insert tales of his own training, but the boy never asked. As the saying goes: "It's you they want to meet, but it's them they want to talk about."

He managed to feign interest until his drink arrived—the boy *was* pretty to look at—while his mind slipped back to the coincidence of fate, the question of Caleb Doyle. He allowed the boy another five minutes and subtly turned the subject there.

"How does your boyfriend feel about your flipping your willy at strange men every night?"

"I don't do it every night." He frowned. "And I don't have a boyfriend. Not anymore."

"Oh? What about this playwright?"

"We broke up. I still love him, but he doesn't love me."

Henry was excitedly blinking, not with his eyes but with his heart. Then he remembered the love cry of *Toby* over the phone. "You're certain about that?"

"Oh yeah. He doesn't know what he wants anymore. Except that he doesn't want me."

Careful, Henry told himself. There's nothing here for you. It doesn't matter if the boy is attached or free. Nevertheless, it was fun to grope around in the underwear of a young man's private life, especially when the young man didn't have a clue.

"I'm sorry," said Henry. "That must be very painful for you."

"A bummer. I never loved anyone the way I love him."

"And what do you love about this Doyle fellow?" *Bad question*— Henry instantly regretted asking it.

"Well, for the longest time, I loved that he loved *me*." The boy looked so solemn. "But now he doesn't, and I still love him, so it must be something else."

"The sex," said Henry, lightly purring the syllable.

Toby lowered his eyes, color filled his cheeks. Henry had made a stripper blush? "Sure. But I liked the sex because it meant we loved each other, not the other way around. Sex by itself isn't that interesting."

But interesting enough for some, thought Henry. "That's a surprisingly romantic view for a man who works at the Gaiety."

"I know. It's weird. But I have a block about sex. I think about it all the time. But I can do it only when I'm in love. Which is one of the reasons why I first started going to the Gaiety. To see how raunchy I could get, doing things I wouldn't dare do back in Wisconsin. And I can get real raunchy there—"

"I found you convincing."

"But not in bed. Not for real. Then I get all—" He pressed his elbows to his sides and jiggled his hands like flippers. "I guess I'm just a stupid, geeky, old-fashioned romantic."

Henry thought this pure-heart-in-the-whorehouse nonsense had gone out with Tennessee Williams. It might only be Toby's way of fending off predators, yet he did not seem imaginative enough to have made it up.

"You must think I'm one sick puppy," said Toby with a proud lift of his head.

"Not at all. It takes all kinds. How old are you?"

"Twenty-four."

He sounded and behaved like someone much younger. "Ah. You have years to learn what the world can teach you."

"And I want to learn. Everything. I need it for my acting."

"You might find it useful for life as well."

"But going back to why I'm in love with Caleb?"

"Yes?" said Henry wearily.

"He's smart. He's read everything. And not just plays. He knows theater, not like an actor but a writer. He wrote a couple of speeches for me for a play I'm in. Before we broke up. I'm still finding out how much is there, layers and layers. It gives me loads to work with."

"You're in a play?" said Henry.

"Yes. Well. A new piece some friends and I are doing."

"I'd love to see it," said Henry. "I truly would. But I can't. The worst thing about a long run is one has no time for friends' work. Alas." He cut off the invitation before it was offered. His prick had led him into more bad theater, fringe and otherwise, than he cared to remember. "And what else do you love about this man?"

"Oh, that he's good-looking."

"Of course."

"In my eyes anyway. I don't think anyone else sees how handsome he is. To them he's just short and skinny."

"As short as I am?" said Henry.

Toby closed one eye and studied him. "No. I think he's shorter."

"And he's successful," said Henry. "That's something you must love about him."

Toby looked confused. "No. I'm happy for his sake he's done well. But it has nothing to do with why I love him."

"Success can be sexy," Henry argued, not without self-interest.

"Like having a nice body or good sense of humor. It can't hurt that his success is in a field that you're just entering."

"No," said Toby. "I'd love him even if he were a stockbroker. Or a garbageman or a dentist."

Now he *was* putting Henry on. Either that or the boy had a remarkable gift for lying to himself.

It was late. Henry was tired. He had finished his drink; Toby's cup was empty except for a brown lick of dried foam. Now was a good time to move on to the next phase.

"I'd love to continue this," said Henry, "but I'm exhausted. You must be tired too. We both put in a very full day's work tonight. We should say good night. Unless you'd like to come back to my place."

Toby stared. Then his face began to twist into various grimaces of regret and apology. "Sorry. No. I can't. I'm flattered! Like you wouldn't believe. That an actor I admire wants to sleep with—I mean, that is what you want. Or am I—?"

Henry raised his hand to stop his noise. "I expected you to say no. But I had to ask. Just to make sure."

Toby looked guilty. "Don't hate me. I told you. I'm not like that. And I didn't lead you on."

"You didn't. And you're right. It's better this way. Wiser. That we not throw away this wonderful first meeting in nasty old sex."

Henry meant to be sarcastic, yet he couldn't tell exactly where the joke landed. He *had* expected to be turned down, yet was oddly pleased when Toby did say no.

"I've enjoyed our talk," he continued. "I'd like to get together again sometime."

"You would?" said Toby. "I would too."

Henry paused, pretending that he had to think about this. "Have you seen *Tom and Gerry* yet? Pure fluff, but quite engaging. Or so people tell me. You showed me yours tonight. It's only fair that I show you mine." He laughed. "What night are you free?"

The boy frowned. "I got rehearsal all week for this play. Except Tuesday. Yes! Tuesday we quit early. Half the cast has a catering gig."

"Tuesday night it is. Very good. There'll be a ticket in your name at the box office. And then I want you to be my guest for dinner afterward."

"You don't have to do that."

"Yes I do. I hate to eat alone."

You transparent old lecher, thought Henry as he paid the check. Surely this boy sees through you.

Outside they bid each other good night. Henry wanted to kiss Toby on the cheek, a professional theater peck, but he restricted himself to a cordial handshake.

"This has been an honor," said Toby.

"Please," said Henry. "It should be a pleasure."

"Right. Sure. It'll be a pleasure Tuesday. See you then."

Henry watched the boy head down Eighth Avenue, walking with a contented, bouncing ostrich stride, his head held high like a ballerina's. The loose seat of his jeans squashed and unsquashed under his ample bottom, the single fold of denim flipping from cheek to cheek. Henry waited to see if the boy would turn around for one last look back. He never did.

Henry turned and started uptown toward his apartment.

What the hell was he doing? What did he want from a playwright's ex-boyfriend? One could understand why he *was* an ex. His contradictions were intriguing, but also maddening. What Henry should want, of course, was to get Toby in the sack. But this felt more complicated than lust. He'd already seen him naked. There was no mystery there. And Henry did not want romance. He did not want to fall in love with Caleb Doyle's ex.

He was surprised that Doyle still lingered in his head, a man he'd never met. But there he was, right behind Toby. And behind Doyle was his sister, Jessie, Henry's little assistant, like a lining up of planets, an omen of high drama. What kind of drama, Henry couldn't guess. If he were a nobler, more sentimental soul, he'd want to reunite the two lovers. But that plot felt old and hackneyed, with no fun and games for poor old Henry Lewse.

20

And how did that make you feel?"

"Guilty. Stupid. I had no business lashing out at my mother. My sister didn't help matters, but I can't blame Jessie. We need her more than she needs us. Our mother, I mean. But I should be glad of that. I wish she took my work more seriously, but I agree with her too. Because it's not real. None of it."

"What isn't real?"

"My work. What I do for a living. My so-called living." He took a breath. "Which is why I want to give up writing and theater. It's time that I do something real."

Seeing your therapist was a terrible way to start the week, and ten in the morning far too early. The mind was too scattered, the tongue too loose. Caleb surprised himself by leaping so soon from his visit home to this new idea.

Dr. Chin, however, took it in stride. "And what do you want to do instead?"

"Shouldn't you be asking *why* I want to give it up?"

She laughed, a light, musical titter. "Oh, there are so many reasons not to write or act or paint. But okay then. Why?"

Caleb was annoyed by her first question, which was the right question, the hard one. "I could give a hundred reasons," he said. "But the real one is that my circus animals have deserted me."

"But you broke off with Toby. He didn't desert you."

"I don't mean Toby. I mean my bogies, my writing demons." Why did people always bring up Toby? "There's a poem by William Butler Yeats. 'The Circus Animals' Desertion'? Where he says he gave his heart to the theater, but he's all burned out and his animals have run off. It's the poem with the lines 'I must lie down where all the ladders start,/In the foul rag-and-bone shop of the heart.' "

"I think I know that one. Vaguely. The way I know most poetry." She laughed again, this time at herself.

Caleb had been seeing Dr. Chin once a week for almost a year. She was a psychiatrist of no particular school, eclectic and pragmatic. He thought of her as "the Laughing Therapist" or sometimes "Dr. Chin, Medicine Woman." She was Chinese, but the southwestern look of her office—Georgia O'Keeffe on the wall, Navajo blanket on the sofa—suggested wisdoms of the Far West rather than the Far East. His mockery of her included fondness and respect. He'd gone through all the usual phases in the therapeutic relationship: angry resistance, giddy infatuation, bitter disappointment. Now he felt at ease with Chin, relatively. She was so transparent, willing to make mistakes and admit them, open in her uncertainty, without guile or harsh judgments. She could be flaky, especially when she wasn't paying full attention, but there were occasional flakes of gold in her musings. Caleb was rarely tempted to lie to her.

"Maybe you should go *there*," she suggested. "The foul rag-and-bone shop."

"Toby? No. Toby isn't the problem. Toby is just a symptom."

"You still believe that he was using you?"

"Or something. He wasn't there for me. He barely knew me."

" 'Using' is such a slippery concept," said Chin. "We all need help from other people. Certainly other people have helped you."

"Yes. But I always knew who they were, and why they were helping. We helped each other. Or maybe we used each other. But we never called it love. We never mistook it for romance. Oh, I don't know. Maybe I'm just not ready for another boyfriend." He frowned and looked away. "I brooded all weekend about Ben."

"That's nothing to be ashamed of."

"But his death was six years ago. I feel like I'm using *him* to justify self-pity."

She thought for a moment. "A little self-pity now and then is no crime. You've been through a very painful experience. It's natural that it reminds you of other painful experiences."

"But I'm measuring Toby against Ben. Which isn't right. I pretend the old love was clear and solid, but I know it wasn't. It began as half-love, make-believe love. Then Ben became sick, and I had to live up to that love."

"Like the couple in your play."

Chin hadn't seen *Chaos Theory*. She disliked theater, distrusted it, which was another reason why Caleb respected her. Unlike his mother, however, Chin read his plays.

"Yes. Yet another way that *Chaos Theory* is about me and Ben," he admitted. "But I was using Ben there too. His spells of dementia in the hospital? I gave them to a schizophrenic. I made them funny. And then I gave my feelings of helplessness to the wife. I made us straight. Which is more universal, you know. More commercial."

"We've been through this, Caleb. You do nobody any good by punishing yourself with these accusations."

"I thought your job was to make people confront the worst."

"In most cases, yes. But some of us *use* the worst in order to avoid looking at things that *can* be changed."

"I'm not fishing for—oh, not compliments, but the it's-okay-be-nice-to-yourself stuff. I hate hating myself. It's boring. But there's nobody else to hate. Except Toby. Only I don't hate him, not really. And Kenneth Prager."

There was a long pause from Chin.

"The reviewer at the *Times*," Caleb reminded her.

"I remember. I thought we'd finished with him too."

"Just a hack, I know. But I can't find anyone else to blame. Except the jerk producers who insisted we open the play before it was ready. Jesus. I finally write an honest play. I make up for a phony play about sex with an honest play about love, and I get kicked in the teeth. Rejected. By a hack at the *New York Times*. It's like you said last week. That he was trashing my life with Ben."

"I didn't say that! I said that for *the world* to reject your play *might* feel like they were denying your experience with Ben. Or words to that effect." She returned to her notes. "I have no idea who this reviewer-reporter-critic person is. And he is not the issue here. *You* are the issue."

Her vehemence surprised Caleb, confused him.

She cleared her throat. "Let's get back to Toby."

"Do we have to?" He tried to sound humorous.

"You said Toby was just a symptom, not a cause. You mean your breaking up with him was just a symptom?"

"No. My falling in love with him. He's a blank. A kid. There's no *there* there with Toby."

"You once said that he was half saint, half whore."

Caleb snorted. "I'm not so sure now about the saint part."

Chin smiled but waited for a serious reply.

"All right," he conceded. "It's true. I was in love with him. But it was like loving a dog. It was all about me, not about him."

"And you blame him for that?"

"No. I blame myself. Or if I blame him, it's only because I was disappointed there was nothing in him to love. Just a blank, an empty space, like an empty stage. Most actors have that, you know. It's where they play their parts. This big hole that they need to fill with make-believe and fame."

She said nothing but sat there, thinking.

"You think I mean a different kind of hole?"

"What? Oh." Her eyebrows twitched. "It sounded like the sexual side of the relationship was fine. And holes are holes." She sighed. "No, I was wondering about your fear that he was using you, combined with your decision to stop writing plays."

"It's not a decision, it's an inability."

"Maybe." She placed her finger over her mouth.

Caleb frowned. "You're saying I *want* to fail? In order to test Toby's love? To see if he'll love me even if I were a flop?"

"It's an idea."

"But I'm not in love with him now. And I'm already a failure." He began to laugh. "So what would the point be?"

"You're right. There can't be any possible connection." Her sarcasm was as light as a feather. "But we'll continue this next week. I see our time is up."

Of course. He should have sensed the end approaching. Chin regularly finished sessions like this, with a new, often pesky notion for Caleb to worry around in his head over the coming week.

As he stood up he could not resist saying, "Shouldn't you be encouraging me to get *out* of art? What's Freud's line? Artists are just weak souls who retreat into fantasy and hope to find there 'honor, fame, wealth and the love of beautiful women'? Or men in my case."

"You're being silly. You know I have the highest respect for art and artists." She opened the door for him.

"You once told me that books and art and plays are nothing but elaborate coping mechanisms."

"I cannot believe I said 'nothing but.' There's nothing wrong with a good coping mechanism. See you next week."

Almost every Chin session ended like this: in a parting volley of unanswered questions and charges. Caleb's head buzzed like a hive as he stepped out on West Tenth Street, their last words orbiting around him as if they'd just had an argument. He liked Chin, he trusted her. But sometimes, for a minute or so, after a final exchange like the one today, she reminded him a bit of his mother.

The sun was bright, the air soft, the street deserted. When he arrived here an hour ago, this quiet block had been dotted with men and women in business suits walking their dogs before they left for work, animals of various sizes and breeds, like four-legged ids on leashes. Now the dogs were locked indoors, asleep and dreaming; their owners were out in a useful world of money. Caleb had no chores or duties, only the challenge of spending another day in his own sorry company. Chin was often the social highlight of his week.

Her suggestion that he wanted to fail in order to test Toby was pure bull. He wasn't in love with Toby. He probably never was.

Love, love, love. Why did everyone always want to talk about love? Even psychiatrists. People wanted songs about it, novels, operas, plays. All of Caleb's plays had been love stories: *Chaos Theory* was about schizophrenia and love; *Venus in Furs* was about literary imagination and love; and *Beckett in Love* was about, well, Samuel Beckett and love. Caleb wished he could write instead a play about quantum mechanics or non-Euclidean geometry. Something pure and abstract, no words, only numbers. There would be no people onstage, only spheres and cubes and tetrahedrons. He wouldn't have to trouble himself with actors.

21

Look at these figures, Frank. Oo-hooo! A Monday-morning sell-off. These clowns don't know shit. Watch the numbers fall. Dumb rats desert a sinking ship. Churchill here. Davey! No, no, no, man. We're not gonna sell. *Au contraire.* I'm planning to scarf up another ten thousand shares when it gets below twelve."

John Churchill sat at his computer, talking to Frank, to callers, to himself. The mike cord of his headset was invisible. He had called Frank over for no discernible reason, unless he just wanted someone to see him at full throttle. Anybody hearing his torrent of words would think they were in the noisy hubbub of a trading floor, but Taurus Capital was otherwise quiet, a long white space with a high ceiling and polyurethaned floor. They were off lower Broadway, in a SoHo loft that was probably once the home of an artist and full of wet canvases and loud music. But money moved in and changed everything. Even Frank wore a necktie here.

"Don't wuss out on me, Davey. You need balls of brass. The dotcoms are not dead. Take it from me, a real dot-commie. Now what about the other hundred Gs you wanted to throw in the pot?"

Churchill was a young/old forty, with salt-and-pepper hair and French cuffs. He spoke like a construction worker, but it was only Ivy League macho: Harvard Business School. Frank knew firsthand that real blue-collars save foul language for real anger and pain. All day Sunday, whenever the lunacy of actors mucking around in their psyches had become too much for Frank, he told himself, Thank God I go back to real people on Monday. But an hour of John Churchill was enough to remind him how unreal most real people are.

"Candy-asses. Sheep. The world is divided between people who lead and people who obey. You're a smart guy, but you'd rather take orders than give them." It took Frank a beat to understand Churchill had finished his call and was talking to him. "What do you want?"

"You called *me* over," Frank reminded him.

"Oh yeah. That's right. I wanted to ask—" He shuffled through a stack of papers. "We spend way too much on Stein. An arm and a leg for one damned temp, sweetness. Darling. How are you?"

Another phone call elicited a whole new personality.

"Oh, baby. You know that's not my department. Where are you? Sweetness. Don't call me during class. Wait until recess. You want Mrs. Cutler to confiscate your phone again? We'll discuss this with your mother. Pets are her department. Love you, darling. This dickhead agency." He found the bill from Tiger Temps. "You've had Stein here four months and you still pay them a percentage? Not smart, Frank. Not smart at all."

"Sorry. Yes. We should fix that. We *could* hire her full-time and give them a finder's fee." Which Frank had proposed three months ago, but he knew better than to remind Churchill of that.

"I hate paying those scumbags another dime. But she'll stay? I don't want to buy her and have her quit on us next week."

"She likes it here," said Frank. "You give her a raise, and you still save money." Frank had started here the same way, hired as a temp, then sold by the agency to Churchill—like a leased Lexus.

"Do it, do it, do it," said Churchill. "You should've done it months ago. Would've saved me a shitload of money."

"My mistake," said Frank. "I'll take care of it immediately." He turned and headed back through the white room.

His official title was "office manager," but he was only a secretary. There were six employees at Taurus Capital, and all were treated like secretaries. They researched the new companies and processed the numbers, but Churchill made the decisions. The man was right, however: Frank did prefer to take orders—here anyway. It was a nice change from the acting life, where he had only himself to blame when things went wrong. It was good to have a boss who could be the target for all bitching and moaning and complaining.

He walked past Donald, Kim, Tony, and Pavel clacking away at their computers or mumbling into their headsets. Leslie Stein had the desk in the far back corner, farthest from the windows.

"Hey, Leslie. For what it's worth, good news from Mr. C."

She didn't look at him but held up one finger, asking him to wait while she finished whatever was on her screen. Frank stayed on his side of her desk, in case her activity was non-work-related. He didn't like to embarrass his charges.

Leslie was not what you'd expect in an investment boutique like Taurus. She dressed in black, wore brown lipstick and red nail polish; her face was full of piercings. Frank wondered if she wore body jewelry downstairs.

"All right, Frank. Done. What's the whoop from Church Lady?"

Frank reported that Churchill was finally hiring her full-time.

"Big whoop. But good. I need the moola. Now I can pay the printer and get my chapbook out of their warehouse."

Leslie was what she looked like, a Downtown poet. But she was good with numbers and not bad on the phone. Her real gift was she didn't give a damn. She had the jadedness of a woman with too many divorces and love affairs, but she was only twenty-five.

"Sorry it took so long," said Frank. "Churchill worried that you might split, but I assured him you were happy here."

"Like a pig in shit," she muttered. "No worse than my other jobs. And here I got another artiste to keep me company."

"Or ex-artiste," he reminded her.

"Hey, I'm going to a club tonight with friends. You want to join us? We can celebrate my whoop-de-do promotion."

"Thanks. But I got rehearsal tonight. Your friends go clubbing on a Monday?"

She shrugged. "They got their own hours. I usually drop out around one. But we're going to a performance piece and it starts early. Ten. Leopold and Lois. An anti–kind of nightclub act."

"Performance piece," Frank grumbled. "A fancy name for half-assed theater."

"That's right. You prefer full-assed theater." She snickered through her pierced nose. "So should I come see your show?"

"Might be too white-bread for you."

"No skin off my ass. Just thought it'd be a good way for me to know you better."

"But only if you let me see your chapbook of poems."

"I don't know, Frank. They might be too scary for you."

They often flirted like this, in a cool, bored, just-for-practice manner. Under different circumstances, if he hadn't met Jessie, he might have pursued Leslie. He *was* her superior, but not that superior. He suspected there was little to gain here except sex. Which was not unattractive. Frank was hornier at the office than he ever was while directing a play or even acting in one.

"And how's your kiddie show going?" she asked.

"Going, going, gone," he told her. "We did it on Friday and again Saturday. So it's finished."

"Sorry I missed it." She spoke in a brutal deadpan.

"It went well," he argued. "It went very well." He wanted to defend the show but knew he'd be wasting his breath.

"Must be a big relief to have it over. No more Mister Rogers, huh? No more visits to Munchkinland."

"Yeah. One down and one to go. Then I can have a life again. But congrats on the raise," he told her. "For what it's worth. Later."

Frank strolled back to his desk, needing to get away from Leslie before he said something stupid and indignant about *Show Boat*. Because he was proud of what he'd done. But Leslie would never understand. Leslie was way too cool.

He pulled out his chair and settled into his corner. Yes, one down and one to go. Thank God. It had been totally crazy this past month, jumping back and forth between two shows and this job. Now *Show Boat* was over. There would be no more breaking up afternoons with two-hour trips to P.S. 41. No more overload of activity, the rush and confusion. Life would be simpler. And Frank was sorry. He already missed the craziness. Which was ridiculous. God knows how he would feel next week when he also finished with *2B*.

He needed to call Tiger Temps but decided to call Jessie first. He wanted to hear her voice. She hated to be called at work, but he had a good excuse today, two in fact: she had left a message on his machine last night, and Allegra had asked him to ask a favor.

The phone was picked up on the second ring. "Henry Lewse," a forceful female voice declared.

"Jessie, hi. It's Frank."

"Oh. Hi."

"Sorry I didn't get back to you last night. Rehearsal ran late."

"Oh. No problem." She did not sound happy to hear from him, which hurt his feelings. He was much too sensitive about her.

"Your visit to your mom went okay?"

"The usual shit. I can't talk now."

Her voice was low, almost a whisper.

Then Frank heard music in the background, a Big Band number from the 1940s, and a clank like the banging of a radiator.

"Henry's already up?"

"Oh yeah. Up bright and early today. Working out on his weight machine. So I can't talk."

"Quickly, then. Allegra wants to know if you can bring your brother to the play. She hopes to get a quote from him if he likes it."

"That's so Allegra," said Jessie. "Well, I already asked him. He said he'd come. But not this weekend. He's got his party on Friday. Remember? Maybe next weekend?"

"Okay. Sure. I'll tell her." Frank was surprised she'd already invited Caleb, but he was more concerned about something else. "Does that mean *you're* not coming on Friday?"

"I'll try. But Caleb might want help with his party."

"I thought we were going to his party *together*?"

"Oh yeah. That's right. I forgot about your play. So you can't be there till late, right?"

"Maybe I can't be there at all," he said.

"Oh, Frank. Don't be like that. I'll come to your show. I'll come Saturday. But come to Caleb's party. You really should."

"I'll try. Look, I better go." He was afraid of what else he might say. He couldn't understand his temper today. "Let's talk later. All right? We'll get together *sometime* this weekend. All right?"

"All right," she said uncertainly. "I got to go too. Oh, quickly. Before I forget. How was it Saturday?"

"It went well. Even better than on Friday."

"Oh good. That's wonderful. They must love you there. Kids and parents both. Sorry. I got to go. But we'll talk later. Bye." Click.

Before he could thank her or stop her or say anything else.

Frank loved Jessie, and she was worth loving, but she didn't make it easy. He gripped the receiver like a blackjack, then returned it to its slot, very gently, like he could never harm a fly.

22

O h, Frank, thought Jessie as she hung up. She'd said something wrong but wasn't sure what. Now he was playing games about whether or not he'd go to Caleb's party. Silly old Frank. He should know better than to call her here.

She decided not to think about it and went back to work.

Henry was around the corner, groaning and grunting at his Nautilus machine. The blacksmith bang of weights was accompanied by old music on the stereo, "String of Pearls."

Monday was a dark night, and Henry usually slept until noon. There was a lunch scheduled for two today, with Adam Rabb of all people, and Jessie assumed she would have to wake him. But when she arrived this morning, Henry was already up, bouncing around the apartment in sweatpants and tank top. "Jessie, *mon amie*. And how are you on this exquisite morning?" Then he put on a CD of 1940s dance music and began his morning workout. She had sniffed the air, but there was no aroma of dope.

Jessie usually enjoyed Mondays. Henry slept late, she did her chores, and then, when he woke up and found an empty night ahead of him, he hung out and chatted. Today, however, started out all wrong. She couldn't enjoy anything, not even Henry's mail.

She read all his correspondence and answered most of it, except for the more personal letters. Her typed reply was clipped to the original letter and left out for Henry to sign. There had been a flurry of personal notes the week after *T & G* opened, but they soon dropped off. Now his mail consisted chiefly of bills, invitations to speak—student, theatrical, or gay groups—requests for donations, petitions, and an occasional fan letter or plea for help *disguised* as a fan letter. People rarely asked for autographed photos anymore, but they did ask for advice. There was one of those today:

> *Dear Mr. Lewse,*
> *I saw you last week when my middle school drama class came to "Tom and Gerry," your smash hit musical. You were wonderful. I laughed and laughed.*
> *I myself want to be an actress and think I have what it takes. How did you do it? If I send you a list of questions on how to structure my career, will you answer them?*
> *Thank you. You are the greatest.*
> *Sincerely yours,*
> *Tiffany Benz*

Nowadays even seventh graders were on the make. When Jessie showed Henry the first such letter, he was amazed. "Is this an American thing? How does one respond? And it's a boy?" The first writer was male. "How old? Hmm. We *could* tell him I won't be able to advise wisely until I see his photo. In either Speedos or briefs."

He was joking, of course, but Jessie worked out a standard reply on her own: "I regret that my schedule does not leave me time . . . hard work and perseverance . . . many good drama schools in this country . . . best of luck."

She wrote this letter to Tiffany and ran it out on the printer.

The clanking stopped. Henry came around the corner, looking disturbed, staring at a CD case in his hand. He was dripping, his tank top and gray chest hair plastered to his torso, the black hair on his head sticking out in all directions. Trim but grizzled along the edges, Henry looked like an old gymnast.

" 'Sentimental Journey,' " he said. "I could've sworn that was Glenn Miller. But I guess not. I have this inexplicable yen for 'Sentimental Journey.' I wonder where could I find it?"

"I'm sure they have it at Virgin," she told him.

"Virgin? Oh, the store. Of course. But what disk would it be on? I suppose they could tell me."

He seemed so helpless that Jessie couldn't stop herself. "If you like,

I could stop by and find a CD on my way home. Or I could probably download it from the Net."

"Can you do that? No, no. Not necessary." Henry seemed to think it was cheating to pull music from his computer. "A regular CD will be fine. I'll go over to Virgin this afternoon myself. It'll get me out of your hair and give me something to do."

"You can do it after your lunch with Rabb," Jessie suggested.

"Oh yes. That producer fellow. What time is—?"

Just then the phone rang. Jessie looked at the caller ID screen: England. She answered on the next ring. "Henry Lewse."

Henry watched eagerly, as if expecting a call.

"Good morning, Jessie. Has our naughty boy dragged his sorry carcass out of bed yet?"

"Dolly. Hello."

Henry's face fell.

"Good morning. Or it's evening over there," said Jessie, stalling while she watched Henry to see if he wanted to talk to his agent.

He waved both hands across his face.

"No, I'm sorry, Dolly. He's still dead to the world. Do you want me to have him call you at home when he gets up?"

"Want and get are two entirely different verbs with Henry." Dolly Hayes had the most wonderful voice, a throaty Joan Greenwood purr. "He hasn't returned my last calls. We haven't spoken in weeks. If I didn't know his bad habits, I'd swear he was avoiding me."

"He's been very busy, Dolly. Is there a message I can give him?" She took up her pen to write it so that Henry could read it over her shoulder.

"We have a nice job offer in hand. Voice-overs for a series of very smart detergent commercials."

Jessie wrote "Voice-over soap ads." Henry pulled the pen out of her hand and scribbled beside it "U.S. or U.K.?"

"Is that for the American or British market, Dolly?"

"The U.K., but it's nothing to sneeze at."

"British. Uh-huh. I'll tell him."

Henry flipped his right hand backward as if to say "Piffle."

"I can understand him turning up his nose at a season in Leeds, but this easy work for excellent money and wonderful exposure."

"I'll let him know." She wrote "Good $, big expose."

Henry worked his hand like a chattering sock puppet.

"Has he met yet with that Rubin fellow?"

"Adam Rabb. No, Dolly. That's today."

"Can you let me know how it goes? I assume it's just another case of commerce kissing the arse of art, but you can never guess where these things will lead."

"No, Dolly. I'll tell Henry to give you a full report."

"So how *is* our boy doing? Up to his eyebrows in the New York fleshpots? Rediscovering his hippie youth? Or is he already smitten with some pretty piece of American tail?"

"He seems to keep pretty much to himself, Dolly."

"Uh-huh." Dolly sounded dubious. "Let me just say, as one chum to another: We all want to protect Henry. He plays to the mother in us. But Henry's worst enemy is Henry. See what you can do to get him to call me."

"I'll do my best, Dolly."

"Thank you, Jessie. Good-bye."

Jessie hung up and turned to face Henry.

"And that's all the silly cow could find?" he said. "They want to use my voice to sell bars of soap?"

"Laundry detergent."

"Stupid cow."

Jessie liked Dolly Hayes. She couldn't understand Henry's antipathy, or why he wanted to drop her for an American agent. "She sounds concerned. She just wants to talk."

"Me mum's dead, thank you. I don't need another. Her only real concern is that I might be leaving her."

"But you are. You haven't told her yet?"

He frowned. "She's a friend as well as a business associate. I don't want her to take it the wrong way." He looked guilty, then covered his unease with a naughty smirk. "But thank you for fibbing for me, Jessie. You're an excellent liar. I should feel terrible for bringing out that side in you."

"Not at all." She laughed. "It's in my job description. Lying."

"You are so good to me. I don't know how to repay you."

And as he turned away, a new thought lit up a corner of her brain. "Actually—Friday night? After the show. Do you have plans?"

"What? Plans? I don't think I—"

"Would you be my date? For a party?" Fuck Frank. If Frank wouldn't go with her to Caleb's, she'd take Henry.

"A party?" He made a face like she'd just asked him to eat boiled dog.

"My brother's birthday. He's giving himself a party. My brother. Remember? You said you wanted to meet him."

"Oh, the playwright! Yes. Of course." *Now* he was interested. He remained confused, but he was definitely interested.

"It's a big party, so I don't know if he'll have a chance to explain algorithms to you. But you will get a chance to meet him."

"Algorithms? Of course. Algorithms. Why not?"

"You'll come?"

"It's the least I can do. I owe you, Jessie. Besides, I need to get out more. And I'll get to meet your mysterious brother."

"Nothing mysterious about Caleb."

"But he is to me. I've never met Mr. *Chaos Theory*."

"Uh, he's still raw about his play," she said uncertainly.

"I will be the soul of discretion there. Trust me. Friday night then. Excellent. Something else to look forward to." Henry returned to the dining room and his weight machine.

Jessie didn't know what to make of his off-and-on interest in Caleb. It did not sound sincere. But why should she care? Henry Lewse was taking her to Caleb's party, which was not just a birthday party but a real New York theater party. It should set people talking.

The clanks and grunts resumed around the corner. Jessie continued with the mail. Only now did she think of Frank again. But this had nothing to do with Frank. Frank didn't want to go to Caleb's party. He had made that clear. She was doing Frank a favor.

"Henry?" she called out. "Shouldn't you be getting ready for your lunch meeting?"

"My lunch what? Oh. I guess." He returned to the door, his face shiny with sweat. "Who's this fellow again?"

"Adam Rabb. He's a producer. Mostly theater, but an occasional movie. Good theater, bad movies. He's famous for being an asshole."

"Aren't they all? And what does he want from me?"

"Dolly says it's just a meet and eat."

"Hmm. He just wants to bask in my stardom. Oh well. At least I'll get a good meal out of it. I suppose I *could* wash."

He disappeared into his bedroom. Jessie shook her head and chuckled. He could be a very witty man.

She opened his phone bill: She enjoyed looking down the list of long-distance numbers and cities, wondering what famous colleagues were represented here. Henry was clearly a phone-call friend, not a letter-writing friend. The new bill included a category labeled Premium Calls. She had her suspicions about what they were but didn't dare ask Henry. She called Verizon.

"Those are what we refer to as adult services," the operator explained. "Did you want to put a block on them? So members of your household cannot call those numbers?"

"That's okay. We want to keep them. I just didn't understand the terminology. Thank you."

Jessie wasn't shocked, only surprised. She thought phone sex would be too techno for Henry. But she gave the matter a shrug, made out a check, and moved on to the next item.

23

Sunlight, brightness, day. Henry had forgotten how bright daylight could get in America, even in New York. He shielded his eyes as he walked up Broadway toward Central Park, feeling like an anonymous vampire strolling through the lunch-hour mob, a stylish phantom in a linen jacket and collarless shirt. He really should invest in sunglasses.

He suddenly began to hum "Sentimental Journey," the tune he had struggled to remember all morning. The other 1940s tunes had blocked it out. Only now when he was outside and walking did the melody return. It was for the boy from last night, of course. Toby. As in Toby Tyler. Who ran off and joined the circus. Henry wanted him for his own little circus. Sex. Just sex. Oh, there may be a dash of sentimental feeling, but that was only nostalgia for his own frisky, heartless, get-laid-every-night years—when he was Toby's age.

Columbus Circle appeared, a weird mix of Piccadilly and Marble Arch. Jessie said that the restaurant, Jean Georges, was in the ugly black building towering over the park. He spotted the building—it was *very* ugly—then followed the crowd into the crosswalk to circle the circle.

Henry regretted he wasn't seeing Toby until tomorrow. If he were seeing him tonight, his dark night, he could make an early start of it. Who knew how long it would take to get the boy out of his panties? He seemed awfully innocent for a stripper, although not so innocent for an actor.

On the far side of the circle, at the entrance to the park, stood an elaborate white monument. A monument to what, Henry couldn't guess. It was a marble cake with gold doodads on top and chalky nudes on the sides. A half dozen living boys, black, brown, and pink, floated and spun around the base. They rode on skateboards and Rollerblades, swerving and pitching and leaping. Henry paused to watch. They were beautiful. They betrayed no awareness of the people around them, no trace of self-consciousness. They were lost in their skill, absorbed by their action. Their baggy jeans hung halfway down their hips, so low that their slender torsos suggested tulip stalks emerging from the bulbs. Very sexual, of course. The whole world was sexual. A naked boy stood on the prow of the monument—he was a statue—with his hands lifted skyward and two pigeons perched on his palms—the pigeons were real. Henry smiled and resumed walking. There is nothing like lechery for putting one in touch with the beauty of things.

He crossed the street to the ugly black building, a black glass monolith with an ugly silver globe out front. Another bloody business lunch. Well, not real business, only pretend. He had done a dozen such lunches or dinners since arriving in New York, the self-important ruses of people with money to meet people with fame. They called themselves producers, but none ever seemed to have produced anything. Henry had learned to expect nothing from these meetings except an opportunity to taste some very expensive wine.

Just inside the plate glass stood a tall, dark, Mediterranean youth in a tux. "Mr. Lewse?"

"Yes?" It was always nice to be recognized, nicer still when it was someone with such pretty bee-stung lips.

"Welcome to Jean Georges, Mr. Lewse. Mr. Rabb is already here. This way, please."

Henry followed the fellow through frosted glass doors into a large, gray room full of blue suits. Watching the bit of seat just below the maître d's jacket, Henry found himself humming one last bar of "Sentimental Journey."

They approached a corner table occupied by a big, sad, badly rumpled man. He slowly stood up—he was *very* big. He hadn't shaved. Or maybe that was his full beard, a sickly shadow. He held out his hand. "Henry Lewse," he said in a low grumble. "This is an honor."

"So nice to meet *you*," sang Henry, wishing the man had introduced himself. He had already forgotten his name.

The man sat back down and gestured at an empty chair. It was catty-corner to him, so that Henry might see the room—or, more likely, the room could see Henry.

"Let me start off by being a total cliché: I'm your biggest fan. You're a great actor, Henry Lewse. A true artist."

He maintained a flat, emotionless mumble, a bored tone at odds with his words. Henry suspected sarcasm, but one encountered that kind of irony so rarely over here.

"I know all your work. *Hamlet* and *Vanya* at the RSC. Your *Godot* with Jonathan Pryce. *Cloud Nine.* You were a wonderful Grandcourt in the BBC *Daniel Deronda.* They showed it here on *Masterpiece Theatre,* you know."

He seemed sincere, despite the affectless mutter. Maybe he was depressed? His clothes were badly disheveled, expensive clothes, a designer jacket and striped silk shirt, wrinkled and rumpled, not like he'd merely slept in them, but like he was his own unmade bed. His slovenliness was such a surprise in a producer that Henry wondered if he might actually have brains.

"I watched the Carol Reed *Oliver!* again last night. Back in your child actor days. When you were H. B. Lewse."

"Oh dear. We have done our homework, haven't we?" Half the boy actors of his generation did time in that infernal show, but Henry had done the flick as well.

The producer smiled: a thin, wan, lipless smile, like he'd just played a winning hand of cards. He opened his menu. "Shall we order? I already ordered wine. Excellent pinot noir," he mumbled into his wrinkled collar. "Had it for lunch yesterday. The charcuterie is good, the lamb first-rate, and the duck is fab."

"You eat here often?"

"Finest restaurant in town."

Henry looked around the room and wondered what Toby would think of it. "Do you know how late they serve?"

The wine steward arrived with a bottle. He displayed the label to the rumpled host, uncorked it, and poured a splash into the man's glass. The man tasted it and nodded. The waiter then filled Henry's glass. Henry took a swallow. It was wonderful wine, sharp and clean. It evaporated in the mouth like flavored air.

"I think we're ready to order."

"Very good, Mr. Rabb. I'll send Victor over."

That's right. The man's name was *Rabb.* And his first name was

Aaron or Arnie or something biblical. Knowing his host's name made Henry feel less defensive, less vulnerable.

"So," said Rabb. "How did you like *Greville*?"

"*Greville*?" Another name he was supposed to know?

"The novel I messengered over last week."

The book that bounced around his apartment all weekend. So here is where it came from.

"Oh that. Yes. Of course."

"Did you get a chance to read it?"

"Yeeees," he said uncertainly.

"And?"

"Interesting. Like a trashy marriage of *Lolita* and *Silence of the Lambs*." Someone had said that, Henry couldn't remember who.

"Ha ha ha," said Rabb. He actually spoke the syllables. He held his mouth open for a moment in a cold, rectangular grin. "I bought that trashy marriage, you know. I'm making a movie of it."

"Are you now?" He'd certainly stuck his foot in it, hadn't he? Henry looked for a way to undo the damage but could come up with no clever phrase, no good joke. So he smiled at Rabb, a long, bland, foolish smile.

Rabb smiled back. "Forget the novel. We have a script now. It's better than the novel."

"I'm sure it is."

Rabb tried to sustain his smile, but it was fading.

"Gentlemen?"

The waiter stood over them.

Both men were relieved by the distraction. They ordered lunch: Henry asked for the duck, Rabb the charcuterie. The waiter departed.

"It's a part that everybody wants."

For a moment Henry thought Rabb was referring to the duck.

"There's no truth to the rumors it's been cast. But we're talking to Oldman and Malkovich. *And* Alec Baldwin. You read the trades?"

Henry nodded, then caught himself and shook his head. He returned to the wine. He was safer with the wine.

"We've gone to Susan Sarandon for the mother, and Julia Stiles for the daughter. I want to keep away from Miramax, because they'll want

Paltrow. But she's not sympathetic anymore. Audiences will *want* her to get killed. Ha ha. But with Julia . . ."

Henry nodded and smiled, but he stopped listening. Rabb's monotone mumble was not only dull but also hard to follow in the noisy restaurant. He was one of those talkers who expect the listener to do all the work. Henry had no interest in "industry gossip." That's what this was, wasn't it? Rabb said they were talking to *other* people, so there was no work here for Henry. Rabb was merely declaring his importance by dropping names. Money people think they possess people by naming them. But the wine tasted heavenly.

"And we'll be shooting on Capri. Have you been? Lovely. I want Daldry to direct. Maybe Hytner, only he's getting awfully mumble mumble. But the English are so much better at this. And not because they're cheaper. We're talking a budget of mumble. The salary for *Greville* will be commensurate with mumble mumble—"

Yes, thought Henry, lifting the glass of wine and examining the color. If I can get Toby to try some, I can get him soused. Well, not soused but more in touch with himself. Then . . .

Rabb had stopped talking. He was frowning. "You don't seem terribly interested in this."

"What? Oh, I'm sorry. It's just that this pinot noir is so good." And you are boring the anus off me.

Rabb studied him a moment, then shook his head and smiled another cool, smug, lipless smile. "You're a sly boots, Henry Lewse. What else have you got up your sleeve?"

"I beg your pardon?"

" 'A wink is as good as a nod for a blind man, eh,' " said Rabb, in a clumsy approximation of Scottish or Yorkshire or something.

Before Henry could ask what he meant, the food arrived, pretty portions on white plates as big as hubcaps.

"Dig in, Henry. Yum."

Rabb attacked his own plate of sausages and sliced meats with surprising enthusiasm. He was no mumbler when it came to eating.

The duck was sliced in neat half-inch diagonals. Henry took a bite and bit into crispy skin. Warm juice squirted the roof of his mouth. He almost burst out laughing. It felt as good as it tasted.

"Your agent is Dolly Hayes?" said Rabb.

"What? Oh yes. Good old Dolly." He could see it now. He'd bring Toby here, wine him and dine him, woo him and win him.

"Very well . . . I should . . . She's in London, right?"

Henry nodded. "Where it's harder for her to play big sister. Dolly is the last of her breed. Not just an agent but a friend. I don't know how much longer we'll remain—"

Rabb leaned over and jabbed his fork into Henry's duck. He stuffed the piece in his mouth.

Henry blinked away his surprise. "The last of her breed," he repeated. "She loves good theater even more than she loves her commission. Sometimes. Which can be admirable," he admitted. "Although in this day and age one needs to give more thought to . . ."

But Rabb appeared too involved with his own food to hear a word that Henry was saying. Who was it who said that the opposite of talking isn't listening, the opposite of talking is waiting? It must have been an American.

24

Once upon a time, Monday nights were dark nights. Every theater was closed, everyone stayed home: actors, audience, and critics. But Kenneth Prager found that no nights were completely dark anymore, certainly not Off-Broadway.

He put in a full day at the *Times* on Monday, writing the final drafts of two reviews that would not run until later in the week. One described CSC's uneven revival of *The Rivals,* the other a vanity musical about New Yorkers and their dogs. "Imagine *Rent* with dog biscuits, or *Hair* with mange, and you get some idea of *Dog Run.*" He tried to be kind to the actors.

It was going to be a slow week. He wanted to review the new Richard Foreman and explore his thoughts about that strange avant-garde dreamer whose performance pieces hadn't changed in thirty years. Repetition became a kind of integrity. But Ted Bickle, the first reviewer, had put dibs in on the Foreman. Bickle was being very piggy with assignments since his return from the hospital.

The copyeditor routed *The Rivals* back into Kenneth's computer decorated like a Christmas cookie with red corrections and green queries, including one asking him to explain, "for our few readers who might not know," what century Sheridan had lived in. Kenneth could have worked at home, but he needed his office in the Times Building. He felt solid here, grounded, safe in his fourth-floor cubbyhole. Other *Times*men and *Times*women softly milled outside his open door. Kenneth was not the boogeyman here, not the Buzzard of Off-Broadway, but a good journalist, a disciplined writer who never missed a deadline. He liked most of the people he worked with, and they seemed to like him—except maybe Bickle.

He went home by cab. He used to take the subway but couldn't anymore. Too many theater people traveled underground.

He ate dinner with his family that night, munching the macaroni and cheese—Rosalind's favorite—that Gretchen had picked up at Gourmet Garage on her way home from the office. He listened to Gretchen ask Rosalind about a boy she was sweet on, Tony, who'd been in *Show Boat* with her. He was startled to learn that Rosalind could be sweet on anyone. Wasn't she too young?

"Does this mean I'll have to start meeting boys at the door with a shotgun?" he teased.

"Oh, Daddy," said Rosalind, baring her braces at him in a grimace of humiliating pity.

Around the time when most family men were thinking about going to bed and enjoying nice long chats with their wives—he wanted to ask Gretchen about this Tony—Kenneth had to go out again. He was expected at Cafe Fez tonight for something called "Leopold and Lois." It wasn't a play, it was—God knows what it would be. The music reviewer had seen it and said it wasn't music. So they were sending Kenneth.

"Good luck, dear," said Gretchen when he kissed the top of her head—she did not get up from the sofa. "Who knows?" she timidly hoped. "Maybe it'll be fun?"

He could only make a pained face and produce a pained noise. "I'll try not to wake you when I come in," he told her. "Good night."

Cafe Fez was just over in the East Village. Kenneth decided to walk. The night was lovely, the air mild and fragrant. A man could be safely anonymous in the bosky shadows of the tree-lined streets.

Fez was in the basement of a large, trendy restaurant near the Public Theater. Reviewers were supposed to be incognito, but the management knew him. "The *Times,* right? We got a table for you." The room was set up like a nightclub, but the crowd was hardly café society. They were all in their twenties, with an extreme sampling of shaved heads and stapled faces. Kenneth had left his necktie at home but feared he still stuck out like a Secret Service agent.

They led him to a table where a man was already seated, a plump young man in a seersucker suit. "Kenneth *Prager*! What a surprise! Never thought I'd see *you* here!"

He held out his hand and Kenneth shook it: a damp, pudgy hand. "Hello, Cameron."

Cameron Ditchley wrote for the *Post*. He wasn't their theater reviewer or music critic, just a renaissance hack whose beat was "Downtown." A florid dandy of another era, he was not yet thirty but looked straight out of *Sweet Smell of Success*. He wore a display handkerchief in the pocket of his jacket. He spoke in an exuberant whine full of random italics.

"I hear this is *fabulous*. But you must have heard *too*, or the Paper of Record wouldn't be sending a man of *your* credentials."

They made shop talk for ten excruciating minutes. Ditchley loved anything he hadn't seen, and hated only shows that had closed. Whenever Kenneth feared he'd become a sell-out, a hack, a whore, he often told himself, Well, at least I'm not Cameron Ditchley.

Finally, the show began.

An old man and old woman stumbled up onstage, or rather, two boys in their twenties, one of them in drag. Leopold and Lois were a lounge act: Leopold played the piano, Lois sang. Leopold wore the bad, sooty makeup of a child playing Grampa in a school play. Lois was more convincing in her blue-rinse wig and teal blue evening gown. Kenneth was not averse to drag; he could appreciate camp. He loved the late Charles Ludlam.

Lois kicked off the act by singing "All of Me"—in the coarse croak of a sick crow. No, it wasn't music. Kenneth scribbled the song title on his notepad. He noticed Ditchley noticing; Ditchley took out his own pen and wrote something on a cocktail napkin. Sitting with other reviewers often made Kenneth feel like they were all taking a test and he should keep his answers covered.

"Good evening," Lois croaked. "Welcome to the musical stylings of Leopold and Lois. Lucky you." Leopold tinkled the intro for a song. But instead of singing, Lois growled, "That reminds me—" and fell into a boozy ramble about her life in music, starting with her childhood. She had a wonderful drunken mother and an even drunker father, who raped her when she was twelve. "Oh, but I got my revenge on him," she said sweetly. "Next time he visited me in bed, I was holding a straight razor under the covers. Ha! Improved his vocal range by a whole octave. Mom, of course, never forgave me. So I left home and went into show business."

It was supposed to be funny, or funny for being so unfunny. The kids around him roared. At the next table, a young woman with brown lipstick and a face full of rings—she was armored like a stag beetle—applauded by pounding the table with her fist.

The show continued in this vein, with more monologues than songs, Lois tossing back drinks and laughing as she told stories about her first husband the junkie, her second husband the cross-dresser, and how Leopold was beat up in grade school, then in high school, then in college, then was thrown off a roof by his boyfriend, "a very nice schizophrenic named—Mike."

"So here we are," she concluded and reached across the piano to clutch Leopold's hand. "Together forever. The way it was meant to be. Isn't life a kick?"

It was a parody, of course, a riff on all the smiling-through-the-tears schtick of a million lounge acts. But the ugliness and pain outweighed the comedy. There was no sympathy here, no pity, only contempt for an old woman's delusions. And there was no love of showbiz either. Kenneth worked hard to find some affection for junk, the poetry of trash. There was nothing but anger.

Lois began to sing "Hey, Jude"—"For the kids," she explained—turning the elegiac Beatles song into a bitter, angry rant.

"Isn't this *fabulous*?" cooed Ditchley.

Once Kenneth caught the note of anger, he could notice nothing else. And the audience ate it up, enjoying the cruelty as if it were bold truth-telling. You'd think the show were an attack on Ronald Reagan or the Vietnam War, not the mocking of two old entertainers.

What were the performers and audience so angry about? Their parents' lives? Getting old? The vicious world of celebrity and entertainment? Whatever the cause, Kenneth felt he'd fallen into something fierce and ugly. It made *him* angry.

When the show ended, Kenneth hurried outside. He needed the meaningless noise of the city at night. But it was late, the city was quiet. He walked home on West Ninth Street, a silent corridor of tall apartment buildings that suggested a high empty room like a deserted theater. Kenneth hated the empty quiet. He walked more quickly. He could hear nothing here except his own sorry footsteps.

25

You: Hello.

ME: Oh!

YOU: What?

ME: You scared me.

YOU: Sorry.

ME: Where are you?

YOU: Right in front of you. Can't you see me?

ME: No. It's too dark.

YOU: Never mind. You don't need to see me. We can just talk.

ME: Who are you?

YOU: Don't you know?

ME: You sound like— Oh my God.

YOU: What?

ME: Words fail me.

YOU: They always did.

ME: But it can't be you. You're dead.

YOU: Thoroughly dead. There's nobody deader.

ME: What's it like?

YOU: Death? It's not like anything.

ME: Are there bodies? Or are you only voices?

YOU: We have bodies. We can't touch the living, but we can touch
each other.

ME: You're not alone?

YOU: No. There's other dead people here. Many, many other dead
people. Which makes me glad. Whoever said "Hell is other
people" was an idiot. Can you imagine the opposite? An eternity

of solitude? Without company or conversation? With no words but your own. Nobody to tell you other people's stories? Forever and ever.

ME: The dead like to hear stories?

YOU: Oh yes. We tell each other stories all the time.

ME: Do you follow our stories too?

YOU: The living? You mean, do we watch you? Like television?

ME: Yes. Do the dead still care about the living?

YOU: Enough-about-me? What-do-*you*-think-about-me?

ME: I didn't mean it like that. I meant—I think about you all the time, Ben. Selfishly, yes. I admit it. But I *do* think about you. Do you ever think about me?

YOU: Why else would I be here?

ME: ——

YOU: What're you doing, Cal? What's that noise?

ME: I'm crying. Don't you remember crying?

YOU: Oh yes. Crying. What the living do.

ME: I'm just so happy to have you here and be able to talk to you again. So this is real. I'm not just imagining you?

YOU: Oh no. You *are* imagining me. But that doesn't make it any less real.

Caleb set his pencil down, blinked a few bright needles of tears from his eyes, and read over his words. You're a funny guy, he told himself. A very strange and funny guy.

26

The buzzer loudly buzzed. "It's me, doll," Irene sang over the intercom. Caleb buzzed her in and returned to the kitchen. He heard the elevator humming in the wall while he finished fixing the coffee.

"Knock knock!" she called out through the open door.

"In here."

Irene Jacobs sailed around the corner, tall and athletic and grinning, a huge macramé bag hung from her shoulder. "Good morning, doll." She kissed him hello and shook a white sack at him. "Not only does your agent make house calls, but she also brings almond croissants."

"Great. I thought we'd go out on the terrace. It's too pretty a morning to waste indoors."

"Fine by me. I love your terrace."

Caleb stacked everything on a tray—plates, cups, the hourglass of coffee—and carried it outside. Irene led the way, peering into his rooms. Caleb wondered if she were adding up costs and figuring out how much longer he could afford to live here.

He set everything on the table in the prow of the terrace. The fieldstone building across the street towered over them like a sunlit slice of granite cake. A whole flock of pigeons spilled softly from the roof, swooped downward, then clapped hands and rose up again. A crow croaked in the park around the corner—the city had begun to attract the loud, black, solitary birds. The billboard for *Tom and Gerry* still stood across the way but was less conspicuous by daylight, blending into the jumble of walls and rooftops.

"Nice," said Irene as Caleb poured the coffee. "Gritty but pretty."

She was an entertainment lawyer, not an agent, but acted as agent and manager for a handful of theater people. A former hippie with frizzy hair and copper freckles, she wore jeans and thrift-shop peasant blouses with her Armani jackets and Fifty-seventh Street haircuts. She was a fierce liberal and tough businesswoman, facing the world of politics and the world of showbiz with the same fuck-you grin.

"You don't look like you been sleeping well." She ran a finger under her own eyes. "Using insomnia to start something new?"

"Nope."

"Really? When I walked by your office, I thought I saw an open notebook next to your computer."

"Must be my address book. I haven't written a word in months."

"In that case"—she scooted her chair up to the table—"you might be interested in this. I got a call. Andras Konrad. Hungarian producer. He just bought the option on *Fear of Flying*. They're looking for a screenwriter. And somebody recommended you."

"*Fear of Flying?*" said Caleb. "That must be twenty years old."

"More like thirty. It's been knocking around forever, one of those jinxed projects that never gets made. It's lost its edge over the years. But the Hungarians don't know that. They think they got a hot, sexy property on their hands."

"No, Irene. Sorry. I can't."

"Why? You said you're not working on anything. And here's something you don't have to take too seriously."

"It's not this project. It's all projects." He took a deep breath. "I'm seriously thinking about giving up writing altogether."

She didn't even blink. "Then this is perfect. You get paid eighty thousand up front. It'll never get made. It's the next best thing to *not* writing—except you get paid."

"Didn't you hear me? I want to stop. I want to give up writing."

She looked him in the eye. "For how long?"

"Forever."

She smiled—her sweetest, you-are-so-full-of-shit grin. "I have a better idea. Give it up for a year. If you can give it up for that long. Then see what happens."

"Why can't anyone take me seriously on this? My sister doesn't. My therapist doesn't."

"Are you still seeing Chin?"

"Yes."

"Isn't she amazing?"

Caleb frowned. "This is just a joke to all of you. Right? Just more neurotic-artist shit."

"Sorry," said Irene. "But I hear it from clients all the time. I hear it from *myself*. 'Oh I shouldn't do this anymore. Oh I should do something real with my life. Oh but there are whales being killed.' Or dolphins. Or owls. Or I should work for world peace. Blah blah blah. We *all* talk like this. But talk is cheap. When you stop writing, you just stop. You don't announce it. It's over and done with. The end."

"But I'm not writing. The end is here."

"Caleb, dear. If this were two years after *Chaos*, I'd believe you. But it's been two crummy months. Give yourself a vacation. You deserve it. You got creamed. It happens to the best. Although I still think you could've given the play a happy ending. And not just for commercial reasons."

"A happy ending would've been dishonest."

She wasn't listening—they'd had *that* talk many times. She hoisted her bag into her lap. "Next bit of business: the party on Friday." She pulled out a heavy manila envelope. "The caterer dropped these off. It's the guest list with the RSVPs."

"How many are coming?"

"Who knows? Theater people never RSVP. They're too busy living in the moment."

Irene had done the dirty work, or rather, hired people who did the dirty work: the caterer and the invitation senders. It went forward with a momentum that had nothing to do with Caleb.

"But they also sent this." She passed him the bill. "Which they want paid in full up front."

Caleb was looking over the guest list, searching out the names that had sent regrets. "Huh. Mary Louise won't be coming? Or David. Or Joe." Nobody involved in *Chaos* was coming, not even the director.

"They probably feel guilty."

"We *all* want to avoid each other," said Caleb. "Like a bunch of kids caught playing strip poker." There was no need to mention the obvious: they blamed him for this flop.

Irene tapped the bill in his hand. "So?" she said. "What do you want to do about this?"

He looked at the amount: twelve thousand and change. It was what they'd agreed on, but seemed much larger printed out.

"They want it all now. By tomorrow. The original deal was half now, half next month."

He began to laugh. "They're afraid I might not be good for it? Broadway bomb and all?"

"I know Jack and his partner. They're being jerks."

"If I don't pay, I might have to cancel the party?"

"What? You want to call their bluff?"

He thought about it, wondering if he really could pull the plug. "Oh, let's pay the jerks," he said. "I want to go out in style. One last bash. While I can still afford it. And I'm still able to live in this cottage in the sky."

"You'll be fine. Unless you radically change your lifestyle, develop a taste for lobster. Or crack. You're solvent—until the end of the year. But I wouldn't turn up my nose at screenwriting jobs, no matter how bogus." She tapped her watch with her index finger. "I should be going. I'm seeing my trainer at eleven-thirty. She'll be so proud. I had an almond croissant in front of me and ate only half."

Caleb walked her back into his apartment.

"So," she said. "*I* pay the gangster caterers. *You* think about *Fear of Flying*. And we see each other on Friday. Trust me on the other stuff, doll. You'll feel better in time. Every writer or actor or director goes through this kind of funk."

"I know. I'm not alone. Which doesn't make it easier."

"Besides, if you give up writing, what else would you do with your life?"

"There's always drugs." He smiled. "Or maybe I could become a Buddhist and join a monastery."

"Oh no. You don't want that. I was in an ashram for six months. Twenty-five years ago and my bowels still haven't recovered. Good-bye, doll." She kissed his cheek and walked downstairs to the next floor, where the elevator was.

Caleb went back out to the terrace and began to load the tray.

Irene is right, he thought. If I *say* I'm going to quit, I'll never quit. I should just stop writing, cold turkey. See if anyone even notices?

There was a loud knock at the front door, a jokey shave-and-a-haircut rap-rap. It must be Irene. Nobody had buzzed downstairs. Caleb walked back inside and opened the door.

"Did you forget some—?"

A large, pale, beefy shape filled the doorway. Toby.

27

Hi. Uh. Sorry. A lady was going out as I was coming in. I should have buzzed. Right? And called too. Sorry."

He stood on one bent knee and hung on one hip. His head was down. He looked at Caleb through a soft fray of hair—a sheepish, sheepdog look. He wore an olive drab T-shirt and jeans.

"Toby. Hello. What brings you downtown?" Caleb spoke calmly, coolly. But he was not prepared for how real Toby looked, large and solid. He had not seen him in two weeks. The oversize image passed straight through his eye into his gut. There had been a time when Toby went from eye to heart, or eye to cock. But today he went straight into the pit of a raw, pink stomach.

"I came for my socks and underwear," he said.

"What?"

"The stuff I left in the laundry. Didn't you get my message?"

"Oh. Right. Yes. The laundry came back last week."

"I forgot. Until I started running out of clean underwear."

He looked paler than Caleb remembered, blonder, almost translucent. He had his old, curious smell, half sour, half bitter, like raspberries and seawater. It was too intimate standing next to him.

"Is my stuff still here? You didn't throw it out, did you?"

"Don't be silly. Elena must've put your underwear in with mine when she put everything away. Come on in. We'll find it."

Toby strolled inside, looking tougher and more confident than Caleb expected. He held his head high, indifferently gazing around at what had been his home away from home, for a few weeks anyway.

"So how have you been?" said Caleb.

"Busy. I'm in a play, you know."

"I remember. That thing with my sister's friends."

"The speech you wrote me? It works great. Frank wanted us to rework it, but I refused to change a word."

"Whatever's best for the play," said Caleb.

They came to the bedroom, as small as every other room, two-thirds of it filled with the double bed. The curtains were open. The big casement window divided the view into squares like a wall map. Caleb waved Toby in. "Underwear's in the bottom drawer. Just go through it and pick out yours."

"You trust me with your stuff?" He looked over at Caleb with a hurt, touched, heartbroken expression.

He was acting, of course. He was always acting. The trick with Toby was to figure out when he was acting out things he only pretended to feel, and when he was acting out things he really felt.

Fuck it, thought Caleb. He stepped past Toby's doggy stare, opened the drawer, and took out fat white stacks of briefs and T-shirts. He set them on the bed. "Here. Find your things. Can't be many. I haven't come across any yet." They both wore briefs, but Toby's underwear should be easy to locate. Not only was he taller and heavier, he wasted money on brands with names like "2(x)ist."

Toby sat sideways on the bed, like a lady riding sidesaddle, bending over the stacks as he went through them.

Caleb stood in the doorway. "So you like living uptown?"

"It's okay. Allegra is ripping everyone off, charging us four hundred each. But nothing I can do about it, is there?"

His T-shirt rode up in the back. Three little vertebrae marked the descent downward.

"You'll get to see the apartment when you come see the play."

He wore no belt. The lip of his jeans stuck out. A slim white tongue of waistband was just visible inside.

"You are coming, aren't you?"

"Eventually. Not the first night, but—later."

Toby twisted to the left. The waistband slid down to the flat-boned isthmus between spine and bottom.

And Caleb lunged. He grabbed Toby by the waist and threw him facedown on the bed. He shook him by his britches, shaking him out of his jeans and underpants. Toby's ass was round and heavy like an old-fashioned medicine ball. He tried to squirm free, but Caleb pinned him from behind. He wedged his chin between the cheeks and rubbed his beard there. "Here is what I love," he said. "This is all I ever loved. Because nothing else in you is real." He buried his nose in the warm, mossy furrow. He pried him apart with his thumbs; he dug in with his tongue. Instantly the boy was up on his elbows, arching his back and grunting like an elephant.

"Would you like a bag for those?" said Caleb.

"I brought my knapsack. I'll put them there. But thanks."

Toby continued to examine neck tags and waistbands. Caleb remained in the doorway. But yes, he could imagine violating him. Rimming or spanking or fucking him, something obscene. Except it would be like sex, and sex could be mistaken for love. And he did not love Toby.

"Oh, almost forgot," said Toby, unrolling a pair of socks and checking for holes. Only Caleb's socks had holes. "Guess who I met?"

"Who?"

"Guess."

"How should I know?" Caleb sighed. "Shakespeare's dog?"

"No. But close." Pause. "Henry Lewse."

Toby did not face Caleb but concentrated on rolling the socks back up. He seemed to be smiling.

"He asked me to come see his show. Tonight. And he wants to take me to dinner afterward."

Caleb didn't believe it. But Toby was not a good liar. So it might be true.

"How nice for you," Caleb said drily. "Where did you meet?"

"He came to my class at HB and gave a talk. And I went up to him afterward and asked a few questions."

At least it wasn't Kinko's. Where Caleb had met Toby when he became a regular there during the rewrites of *Chaos Theory*.

He was staring at the back of Toby's neck, the downy white squiggles under his haircut. He is not going to make me jealous, he told himself. But Henry Lewse? Henry "the Happy Whore" Lewse? Toby was crueler than Caleb had ever imagined possible.

"So that's why you need clean underwear. For your date."

Toby snapped his head around. "What an ugly thing to say. And it's not a date. It's just dinner."

"I remember dinner with a playwright and where that ended."

Here, in fact, in this very room. Which was easy to forget in daylight. Or no, the curtains were wide open, the sun bright the next morning when they woke up together. Toby had shown no embarrassment over the hundred windows across the way, like a wall of eyes, and what the neighbors might think of two nude men in this airborne display case. He had actually seemed proud to be seen naked with Caleb by a city that might or might not be looking—a surprising attitude for an earnest, wholesome kid from Wisconsin. It was Caleb who wrapped himself in a blanket while Toby stretched and smiled and stood at the window.

The room suddenly felt as bleak and empty as a crime scene.

Toby said nothing but sat very still with his back to Caleb. He stuffed his underwear into his knapsack. "I'm finished," he said. "I should let you get back to work."

Caleb wanted him to go—out of this bedroom, out of his life. But not yet. "I'm not working on anything," he confessed. "Let's go out on the terrace. I think there's some coffee and almond croissants left."

"Oh? All right. Sure. I got time." Toby hoisted his pack and followed Caleb out to the terrace.

He looked less sexual in sunlight, more opaque. He didn't want coffee, but he wolfed down a sweet pastry almost as soon as he sat.

"Oh. Almost forgot," he said and paused to suck a crumb from his teeth. "Happy birthday."

"It's not until Friday."

"Your party is Friday, correct?"

An insincere, actorly note had entered Toby's voice; Caleb waited to see where this was going. "Yes?" he said.

"Who's catering?"

"I don't remember. How come?"

"I thought maybe I could get a cater-waiter job. So I can come to your party after all."

And he began to laugh, like it was a really clever joke.

"Wouldn't that be a hoot? I'll be at your birthday. As nothing but a waiter."

"Don't be silly. If you want to come to my party, come. Nobody's going to throw you out."

"I thought you wouldn't want me here."

Caleb didn't, but he accomplished nothing by feeding Toby's private soap opera. "I assumed you wouldn't want to come. Who wants to see his ex-boyfriend having fun with other friends? But if you want to play masochist, I'm not going to stop you."

"I'm not playing, Caleb. It's what I feel. It hurts that you don't want me. But I want to feel that hurt. I want to experience every minute of it. Until it's over."

Toby spoke in a haughty, hammy manner, yet Caleb feared that every word was true.

"And that's why you have a date tonight with Henry Lewse?"

"I told you. It's not a date. It's just dinner."

"If you're chasing Lewse to make me jealous—?" Caleb shook his head. "It won't work. Forget about me. Go after him. For his own sake. He's important. He's famous. He's a good actor." Or was. "He's openly gay. He's not bad-looking. You can do a lot worse than Henry Lewse. *He's* still a success."

Toby sat in his chair, staring at Caleb, glowering at him.

I am being such a shit, thought Caleb, but it's the only way.

"In fact, why not bring him to my party? The glory of British theater. Show him off to people. And they'll all think: Lucky Toby. He dumped a loser and found a winner."

"Go to hell," said Toby. "I don't want Henry Lewse. I want you."

Caleb let out a sigh. Not even being a total asshole could drive Toby away? "Well, you can't have me. I'm sorry."

"Don't you get it, Caleb? I love you."

"I know. You've told me. Repeatedly. But I *don't* love you."

"Why? What did I do wrong?"

"You didn't do anything wrong. I just don't love you. It's a simple, nonpejorative fact."

"I know why. It's because you're in love with someone who's dead."

Caleb kept his temper, unlike last time. "Ben died six years ago. This has nothing to do with Ben."

"And you know why you're still in love with him? Because you didn't love him enough when he was alive."

Caleb clenched his teeth to stop himself from shouting. "What a shitty thing to say. What TV talk show did you hear that on? What do you know about it anyway? Not a damn thing!"

The depth of his anger took Caleb by surprise. And it must have shown, all of it, because Toby looked stunned, frightened.

"I'm sorry!" Toby bleated. "But I'm in love with you! It makes me say shitty things."

Caleb turned away, regretting his temper, his words. "You should go home, Toby. Or go to work or go wherever you should be right now. We're not good for each other."

"You don't want me to come to your party?"

Caleb began to laugh. "Fuck the party. Come. Don't come. I don't care. But today? Just go. Please. I'm tired. I'm in a shitty mood."

Toby slowly stood up, blinking and making faces. The actor was "thinking."

"All right. I'm going," he announced.

Caleb walked him back inside, escorting him to the door.

"I apologize for what I said about Ben," said Toby. "I had no business saying it. I'm sure you loved him very much."

They came to the front hall.

"Good-bye," said Caleb and held out his hand.

"What?" Toby stared at the hand. "You can't hug me? You're afraid I might kiss you?"

"No, Toby. Maybe later, but not today."

Toby stepped backward down the stairs, holding his own hand high and out of reach. "Then I don't want to touch you!"

"Fine then. Have a nice night with Henry Lewse. Be safe." Caleb didn't intend to be sarcastic, but it did sound sarcastic, didn't it?

Toby stopped at the foot of the stairs in front of the elevator.

"You don't get it! But you will! Years from now! You'll understand! I could have been the best damned thing that ever happened to you!"

He turned and hurried down the next flight of stairs. He knew not to spoil a good exit line by waiting for the elevator.

Caleb softly closed the door and locked it. And he smiled.

Because it was ridiculous, it was absurd. Here was this cute, sweet, sexy kid, and *he* wanted Caleb. What did it matter that he was thoroughly self-absorbed? And so needy that he could be jealous of the dead? He was young, attractive, affectionate, and available. He was also boring, but you weren't supposed to notice that. Sex was such a dirty trick. It made people exchange their peace and quiet for lots of bad company and dull conversation.

At another time, however, in a more generous mood, Caleb might have let himself be loved—for as long as Toby's love lasted. This was first love for Toby, or rather, first requited love, even if it was requited only in lust. But a response of any kind was so new and surprising for the boy that he might have taken months to recognize that he and Caleb were all wrong for each other.

Let him be Henry Lewse's problem, Caleb told himself. Lewse must have a good hard heart. He was an actor and a celebrity. He probably went through cute boys by the dozen, like doughnuts.

28

"I luf you like a pig lufs mud."

The sentence popped into Jessie's head on the subway, complete with foreign accent. She didn't know what it meant or where it came from. It sounded like Greta Garbo.

"This is a message for Jessica Doyle. Allegra here. Wondered if you're free for coffee this afternoon. I need to pick your brain." *Beep.*

The recording was on Henry's machine when Jessie arrived. She could guess what this was about: Caleb and *2B*. If you scratch my back *again,* I'll scratch yours—one day. Which was so Allegra. But Jessie liked Allegra. You always knew where you stood with Allegra.

"Allegra, hi. Jessie here. Coffee sounds good. How about three? We can meet somewhere in Central Park. It's way too pretty a day to waste inside. Call me back and let me know."

Clank clank clank.

Henry was in the dining room, already banging on his weights.

Jessie went to work. She checked his schedule and made a dental appointment and a few restaurant reservations. He was having dinner next week with Christina Rizzo and Rufus Brooks, the hunky Hollywood hack. Then the lobby sent up a messenger with a package that needed a signature. Jessie signed Henry's name. Not a full forgery, but she knew how to evoke his lazy squiggle. A flat cardboard envelope, it was from Adam Rabb.

Henry came around the corner. "Jessie, *mon amie,* what do you think?" His tank top was raised and he was frowning at his stomach.

"Uh, fine." Hardly a washboard or six-pack, but the muscles looked solid under the light grizzle of gray hair.

"Not too much tummy?"

"Oh no. It's the belly of a man ten, no, twenty years younger." She could never remember how old Henry claimed to be from one week to the next. "Big date tonight?" she asked.

"What? Oh no!" He laughed. "Alas. Just need to tone up. This play's left me flabby." He jerked the shirt back down.

No, he must have a date, if not tonight, then sometime soon.

"I luf you like a pig loves mud," she said, slowly and deliberately, so Henry would know she was quoting.

He stared at her. "I beg your pardon."

Jessie blushed, then laughed. "It's from a movie. It popped into my head this morning on the subway. I don't know what it's from. I think it's Garbo."

"Are you sure? It sounds like Dietrich."

"That might be just my bad accent."

He thought a moment. "No. Sorry, my dear. I'm a very poor queen, but I don't recognize it. What's that?" He pointed at the package in her hand.

"Oh. It just came." She passed it to him. "From Adam Rabb."

He weighed it. "Words, words, words. Ugh. He said he'd be sending me a script. So I can read the part they're giving Malkovich."

"There's no part for you?"

"Oh, maybe the butler." He thrust the package back at her. "But my body's not completely beyond hope? Yes? Well, back to the rack," he declared, and returned to the dining room.

Jessie tugged the screenplay from the cardboard—"*Greville,* based on the novel by"—and set it on the table with all the other unread books and scripts and plays that people sent to Henry.

He *must* have a date, she decided. About time too. He was a hardworking actor in a foreign city; he deserved to get laid. She felt mildly miffed, oddly annoyed, but only because she didn't know who the man might be. It could be fun to find out.

"I'll do what I can to get him there. But I can't promise anything."

"Right right right," said Allegra. "You can lead a horse to water but you can't make him drink."

"And you can lead a whore to culture but you can't make her think," Jessie added.

"What?"

"Sorry. Old Dorothy Parker joke. Hmm. Good cappuccino."

They sat on a bench just inside the park under the trees behind the *Maine* Memorial, the weird white monument that faced Columbus Circle like an old set from *Ben Hur*. They were drinking mocha cappuccinos, which Allegra had brought today instead of coffee, making clear just how important Caleb was to their show.

"But the show's looking good?" asked Jessie.

"Real good. What does Frank say?"

"Nothing really. We've hardly seen each other this week."

"Oh?"

Jessie shrugged. "We've been busy."

"You haven't broken up or anything?"

"It's too soon for there to be anything to break."

"Good good good." Allegra took a sip through the flute-hole in her lid. "I think you guys are made for each other."

"Uh-huh," said Jessie dubiously.

She had known Allegra six months, ever since they met at HB Studio, when Jessie was a secretary there and Allegra was taking classes. Jessie understood from the start that this friendship was built on use—she *was* Caleb Doyle's sister—but Allegra was a very nice user. The Dorothy Parker joke was not consciously directed at her. She was very pretty, with black hair, pale skin, and red lips, very delicate, even today when she wore jeans and a man's shirt.

"You look fine, girl. *So* fine," crooned a bike messenger in boxy blue eyeshades as he walked his clicking bicycle past. Jessie assumed he was looking at Allegra.

"We're in the home stretch," said Allegra. "I wish we could do a full rehearsal tonight, but half the cast has a cater gig. Frank's using it to go one-on-one with Toby. Who needs the attention."

"Toby's no good?"

"No. He's just slow. Like Christmas."

Jessie was relieved. She had introduced Toby into the circle. "Sounds like fun," she said. "Hard work, but fun. I'm sorry that I'm not part of it."

"I'm sorry you aren't either," said Allegra.

The idea of working with them often crossed Jessie's mind. But doing what? She couldn't act—she was too cerebral. She couldn't write—she was too self-critical. She couldn't direct—she was too impatient. She *could* stage-manage, but it was too much like being the mommy, and she was tired of being the mommy. She sometimes seemed to be everybody's Stage Manager.

"Maybe next time," said Jessie.

She should be going. They had said everything they had come here to say, and it looked like rain. The sky had been clouding over since noon. The clouds were gray, the grass as green as house paint.

Allegra sucked out the last dribbles of cappuccino but then leaned back on the bench, not ready to go yet. "Oh life," she said, watching people pass. "Working on a play makes me itchy. Frisky."

"How're things with Boaz?"

"Oh, Boaz is Boaz."

Jessie assumed they were talking about sex. "I hardly know Bo. But he seems nice. Sexy. In a hetero Nijinsky kind of way." Then she saw the deliberate, faraway look in Allegra's eyes. "Oh. Problems?"

Allegra took a deep breath. "I probably shouldn't tell you—" She bent forward, folding herself over her crotch. Here was the real reason for the mocha cappuccinos. "I've been messing around. With somebody else."

Jessie almost said "Frank?" But it couldn't be Frank. "I'm sorry," she said. "I won't ask who. None of my business."

"It's Chris."

Jessie shook her head. She didn't know any guys named Chris. Then she squinted at Allegra, hard. "Chris Jamison? Big butch Chris?"

Allegra was smiling. "Are you shocked?"

"No. *Surprised,*" she admitted. Chris was bulky but beautiful, like Paul Robeson with breasts, while Allegra was so delicate, like a Cuban china doll. "I didn't think she'd be your type."

"I'll say! She's a woman." Allegra laughed. "I mean— It's not like I've never been there. Hey, I was a theater major. And my taste in women friends has always been better than my taste in men," she admitted. "Except I like men being dumber than women. It makes them easier to be around. Less work."

Jessie didn't know what to say or where to begin. "But you all live in the same apartment."

"And I sleep with Boaz, and we still fuck. Which is weird with Chris right down the hall. But it's not like Chris and I are lovers. We've had sex twice—well, one and a half times. It began with a back rub. But she's sworn off straight girls. They're nothing but trouble, she says. And I see her point. But I can't stop thinking about her. I don't know if it's love or horniness or preshow jitters. But I'm fixated. She has so much presence. She's not fat. I know it looks like fat, but when you're in bed with her, wrapped in her, surrounded, it doesn't feel fat, it feels— metaphysical."

Jessie listened with her chin in her hand, looking sympathetic, suspending judgment, feeling full of human interest, and all the while thinking: Everybody is getting laid except me.

29

I am too talented for my own good. What would you do in my shoes? Business or theater? It's a hard choice. I walk into a room and people know. *I am not nothing!* I'm someone important. Someone of value. And you know why they know that? Because I'm a positive—"

"Wait. Stop. Go back."

"What?" said Toby.

"Why did you do that?" asked Frank.

"Do what?"

"Shout the line?"

"Which line?"

" 'I am not nothing.' "

"I didn't shout it."

"You did."

"I didn't."

"All right," Frank conceded. "But you overemphasized it. Made it too important."

"But you said it was important."

"Yes, but—" Frank took a deep breath. "Never mind. Let's not argue. We just need to find a way to make this scene work."

They stood in the big, half-bare living room on West 104th Street. Frank had come straight from the office and still wore a shirt and tie. Toby wore his usual loose jeans and dark T-shirt, his chest stamped ABERCROMBIE. They were working on his monologues and had come to the fourth one, where confidence falls apart and fear bursts into view. Patience was running low.

Toby shook his head. "Sorry, Frank. I'm in a real crappy mood today. Life sucks. But I need to forget Toby and focus on 'Toby.'" He made quotation marks in the air with his fingers.

Frank agreed the problem was there. The hardest role for almost any actor to play is him- or herself. You play yourself anyway, whether you're Lear or Seinfeld, but you can usually be more accurate when you are pretending to be someone else.

"All right. Let's try it again. Wait. Let me—" Frank turned on the lamp by the television. It was only six, but the sky had been clouding up all afternoon, threatening rain without ever delivering. The rooms had grown dark and gloomy. Nobody else was home. Allegra was out, and the others were off at a big catering job.

"And carry this," said Frank, taking his sports coat from the chair. He disliked it when actors hid in props, but they needed something here. "And put this on." He took off his necktie, and Toby knotted it around his neck—it hung like a red-striped candy cane over his T-shirt. "Now pretend I'm Chris. I'm going to sit here like Chris. And I want you to come in and convince me that you have the most wonderful fucking life on the planet."

Frank sat in front of the TV. Toby came around the corner.

"Hey, hi. What's on? Boy, did I have a great day. Had a great audition. *And* an excellent job interview . . ."

Frank listened closely. But there was no change, no growth. The monologue was as wooden as ever.

"How about a break?" he said. "Do you know if there's any juice or soda in the fridge?"

Toby followed him into the kitchen. "I'm sorry, Frank. I got a grip on the other scenes—I think. But this is the important one, and I have a block about it. I don't know why. Maybe I'm afraid of expressing too much."

"Better too much than too little. We can bring it down later." Except Toby's "too much" really was too much.

"I wonder if I'm feeling too rejected to 'play' rejected. Because I really am bummed out this week. I'm overdosing on no."

"Here." Frank handed Toby a glass of orange juice. He disliked mucking around in real emotions—this was theater, not group therapy—but he decided to listen to Toby, on the off chance that he might hear something he could channel back into the monologue.

"I'm told I'm too white-bread for one part. Or too faggy for another. And then I get dumped by the man I love. New York just chews you up and spits you out. I don't know why I even moved here. I should have stayed in Milwaukee. They have good regional theater. But if you're famous in Milwaukee, who are you? You're somebody who's famous in Milwaukee."

The boy was so naked, so needy. Why would anyone this vulnerable expose his ego to the acid bath of theater? But Frank knew why. He'd been there himself.

"I'm sure glad I don't have to be famous anymore," said Frank.

Toby stared. "But you never were famous."

"No. But I thought I needed to be famous. Before I could be happy. And then I found I could be happy without fame."

Was he happy? He waited for Toby to challenge him there, but the boy only nodded obliviously.

"Well, I don't *have* to be famous," said Toby. "But I won't turn up my nose at it. It'd make Doyle see how wrong he was."

Maybe here, thought Frank. They might find Toby's missing key in his experience of love gone wrong. "It's rough," he said, "being dumped by someone you love. Let's go back to the living room."

Toby followed him. "I saw Caleb this morning. Big mistake. I just dropped in. I should have called. But he hardly noticed I was there. Like I was last week's laundry."

"Uh-huh. So what do you feel when you tell people things are fine, even though you've just been dumped?"

"But I don't tell anyone things are fine. Because they're not."

"Right." Frank paused to think of another approach.

"I don't know what I did wrong," Toby argued. "It's like he doesn't want to be loved. Like he thinks he doesn't deserve it. You're seeing his sister, right? Is she fucked up, too?"

They had Doyles in common, didn't they? "Oh, Jessie is—complex. But I wouldn't call her fucked up." And Frank would never claim that she *deserved* his love.

"The whole family's twisted. They can't love anyone who's actually there. In the present, in the now. Caleb's still in love with a dead guy. Isn't his sister divorced or something?"

"Yes. Only she never talks about her ex." Frank had his own theories about Jessie, but he was not going to share them. "They're an odd pair. Special. Different. And different from each other too." He thought of Jessie now not as an image but as a sound: her sharp, witty laugh. "She's smart. Practical and funny. And pretty. But she's not ready to love anyone at the moment. Which is her prerogative."

"Sounds like her brother," Toby said nastily.

Frank lifted an eyebrow at Toby. "Maybe Caleb isn't rejecting love. Maybe he's just rejecting you."

He said it as a joke—he pretended it was a joke, anyway—but Toby looked insulted.

"No! Absolutely not!" Toby recovered with a scornful laugh. "No way. He accepted me when love was new. When it was fun. But then it turned serious and it put him off. Because he has intimacy issues."

"But his play just went down in flames," said Frank. "He might not have all that much love to share these days."

"Uh-uh," Toby insisted. "He has intimacy issues. It's a gay thing. You can't understand, you're straight."

He knew Toby only wanted to shut him up, but Frank hated hearing this line from gay friends. It was even more annoying than when they said, "Just how straight are you?" after Frank made a good joke. But the truth was that Frank *didn't* understand gay men. In particular, what did they see in other men? What did women see in men for that matter? Men are so ugly and unlovable. Frank sometimes wondered if a hetero male were simply a self-hating man.

"What time is it?" said Toby. Almost seven. "Good grief. I have to be midtown at eight."

"I thought you were free all evening?"

"Since it was just me, I thought we'd rehearse only an hour or two. So I made, uh, plans."

"You can't call and tell them you'll be an hour late?"

"No, because— Because I can't, that's all."

Frank was actually relieved their sticky one-on-one was almost over. Even so: "I wish you'd told me. I could've made other plans."

Such as getting together with Jessie. He knew that she loomed large in his thoughts only because they'd been talking about Doyles.

But it was too late now. And it was a weeknight. There is nothing more unromantic during the first weeks of a relationship than seeing your beloved on a weeknight.

"All right, Toby. One more time then?"

They went back to the beginning. Frank became Chris again. Toby came out and launched his first speech. And it went better. Toby was in a hurry, which often helped. Then they came to the final monologue.

"I walk into a room and people know I'm not nothing. I'm someone important, someone of value. And you know why they know that? Because I'm a positive person."

The speech raced like water over a flat rock of uncertainty. It was alive. Yes, that's what the scene needed, real fear. Had Frank frightened Toby with the idea that Caleb was not rejecting love, he was rejecting Toby? Frank didn't care so long as it worked.

Toby delivered his last line, "Everything is fine. Everything is great." He stood there, exhausted, blank. And Frank had an impulse—either as himself or Chris, it didn't matter—but he got up and set a timid, sympathetic hand on Toby's shoulder.

And Toby seized him, hard. He threw both arms around him and held on tight. Frank had never guessed the boy was so solidly built, like a refrigerator.

But it felt right. It felt good. It felt so good that Frank feared it might not be acting. Here they were, two men in love with a brother and sister, sharing a bear hug of panic.

"Blackout," Frank whispered in his ear.

Toby released him. Frank could breathe again.

"What do you think?" Toby asked nervously. "Did it work?"

"Definitely." So the boy *had* been acting. Good. An acted emotion is easier to repeat than a real one.

"It felt right to me too," Toby admitted. "I'm getting there. I think I have a handle."

"Want to try it one more time?"

"I can't. I need to shower and shave for my—thing. But tomorrow. Okay? I have a handle now. I'll be even better tomorrow. With the others here." And he hurried down the hall to his room.

Fine, thought Frank. See if I care. But it was good to stop here. They could work on the scene tomorrow.

Frank was glad to finish early. He could go home to Hoboken. He was glad to have a free night ahead of him. He could watch television, he could listen to music. He needed to save Jessie for the future, when his plate wasn't so full.

Besides, it looked like it was going to rain.

30

Jessie rode the subway downtown from Columbus Circle. The train was packed at rush hour. Standing the whole way, she found herself thinking first about bodies, then feet, then food.

When she got off at her stop, Houston and Varick, she heard a sloppy clatter like applause overhead. She timidly went up the stairs toward the noise.

Rain fell through the sky like a curtain of needles. It bounced all over the sidewalk like marbles. The street was bright with rain, varnished with wet. People crowded together in doorways, looking, waiting, then dashing to the next doorway and waiting some more. Cars and trucks kicked up a dense spray like smoke. The gutters and puddles teemed with bubbles.

Jessie grabbed a newspaper from a trash can, covered her head, and ran. It was a warm city rain, with a peculiarly sweet smell of iron. Her building was three blocks away on Vandam Street. Fucking Mother Nature, she told herself. But it was only rain, only water. She began to laugh at herself. She was soaked when she reached her front stoop. She shook herself off in the vestibule like a wet dog.

The neighborhood was a limbo zone of factory lofts, office buildings, and town houses, south of the Village, west of SoHo. Her building was a five-floor walk-up shelved like an old book between two printing plants. There were rumors that Leontyne Price lived in a town house across the street, but Jessie had never seen her.

She climbed the steep stairs to the top floor.

Her home was an illegal sublet with no lease, a shower in the kitchen, and a toilet in the hall. But it was all hers.

The front door opened directly into the bedroom, which was dark.

The windows faced air shafts, and the place was in shadow even on good days. There was the loft bed overhead that Charlie had built, strong and solid. He was a better carpenter than a husband. The kitchen was on the left, the living room on the right: a square space with a ratty sofa, a spongy easy chair patterned like a cow, and a stage-prop fireplace from a production of *A Doll's House*. The bookcases flanking the mantel were full of videos, mostly old movies taped off cable. Over the mantel hung a framed poster for *Venus in Furs,* an art nouveau woodcut of a female face in a mink halo. "Like Mame with a whip," Caleb joked when he gave her the poster.

Jessie turned on lights, then music, then took a shower. The spray from the faucet joined the soothing crackle of rain outside. She pulled on panties and a sweatshirt so she could be comfortable while she decided what to do this evening. She considered calling Greta, her downstairs neighbor, but Greta was out of town. She was sorry she hadn't suggested dinner to Allegra, but she'd reached her Allegra quotient for the day. Sex, sex, sex: that's all Allegra would want to talk about; Jessie was tired of sex talk. She was sorry that Frank had rehearsal tonight. But she didn't need anyone. She could stay in.

There was some broccoli in garlic sauce in a plastic tub in the refrigerator. She sniffed it—it seemed safe—and stuck it in the microwave. She went out to the living room and found the book she'd been reading, *Hope Against Hope* by Nadezhda Mandelstam. A memoir of Russian poets under Stalin—Osip Mandelstam, Anna Akhmatova, and others—it had been recommended by Caleb, another of those sad artist biographies he read whenever he was blue. Jessie curled up on the sofa with her bare feet tucked under her bottom and entered a harsh world where people wore rubber raincoats, ate hard-boiled eggs, wrote harrowing love poems, and betrayed one another to the secret police. It sure put things in perspective.

The microwave began to beep. The phone rang.

She answered the phone. "Hello?"

"Jessie?" Rain sizzled like static. "Hi. It's Frank."

"Oh hi!" She was surprised by how pleased she was to hear from him.

"I was downtown after work. Happen to be around the corner. Thought I'd call to see if you're free. You eaten yet?"

"I'm eating now." But she wasn't. Not yet. Why did she say she was? "Hey. Why don't you come join me? Pick up something at the diner on the corner, then come up here and we can eat together." "Oh?" He hesitated. "All right. Sure. Need anything?" "No. I'm fine. See you shortly." Click.

What was Frank doing down here? He didn't just *happen* to be around the corner. He should be uptown rehearsing. He had come to see her, of course. But had he come to talk? Or for more? She was surprised by how quickly her body wanted a larky, friendly fuck.

She turned off the lamp in the living room, then turned it back on. It was still light outside despite the rain. She didn't want the room to be pitch-dark, but everything looked shabby in the electric glare. She considered brushing her hair and pulling on jeans. Nyaah. She felt kind of sexy in the sweatshirt that hung over her panties like a miniskirt. But she slid *Hope Against Hope* under the sofa, for fear Frank would think she was way too serious.

He buzzed sooner than expected.

"That was quick," she called down on the intercom.

"I didn't need much."

She buzzed him in. A moment later, he knocked.

She opened her door. "Howdy."

And there he was. He was still dressed for work in a coat and white shirt but no tie. He held a paper bag in one hand. A small, cheap collapsible umbrella hung from the other hand like a dead bat.

"I didn't know if you'd be home," he said. "But I figured I had nothing to lose." His gaze drifted down, then snapped up again.

And Jessie thought: This is Frank. What was I thinking? I can't just fuck Frank. She was sorry that she hadn't pulled on jeans. She didn't look sexy, but lazy, slobby, slutty.

"Come on in," she said. "Make yourself at home."

He left his umbrella on the floor in the hall and strolled in. He glanced up at the loft bed. His feet made a slurping, sucking sound.

"Wasn't there rehearsal tonight?"

"Dwight and Chris and Melissa had a cater job. So I just rehearsed Toby." He entered the living room, saw the sofa, then the cow chair. "You can be only so long with Toby without going nuts."

He went to the cow chair and sat there. No, he didn't want to fuck tonight either.

"I just put my food *back* in the microwave," said Jessie. "Would you like something to drink? Beer? Tea? There might be some wine."

"Beer sounds good."

She went into the kitchen, took out her broccoli, and opened a Rolling Rock. No, no, no, she told herself. Let's have a nice friendly talk and save the other stuff for another night.

When she returned, Frank was sitting in the cow chair, looking at her tapes in the bookcase and eating an apple. That was all he had in his paper bag, an apple.

"You have some good movies here."

"That's right. You've never been here."

"No, we've been to my place, but not yours." He smiled at her when he took the beer, a nervous, worried smile.

She sat on the sofa and stuck a forkful of broccoli in her mouth.

He had come to her tonight. He was in *her* space. That must be why he had such sexual weight. Horniness kept changing its mind.

"I hate to ask this but—" He looked at her more seriously. "Do you mind if I take off my shoes and socks?"

"What?"

"They're sopping."

She laughed. "Like I'm formal?" She tugged her sweatshirt over her knees. "Go ahead. Be comfortable. It's not like we're strangers."

He tugged at the laces of his tennis shoes.

"Southerners," she teased. "You're so fucking polite."

He made a face as he unpeeled his socks. "Hey. I lost my manners back when I lost my accent." His feet were white and soggy.

"Uh-uh. You still have the manners." Was that what was wrong with Frank? He was too nice? "But you're right. You have almost no accent. How come?"

"I've been doing theater since high school in Memphis. It just rinsed out on its own." He shrugged. "How's your mom? You saw her on Sunday?"

"Crazy as ever. Let's not talk about her. You sure you don't want more to eat than just an apple?"

"Not hungry. I could lose some weight. Nine-to-five jobs are fattening. I eat lunch just to get out of the office."

He was right about his weight. She wouldn't contradict him there.

"You poor guy. I hate to think of you giving your days to a stupid stockbroker."

"No worse than you giving your days to Henry Lewse."

She sighed. "But he's theater. He's a way to get close to something I love."

"If you were me, you'd know to run from it."

"Get out of here. You love theater. You have a gift for directing."

"I don't have any gift."

"You do. You just need some luck to go with your gift."

He looked at her, surprised, even touched. He took another bite of apple, another swig of beer. "Cute outfit you're wearing."

"Thought you'd never notice." She knew he was flirting only because their talk had gotten too serious, but she didn't want to be serious either. "Oh! You won't believe what Allegra told me today!"

"What?"

"Oh— No, forget it. It's not *that* interesting."

Just in time, she recognized what was at stake. This was not just fun gossip. She could not betray Allegra. And she should not spook Frank by tattling about the love lives of his actors.

"Hey," she said. "Your trousers are soaked."

And they were: black up to the knees.

"Only the cuffs."

"You can take them off too, you know."

He looked down at his slacks, then up at her. "But if I do that, I might give us the wrong idea."

She hadn't intended her proposal to be sexual. But it was, wasn't it? She grinned. "And what's wrong about that idea?"

"Nothing. Except it's a weeknight. We get so little time together, I thought it might be nice to just talk."

"Yes. Good. Right. That's what I want too," she claimed. "Do whatever makes you comfortable."

He looked skeptical, maybe of her words, maybe of his own.

"But if you want me to be comfortable—" he said.

And he stood up. He turned his back to her. He unbuckled and unzipped. He stepped out of his trousers and there was a glimpse of off-white boxer shorts. His hairy legs looked cute with his coat and shirttail. "Where can I hang these?"

"Just drape them over the back of that chair."

Which he did. And he sat back in the cow chair, as if nothing had changed, as if he didn't have something jutting in his lap. He crossed his right leg over his left. He was still smiling, but it was an uncomfortable smile, directed at himself, at her, at his penis.

What the hell were they out to prove? That they could sit around in their underwear without pouncing? She folded one leg under the other, keeping her knees together. She wished they didn't feel like an old married couple.

"Oh oh oh," she suddenly said. "You might know this. A line from a movie has been going through my head all day. 'I luf you like a pig lufs mud.' Sound familiar? Is it Garbo? Dietrich?"

He thought a moment. Then he broke into a smile. "Uh-uh. It's Ingrid Bergman. It's—oh what's the name?" He snapped his fingers.

"*Gaslight? Casablanca?*"

He shook his head. "No, period piece. A comedy. And she's beautiful, like always, but funny too, which makes her even more beautiful. She's a fortune hunter, and she has a great name. *Clio Dulaine!* And she's in love with Gary Cooper."

"*Saratoga Trunk!*" cried Jessie. "It was just on AMC. How could I forget? And there's a dwarf, and a mulatto housekeeper. And you're right. She is beautiful. But not half as beautiful as Gary Cooper."

One met so few men, or women either, who really enjoyed old movies. Gay men thought they did, but most of them knew only a few obvious titles and the same tired scenes. The occasional straight man who loved old movies was usually ashamed of knowing so much. But not Frank.

"I luf you like a pig lufs mud," Frank repeated. He was staring at her.

"What?" But she knew what.

"Too bad it's a weeknight."

"You keep saying that."

"It's just— I don't know. There's usually something too rushed and utilitarian about sex on a weeknight."

"What makes you think I want to go to bed with you?"

He considered that, then nodded. "Good. If you're not interested, we have nothing to worry about, do we?"

She propped an elbow on a knee and set her chin in her hand.

They were both playing bluff with their lusts. "Hey," she said. "It's early yet. Want to be utilitarian?"

He smiled. "I don't know. I keep changing my mind. From minute to minute."

"Me too." Her throat was tight, her words squeaked.

And they sat there, gazing at each other across the room, waiting for someone to make the next move.

Finally he stood up. He came toward her. He was still smiling.

She scooted over on the sofa.

He sat down beside her. He slipped an arm behind her back.

"Hello," he said.

"Hello yourself."

She leaned into the heat of his body. She was surprised by how warm he was. He seemed as large and comfortable as a dray horse. She looked up at a chin peppered with evening whiskers. "Should I brush my teeth?" she whispered. "Broccoli with garlic sauce?"

"I love broccoli with garlic sauce." And he kissed her.

His mouth tasted like apples and beer. She could feel his kiss take root in her crotch, twist and knot there, then climb like a vine into her breasts.

Oh yes, she thought. This is what I want. This is what I need. Sex. Good friendly sex. Sex with a good man, a nice guy who loves me more than I love him. Which was too bad. But better this way than the other. And there's no telling what either of us will feel on the other side of the finish line.

31

He climbed deep into her kiss. He pressed her pillows of breast against his chest. His hands were under her sweatshirt, stroking a bare back where a bra should be, fingering the soft sawtooth of spine. He inhaled shampoo and hair. She felt wonderfully small in his arms, sweetly portable, as if he could hold her and keep her always.

His body was thinking: Sex, good dumb animal sex. But his mind was thinking: Love, Jessie, the future. His mind and body had been fighting ever since he arrived here. His body had won, but his mind now found itself hoping that the body could win love if the sex were good enough.

"Let's move this up to the bed," she whispered.

"There enough room up there?"

He sat up. She slipped out of his arms. He watched her scurry into the bedroom and up the ladder. A pair of frayed panties peeked out from under her sweatshirt as she popped into the loft bed.

He stood up so quickly that he felt dizzy. He shook off his coat and began to unbutton his shirt.

"What're you doing?" she called out.

"Getting comfortable."

It didn't look like there was much maneuver room up there. The poster for *Venus in Furs* faced him on the wall down here; he disliked undressing in front of it.

His boxer shorts and T-shirt looked grubby—he saved his good underwear for weekends—so he shucked them before he started up the ladder. The rungs bit his bare soles.

"Oooh," she moaned as his nudity climbed into view. "*I* wanted to strip you."

"I'll make it up to you."

He drew her against him. And there was pure pleasure, the mindless joy of being in bed with a woman, any woman. Then the woman became Jessie again, and it was even better.

Her sweatshirt disappeared, then her panties. He sat back on his heels to take her in with his eyes. There was more room up here than he expected. The window peering over the top of the platform bed provided enough light for him to see her: she lay on her back, a beautiful shape wearing only a haircut, a smile, a cross-eyed pair of teacup breasts, a triangular ginger beard.

"Uh-huh," she purred. "So you do like older women?"

"No. I like you." He wished she wouldn't play that game; she was only two years older. He lay down again, hoping to persuade her that his like was love.

It was better than the first time, but more complicated, less innocent. He felt more strongly about her. When he nuzzled and suckled a breast, he wanted to think it was her heart that his lips felt in the thickness behind the nipple. When she took him in her mouth, he was not only physically excited, but also emotionally touched. She held him in one hand, used her other hand to hold her hair off her forehead, and cut her eyes at him, as if to say: See how much I like you? But it was confusing to watch the woman he loved take a dick in her mouth, even if it was his dick. He regretted that she did it so well. He could not help thinking of all the gay men in her life. Did they give her tips? Did she hope to hold her own with them? He gently lifted her up and kissed her forehead and eyelids. Then he laid her on her back and bowed down to her sex.

Oh yes, this was what he wanted. Her beard lightly scrubbed his chin and lips. He opened her with his thumb, he found her with his tongue. He was in charge now. He could be obscenely intimate with her private fingerprint of salts and hormones, kissing and twirling her. He could taste her in the back of his throat, a pleasantly bitter flavor as if an aspirin were lodged there.

Her breathing deepened, her stomach rose and fell. A finger joined his tongue and he felt the little ridges like the ribbed roof of a dog's mouth. He loved the architecture. Then the ridges began to rise like the ribs supporting the roof of a cathedral. Her breathing sharpened and grew louder as the cathedral opened inside her. She lifted herself against his mouth, she gripped his shoulders. And Frank was in heaven. She was taking his love, loving his love. She threw her head back and opened her throat, pressed her heels against his ribs and rode his mouth to glory.

When she was done, when she lay flat on the bed, catching her breath, she looked flaccid and boneless, like he'd removed every bone from her body. He gently wiped his mouth off on her thigh. He crawled up beside her. Her face was pink, her eyes blissfully shut. She drew deep breaths through an open smile.

"And you said you don't like sex."

"Hmm?" Her eyes remained closed. "I never said that."

"You act like it. Sometimes."

"Maybe. I can be stupid sometimes." She groped around until she found him. "You now. Put on a condom. While I'm still—warm."

"Not yet. I don't want to finish yet."

"We have work tomorrow." Her hand pumped him. "Both of us."

He held her hand and stopped her. "You should rest," he said. "You just had quite a workout."

"Hmmm."

He could come in her hand or even her smile, he was so excited right now.

"Did you bring any condoms?" she said.

"Uh-uh. I didn't think we'd end up in bed." He wanted her to know that he didn't come here just to get laid.

"I think I got some. In my purse."

"*Why?*" he said sharply. "In case Henry needs them?"

She opened her eyes and stared at him. "Hell no." She laughed. "Henry can carry his own rubbers."

Why had he said that? Why had Frank brought *him* into their bed? He had no business being annoyed that Jessie carried condoms. Every straight woman should. He'd love to fuck her without one. He'd love to get inside her with nothing between them. He'd love to get her pregnant. Which was a stupid thing to think.

"I'll get your purse," he whispered. "In a minute. I don't want to leave you yet." He gathered her up and turned her on her side. He pressed his front against her back and held her from behind. He burrowed his nose in her hair and lightly flicked her nipples.

"Careful. I'm very tender and ticklish," she murmured.

"I luf you like a pig lufs mud," he repeated. And so she wouldn't think he was only quoting Ingrid Bergman, he added, "You are so fucking beautiful."

She made a pinched, irritable noise. Then she wiggled her bottom against his cock. She reached back to stroke his hip. "What's the dirtiest thing we can do with each other?"

"Let's not think like that." It was as if she wanted to fight his words with sex.

"You want to fuck me in the ass?"

She said it so matter-of-factly that he tried to be equally blithe. "Hmm? Not tonight."

"I thought all guys wanted that. Straight guys too."

There, she said it. The thing at the back of Frank's mind was in her mind too. Gay sex was everywhere.

"What if I finger-fuck you?" she said. "Or rim you? I've never rimmed anyone before."

He rose up on one elbow. "Why're you talking like this? Why do you want to make this dirty? I'm not a gay man. And neither are you. What do you want to prove?"

She turned around and blinked at him. "I want to make you feel good."

"No. It's something else. You want to prove this is just a good, dirty fuck. You don't want to admit that I'm in love with you."

Her mouth hung open. She looked down at his cock, as if that could explain him. "Here," she said. "You think too much."

"No." He pulled her hand away. "Listen. Can't we talk?"

"Now? Jesus. I feel so good right now, Frank. This is great. This is fun. Why do you want to mess it up?"

"Because it's not just fun for me. I love you."

She looked at him, but said nothing, not "I love you too" or even a safe, polite version like "I love *being* with you."

"Is that so awful?" he demanded. "That a straight man can love you? Or are you so hung up on your gay brother and gay boss that being with a man who can love you is paralyzing!"

She stared at him. She slowly sat up, gathering her legs to her chest. "Fuck you," she finally said. "Go ahead. Call them fags. That's what you're thinking."

"No! I don't care about them. I care about you. I don't want to fuck you in the ass or any of that—stuff." He almost said "faggot stuff" but caught himself. "I want to be with you and have you with me, without any of this other shit in your head."

"It's in your head, Frank, not mine!"

He sat up too, hiding behind his knees. If they were in a normal bed, an earthbound bed, one of them would have left by now. But they were trapped up here on this platform, naked and angry.

"I'm not in love with Henry!" she declared. "And I'm not in love with Caleb. He's my brother, dammit. I know him too well."

"I didn't say you were in love."

"Just because I don't love you the way you want to be loved, you think I must have a sick incest thing for my fag brother?"

"You call him a fag. I never did. And I never said you were in love with him *or* Henry. I didn't mean—" But had she just said what he thought she said? "You do love me? In *some* way?"

She lowered her face behind her knees. "I don't know what I feel. I *wanted* to love you. Maybe. But I sure the hell can't now. Not after hearing what you think of me."

He was tempted to backtrack, tell her he was sorry, plead with her. But no, he refused to be tricked into taking the blame.

"Bullshit. You're not ready to love me. You're not ready to love anyone. Or let yourself *be* loved. Because you're too in love with success—Caleb's success, Henry Lewse's success—to make your own life. And you know why you need success? Because you don't like yourself enough. Well, I like you. I love you. And if you had any brains at all, you'd understand that that was success enough."

She looked stunned, confused.

Frank was amazed at how articulate anger had made him.

Jessie looked down at the mattress, eyebrows and mouth pinched tight. Finally, she found what she wanted: her sweatshirt. She pulled it over her head and yanked it over her nudity. "Okay," she said. "You win. I'm a self-hating piece of shit. Now get the hell out of my bed before I push you off."

162 | CHRISTOPHER BRAM

"Jessie, I didn't—"

"Fuck off. You made your point. Just get the fuck out."

He scuttled over to the ladder but stopped at the edge.

"I go to bed with a guy I like," she muttered at the mattress, "and he dumps his righteous shit on me. He stuck his tongue up my twat, so he thinks he has a right to lecture me on what a mess I've made of my life." She looked at him. "You're the mess, Frank. You can't succeed at what you love, which is theater. So you walk away from it. And you expect me to walk with you. No way. I won't be your fucking consolation prize because you failed as an actor."

"What the fuck does that mean?" cried Frank. "This has nothing to do with that! I love you for you."

"Yeah? So why aren't you in love with someone who doesn't know shit about theater? Who has no ties, no knowledge, nothing?"

His mind was blank with anger, white with rage. He did not know how to answer. He started down the ladder before he threw something at her. "Fuck you," he said and tripped on the last rung.

He did not fall far but slammed against the wall. He stumbled out to the living room. He began to pick up his clothes off the floor and pull them on. *Venus in Furs* leered from the wall.

"I know three Obie winners!" Jessie called out. "I work for someone who's sure to win a Tony! But what have *I* done? Not a damn thing. It must make you feel *real* good. To love somebody who's an even bigger loser than you are."

"I am not a loser and neither are you. You are so full of shit."

"If I'm full of shit, why're you in love with me?"

"Because I didn't know there was so much shit that I'd never be able to save you from it."

"My hero," she sneered. "My savior." Their words sounded even more vicious when they couldn't see each other's face.

His sneakers were cold and wet. Frank pulled them on without the socks. He wanted to throw his sopping socks at Jessie or stuff them into her broccoli, but he left them on the floor.

"All right. I'm leaving," he announced.

"Good. I have nothing more to say."

"Neither do I."

He stood under the loft bed. All he could see was a bare foot at the edge of the futon, big toe angrily snapping against the index toe.

"I'm just glad," she said, "that I learned tonight what you really think of me. Before I cared enough about you for it to hurt."

"Fuck you," he told her foot and slammed the door behind him.

It was still raining outside, only a light drizzle, but Varick Street could not have looked more desolate. Everything was closed for the night, so it was all black or gray, with occasional sparks in the puddles where rain struck. Frank kept opening and closing the five-dollar umbrella he'd bought on his way downtown, but the spokes were broken and the thing made no sense anymore. He tossed it in the trash, then clutched his coat around his throat and walked more quickly, heading north to Christopher Street to catch the PATH train.

It was not even nine, but he'd already made a full night of it. Bad sex *and* a vicious argument. Which was better than most people do over a weekend.

Fuck her, he thought. He didn't need her. What did he see in her anyway? She was a basket case. So what if she were funny and smart and pretty? He loved her—*had* loved her—*despite* her theater thing, not because of it, and not because he hoped to break her of it. That was bullshit. Wasn't it?

It was definitely bullshit when she called him a fag hater. He had nothing against gay men. He liked them, he envied them, especially now. They could get laid whenever they wanted, with no complications or heartache. But Frank hadn't even gotten his rocks off tonight.

32

Henry Lewse stood on the bright stage of the Booth Theatre, wearing a yachting cap and wagging dinky pretzel eyeglasses at the female lead as he *talked* a song at her:

> It's awful to be rich.
> You may not own a stitch.
> But sing about your poverty
> And folks will give you sympathy,
> While I can never bitch.
> How awful to be rich.

Toby sat in the sixth row, in a blue blazer and red striped tie—Frank's tie, which he had forgotten to return after rehearsal—slunk down in his seat. He felt very grave and professional watching Henry Lewse perform. What a fine actor, he thought. What a great man. Why was he wasting himself in crap?

Toby hated *Tom and Gerry* almost as soon as the curtain went up. It was so silly, so unrealistic—even for a musical. And adding to the pain, each and every male actor, from the lead down to the Pullman porters, made Toby think: I could be him, I could do that. It hurt like hell that he wasn't onstage with the others.

But he didn't feel like that with Henry. No, Henry was brilliant. Henry was irreplaceable. Henry was his friend. The man seemed so much larger here, magnified by lights and audience and laughter, than he had visiting the Apollo Room at the Gaiety.

"I suppose your husband is big," said Henry.

"Oh, quite big," said Gerry, the runaway wife.

Henry sighed. "One of the tragedies of this world is that the fellows most in need of a thrashing tend to be enormous." A perfect note of absurdity made the dry words hilarious. Not that Toby laughed, but he felt the line click. And the audience laughed—good, strong, hundred-dollar guffaws, which was how much tickets cost.

As soon as Henry stepped offstage, Toby went back to hating the play. It was a bored kind of hatred, a bad mood that dug up all the dark thoughts he'd been having today. About Caleb, of course, who not only broke his heart but also accused him of being a whore who'd go to bed with a Broadway star. Ridiculous. Then Frank, who said Caleb wasn't rejecting love, he was rejecting Toby. What did Frank know? And here was Henry Lewse himself, who assumed that just because he was a rich and famous actor, he could snap his fingers and Toby would come running. If he thought dinner and a ticket to a bad musical were all it took to get into Toby Vogler's pants, he was even dumber than the others.

Henry reappeared and Toby couldn't hate him anymore. Hackensacker and his sister, the much-married Princess Centimillia, sang a duet, "Loving Lovely Love," where Henry took the dumb rhyme of "matrimony" and "baloney" and made it funny with a deft little pause. But Henry Lewse onstage was different from the fellow who'd meet Toby after the show tonight, magical and airy. Did some of that Henry rub off on the letchy, earthy, human Henry? The letchy Henry was the only Henry that liked Toby.

The show got better before it got worse. The ending was real stupid, with the introduction of identical twins followed by a double wedding. But when the curtain came down, the audience jumped to its feet. They couldn't wait to give it a standing ovation.

Toby remained stubbornly, righteously seated—until Henry came out. Then Toby rose, and his beating hands joined the others. When he heard a few hollers, he let out one of his own. "Bravo!" he cried, but was ashamed his voice sounded so thin.

Henry stood twenty feet away, smiling, bowing. And then he saw Toby. Yes, he must have seen Toby because he winked. Toby almost burst out laughing, he was so tickled. He turned to the middle-aged couple beside him to see if they saw that. But no, they were busy picking their programs off the floor.

And then it was over. The cast stepped backward, the curtain fell, the lights came up. All over the auditorium people were smugly smiling and sighing, as if after sex. Toby joined the throng moving toward the row of open doors, although nobody was in a hurry to get outside. It was still raining.

Toby opened his umbrella, stepped into the patter, and went around the corner to Shubert Alley. It felt good to be out in the cool air and tapping rain—so good that he was tempted to keep walking and head home and forget about dinner with Henry.

He came to the stage door. He was surprised that nobody else stood there: no friends or fans or autograph hounds eagerly waiting under the dripping eaves.

People began to come out. Toby had to look twice to recognize cast members: he saw Gerry behind a young woman's yawn, the Princess Centimillia in a motherly profile. Toto the gibberish-talking houseguest was just another East Village homo—he actually cruised Toby as he walked by. Then came Henry, who had started the evening as Henry, turned into Hackensacker, and now was Henry again. He wore denim, just like the night they'd met.

"Tobias! Hello!" He lifted both arms, uncertain if they were at the embracing stage yet, then lowered one arm and shook Toby's hand. "I forgot it was tonight. Such a nice surprise to spot you at the curtain call. So. Did you like it?"

"I liked *you*. You were wonderful. Henry." He almost said "Mr. Lewse," but no, he would call him Henry tonight. "You turned a pig's ear into a silk purse."

"You think so? Well, it's not great theater, but it does provide one with opportunities. I try to make the best of them. I'm just glad you enjoyed it."

"Everybody did. The audience loved you." Which was true, but Toby feared Henry wouldn't believe him when there were no other fans. "Uh, I'm surprised I'm the only one out here."

"So you are, so you are." He looked around. "It *is* a weeknight. And it's raining. And stage-door Johnnies are a thing of the past. Except in *your* line of work." He smiled. "I see you brought an umbrella. Very smart. Shall we?"

They stepped out into the rain. Henry stayed close, but he didn't touch Toby, only the slender shaft of his umbrella.

"Let's catch a cab. And then, if you don't mind, I'd like to swing by my place and change into something more spiffing. Jean Georges is a coat-and-tie kind of restaurant, even at midnight. I look rather grungy in my blue jean layabouts. Like rough trade."

"Sure," said Toby, even as he thought: Don't give me that change-my-clothes crap. You just want to get me home and get me into bed. It'll serve me right. It'll serve Caleb right too.

Henry flagged down a cab. "West Fifty-fifth and Broadway," he told the driver, then fell back into the cushions and grinned at Toby. But instead of pouring on the flattery, as Toby expected, he fretted about his performance. "You think it went okay? I wish I could say the same. I *had* it a few weeks ago. Now it's beginning to slip." He shook his head. "The hardest thing about comedy is keeping it new. With drama you can explore, build, try other approaches. But with comedy there's usually only one way to do it, and once you find it, things start to go downhill."

They arrived at a brand-new apartment building and entered a glassed-in lobby with a doorman in a white shirt.

"Good evening, Mr. Lewse. Good show tonight?"

"I've done better. But I've done worse too. Thank you for asking, Mike."

Toby watched the doorman's face for a smirk or scowl, something to indicate what he thought of Henry Lewse bringing a young male home, but the man betrayed no reaction.

As they rode up in the elevator, Toby decided: Oh, all right. Go ahead. Take me to bed. Let's get it over with.

He smiled and nodded at Henry Lewse. Henry Lewse smiled and nodded back.

The elevator doors opened and they walked down a carpeted hall-way. Henry unlocked a door. "My home away from home."

Toby followed him inside. Everything was in whites and grays, with one room filled by a sinister steel contraption that Toby didn't recognize at first. "You have your own Nautilus machine?"

"It *seemed* like a good idea at the time. The convenience. Exercising at home, however, you don't meet as many interesting men as you would at a gym. Go ahead. Give it a test drive."

Toby entered the room, but he did not go to the machine, he went

toward the huge windows that looked out on the city. They were fifteen stories up and buildings stood all around. The illuminated peaks
seemed to steam in the rain.

"Oh wow. It's like one of the Batman movies."

"You think?" said Henry. "Not *Blade Runner?*"

Toby stood there, looking at the view, at his reflection, at the reflection of Henry Lewse in the doorway behind him. He waited for Henry
to come up, embrace him from behind, and—

"Excuse me." Henry's reflection turned away, entered another
room, the bedroom, and *closed* the door.

Toby was confused. He was hurt. What's going on? Had Henry
Lewse changed his mind? He doesn't want to seduce me?

Toby went to the bedroom door. He lightly knocked. "Henry?"

"Yes?"

"Here's a suggestion. You want to skip going out and order in?
Pizza or Chinese food?"

The door popped open. Henry was barefoot but in his jeans and a
sleeveless undershirt. An ugly unmade bed gaped behind him.

Toby expected a lewd smile, but the old man only looked confused. "Are you sure? I wanted to take you to Jean Georges. I hear it's
very good. And it's so rare I get company for dinner."

"Seems like so much trouble," said Toby. "And it's expensive. And
late. And I'm not that hungry."

"We *could* stay in," Henry offered. "There's first-rate Chinese
nearby." He let out a long, mock sigh. "You spoil my plans. I was going
to wine you and dine you, stupefy you with food, then bring you back
here, show you some dirty pictures, and take advantage of your innocence. But I suppose none of that appeals to you?"

He was smiling. He sounded deliberately absurd, a bit like Hackensacker, in fact. Toby didn't know what to say.

"I see," said Henry—Toby couldn't guess what he saw. "Well. First
things first." He led Toby into the kitchen and took out a Chinese take-
out menu. "I don't know about you, but I'm famished."

He picked up the phone and placed an order.

"Scallion pancakes. Crystal shrimp dumplings. General Tso's
chicken. Broccoli with garlic sauce." Everything sounded new and
wonderful when read out in that deep plush voice. "That should be

enough, don't you think?" he asked Toby. "Fifteen minutes? Thank you." He clicked off the phone. "There. We've taken care of dinner. Would you like a drink? Oh sorry. You don't drink. Only hot cocoa."

"No, I'll have a drink."

Henry gave Toby a surprised, disapproving look. "That's a bad idea, don't you think?"

"Why?" Was he kidding?

"If we both start drinking, we might forget who we are, and who knows where *that* might lead?"

Toby laughed. "Isn't that where you wanted it to go?"

"Of course. But I presume you don't."

Toby could feel himself stirring in his trousers.

"Maybe I do. Tonight."

"You're just being polite," said Henry.

"You don't know what I want," said Toby with a nervous laugh.

"Do *you* know?" asked Henry.

Toby stood by the refrigerator, Henry by the stove. He did not look so old despite the gray hair peeking from the neck of his undershirt.

Toby stepped forward. He slipped his thumbs into the denim belt loops. He pulled Henry toward him. He'd forgotten how much taller he was than Henry.

"What's this?" said Henry. "And this? And what about—"

Toby silenced him with his mouth. He was startled by the lively tongue inside, but he pressed on and embraced Henry harder. Without thinking, he shoved a hand down the seat of a famous man's jeans. He stroked a cool, hairy butt, not as hairy as Caleb's, and not as solid as Toby liked, but not flabby or clammy either.

He broke off the kiss so he could think more clearly. "Wow. Double wow. I can't believe I'm doing this with an actor whose work I admire so much."

"My boy— If you're going to blow smoke up my ass, wouldn't you be more comfortable doing it in bed?"

33

Peach skin. Blond haze. Freckles. The body stretched out before
him, nearly level with his eyes, a lion-colored landscape, a Sahara of
flesh. The slope of abdomen rose in the distance to the ridge of rib
cage. Down below was a belly button like a water hole and, closer still,
just under Henry's nose, a pale briar of pubic hair.

It's remarkable how sexless sex can be after the first half hour.
Henry had to remind himself that the rubbery stiffness filling his
mouth was Toby Vogler's penis. He pictured Toby himself on the other
side of his rib cage, head on a pillow, hand behind his head, frowning at
the ceiling. The boy was not a terribly demonstrative bedmate, offering
little more than an occasional murmur from the back of his throat, like
a dog chasing rabbits in its sleep.

Toby or not Toby. That is the question.

Here he was, the Hamlet of his generation, down on all fours
between a muscular pair of American legs, trying to make it talk.

Toby lifted his hips, took a sharp breath, and seemed to swell
against Henry's tongue. But no. He was only readjusting his buttocks,
as if one cheek were going to sleep.

"Put your hand here. No. Here," Toby commanded.

Henry had lost his own erection days ago. All he wanted now was
to hear Toby groan and see him spurt. Orgasm had become a point of
honor.

He was not entirely surprised. He had been caught off guard when
they first arrived at the apartment and Toby started dropping hints, as
light as crowbars, that he expected Henry to make a pass. It was a bit
unnerving, like seeing a chess piece move itself, yet promising. But then
they kissed and Henry could not find Toby's tongue. He had to chase

around his mouth before he caught it. When he opened his eyes, wondering what was wrong, he found Toby's eyes already wide open in front of him, like the eyes of a terrified horse. Toby quickly shut them, suggesting a child feigning sleep, and Henry wondered, Am I like kissing Hitler?

But Toby did not flee. He let Henry take him to bed. He let Henry undress him. But he had looked sexier in clothes.

His trousers, for example, were not as loose as the ones he wore the night they met; the fold in the middle of his bum was smaller, though it too flicked back and forth when he walked, but more quickly, like the tail of a puppy dog. Inside the trousers were underpants, white with some kind of mathematical formula on the waistband—as if his playwright used him as a notepad. Henry had been overjoyed to kneel down, rub his face in white, then slide the underpants down and release a cock as excited as his own. It had been downhill ever since.

If I were his age, thought Henry, and my prick were in Olivier's mouth, or even Gielgud's, the history alone would be enough to make me pop. What was the name of the boy who'd sat naked in his lap and asked to be jerked off while they watched a video of Henry's *Hamlet*? Now that was kinky, that was fun.

The phone rang.

"Want me to get it?" said Toby. He was closer to the nightstand.

"Hello? Oh. It's our food. Shall I tell them to send it up?"

Henry had forgotten about dinner. It seemed like hours ago that he had ordered food. He nodded. His mouth was empty now, but numb. His tongue forgot how to shape words.

"Sure. Send him up," said Toby, who was hardly winded.

Henry sat up, curling and rolling his lips back to life. He looked down at his bedmate. The boy stopped being a problem in hydraulics and became a person again, albeit a person with an erection—it lay bright red on his stomach like the club from a Punch and Judy show. Toby gazed up at Henry, trying out different expressions: an amused smile, a sad frown, an apologetic smirk.

The door buzzed. "Right back," Henry said hoarsely and threw a towel around his waist.

He opened the door on a Chinese gentleman in a yellow slicker, a middle-aged fellow who instantly averted his eyes.

"Oh, sorry," said Henry. "I'd given up on you. I was just about to step in the shower."

The fellow nodded. "Sure, sure. No problem. Twenty-five ten."

Henry was counting out the money when he noticed the man peeking from under his eyebrows into the apartment. Henry sniffed the air, wondering if the man could smell Toby on him.

"Thank you," said the man when he took the money. "Enjoy. Enjoy all things. Much good. Our age. Good night."

Henry carried the shopping bags of food back to the kitchen. Our age, indeed, he thought.

Toby appeared in the doorway. He was still naked.

"I'm sorry," he said. "Don't hate me."

"Nothing to hate. It happens." Henry was confused by how sad he felt to see him here, the boy from the Gaiety, standing nude in his kitchen. Be careful what you wish for.

"I guess I'm just feeling so awed to be with an actor that I admire so much."

"Oh please. I'm not your type. Simple as that. You like me enough to get hard, but not enough to get off." He hesitated. "Not to put too fine a point on it, but I *am* old enough to be your father."

"I like you. Really. But I guess I'm still in love with Caleb."

"Yes. There is that." Henry was actually glad to remember this other reason.

"Did you want me to go?"

"Don't be ridiculous. We haven't had dinner yet."

"I'd like that." He looked relieved. "Should I get dressed?"

"Or stay as you are. Whatever makes you comfortable." Henry smiled, daring Toby to remain naked, even though he felt judged by the boy's body. "I think I'll be a nudist myself tonight," he declared, undid his towel, and tossed it. He slapped his solid, youthful stomach.

Toby frowned and looked away.

"But *you* get dressed," said Henry. "It'll be like the night we met—with the roles reversed."

That cinched it for Toby. "No, I'll stay like this," he said. "I should probably wash my hands."

"Good thinking."

Henry knew he should be feeling angry and defeated right now, but he felt fine. Somewhat sad, but not terribly so. He had reached the point in life where even bad sex was good sex.

A few minutes later they were sitting at the kitchen table. Henry briefly considered eating in the dining room, but it would've been too peculiar seeing their genitals through the glass tabletop. He served up the food. "A nice paradox, don't you think? There's something absurd about a naked actor. Two naked actors is even more preposterous."

"Could you pass the salt?"

They began to eat. The crunch of broccoli in the silent kitchen suggested two dinosaurs devouring a forest.

" 'We're actors. We're the opposite of people,' " Henry suddenly announced. "Who said that? It's not original."

"I'm not a real actor," said Toby. "Not yet anyway."

"But you are," Henry insisted. "The child is father to the man. Wishes are horses. All that stuff. But actors aren't so different from other people. Not at all. Whoever said that was talking nonsense. Once upon a time, maybe, when everyone else was God-fearing and selfless. We were freaks of vanity, monsters of egotism. Unlike the rest of humanity. Now, of course, everyone's a narcissist. Every nobody and somebody needs to strike a pose in the public mirror. Amateurs."

Henry was talking only to hear himself talk, happily filling the silence. But during their first meeting, Toby had done most of the talking. The boy must be feeling very low if he could say so little.

"You are a real actor," he assured Toby. "I recognize the need in you. The hunger. And your interest in craft. It's craft that separates a professional narcissist from an amateur."

Toby took a deep breath. "I saw Caleb today. My ex?"

"Oh?" Henry speared a dumpling and plopped it in soy.

"I left some stuff at his place and had to pick it up."

Henry shoved the dumpling in his mouth. "And he was wonderful," he muttered around the dumpling. "And now you're in love again?"

"No. He was awful. So cool and casual. Like I was nobody. But I said some things I shouldn't have said."

"Such as?"

"He had a boyfriend who died of AIDS. Six years ago. He's still in

love with him. You can't compete with a dead person. They're too perfect."

"Quite true." Henry had forgotten about Doyle's dead lover, but
he doubted that the widower was still in love, not at his age.

"I said he loved him dead only because he didn't love him enough
when he was alive and sick."

"Oooo. That *is* bad."

"Real shitty. He told me to get out. He must hate me now."

"You poor guy."

And Henry did feel sympathy, but for Doyle, not Toby. He was suddenly impatient and exasperated with the boy, and hurt.

"And that's why you were so eager to go to bed with me tonight?
To get even with him."

Toby stared. "No. I just—I saw you in a show and you were great,
and I thought it'd be fun, and make me feel better if— I like you,
Henry. I wanted to make you feel good."

"Of course you did," he said sharply. The boy hadn't done a damn
thing for him. "Could you have orgasms with your playwright?"

Toby winced. "That's awfully personal."

Henry shrugged. "Under these circumstances? I would think we
could say absolutely anything to each other."

Toby shifted around on his chair, *acting* naked.

"Did you fuck?" said Henry.

Toby looked down, his mouth pinched tight at the corners.

Henry leaned closer and softened his voice. "Or did you prefer
frottage? Blow jobs or mutual wanks? What *do* you like?" If they
couldn't fuck in the flesh, they could at least fuck in words.

"Crap!" Toby cried. "Crap, crap, crap!"

Henry leaned back in alarm.

"I can't do anything right! I can't be a good actor. I can't keep a
boyfriend." Tears garbled his speech. "I'm not even good sex!"

He was crying. There were actual tears on his cheeks. Henry
scolded himself for being so cruel. He had never guessed his stripper
could be so softhearted.

"Why am I a loser? Why does the world hate me?"

"There, there," said Henry. He scooted his chair next to Toby's and
lay an arm over his shoulder. "There, there."

"Why am I such bad sex?"

"Nobody said you were bad sex. Every man has problems down there. You're not in the mood tonight. You're in love with someone else. Besides, an orgasm is only external behavior."

The boy continued to sob and shudder. "Damn him," he snarled. "Damn him, damn him, damn him."

Henry held Toby against his chest. "This is why *I* never fall in love. You think about Him all the time. Not a real Him, an imaginary Him. The most hurtful Him. A Him who makes *you* feel like an absolute shit."

Toby twisted his face around. His eyes were red, his upper lip slick with mucus.

"You never fall in love?"

"Almost never." He passed Toby a paper napkin. "I fell in love constantly as a boy. But then I understood that it was useless to be unhappy. Life is short. I refuse to take myself—or anyone else—so seriously that they will cause me pain. Oh, I allow some suffering, for the sake of my work. But nothing too awful and human. It worked for Noël Coward. It worked for Oscar Wilde—well, up to a point. It's worked pretty well so far for Henry Bailey Lewse. Knock on wood." Which he did.

"You must get real lonely."

Henry was startled that Toby took his speech literally. Did he not hear the irony and wishful thinking folded into his philosophy?

"Not at all. I have my friends and mates and colleagues." He laughed, kissed Toby on the temple, and released him. "I'm not nearly as lonely as you, my boy. I'm more self-sufficient. Besides, I get to break my heart playing at love for audiences. An actor does not need to feel a lot, you know, he needs only to feel accurately."

"Maybe that's why I'm not a better actor. I feel too much."

"It's possible." Henry studied Toby, wondering how much of his drama was real, how much was put on, and if the boy could distinguish one from the other yet.

Toby resumed eating, so Henry resumed too. He was surprised the food was still hot. Their little scene had not lasted so long that anything got cold.

"I'd like to spend the night," said Toby.

"Oh?"

"I don't want to sleep alone tonight. But I won't have sex with you. I'd like to, but I can't. I hope you understand."

"I understand," said Henry. "Well, I don't. Not really. But I'll accept your terms. Tonight."

He glanced at Toby and looked him up and down. The boy's nudity had grown as natural and meaningless as the nudity of a Labrador retriever. But he was pretty. Henry enjoyed looking at him.

"Toby?" he said. "Do you use chemicals?"

"You mean drugs?"

"Nothing unnatural. I was thinking of grass."

"No way. Not me. I've never done anything like that. I don't see the point. That's not why I am the way I am tonight."

"I'm not accusing you. I was just— Oh never mind."

He should've guessed that Toby was so square he wouldn't understand that Henry partook, much less want to join him. It was just as well. There was no telling what kind of demons would slip into Henry's head under the warm muzzy fog of a high while he shared his bed with this big blond Labrador of an American boy.

34

ME: Who do you see there?

YOU: Why do you want to know?

ME: I'm curious.

YOU: You're not jealous?

ME: No. I was never jealous. I don't have a jealous bone in my body. Have you met anyone famous?

YOU: A few, but not many. The unknown dead outnumber the famous a trillion to one.

ME: Who then? Tell me.

YOU: Janis Joplin.

ME: Why? You were never a Joplin fan.

YOU: I didn't *want* to meet her. I simply met her. Death is like life. You cannot anticipate what happens.

ME: So what's she like?

YOU: Short. Much shorter than I ever imagined. And confused. She spends her time looking for her mom, whom she adores. But Ma Joplin is tired of Janis and hides from her.

ME: What about people we knew? Do you see our friends?

YOU: Oh yes.

ME: Who?

YOU: All of them. And more. Guys whose names I never knew.

ME: Allen?

YOU: Yes.

ME: Stan?

YOU: Of course.

ME: Cook? Ethan? Danny?

YOU: They're all here.

ME: Phil Zwickler? Vito? Bob Chesley? Bob What's-his-name, the actor with the two-toned ponytail? Charles Ludlam? Tim—not Craig's Tim, but the other Tim, the Tim whose boyfriend died soon after he did and whose name I can never—

YOU: Tim Scott?

ME: No, he was a painter. This Tim was an actor. He produced the terrible plays his boyfriend wrote before they both died.

YOU: Whatever their names, they're all here. Every last one.

ME: And you hang out with them?

YOU: Not anymore. The first two or three years I saw some of them regularly. Especially Stan and Danny. We were what we knew. We wanted to finish telling our stories. We needed to compare notes.

ME: Notes on what?

YOU: At first we talked about hospitals. It was like those awful parties where businessmen talk about their least favorite airports. But what we mostly discussed was what it was like to "pass over." The fear, the pain, the exhilaration, the relief. We all needed to tell that tale, even though we were afraid we were full of clichés. It's the dead person's answer to the coming-out story.

ME: And how people treated you? Do you talk about that? Who loved you, who didn't? Who was kind, who was cold?

YOU: There you go again. "What do the dead think of us?" The living are so biocentric.

ME: We think about you. We want to believe that you think about us. Even if you think about us badly.

YOU: The rules are like this: You have to think about us, but we don't have to think about you.

ME: Hardly seems fair.

YOU: Death, like life, is not fair.

ME: But you don't see our friends anymore?

YOU: No. I used to see everyone, then only Stan and Danny, then we grew tired of each other. Eternity is a long time. So I started meeting people I didn't know in life but had wanted to meet. Like Anthony Reisbach.

ME: Who?

YOU: A beautiful kid at school. I didn't teach him—he wasn't smart enough for advanced math—but I noticed him. Sweet, apple-

cheeked jock, soft-spoken and graceful. He drowned in a
swimming pool the summer after he graduated.

ME: You were never a chicken hawk.

YOU: No, but one's tastes get more diverse in eternity.

ME: Are you in love with him?

YOU: The dead don't fall in love. Not in the way that you mean, lust
and obsession. I enjoy his company.

ME: But you told the truth when you were alive and said you never
fell in love with any of your students?

YOU: I told the truth. They were such babies. You would have heard
about a crush if I had one, Cal. I always told you about each and
every man I ever lusted after or tricked with.

ME: I'll say.

YOU: Don't pout. I never rubbed your nose in it.

ME: But you weren't shy about it either.

YOU: I wanted you to know that it was only lust, only sex. Our love
stopped being about sex long before I got sick.

ME: I know. I'm sorry.

YOU: Don't apologize. I liked sex more than you did. It's as simple
as that. And there was too much other life between us. It crowded
out the sex. You gave me enough love in other ways.

ME: I have to ask. Is there sex in death?

YOU: That's funny. I'd made a bet with myself that your first question
would be: Are there books in death? Libraries? Can the dead read?

ME: I'll get to that. But is there sex in death?

Caleb looked up from his notebook. The rain beat against the casement window. The traffic slurred in the street far below. The lamp cast
a halo on his desk. He tapped the eraser end of his pencil against his
mouth. Should there be sex after death?

He didn't know what he was writing here, if these night thoughts
were therapy or a verbal exercise or useless nonsense. They definitely
weren't art and would never become public, although his sense of craft
could not stop him from revising and improving sentences. Last night,
when he wrote the first pages, had been eerie and exciting, not eerie
like ghosts but like what he had felt when he was sixteen and wrote his
first paragraphs of pornography, creating bodies out of air and words.

He returned to the spiral notebook tonight feeling slightly guilty, like a kid who was about to jerk off. Writing and sex and necromancy were hopelessly tangled together.

But should the dead have sex? He didn't know. He decided to skip it. In his head he heard Ben toss out the next question.

YOU: When you remember me, do you think about the sex?

ME: Very rarely. Or no. Never.

YOU: How then? What do you remember?

ME: Strange. I've never sat down and tried to remember you on paper like this.

YOU: So try it now. What do you remember?

ME: Your smile. I know it sounds sappy, but the first thing I remember is your smile. Like when you laughed at a good joke. I knew you were happy, which made me happy, and the world was right with itself.

YOU: I'm like the Cheshire cat? Everything has faded except my smile?

ME: Don't put words in my mouth.

YOU: Why not? You're putting words in mine.

ME: Fair enough. But I remember your smile first because I'd prefer not to remember some of the other things.

YOU: Like?

ME: Your bad moods. Your bossiness. Your bully tendencies. Your habit of playing the schoolteacher even at home.

YOU: But you liked being bossed.

ME: Sometimes. I liked having someone make my decisions. So I could save all my thinking for my work. It wasn't good for me.

YOU: You should've bossed me back.

ME: Maybe. But it wasn't in my makeup. I thought you were so tough and wise and together.

YOU: I wasn't.

ME: No. But I didn't know that. Not until you got sick.

YOU: We don't have to talk about that.

ME: You want to avoid that, don't you? Because you were embarrassed to be sick. Humiliated. I remember the first or second time you were in the hospital, before we knew it wasn't a onetime thing but

was going to be our life for three years. And you shit on yourself.
Big deal. So what? You were in your hospital gown. You couldn't
get to the bedpan and you let out a squirt. Bright orange—
YOU: Don't!
ME: Shit. Highway-safety-orange shit. You got a splash on your nice
argyle socks, and you went nuts. It was like the end of the world.
You tore off your socks and told me to throw them, toss them, you
never wanted to see them again. As if that would solve anything.
YOU: I wanted things to be clean. I needed things to be orderly.
ME: You were afraid of confusion. You were terrified of mess.
Which was why you loved math. And Bach. And Japanese food.
But you contradicted yourself, Ben. You taught math to *teenagers*.
And you loved *me*. Who was a total mess. Emotionally, physically,
mentally. You scolded me like I was ten years old, about leaving
papers around or needing a haircut or not changing a dirty shirt—
YOU: You miss me, don't you?
ME: Of course I miss you. Why else would I be wasting my time on
this stupid writing exercise? I thought I could write myself out of
my bleak mood, but it's not working. I'm tired of being sad, I hate
myself for being unhappy.
YOU: Why do you think you need to be happy?
ME: Aren't we supposed to be happy? Isn't that why we're here?
We're obligated to be happy like we're obligated to succeed.
Happiness is the point of life. Are the dead happy?
YOU: We transcend happiness. Unhappiness too.
ME: Wait a minute. "Why do you think you need to be happy?" I
know that line. It's Osip Mandelstam. His wife quotes him in *Hope
Against Hope*. They were sent to Siberia by Stalin. They were
feeling suicidal, and Osip told her, "Why do you think you need to
be happy?"
YOU: Death is a kind of Siberia. But you get used to it.
ME: No. Not that. What I'm saying is that you didn't make it up.
You've been reading over my shoulder.
YOU: Yes. And you read such gloomy books. No wonder you're
depressed. You need to lighten up. You should go to the movies.
Or the theater. See a nice comedy. I hear this new musical, *Tom
and Gerry*, is very funny.

35

The rain fell all night. There was rain in her sleep, rain in her dreams. Rain was gargling in the downspout by her window when Jessie woke up the next morning.

Perfect, she thought. Shitty weather for my shitty life.

She lay in bed for the longest time, remembering all the awful things that had been said last night: "You self-hating asshole." "You righteous loser." "You love fags because you hate yourself." "Well, you love me because you love your own failure." And so on and so on. Not those words exactly, but ugly, poisonous words with the same effect.

What an idiot she'd been to open herself to Frank. You think sex will be fun, a good time, a vacation where you can climb out of your head and into your body. But a man gets you with your pants down when he gets your pants down.

And this warm, smelly bed was the scene of the crime. That fact was enough to get Jessie moving. She rolled off the futon and stumbled down the ladder. She went into the kitchen, turned on the shower, and stepped in, hoping the hard spray would wash away her sour stupidity. It felt wonderful for the first minutes, until she looked down at her pale white legs and pictured a pair of crocodile eyes watching from between her thighs.

The city was slick with rain, its colors bright and runny. Smears of red and yellow light floated on the bleary khaki pavement under the shop windows on West Fifty-fifth Street.

"Good morning," Jessie sang at the doorman of Henry's building. She shook her umbrella dry, then closed and tightly furled it while she waited for the elevator. She was glad that she had a job to go to today, relieved that she had work to do.

She took out her keys as she went down the hall. She found the right key and unlocked the lock. She opened the door and heard the clank, clank, clank of the Nautilus machine.

"Good morning," she called out. "You're certainly up early on this dark and shitty morning."

There was no answer, not even Henry's usual grunt.

She turned on her computer and hung up her raincoat. Pressing the palms of both her hands against her cheeks, she rubbed her face, as if to rub away all anger or bitterness, and stepped around the corner to ask Henry if he wanted—

But it wasn't Henry on the weight machine. Henry did not have a burly, porpoise-smooth body. Or wear such snug white underpants. A stranger—it *was* a stranger—straddled a bench with his beefy back facing Jessie. He lifted a column of weights with two thick arms. Black cordless headphones covered his ears. The music was turned up so loud that Jessie could hear it buzz like a dance club full of bees.

He finished his set, stood up, and turned around. He jumped six inches in the air when he saw Jessie.

"Toby?" He looked like Toby Vogler, but Jessie had never seen Toby undressed. Everyone looked different naked. And she never expected to see *him* here.

He caught his breath with one hand pressed over his heart. "Jessie?" He squinted at her, then lifted the muffs of his headphones an inch off his ears, as if that would help him see. "What are you— Oh!" His eyes darted down and he saw he wasn't dressed. He clamped the headphones back on, as if the music could clothe him. His face turned pink, then his neck and shoulders. "Sorry. Forgot that you— Mmmm!" He hunched down, not completely but just enough to suggest modesty. He fled into the bathroom and closed the door.

Jessie stood there with her mouth half open, adding it all up. Her brother's ex-boyfriend was here? In his underwear? In the morning? After spending the night with Henry? The little gold digger. Allegra joked that he was more cupcake than beefcake, but the cupcake was sleeping his way up the food chain.

She couldn't wait to tell Frank. But then she remembered that she and Frank hated each other. She was angry all over again.

The bedroom door popped open. Henry strolled out in his terry cloth bathrobe. "Oh? Jessica. You're early this morning." He peered into the dining room at the Nautilus machine. Rain tapped against the plate-glass windows. "What a dreary day," he said. "It's like bleeding Edinburgh out there."

"If you're looking for your guest," said Jessie, "I scared him off. He's hiding in the bathroom."

"Oh?" Henry acted so nonchalant, so irritatingly innocent.

Jessie refused to play along. "How do you know Toby?"

"What? *You* know him?"

"Of course, I know him! He was my brother's boyfriend!"

"Oh dear." He lowered himself onto the nearby sofa, as if this were a great shock. "New York certainly is a small town."

"You didn't know?"

He began to chuckle, a sincere, humorous noise joined by a guilty smirk. "Oh I learned it soon enough," he admitted. "But I didn't know it when we met. We met in a club, you see. A couple of nights ago. It never crossed my mind that *you'd* know him too." He continued to laugh as he shook his head at himself. "Oh what a tangled web we weave. But it's nothing serious," he insisted. "Not in the least. Just a friendly, one-night, hello-good-bye sort of thing."

"I didn't think it was serious. Not with Toby."

He lifted his eyebrows at Jessie, intrigued by her comment.

But she declared the conversation over. "I got work to do. And today is Wednesday. You have a matinee today."

"Oh yes," Henry said wearily. "Work, work, work. It never ends, does it?" He slowly stood up. "I should get him out of the loo."

Jessie went into her corner and sat down. She heard Henry at her back, lightly knocking on the bathroom door.

"Toby? Toby? It's safe to come out. We really should be going."

He was being so nice to his little trick, his conquest. Jessie was startled by how hurt and angry she felt. It wasn't out of loyalty to Caleb—no, Caleb was finished with Toby. And it was no business of hers who Henry fucked. It was just annoying that the boy had made his way here, into *her* world, *her* turf.

She checked the answering machine. She thought there might be a message from Frank but was glad that there wasn't.

"Jessica. Dolly Hayes here. It's Wednesday evening here so it must be morning there. I just spoke to Adam Rabb. We have something that needs to be discussed sooner rather than later. Have Henry call me immediately. This is no time to play phonesie."

The bathroom door opened and Jessie heard Henry say, "I'd love to 'hang,' but I have a matinee. Don't you have a job to get to?" The bedroom door closed and the voices were reduced to mumbles.

I should've been a man, Jessie told herself. Fags have it so easy. Look at Toby. Dull, vague, not-so-bright Toby. But because he has a dick and a pretty face, men like her brother and Henry Lewse fall all over him. Henry never paid that kind of attention to *her*. And to think she wanted Henry's respect. How can you respect the respect of a man who could follow his wiener into spending hours and hours with Toby Vogler? What could they possibly talk about? All right, they probably didn't talk. Toby must be good sex. He was too dull to be anything else. But she had gotten her own ashes hauled the night before, and orgasms now seemed as meaningless as sneezes.

The bedroom door opened and Henry escorted Toby through the living room. Toby looked surprisingly dressed up in a blue blazer and good slacks. "Uh, see you later," he told Jessie as they walked by.

"Yeah, right," said Jessie.

She heard them exchange good-byes at the front door. It sounded like they were setting up another date, but she couldn't be sure. There was a teeny *tsk,* like a kiss, and the door closed.

Henry walked back through the living room. "Buba ba, bu ba, bu ba, bu baba"—he mumbled "Sentimental Journey" again, but in a dry, joyless manner. Which was odd for a man who'd just gotten laid.

"Henry," said Jessie, saying his name flatly, as if saying, *Hey you.* "Dolly called. She wants you to call back. She says it's important."

"I'm in no mood to talk with that cunt," he muttered.

He was as irritable this morning as Jessie. By what right? He'd spent the night with a pretty boy bimbo. And he used the *c* word, which Jessie hated. Often it was just thoughtless, but today it sounded deliberately vicious.

"That 'cunt,' as you call her," said Jessie, "stood by you loyally for years. Just because you're planning to dump her doesn't mean you can't call her by her name."

"What was that?" Henry stood across the room, scrunching one eye at her. "Oh please. I'm in no mood today for your oh-so-American sensitivities."

They had stepped on each other's toes before, but then there were always apologies or laughter or something to soothe the insult. That wasn't happening today. Jessie was actually glad that they weren't making nice.

"No, you're right," she said. "English bluntness is more honest. Let's call a cunt a cunt, and a fag a fag."

Henry tilted his head to one side, as if he hadn't heard right. "What's this tone? Why are you talking like this? Are you angry because I slept with—" He had to snap his fingers at the front door while he rummaged in his memory.

"Toby."

"I know *his* name! Your brother, I mean."

"Caleb."

"Yes, him. You're angry because I slept with your brother's ex-boyfriend. Is that what this is about?"

"Why should I give a fuck who you fucked? He's nobody to me. Just a big twink. If you want my brother's sloppy seconds, it's no skin off my nose."

Henry took a deep breath. "None of this is any of your damn business."

"No. It's not," said Jessie. "So why don't you let me get on with your business that *is* my damn business and stop talking about this other business." She turned around and faced the computer, letting her body declare the discussion over. But her mouth could not help adding, "Gay or straight, all men are the same. The little head is always thinking for the big head."

Henry was silent for a moment. She could feel him behind her. He stood six feet away, but she sensed a rise in temperature.

"Yes, well," he began, "you might try following your own little head sometime—or whatever the *womanly* equivalent is called." He loudly avoided the *c* word. "Because then you might have a life of your own and wouldn't be such a nosey parker fag hag about mine."

"Fag hag?" She turned around. "Fag hag? I'm just a cunt and a fag hag to you?"

Sticks and stones, she thought, and the rest of it. And they were only words, and she used them herself, and they rarely caused real pain. But today they felt like deadly weapons.

"You old queen," she continued. "I balance your books. I write your letters. I buy you your pot. And do I get respect? Do I get thanked? No. I get called a fag hag and a cunt."

"I never called you a cunt!"

"No, but you thought it!"

"I'm certainly thinking it now!"

"See! See!" She jumped to her feet and waved her hands at him, at the room, at the world, without knowing what she'd say with the gesture. "I'm tired of this bullshit. I'm sick of being invisible. A third-class citizen. A nobody. I'm done with you, Henry. Finished. I quit."

He became very still. All the life went out of his face, except for his eyes, which looked straight at her, a sad, calm gaze that held her while he hunted for the right words, the right emotion.

"Good," he finally said. "Because this old queen is done with you." His eyes turned small and black and angry. "This old, *old* queen does not need to see your cunty puss ever again."

Jessie was shocked by his response. Her words actually meant something to him?

"Go ahead! Quit! You think I'll miss you? You and your cunty competence? Your cunty condescension. This cunty city and its cunty theater. A man can't even get laid in this cunty, huggy, touchy-feely town. I don't need any of you in my life!"

Anger poured off him like the heat of a fire. It was all words, hot yet controlled, with more emotion in the pitch of his voice than in the meaning of his words. Imagine being cursed by Richard Burton or Jeremy Irons. The anger of Henry Lewse was both a terror and a privilege, like standing under a roaring lion. His morning breath was as foul as a lion's.

Jessie sustained her own anger so she could hold out against him. "And I don't need you!" she said. "Or your shitty job and its shitty paychecks. Good-bye. I'm gone." She reached for her raincoat, she grabbed her umbrella.

"Who are you to walk away from me?" he demanded. "You're nobody important. You're only a secretary! An *assistant!*"

His words should have stung, but she recognized she was hurting him by quitting. She took her satisfaction there.

"Right. I'm just a cunty cunt and a faggy fag hag." She opened the door and stepped into the hall. "And you're a total asshole."

She plunged down the hall, ecstatic with anger, drunk with rage. She felt more real than she had felt in years. She had done it. She was free. She didn't need Henry.

She wondered if he were watching. She wanted to see the look on his face, but did not dare turn around.

She heard the slam of the door at the end of the hall.

36

Henry flung the door into its frame. The wood and steel slammed together beautifully.

And he stood there, catching his breath, letting his emotion subside, satisfied the scene had played out so clean and sharp.

Then he thought: Now what? He had just fired his assistant. Or no, she quit—it was one of those simultaneous acts where cause and effect merged. Was that what he wanted? He waited a moment, expecting Jessie to come back so they could discuss the scene and understand what was appropriate or inappropriate here. But this wasn't a fictional piece they could do again. She did not return. Which gave Henry a whole new reason to be angry with her. The silly bitch—he was careful not to think cunt—had quit. Damn her.

He did not need this today. His inner life was already a muddle. Did his outer behavior have to be a muddle as well?

She had left the computer on. Henry stood beside it, looking at the TV part, trying to remember what button one pushed to turn it off. He collapsed helplessly into the armchair. "Oh, Jessica."

What would he do without her? How would he get through his days? He'd have to hire a new assistant, wouldn't he?

But today was Wednesday. He had a matinee in two hours and another performance this evening. There was no time for life on matinee days. Life would have to wait until tomorrow. He had not even showered or shaved yet.

He went into the bathroom, prepped his face with hot water, then sculpted shaving cream over his chin and cheeks. He hated shaving with a safety razor and preferred an electric, but he needed a close shave for a show, what with all the makeup and cold cream.

While his whiskers soaked in foam, Henry faced himself in the mirror, a shabby fellow with dyed hair and a creamy white beard, like a punk King Lear, but gentler than Lear, sweet and harmless.

Why did Jessie quit? Was it something he said? Well, of course, it was something he said. They'd both said too much. So he was just an old queen? Old Queen Lear. But his words had been nastier than hers. How had he allowed their argument to get so out of control?

He held the safety razor under the hot water, lifted his chin, and slowly drew the blade up his throat.

I am such an anus, he thought. Why had he lost his temper? Because of Toby. If only Toby had been better sex.

He rinsed the blade under the tap and began a new swath.

In heartier, lustier times, he would've just fucked the bumptious boy and been done with him. Now, however, he was in his fifties; his cock was no longer the be-all and end-all of sack time. He had to think about *their* pleasure, *their* satisfaction. Which could be quite enjoyable. But if they weren't enjoying it, then he couldn't and it was no longer sex. Which was what had happened last night. Which should have been the end of it. But Henry wanted to see Toby again. He needed to see him again.

The blade scratched beside his ear, a loud, gritty, sandy sound.

Why see Toby again? He couldn't fuck the boy, he couldn't eat him. The boy was useless to him. Yet Henry wanted to see Toby again. So badly that he'd even agreed to go see his bunch-of-unemployed-actors-put-on-a-show-in-somebody's-cellar kind of play. Toby said they were doing an after-midnight performance on Friday and he was sure he could get Henry in.

He knocked the razor against the sink to dislodge a clot of soap and whiskers. It rang like a spoon on a glass calling a room to order.

He must be falling in love with Toby. Or something.

Whatever it was, the whole business made Henry angry, testy. And he had taken it out on his silly-billy assistant. Didn't she know him well enough by now to ignore his uglier moods?

When he finished shaving and splashed cold water on his face, he saw a new face in his mirror: Queen Lear. Was that such a bad thing? She'd be kinder than King Lear, wiser and better tempered. Or maybe not. Maybe she'd be just another bitch.

He took a quick shower, then dried himself and dressed in his usual sloppy going-to-the-theater clothes. His sole nod to fashion was a nicely tailored Burberry trench coat for the rain.

Passing through the living room, he saw the computer was still on. Oh, Jessie, he thought. The hell with you. The hell with Toby too. He left the machine running and hurried out the door to the elevator.

Downstairs the rain continued to fall, a gauze curtain of water. Go ahead and piss. He opened his umbrella and plunged in.

His reprise of temper surprised him. But it was Wednesday. He had two shows ahead of him and would have no time for life today, no emotions until Thursday. Thank God.

At the first crosswalk, waiting for the light to change, he felt himself being watched. He leaned his head back and peeked across the ridge of his nose. He saw a short, gawking, white-haired woman under a bright yellow umbrella that gave her a look of jaundice.

"Hey," she said. "You're somebody, aren't you?"

He took a deep breath. He turned to her. He smiled and nodded. "Yes. Henry Lewse. So nice of you to recognize me."

She continued to stare. "Why would I know you? You on TV?"

"No, madam. Theater. But thank you just the same." He looked back at the crosswalk light, wishing it green.

"It can't be theater. I don't go to theater anymore. It's too expensive. Where else?" she demanded. "Help me here!"

He faced her again. "How the hell should I know! Maybe you bloody dreamed me!"

She didn't even blink. "You don't need to get nasty about it."

37

YOU: Let's talk about success.

ME: All right. Yours or mine?

YOU: I'd say yours. After all, I'm dead.

ME: Success means nothing to the dead?

YOU: No. We're free of that rat race. We don't have to live anymore with those two imposters, success and failure.

ME: I like that. "Those two imposters." Who said it?

YOU: I thought I just did.

ME: But before you. It's not original with you. Or me either.

And it wasn't. Caleb stuck his pencil in his mouth and thought.

He was back in his office, back at his game of words. This usually went better after dark, but a rainy day was almost as good as night. A green grayness filled the city like aquarium water. Falling rain continued to strike the patio outside his window in perfect splashes that resembled tufts of grass. Caleb wondered if this bad weather would last through Friday. Wouldn't it be awful if he had to cancel his party?

"Those two imposters, success and failure." Where had he heard the phrase? It sounded good. And not just good, but true. He bent over the notebook again to see where the phrase would take him.

ME: I've learned firsthand that success is not entirely real. It's never complete. No matter what you get, you want more. But failure is an imposter too?

YOU: Like success, it's only temporary. And all in the eye of the

beholder. What feels like failure to you is going to look like success
to someone else.

ME: That's something I still don't get. That there are people out
there who think I'm a success. Who envy me.

YOU: The only complete failure is death.

ME: But you're dead. Is it really so bad?

YOU: Not half as bad as being sick. And I suspect it's not half as bad
as starving or being an alcoholic or a paranoid schizophrenic or
getting persecuted by Stalin's secret police.

ME: This isn't helping me.

> The downstairs buzzer buzzed.
> Caleb cringed, then sat very still. He wasn't expecting anyone. The
> mailman would leave packages in the foyer. A messenger would come
> back later. He remembered his last unexpected visitor.
> He waited. There was no second buzz.
> He relaxed and went back to the dialogue. But the voices in his head
> were gone. There was nothing now but gray pencil words on green-
> tinted paper. He thought a moment and a new question came to him.

ME: So what did you think of Toby? Was I unkind to him?

YOU: You're asking me? The dead boyfriend?

ME: You were always more experienced in the kiss-the-boys-and-say-
good-bye department.

YOU: All right then. You want my reaction? In the game of love, we
all need to be slapped now and then. Especially when we're young.
When we think we're the center of the universe. It's part of our
romantic education.

ME: So you're saying I did the right thing?

YOU: I'm saying you should have hurt him more. Slapped him
physically and emotionally. You should've caressed his heart, then
pinched it. Kissed it, then drop-kicked it like a football.

ME: Where's this coming from? You were never cruel when you
were alive. Not knowingly.

YOU: But now I sometimes wish I'd hurt you knowingly instead of
accidentally. A deliberate kick is more real and intimate than an

accidental one. But you should understand that. You're the man who wrote *Venus in Furs*.

ME: But I identified with the husband, not the wife.

YOU: You wrote the wife awfully well. You must have wanted to slap me around a little. Too bad you never did.

38

Downstairs in the foyer of One Sheridan Square, standing by the buzzers and intercom, Jessie blankly watched the rain hit the black asphalt in tiny white explosions. She was no longer waiting for an answer, she was just waiting. She considered taking out her cell phone and calling upstairs, but if Caleb wasn't home, he wasn't home. Too bad. He would've enjoyed hearing how she'd just told his favorite Shakespearean sellout to go to hell.

She opened her umbrella and stepped outside. But where to go? She did not want to go home. She did not want to be alone with her brand-new freedom. She was proud of quitting, but where's the joy in pride when you can't share it with anybody?

Stopping at the corner while a chocolate brown UPS truck lumbered past, she looked back at Caleb's building. It loomed over the little triangle of iron-fenced garden like a cliff topped with a castle of solitude. She could see no windows up there, only a few shrubs and the old water tank on stilts.

Maybe it was for the best that Caleb was out. Telling him how she'd quit would also mean telling him she'd seen Toby. There was no dignity in ratting on Toby. It might suggest she'd quit because Henry was bonking the twink. Or worse, that she had rushed downtown to tell Caleb because misery loves company.

But she wasn't miserable. No. She was happy that she'd quit. Really. The action was wonderful, spontaneous and real. But the adrenaline high of high drama was beginning to wear off. She could see the downside of storming out. Her bank account, for example. And the job market wasn't especially great right now. She didn't have a clue about what she could do next with her life.

There was a Starbucks around the corner, facing the newsstand at the subway entrance. She went in, thinking she could hang for a half hour or so and try Caleb later—if she decided to try him again. The place felt surprisingly cozy for a Starbucks. The walls were exposed brick, russet and orange. Lunch hour was over and only a handful of people sat at the tables, reading books or newspapers or working at laptops. There was a harsh stink of wet wool under the aroma of coffee. Jessie bought a cappuccino and almond croissant—she might not be able to afford such treats in the future—and went over to an unsorted stack of the *Times* from the past few days. She found three different Arts and Leisure sections and took them to a table by the window.

The cappuccino was foamy and fragrant, the croissant soft and sweet. Rain dribbled down the window glass like fake tears.

Jessie knew she should be thinking about her life and what to do with it, but she went straight to the movie ads. Dreamer, go to the movies. The only half-decent program was down at Film Forum: *The Decalogue,* Parts Seven and Eight. She'd seen all ten films already. She couldn't remember which of the Ten Commandments these two episodes addressed. Thou shalt not covet thy neighbor's goods? Thou shalt not worship false gods? Whatever, moral drama from Poland was not what she needed today.

She turned back to the theater page.

There was *Tom and Gerry.* She should be inured to the image by now—the quarter-page advertisement featured the same art deco couple that floated on the billboard outside on Seventh Avenue—but the sight gripped her heart and squeezed it.

Fuck this, she thought. Your fight was over piffle, but you were right to quit. He took you for granted. He barely noticed you. He's probably not even fully aware yet that you're gone. He won't notice until he starts drowning in unpaid bills. So why are you so sad? What kind of a masochist are you?

She squeezed her eyes shut and turned to another page. Her eyelids opened on a review of "Leopold and Lois."

"Night Clubbed" said the headline. The reviewer was Kenneth Prager. The opening sentence read: "Like their namesakes, Leopold and Loeb, the musical couple of Leopold and Lois are murderers."

Jessie was not a fan of Leopold and Lois. They were too East Village superironic for her taste. A bad review might be just what she needed right now. There is nothing like seeing untalented success get kicked in the butt to raise one's spirits on a bad day. She folded the page back and began to read.

"You think you're all alone, a stranger in a strange city, and then you remember you're not alone."

The male voice behind her was a bit too loud and clear, like someone talking on a cell phone. She didn't bother to turn around. "Jessie? Hey. It's me."

Now she turned.

He stood over her, a tall, thin geek with stringy brown hair gathered in a long, loose ponytail.

"Charlie?"

He was grinning like a fool, as if she should be pleased to see him. "Not bad," he replied, assuming she'd asked how he was doing. "And yourself? May I join you?"

"Uh, sure."

He folded his elaborate length into the chair across the table. Jessie hadn't seen Charlie Walker in almost two years, but he looked much the same. Forty going on eighteen. He still wore a black T-shirt and black jeans and long hair, like a slacker out of college. Charlie Walker was her ex-husband.

"You could've knocked me over with a feather when I saw you sitting here. Small world."

"Are you living in the city again?"

"Oh no. Just visiting. Doing sound for a trade show. I tech for Pfizer and other forces of evil."

Charlie dressed like a musician, but he was a techie, a sound engineer who'd been doing theater work when Jessie met him ten years ago. Techies are more practical and less ego-naked than artist types. Which she enjoyed for a while. But then Charlie found that work was steadier and the pay superior in the corporate sector. Dull practicality swallowed him like a wolf.

"We're up at the Javits Center, waiting for a mixer console that won't arrive until five. So I thought I'd come downtown and check out old haunts. This used to be my favorite Greek coffee shop, you know. But they paved paradise and put up a Starbucks."

He was staring deep into her eyes. It was an old habit of his, a meaningless tic that Jessie blamed on herself. When they first got together, she had told Charlie that he was too skittish and needed to look people in the eye more often. Which he began to do with a vengeance. He did it with men as well as women, and gay guys like her brother often got confused. His blue pupils were as pale and shallow as a wash of watercolor. He could be sexy in a lazy, laid-back, lullaby manner. He regularly bored women into bed.

"Are you still with— I'm sorry," said Jessie. "I can't remember her name."

"Justine. Oh yeah. We own a house in Trenton now. Real estate is real cheap out there. And we got married."

"Oh?" A half dozen emotions flew around her head, none of which she could express in words. All she could do was squint.

He chuckled, then shrugged. "Just because it didn't work with you and me doesn't mean marriage is bad. And ours ended amicably."

"Yeah, well, we didn't have any money or property to fight over," said Jessie. Or illusions or heartbreak or love.

"We didn't have a pot to pee in," he agreed and chuckled again, his old, annoying, cartoon rasp, like he had a throat full of candy wrappers. "So. What have you been doing? How's your life?"

"My life's okay." There could not have been a worse day to run into an ex-husband.

"Where you working? You still reading scripts at whatsit's?"

"Manhattan Theatre Club. No. That's like three jobs ago." She studied the pitted foam in her cappuccino. "I'm the personal assistant to an English actor in a Broadway show. You know Henry Lewse?"

"Uh-uh. But you know me. If they're not in a *Star Trek* movie, they fly under my radar."

"Well, he's nobody important," said Jessie.

But this truth did not correct the lie. And the lie made Jessie feel more deeply than ever what she had lost. "You're an *assistant,*" he had sneered. "Only an assistant." Now she was the assistant to nobody, which made her nobody.

"You kept our place downtown?" said Charlie.

"Oh yeah."

"Good. That was a really good apartment. Cheap."

"It should be. It's an illegal—sublet." Her voice caught in her chest. The sudden thickness there annoyed her. She had no job now, no husband, no boyfriend, not even an apartment with a lease. "But you're happy in Trenton?" she said.

"Oh yeah. Trenton's cool. We got space. We got a garage, where I can mess with my electric bass. Justine has a garden. Work's dumb but the money's good. I'm not surrounded by techno whizzes who make me feel like a flop. I just go with the flow."

"The tao of Trenton," said Jessie.

He laughed. "To be sure. We can all find peace in our inner Trentons."

Jessie opened her mouth to laugh with him—and she burst into tears.

Charlie grinned, as if these were joke tears.

Her throat closed up and the hot water spilled out. "Oh shit," she croaked. "Why am I—?" She tried to laugh at herself, but each breath only brought up another sob.

Charlie finally understood. He leaned forward, tried to show concern but could only resume his old gaze-into-their-pupils look. He reached across the table and took her hand.

"Jessie? What's wrong? You're not crying about Trenton."

And she scornfully laughed, which brought up a fresh volley of sobs. "Fuck," she sputtered. "Fuck, fuck, fuck—" She pulled her fingers out of his hand and grabbed a napkin to cover her eyes. She pressed the heels of both hands against the sockets. A moment passed and she regained herself. She lowered the napkin.

"It's not about seeing me?" said Charlie.

"Oh no. Not at all."

"I didn't think so."

She stretched her jaw wide, took a deep breath, swallowed, and blinked. Her eyelids felt raw. The coarse brown napkins at Starbucks were not designed for crying jags. "Sorry," she said. "Sorry. I'm having one of those days where I absolutely hate my life."

Charlie nodded, as if this were a perfectly reasonable thing to feel. He seemed uncomfortable but not distressed. Which was so like Charlie. His manly stolidity was one of the things Jessie had liked about him, when she didn't despise it.

"How long were we together?" he suddenly asked.

"Three years." She sniffed up a last noseful of tears. "And were married for one." But Charlie was never quite a husband, he was more like a stunt.

"Is that all?" he said and resumed his sweet, friendly, stupid look. "Feels longer than that. Much longer."

39

Hello, Henry? Jessie? Somebody? Please! Dolly Hayes again. I've been calling and calling. Nobody calls back.

"Adam Rabb has rung up five times in the past two days. Arrogant twit. He talks like a man who thinks he's done the world a favor by living in it. Which is no hair off my dog. But he's given us a twenty-four-hour ultimatum. I told him I can't reach you, Henry, but he says he'll withdraw the offer if we don't respond by ten tonight. Your time.

"It's a sweet deal, Henry. If you truly want to sell your ass for a high price, here's your chance. But if we don't get it, you'll have nobody to blame but yourself."

40

Like their namesakes, Leopold and Loeb, the musical couple of Leopold and Lois are murderers. Their victim, however, is not poor little Bobby Franks, but the pop culture of their parents' generation. This show, a parody without laughs, a ninety-minute tantrum, is probably more in need of therapy than a review. Even so—' "

Dwight lowered the *Times*. "Leave it to a straight man to not get it. I saw that show. And it was funny. I mean, get-a-heart-attack-and-die funny."

"I feel no sympathy for them," said Allegra. "They got a *Times* review. We won't."

"Be grateful for that," said Frank.

" 'Even so,' " Dwight continued, " 'your pleasure or exasperation or probable boredom will depend upon your memories of the forgotten worlds of nightclubs, Las Vegas and Merv Griffin . . .' "

Rain continued to drip and drool outside. It was only six o'clock but felt as dark and dreary as a six o'clock in November. All the lights were on at West 104th Street. Frank was sunk in an armchair in the corner, trying to think himself into the right mood for work. Tonight was Wednesday, the first show was Friday, but he didn't care if this thing lived or died. He was in a foul mood tonight, a dangerous indifference.

" 'The lack of feeling for this deluded couple is chilling. Yet the audience treated the show as howlingly funny.' "

"Enough!" cried Frank, and he forced himself out of the chair. "Let's go. We got tons to do tonight."

"But Toby's not here," said Allegra.

"Screw Toby. Boaz, can you read Toby's lines?"

"No," Boaz said flatly.

"Bo? Sweetie?" said Allegra. "Darling?"

Boaz too was in a bad mood. His squashed good looks looked more squashed than usual. "Music," he said. "I must burn a CD with *all* the show's music." He showed them a shopping bag full of CDs. "I am out of here," he said and left.

"What's going on?" said Melissa. "Is it the weather or moon or did everyone get up on the wrong side of the bed today?"

"Fuck it," said Frank. "I'll read Toby's lines. Come on. Move it."

They all got up, shuffled into positions, and began their first scene, the leisurely opening.

Chris and Melissa marched back and forth between the kitchen and bathroom. They passed each other without speaking. Frank sat in a folding chair in the middle of the living room and watched.

"Great day," grumbled Melissa, the first line of the play.

"No, it's not," said Chris.

"I was being sarcastic," said Melissa.

"Sorry. It's too early to appreciate your dry wit."

I luf you like a pig lufs mud, thought Frank.

Except he didn't. Not anymore. Never again.

Ingrid Bergman's words had come out of nowhere. Frank's mind was like ice and his attention kept sliding off in all directions.

He had woken up this morning feeling like whale shit—which, as his father used to say, is at the bottom of the ocean.

"I won't be your fucking consolation prize because you failed as an actor."

There is nothing crueler than being naked with a woman you love— doubly naked with an erection—and getting chewed up and spit out.

"It must make you feel good. To love somebody who's an even bigger loser than you are."

Sometimes when Frank replayed the scene in his head, he concentrated on the wrong things *he* said—"You are so hung up on your gay brother." But most of the time he treated the fight as all her fault. Never fall in love with someone who's permanently wounded, he told himself. They cannot love you back.

He could not tell Allegra and the others what had happened. They knew too much already. He did not want to have a flock of actors cackling about his love life like a ditzy Greek chorus.

Dwight came out from the bedroom—they were already at his first scene—half humming, half singing "Losing My Religion." In his exchange with Allegra he overdid the gloom, but Frank didn't stop him. He didn't trust his instincts enough to criticize anyone today.

Toby's first monologue with Chris followed. Chris sat in front of the television and Frank read Toby's lines. Remembering how much time and attention he had given the boy last night, he was furious with the dweeb for being late.

" 'Hey. How are you? You have a good day? I had a great day,' " said Frank.

Under the smart-ass banter and jokes, all three stories were about people who were depressed. Which was supposed to be darkly funny, but Frank today found depression only depressing.

They came to the scene where Allegra and Dwight pounce on each other. It could be—it should be—wonderful. Two friends are sharing troubles, swapping sorrows like a pair of Eeyores, and suddenly they're all over each other. But instead of striking the moment like lightning, Allegra and Dwight muddled around it, knocking into each other and bumping noses.

"What are you guys afraid of?" said Frank. "Go for it. Give the line. Pause. Then suck face."

Dwight and Allegra paused, looked into each other's eyes—and broke into giggles.

"You are such babies," Frank grumbled. "What's the big deal? You're depressed and horny."

"But we're also good friends," said Dwight.

Frank stood between them. "The scene's not about friendship!" he said. "It's about fucking!"

"You think it's so easy," said Allegra. "You do it."

"All right then. Like this!"

And he grabbed Dwight by the collar, pulled their faces together, and jammed his mouth into Dwight's. Teeth clicked against teeth; his tongue plunged into warm wetness. Frank kissed hard and deep, even as he thought, This is Dwight's mouth. What am I doing in Dwight's mouth? Why is my kiss so angry?

He released Dwight, turned to the side, and spat the kiss out. "There," he told Allegra. "And people call *me* homophobic."

He noticed everyone staring.

"Jeez," said Dwight with a nervous laugh. "I never knew you cared." But his face was bright red; he looked disturbed, unhappy.

Frank wiped his mouth with the back of his hand. "Sorry. I got carried away in the moment. *Your* moment. So give yourself to the moment. Both of you."

They did the scene again. And again. The moment still eluded them—they lacked the anger that had driven Frank—but they mastered the logistics.

Frank was starting the next Toby monologue when there was a knock on the door. Frank automatically opened it and Toby entered, tiptoeing and making sorry-I'm-late faces. Yet he looked oddly pleased with himself. He tossed his coat at the corner and promptly took over from Frank.

" 'What are you watching? Good show? I think I have an audition for a cop show. Not that one, but another . . .' "

"Sorry I'm late," he said when they finished the scene.

"Where were you?" said Dwight.

"Kinko's. My shift ran late."

"Let's keep going," said Frank. "We're rolling now."

They continued, but they weren't rolling, not really. Everything felt muffled and half-there tonight, underwater, except for Toby's scenes. There was a new confidence and precision in his monologues. He actually remembered what he and Frank had worked out. Frank noticed the surprised looks of the others, then sensed them giving their scenes a bit more concentration, as if to catch up with Toby.

Chris and Melissa stumbled around each other in the kitchen, and Frank had an idea. "Think Laurel and Hardy," he said.

He was afraid Chris might be insulted—she would know which of them was Hardy—but no, she loved the idea. "Lesbo Laurel and Hardy? Yeah. I can work with that."

Her hint of slapstick and touch of graceful pomposity gave the scene more life, made it flow just a little better.

Then Toby performed the fourth monologue. He had his big breakdown and threw his arms around Chris exactly as he'd thrown his arms around Frank. Chris knew how to play that too, hesitating, then timidly hugging him back.

The trashing of the kitchen followed. It was lame, not only because the cast held back but also because tonight's flashes of life made the thing look more clunky and mechanical than ever.

They finished and Frank said, "We're getting there. It's not *completely* shabby." And he no longer felt completely like whale shit. "Let's take a break."

People scattered, windows were opened, cell phones were turned back on. Allegra came up to Frank.

"That was some kiss you gave Dwight," she said.

"I was just illustrating."

"That's what I thought. But you hurt his feelings."

"What?"

"He thinks you're making fun of him for being gay."

"For crying out loud." Frank couldn't believe this. "Why does everyone suddenly think I give a damn who does what with—?"

"Talk to him," she said. "We don't need another bad mood/loose cannon around here."

Frank saw Dwight and Chris leaning out the windows and smoking their cigarettes: Chris's rear at one window, Dwight's at the other. It was too wet for them to climb out on the fire escape.

Frank came up beside Dwight. He quietly stuck his head out. "Hey, friend. Sorry if I spooked you back there."

Dwight did not even turn to look. "It was like you don't take me seriously, Frank."

"I take you very seriously."

"If I frenched you, you'd be howling bloody murder."

"I wouldn't," he insisted. But they were standing so close that it was uncomfortably imaginable.

The fire escape formed an iron cage around their heads and shoulders. Contact lenses of water glittered on the rail. Chris leaned out her own window five feet away, up to her elbows in room light.

"Look. I wasn't thinking," said Frank. "But I wasn't frenching you. I was Allegra's character frenching your character."

"Now I know how girls feel when they get felt up. You and I are friends, Frank. You can't get your jollies by doing stuff to me."

"Dwight! I got no thrill out of kissing you." The kiss was not without emotion, but the emotion had nothing to do with Dwight. "Look. I apologize. I'm sorry. It won't happen again."

Allegra thrust her head through Chris's window. "Hey! Toby has some really interesting news."

It was getting crowded out here. Frank was set to withdraw his head and continue this in the living room. But Toby's head popped out beside Chris's and Allegra's.

"Uh, Frank?" he began. "I was asking Allegra—what are the chances—? Could we put on an extra performance on Friday? For, um, a friend of mine who can't come to the nine o'clock show?"

Dwight and Chris groaned together.

Frank said, "Sorry, Toby. If they can't make it, they can't make it. We may be small potatoes, but we're not so small we can give a command performance for anyone who asks."

"No, no, Frank," argued Allegra. "You should hear this. Toby, tell him who your friend is."

"Uh, Henry Lewse."

"*Henry Lewse!*" cried Dwight. He turned to Frank, wide-eyed, then back to Toby. "Mr. Eve Harrington! Yo!"

"Eve who?" said Toby.

"Dwight, shut up," said Allegra. "What do you think, Frank?" She drew herself back inside.

Frank came back in too, blinking at the bright room after the darkness of the fire escape. They all returned to the light.

"Henry Lewse," repeated Allegra. "He comes to watch and he loves the show. And we get a quote from him."

"What if he hates the show?" said Dwight.

"How can he hate it?" said Allegra. "His buddy's in it."

"He's a nice guy," Toby assured them. "He'll want to help us."

Frank couldn't believe what he was hearing. Henry fucking Lewse. He couldn't escape him. And the others all turned into performing dogs who couldn't wait to do back flips for the guy. He looked at Chris, trusting her to see things differently.

She only shrugged. "I don't mind doing an extra show."

"Me neither," said Dwight. "For Henry Lewse. Wow. It'd be like being watched by Michael Caine. And you're *dating* him?"

"Nooooo," Toby softly mooed, lowering his head. He looked guilty, but proudly guilty, triumphantly guilty. "We met and had coffee. Twice. He's really interested in young actors. In their careers."

"Their ca-whats?" said Dwight.

"Look," said Allegra. "I don't care how we know Henry Lewse. But I'm not going to look a gift horse in the mouth. What do you think, Frank? Extra show on Friday? What do we have to lose?"

And they all turned to Frank, curiously, expectantly, hopefully.

41

"Hello."

"Toby?"

"Oh. Henry. Hi."

"Good. You're still up. I didn't want to call too late."

"I never go to bed before one. Hey, I asked my friends about Friday night? And we *are* putting on an extra performance. And there are tickets. So can I give you one?"

"Of course. Yes. That'd be lovely."

Silence.

"Are you free tonight, Toby? Would you like to come over?"

"It's awfully late. It's almost midnight."

"I know. I just thought you might want— Oh. Never mind."

"But I enjoyed last night."

"Did you now?"

"I did. Honest. It was cozy. Like a sleepover."

"Hmmm."

"I'm sorry I can't give you more, Henry. Can you deal?"

"Would you like another sleepover tonight?"

"Sorry. I need my sleep."

"You seemed to have no trouble sleeping last night."

"I have this play. Remember? Like you have yours. But you will come see it on Friday? You promise?"

Pause. "I wouldn't miss it for the world."

42

The sun was up, the sky was blue—the powder blue of skies in children's books. Jessie walked in a green, green cornfield, glad to be out of the city, pleased to have escaped her obligations, wondering what to do about the little hippopotamus. Roughly the size of a baby pig, he waddled behind her like a private remorse, a pet regret.

There was a strange knocking in the sky, a rapping like the old-fashioned thumps of a cane signaling the start of a play in *The Children of Paradise*. All at once, blue sky and green landscape pulled loose and flew up like a curtain. It's the end of the world, thought Jessie, terrified. The painted canvas of earth and sky vanished overhead. All that remained was a vast starry darkness. And an audience.

She stood onstage in a theater as big as the cosmos, as infinite as outer space. Her hippo remained beside her. Boy, do I have a witty unconscious, she told herself. Because she was beginning to suspect that this was only a dream. She hoped it wouldn't be one of those silly actor dreams where you forget your lines or don't even know what play you're in.

She looked out at the audience. It was all men, an ocean of men in tuxedoes. Which pleased her. She always enjoyed being the only girl at the party. She saw Caleb sitting in the front row. And Mr. Copeland, their high school drama teacher. His eternal boyishness was gone, and he looked as old as their father would be if Dad were still alive. Beside Mr. Copeland sat Frank, in a scowl of folded arms, disgusted with her for appearing in public with a hippopotamus.

But where was Henry? She could not see Henry. He hadn't taken the trouble to come. The shit.

The little hippo at her feet abruptly cleared his throat. He was looking up at her with soft, kind eyes. He slowly opened his wide pink mouth. He was going to speak: he would tell her everything.

But before he could explain the meaning of it all, the cane resumed knocking. Thump, thump, thump. As if the play had still not begun. There was another play behind this play, the real play, God's play, and God was losing His patience.

Jessie suddenly woke up in her bed.

Knock knock knock. Someone was banging at her door.

"Wha? Huh? Who?"

A muffled male voice replied, "It's me. I've come to apologize."

She was sitting up. She lifted and pulled at her blankets, but it was gone. The hippopotamus of wisdom was nowhere in sight.

"Minute. Just a minute," she croaked at the door. Her voice was hoarse and dry. She started down the ladder. Someone had come to apologize? But so many people owed her an apology.

She unhooked the chain and opened the door.

And there in her hall was the long, unshaven face of Henry Lewse. He held a wet umbrella in one hand and a large paper funnel in the other.

"Here," he said and gave her the funnel. "I'm sorry about yesterday. That was very stupid and uncalled for."

Jessie wondered if she were still dreaming. She folded back the paper; the funnel was full of flowers. Not dream flowers, but real ones, plain white daisies with dusty yellow centers.

So this was the real Henry Lewse in her shabby hallway. He looked as incongruous here as a rose in a bowl of brussels sprouts.

"Sorry," he said. "I tried calling. But I only got your machine."

"I turned my cell phone off."

"I see. Yes. Well." He cleared his throat and looked down at his shoes: baby blue Nikes.

Jessie realized she should probably ask him in. But she didn't want to let Henry Lewse enter her grubby privacy. So she just stood at the door in T-shirt and panties, talking to her boss. Or rather, her ex-boss. Or maybe not quite ex-boss.

"I thought we could go out for breakfast," he finally said. "And then we can talk and iron out our differences."

"Oh? Yes. We could," she muttered.

"Where shall we go?"

"Uh, there's the diner downstairs. Why don't you just go there? Get a cup of coffee and I'll meet you. All right?"

"Downstairs?" he asked dubiously.

"Yes. Go out the front door, turn right, and it's at the end of the block. I'll get dressed and join you in fifteen minutes."

"Fine then. See you in fifteen." He smiled at her, a bashful, guilty, irritated smile. Then he leaned into the apartment, grabbed the door, and pulled it shut. He had been embarrassed talking to his undressed assistant?

She remained by the closed door, staring at the cone of daisies in her hand, wondering again if she were awake or dreaming. She looked at the half window under the loft bed. It was still raining. She looked at the clock in the kitchen. It was after ten. Which was late for most people, but early for Henry. Nevertheless, he had come all the way downtown to apologize to her. Jessie was surprised, touched, and suspicious.

Not until she stood at her sink, splashing cold water on her face, did she remember her little hippo. What the hell was that about? When did her unconscious get so fucking whimsical? And what fine truth was he going to tell her?

·

43

The Vandam Diner was on the ground floor of an old printing factory, a stark space with a high ceiling full of heating ducts and a few Impressionist posters on the walls. Jessie had suggested the place only out of habit, but she liked the idea of Henry waiting for her in such an ugly, commonplace setting.

She saw him inside, seated in a booth under the fluorescent lights. He did not appear insulted. He looked up when she came through the door. And he broke into a smile. "Oh good. You came."

"You didn't think I would?"

Ali, the Pakistani manager, came over. "Good morning, Jessica." He set her usual cup of coffee on the table. "This is your friend?" He sounded concerned, as if afraid this older man were a lover.

"Henry Lewse," she said. "My boss. This is Ali Mohran. Who feeds me when I don't feel like cooking. Which is most of the time."

The two men nodded at each other but said nothing.

Jessie ordered her usual English muffin and Ali departed.

She watched Henry, waiting for him to speak, feeling he should make the first move. She was in a position of power here and wanted to enjoy it while it lasted. She blew on her coffee and sipped it.

Henry smiled the same mixed smile that he'd smiled upstairs, an uncertain combination of bashfulness, annoyance, and guilt.

"Jessie?" he finally said. "Why did we lose our tempers yesterday? What were we fighting about?"

"I have my theories," she said. "What do you think?"

He took a deep breath. "I think I made a very bad mistake." He leaned forward on his elbows. "Jessie. Please. Will you come back? I need you. And not just for my bills or business, but as a friend."

"A friend?"

"Yes. Someone with whom I can talk."

"But I'm only an *assistant*." She hissed the syllables at him.

He frowned. "I said far worse things. Which we don't need to repeat."

"No. We don't."

"I was a total anus yesterday. But I was in a terrible mood. I was feeling old and stupid and unloved. When you got all shirty with me, I forgot myself. I was unkind. Terribly unkind."

"I wasn't very civil myself," Jessie admitted. "*You* felt unloved?" She remembered Toby happily bopping around the apartment in his underpants.

"I know I take you for granted," said Henry. "I apologize. What else can I say? I'm an artist. And like all artists, I can be terribly self-absorbed. But now and then, I do remember you, Jessie. And I appreciate you. I do."

"Yes, well—" Jessie lowered her head. She knew she was being bullshitted, but she couldn't help smiling. After all, Henry wanted her back badly enough to go to the trouble of bullshitting her.

"Will you come back, Jessie? I can't promise you an entirely new man. But I will try, now and then, to show you the appreciation that I know you deserve."

She could not say no. But she did not want to give in so easily. "Let me think about it," she said. "We said some very bitter things to each other yesterday. And I can't pretend that I don't still feel hurt."

"Those things were said from feelings of the moment. My long-term feelings for you, Jessie, are feelings of respect and admiration."

"Yeah, right."

He drew his lips together in a pout, annoyed she was not yet in the palm of his hand. "But you will think about it?"

"I'm thinking about it now," she said coldly.

Ali brought Jessie her muffin. "Thank you," she told him, as sweetly as possible for the sake of contrast.

Henry folded his hands on the table. "I would offer you a raise, Jessie. But I know that this isn't about money."

"No, it's not," she admitted. "But money might help me think better." She was smiling again. Henry could be so cheap. He had only the vaguest notion of money, but he usually erred on the cheap side.

"All right. What do I pay you a week?" he asked. And before she could answer, he said, "I'll pay you a hundred dollars more."

My God, she thought. He really does want me.

"Will you come back? Does that change your mind?"

"I told you," she insisted. "I have to think about it."

He frowned. "Your muffin's getting cold," he said. "Eat. Eat." He waved his hand at it.

She tore open a squib of honey and dripped it over the pores.

Henry watched her. He began to smile again, a timid, half-embarrassed smile. As if he knew she was going to say yes.

Then he said, "What do you know about Tobias Vogler?"

"Tobias? Oh. Toby."

"Yes. Him." He spoke dryly, coolly.

He's played me so smoothly, thought Jessie. Here is what this visit is really about. Not me, but Toby. She almost burst out laughing. Henry was so transparent.

"I know little about him," she admitted. "Except that he saw Caleb for six months. And Caleb dumped him." She made a scornful snort. "After the other night, you know him far better than I do."

"One would assume," Henry muttered. "Only, not to put too fine a point on it, our knowing was rather imperfect."

"Oh?"

"We don't need to go into the details."

"Hey. God is in the details." She took another squib and squirted more honey on her muffin. "What? He wouldn't go to bed with you?"

"He went to bed with me. He just didn't want to do anything."

"Ah. He couldn't get it up?"

"No, it was up. We couldn't get it off. And believe me, I tried."

Did she really want to picture this? She asked the questions in order to embarrass Henry, but Henry was beyond embarrassment.

"So he must like you *some*," she said.

"Oh he likes me. But only for my fame, so called. My presumed stardom. If he only knew. But that doesn't bother me. I no longer expect to be loved for myself, you know."

She blinked. "Really?"

He shrugged, but then shifted around to sit sideways in the booth. "Do you know what the sickest thing about this situation is? What's most preposterous after Tuesday night?"

"You want to see him again."

"*Exactly.* And not just want. *Need.* I must see him again. Damn. I must be in love." He laughed at himself, a scornful crow of a laugh. "So much so that I've even agreed to go to this thing that he's in. Some sort of studenty performancy thing."

"Oh."

"Ah, the avante-garde piffle that one sees out of love."

"It's not so avant-garde," she assured him, even as she thought, Why does this hurt? Why isn't this funnier? "But Toby didn't stay with you last night?"

"No. Yesterday was a matinee day. I don't even know my own name on matinee days. But I woke up this morning alone. And I wanted to talk, Jessie. With you." He was facing her again, with moist blue eyes, like an apologetic Siberian husky. "Then I remembered what we'd said to each other and you weren't going to come in. And I felt very sad. Very stupid and very wrong. And here I am."

"And that's why you want me back?" she said. "So you can have somebody you can talk with about your broken heart?"

"Well, yes," said Henry, without a shred of shame.

"Am I supposed to feel flattered?"

"I'm only being truthful," he explained. "This boy is just one of several things that I want to talk about with you. And talk is just one of several things that I miss about your company."

It was hard to say which was weirder, Henry's blunt honesty or the fact that Jessie did feel flattered.

"But enough about Toby," said Henry. "Let's get back to us. When do you think you can tell me your decision?"

"I can tell you now," she said.

"Yes?" He lifted his chin at her.

"A hundred more a week?" she said.

"That's fair, isn't it?"

She closed her eyes. She deliberated over teasing or toying or bargaining for more money. But she found herself nodding instead.

"You *will* come back?" he said.

"Why not?" She opened her eyes and laughed. "I was never really gone, was I?"

"Excellent. When? You can take the rest of the day off. Or, if you like, you can ride back with me by cab."

"I'll ride back with you. Why not?" she repeated, with a resignation so dry it sounded bitter even to her ear. "Let me just finish my breakfast first."

"Whatever you want, Jessie. It's all yours. Anything your heart desires."

Henry was just as the critics said he was: a pure actor, as clear as water, as transparent as glass. Every thought or emotion read perfectly. He needed her only because he needed an ear. But that was something, wasn't it? It was good to be needed. It was better than being alone. It even felt good to be used. Being used brought you deep inside the machinery of the world.

44

The city was still dark and glossy with rain as they rode uptown in the taxi. A string of tiny ruby lights glowed over the long, straight avenue. Then, one by one, the rubies turned into emeralds.

"No big crises while I was away?" asked Jessie.

"Not at all," Henry told her. "But you were only gone a day."

"Feels longer."

"It does," he agreed. "I'm so glad to have you back."

And he was. He was feeling very moral right now, very proud of himself for being humble enough to go downtown and apologize to an assistant. You can be a charmer when necessary, he told himself.

All day yesterday and most of last night, he had felt it tug at his thoughts, the sense that he-they-someone had made a terrible mistake. He'd forget, then remember, then forget all over again. The joint at bedtime, for example, reminded him of Jessie—she had bought excellent grass—then softly erased her, and he decided to call Toby. But this morning he went into a mild panic as he understood that no one was coming in today. There would be nobody to take care of him. Worse, there would be nobody to talk to. So he needed to set things right. Everything would be fine. So long as you do not let pride stand in the way, there is nothing that cannot be revised or repaired or corrected. Except death.

They arrived at the building and rode up in the elevator. Jessie unlocked the door—she had kept her set of keys. Henry went to the kitchen to make himself a pot of tea. Jessie went back to her desk.

"*Henry!*" she called out. "There're fourteen messages here. Don't you ever check your machine?" Without waiting for an answer, she pressed a button and started it: a motet for computer and human voices.

Henry filled a kettle and thought, Yes, this is how life should be lived. An assistant handles the dull stuff and I devote myself to love and art and beauty. I wonder what Toby's doing right now?

"Henry? Come out here. You better listen to this."

He found Jessie sitting at her desk with a fist at her mouth. She was staring at the answering machine. It was already playing its next message. A familiar female voice with a Yorkshire burr pleaded with the silence.

"Henry? Jessie? Somebody? Please! Dolly Hayes again. I've been calling and calling. Nobody calls back. Adam Rabb has rung me up five times in the past two days."

"Adam who?" asked Henry.

"Rabb," said Jessie. "The producer you had lunch with Monday."

Dolly's voice turned cold as piss. "It's a sweet deal, Henry. If you do want to sell your ass for a high price, here's your chance. But if we don't get it, you'll have nobody to blame but yourself." *Beep.*

The computer voice added, "Wednesday. Five-fifteen, P.M."

Another message from Dolly followed.

"Very well, Henry. I tried. It's eleven here, so it must be six there. I just got off the phone with Rabb. I told him you hadn't called back. So he told me and I quote, he was tired of us jerking him off. There are other Grevilles in the sea."

"Oh shit," said Jessie.

"Oh shit," Henry agreed.

"I was tempted to lie and say you and I spoke and you're considering the offer. But I decided against it. In part because I don't like lying. But also to teach you a lesson, Henry. I trust *this* message will get a reply out of you. But I'm going to bed. Good night!"

"Greville?" said Henry. "Remind me again what a Greville is?"

"A novel. Big bestseller. The next *Silence of the Lambs.*"

"Oh shit," Henry repeated.

Other messages followed, all unrelated, none important. The voices twittered away while Henry lowered himself to the sofa and let the terrible news sink in.

And it was terrible news. So close yet so far away. You want to be a realist, you want to be a whore, and a man shows up with a big bag of money but you're off in the lav having a wank. Nevertheless, Henry experienced the strangest tickle. He had just lost something big. And he took a peculiar satisfaction in losing. Losing felt so solid and real, more interesting than winning.

"I look forward to seeing you next week," Rufus concluded— Rufus Brooks was calling from Hollywood, where Henry would *not* be going anytime soon. "Until then." *Beep.*

"Thursday, ten-twenty, A.M.," said the computer. It was the last message. The silence that followed was very deep.

"I'm sorry, Henry. I'm really sorry," said Jessie. "We blew it."

He nodded, then squinted at her. "We?"

She made a face; she couldn't look at him. "If I hadn't quit yesterday, maybe we would've heard from Dolly and you could—"

"Don't even consider it! Not your fault. No use crying over spilt milk." But she was right. It was her fault. Partly. If he changed his mind and became angry over losing this role, he could blame her, couldn't he?

"But Adam Rabb offered you the part at lunch?" she asked.

"Did he?" said Henry, trying to remember the lunch. French food, wasn't it? With very good wine. "We discussed a movie, but he never offered me a part. Not in so many words."

But before he could work it out, the phone let out a loud electronic chirp.

Jessie glanced down at the caller ID. "England," she said and grabbed the receiver. "Hello? Dolly."

Henry waved his open hands back and forth across his face.

"Yes. I just got your messages." She winced at Henry. "I took yesterday off. Doctor's appointment. No, you're right. I couldn't have chosen a worse time. I'm fine now. Oh yes. Right in front of me."

Henry angrily shook his head, then stood up, intending to flee.

"I'm sure he will. Here." She held out the phone.

"Henry!" a tiny voice buzzed in the earpiece. "Henry! Are you there? Talk to me, Henry!"

He glared at Jessie and took the phone. He turned his back to her. "Dolly, dear. Good morning," he said in his creamiest tones.

"Finally." Her voice was as sharp as a school bell. "Where the hell have you people been? Don't you ever check your messages? Bloody hell, Henry, you still live in the Stone Age!"

"We just got in, Dolly, and played your messages. Jessie was at the doctor's and we—"

"Stuff the doctor, Henry. I'm in no mood for your games."

He took on a somber demeanor. "So this *Greville* thing is dead? I'm sorry. There's no way we can get back to this producer?"

Dolly let out a long, exasperated sigh. He imagined it racing through the cable under the Atlantic, terrifying whole schools of fish. Or did phone signals travel by satellite nowadays?

"What's the saying?" said Dolly. "God looks out for fools, drunks, and Americans? You belong to only one of those categories. Even so."

"What do you mean?"

"Your bad manners are golden, Henry. Rabb assumes we have other porridges cooking. And he believes that once you win your Tony next month you'll be untouchable. So he has given us yet another chance. And another ultimatum. Will you play Greville? Yes or no? He needs to know by today. And to persuade you that he's in earnest, he has named a price. He is offering three million."

"Three million," repeated Henry. Such a large, improbable number. "Is that dollars or pounds?"

"Only dollars, darling. So the answer's no?"

"No, I'm just—" It took him a moment to recognize her sarcasm. "Three million dollars?" he repeated. "You're not joking?"

He noticed Jessie watching him, staring at him, with a look of wonder that made him understand this truly was remarkable news.

"So do I call him back?" said the voice in his ear. "What do I tell Mr. Rabb?"

His mind was as blank as a shovel. "What do you think?"

"What do you think I think? I think you should do it! I think you'd be a fool to say no to this kind of money."

"But you thought I was a fool to pursue this sort of thing in the first place," he told her.

"Only because I thought you'd be miserable, Henry. And maybe you will be. But in the course of learning that, you'll put three million dollars in the bank. You could do worse. And it's not a bad script. Don't you think?"

"Oh yes. Not bad. Considering." Was this a trick question? How low would she let him go? What kind of villain was he playing? A

Shakespeare-quoting werewolf? A geek with razor blade fingers? Or no, this was supposed to be a suave pervert à la James Mason.

"So are you in or are you out? Rabb needs an answer by one. It's already twelve-thirty."

"Today?"

"Yes, today. He's tired of being dicked with. His word. Maybe we could *dick* him a little more, but I prefer not to press our luck."

"I can't have a couple of hours to think it over?"

"Oh, Henry. You haven't read the script yet, have you?"

"Of course, I've read it! Don't treat me like a child!" He took a breath, he regained his temper. "*Silence of the Lambs* meets *Lolita*?" He looked at Jessie as he remembered that this was her phrase. "Very well then. Yes. Why not?"

"You agree?" she sounded surprised.

"Yes. This Greville sounds like my kind of guy." Without intending it, he fell into an American accent.

"Good. I'll call Rabb right back."

"Good," he told her.

"All I ask, Henry, is that you remain in the vicinity of your phone this afternoon. And talk to me. In case there's further negotiating. Will you promise me that much?"

"I'm not going anywhere until my show this evening."

"Good. So. Touch wood. Here goes nothing. Can you give me back to Jessica?"

"Certainly." He passed the phone to Jessie.

"Yes?" Jessie told the mouthpiece. "I see. Uh-huh." She frowned at Henry like a concerned mother. "Gotcha. I'll keep you posted. Exciting stuff. I won't drop the ball, Dolly. I promise. Bye."

She gently parked the phone in its slot. Then she slowly sat back up and stared at Henry.

"A movie!" she cried. "A movie!" She leaped from her chair. "And you got the lead!" She threw her arms around him. "Three million dollars, Henry! Three *fucking* million dollars!" And she began to jump up and down, expecting him to jump with her.

45

Henry had never guessed his assistant was so wiry and muscular, her grip so strong. He was touched she could be so happy for him.

She stopped jumping. She let go and stepped back. "Sorry. I got so excited and forgot myself." She tucked her offending hands into her armpits. "But— Wow. Right?"

"Exactly," he told her. "Wow."

She stepped away, looking embarrassed, confused. "Only money. We can't be silly about it. And it's your money, not mine. But hey. I'm happy for you."

"Thank you, Jessie. Thank you very much." He blinked and tried to laugh, but all he could produce was a mild chuckle. "It's so unexpected. It doesn't feel real. It's not like I did anything to get it."

"No, you didn't. So where's the script? I want to read it. Let's see what kind of monster you're going to be."

"Good idea," said Henry. "I should probably read it myself."

They hunted around and found it in the stack on the sideboard in the dining room. A swatch of pages without a cover, it was held together with brass fasteners.

"Here," said Jessie, and she undid the fasteners. "So we can both read it. I'm a fast reader. I'll start and pass the pages to you."

Henry sat on the sofa, Jessie in the armchair. She began to read. Ten seconds later, she handed a page to Henry. More pages followed.

Henry could not keep up with her. She set the pages at his feet.

Movies were a foreign country for Henry, a land he visited rarely and briefly, playing character parts that lasted only a scene or two. His one major role was in the BBC adaptation of *Daniel Deronda,* where he played a cold, sadistic Victorian husband. Good, clean fun. However, acting for the camera was much as Olivier or Richardson or somebody described it: you never perform, you only rehearse. And they film all your rehearsals and use the best. Henry had no practice reading screenplays. He read this one much as he read plays, skipping the stage directions and concentrating on the dialogue. But it was all stage directions and little dialogue. The title character, however, did get a juicy line or two.

"They go to Capri," said Jessie, setting another page on the floor.

"So you get to go to Italy when they film."

No, this did not feel real. It felt nothing like a plausible acting job. First because it was a movie, second because of the money. Three million dollars. Three *million* dollars? No wonder he felt light-headed. It was as if he'd just knocked back a very large martini.

"What a pretty fantasy," said Jessie. "A man loves a girl so much that he wants to kill her mother."

It settled in deeper: This is big money. You're going to be rich, Henry Lewse. The very idea of millions of dollars enlarged his mind. He felt giddy and new. But I'm still the same man, he told himself, the same fool but with money. What is the emotion of being rich? His months of playing Hackensacker should have given him practice.

"You're smiling," said Jessie. "Are you at the scene where he's in the closet full of the daughter's shoes?"

"No. I was just—" He shrugged and dove back behind the sheaf of pages.

His happiness was ridiculous. It was only money—hypothetical money. He hadn't even signed a contract yet. Nevertheless, he was feeling very good, with a lightness in the chest that he rarely felt except when he knew he was going to get laid soon.

The phone chirped again. Jessie jumped up and read the caller ID. "Nope, not England," she said and let the machine take care of it.

"This is David Blackwell at *Variety*. We understand that Mr. Lewse was offered the lead in the film adaptation of *Greville*. We'd like to run this in tomorrow's edition but need to confirm—"

Jessie snatched up the receiver. "This is Jessie Doyle, Mr. Lewse's personal assistant."

Henry was surprised by the imperious tone she took.

"Yes. He has been offered the part. Yes, he is interested. What? Yes, you can quote me. Doyle. *D-o-y-l-e.* Thank you." She hung up and looked over at Henry, blinking in surprise.

"Word travels fast," said Henry.

"I'll bet it's Rabb," said Jessie. "He must be publicizing this to lock you into the project."

She was very savvy. Henry was impressed.

He returned to the script. Knowing *Variety* cared, he paid closer attention. He came to a scene where Greville shares a hot tub with the mother and eighteen-year-old daughter and tries to flirt with both without giving the game away. The scene had possibilities, not least because Henry would get the chance to show off his body work.

The phone rang again. Again Jessie answered it.

"Ditchley? Cameron? Oh, 'Page Six.' Yes, of course." She flexed her eyebrows at Henry like semaphore signals, only Henry had no idea what her message was. "I'd be happy to confirm or disconfirm any rumors, Uh-huh. That is correct. Mr. Lewse has been offered the title role of Greville. Uh-uh. Susan Sarandon? Yes, of course. Mr. Lewse can't wait to work with her."

She pressed the button of the receiver but did not hang up. "Oh my God," she said. "Rabb must've had a press release all set to go. Did you know that you're cast opposite Susan Sarandon? This could be the start of a very busy—"

The phone chirped again; she hit the button.

"Hello. CNN? I see. His personal assistant. An interview? Really? I'll have to check with Mr. Lewse."

The phone continued to tweedle and chirp as more people called. Most only asked for confirmation, but others requested pieces of Henry. *Entertainment Tonight* wanted a press kit and maybe an interview next week. *Good Morning, America* wanted an interview tomorrow; something called *E!* wanted an interview tonight.

It was impossible to read a script with the telephone trilling away. Henry was tempted to go to the bedroom, shut the door, and let Jessie handle this—she handled the calls anyway—but it was too exciting. He didn't want to miss anything.

"My God," said Jessie after the twentieth call, giggling at the lunacy. "You're like a run on a bank. It's free-money day at First Henry Lewse. This Adam Rabb must be *very* connected."

He laughed with her. "It makes no sense. I'm famous for starring in a movie that hasn't even been made yet?"

"That's the best kind. An abstract movie. Pure potential." She shook her head. "Your little friend is going to kick himself for not going to bed with you."

"Who? Oh. Toby. You think?"

What a wonderful idea. Success would bring the boy around. *Greville* would win him Toby. Or maybe Henry wouldn't need the love of a pretty little nobody once he had fame and fortune.

"But he *did* go to bed with me," he reminded Jessie and himself. "Not to put too fine a point on it."

46

The bed was piled with naked parts: bottoms, breasts, a leg, a gut. Frank sat at the foot of the bed, staring at skin, thinking about flesh, the ugliness of it. Without love or lust, the human body was as appealing as a mound of raw pizza dough.

"Does it have to have been bad sex?" said Allegra. "Can't they have had good sex?"

Allegra and Dwight were sprawled on the bed, Dwight on his back, Allegra facedown across Dwight's middle. Her pouty butt was in the air, her T-shirt yoked around her neck. Their jeans and underwear were tangled around their ankles.

Chris, Melissa, and Toby stood by the wall, approximating an audience. Boaz was out in the living room, rigging up the stereo. He refused to watch Allegra do this scene.

Tonight was their last chance to get things right. Tomorrow was opening night, but they hadn't done a tech yet, much less a dress. They were still working out the undressed portion of the program. Nothing was going right.

"Frank?" said Allegra. "Frank? Hello out there? We're waiting."

"If we're like this for much longer," said Dwight, "Allegra's gonna turn me straight."

"Not before you turn me homo," said Allegra.

Dwight began to laugh, as if that were the most wonderful joke in the world. Frank didn't get it.

"No," Frank finally said. "You just look silly."

"Gee, thanks," said Allegra. She rolled off Dwight and wiggled her jeans and panties up. Dwight was even quicker about covering up, turning around so nobody would see his privates.

"Allegra has a point," said Chris. "Why does it have to be bad sex? Why do they have to look ridiculous?"

"Because it's a comedy," said Frank. "And they don't love each other."

"You can have great sex with someone you don't love," said Chris. "You don't even have to like them. Which *I* think is funny."

Dwight told Frank, "Just because *your* love life is in a dark place doesn't mean *we* should suffer." He thought he was only making a joke.

"Fine. What do you guys suggest? How do you want to represent great sex?"

"Let's go back to the original idea," said Allegra. "We're naked and we're under a sheet. And it's after sex and we're blissed out."

"And smoking cigarettes?" said Toby. "That is so tired."

She ignored him. "We're breathless, we're catching our breaths, we can't believe it was so great. And then we see who we're with, and we slowly become ourselves again."

"Since we're under the sheet," said Dwight, "can I keep my underwear on?"

Melissa groaned. "I hate plays and movies where people fuck like crazy, then get up and are still wearing underpants."

Frank thought about it. "Take everything off," he said. "Both of you. And scatter it around the bed. Then, as you do the scene, you're not sure whose clothes are whose. You pass things back and forth. Starting with your underwear. Now *that's* funny." And pathetic. He was determined to include some pathos here.

"I like that," said Allegra. She turned to Dwight. "We can have fun with that, don't you think?"

Frank led the others back down the hall where the audience would be. Nobody was very interested in seeing Allegra and Dwight naked again; they were only "acting" the role of an audience here.

"I wish I was doing Dwight's part," said Toby. "I could make naked funny."

"Toby," said Frank. "Just focus on your scenes, okay?"

Another day, another set of problems addressed and solved, maybe. Toby forgot half of what they'd worked out two days ago. Dwight was dropping lines. Chris and Allegra were resisting Frank just to be difficult. Tomorrow was opening night and nothing was working, but even if it did work, what would they have? Dog meat. Frank had spent four weeks of his life trying to turn a piece of unwatchable dog meat into watchable dog meat. He could not wait for this show to be over. He could be free again, but free to do what? Jessie was over. Jessie was dead. There was no chance of Jessie anymore. There was nothing but his stupid job and this stupid show.

"We're ready!" Allegra called out.

"All right," said Frank, and he led the others down the hall, grumbling, "Let's see what they have for us this time."

47

YOU: You must know everything.

ME: Is that a moral command or a sarcastic comment?

YOU: You think you have to be a polymath in order to succeed.

ME: I just want to know stuff. History, religion, physics, math.

YOU: But you know only the names. You want to talk about Fermat's equation, Riemann spheres, the Mandelbrot set, and the rest, but you can't even take the time to learn elementary calculus.

ME: I like the metaphors. Hedonic calculus. Moral arithmetic. Irrational numbers.

YOU: But they're just metaphors.

ME: And the clarity. The finalities. When you spend your life playing at questions that have no final answers, it's a relief to know that ten times three is thirty, or thirty squared is nine hundred.

YOU: There's something sick about a playwright wanting to do numbers instead of words. Anything to avoid actors, huh?

ME: Words are so sloppy. I want to be precise.

YOU: If you knew some real math, you'd understand there is no deep truth in numbers. It's a closed system, a tautology. You're like those literary critics of forty years ago who went gaga about quantum physics, thinking it proved everything was subjective, which it didn't. Your discussion of fractals in *Chaos Theory* was pure nonsense, you know.

ME: Not that anybody noticed. They were too busy hating my drama to catch the mistakes in my math.

YOU: You made a botch of my dementia too. I was your model for schizophrenia. All the absurd, irrational things said in my fevers?

ME: And witty things too. "The tune goes round the tangent, but it comes out the cosine of bliss." That was a direct quote.

YOU: You turned my dementia into lyrical schizophrenia: theater madness.

ME: Would you rather I told the truth?

YOU: No. The truth was awful. The truth was boring. Just a sick man in a hospital room. Sleeping, sleeping, sleeping. Then waking up and talking paranoid shit about his doctors or his family. Or getting well, but only for a month or two, and only well enough to hate his body for betraying him. Or hate his brain for abandoning him—

ME: Or hate his life partner for going on in life.

YOU: I never hated you.

ME: But you didn't love me. You withdrew from me. You shut yourself off. I remember sitting beside your bed in Intensive Care in the last days—

YOU: No hospital porn. Please.

ME: And you told me to go.

YOU: I didn't.

ME: You did. You whispered, "I don't want you here."

YOU: I didn't want you to see me die.

ME: You were embarrassed by your death. The way you used to be embarrassed about being seen on the toilet. You did not want me, who loved you most of all, to see you suffer that final humiliation.

YOU: I looked awful.

ME: I was used to it.

YOU: I wanted to protect you.

ME: You wanted to die alone. You were ashamed of dying. Or bitter over my being alive. Or something, I don't know what. But I was hurt that you could not share your death with me.

YOU: Why're you so angry? I'm the one who's dead.

ME: Only the dead have a right to be angry?

YOU: Yes.

ME: You have all the rights and I have none?

YOU: You could always join me here.

ME: Don't think that I haven't considered it. But there's nothing like the death of someone you love to spoil the cozy fantasy of death.

Caleb stared at what his pencil had just scratched on the page. Here was the crux of his sadness and pain, in the unfinished business of Ben's death. Ben could sleep with all the guys that he wanted, and Caleb could accept it. But then he wanted to die alone, and that hurt.

YOU: You sound like you're depressed.
ME: I am.
YOU: You should see a doctor.
ME: I am seeing a doctor.
YOU: What can I do to help?
ME: I don't know, Ben. I just don't know. I don't know anything about anything anymore. (Pause.) But thank you for the offer.

48

The audience for *Tom and Gerry* was in a peculiar mood that evening. They were *too* responsive. They laughed at everything. Henry enjoyed it at first, but it became confusing, annoying, like making love to someone who was ticklish.

"You're sure full of beans tonight," the Princess told him in the wings while they waited for the curtain call.

"Am I?" But then he remembered that he had cause to be full of something. Nobody knew his good news, of course, but he was reluctant to tell it, for fear that he would gloat.

They took their bows and quickly dispersed backstage. Henry opened his dressing room door and found Jessie sitting there, talking on her cell phone. She signaled hello at him with her index finger.

"Uh-huh. Uh-huh. At what time? Fine."

He squeezed past her and sat at his dressing table. He was not entirely sure that he wanted Jessie here. He'd like to be alone—for a few minutes anyway. He covered his face with cool, smelly cold cream and watched the highly competent woman in his mirror. She looked so tickled, as if she were laughing at him or herself or the world, he couldn't tell.

She finished and snapped her phone shut. "So how did it go? You must've felt distracted by your big news."

"I forgot. Believe it or not. But I always forget everything except the show." He wiped his mouth so he could speak without tasting cold cream. "You didn't have to come get me. You put in a full day today. I'd think you'd like some time to yourself."

"Not me. And it hasn't stopped. Not even while you were onstage.

I got a big surprise for tomorrow. Do you know who Rosie O'Donnell is?"

He thought he'd heard the name.

"She wants you on her show tomorrow morning."

"I thought I was doing that *ET* thing."

"*Entertainment Tonight* is at eight. Rosie tapes at ten. Somebody canceled. She jumped at the chance to get you. And we can fit her in. Oh I went ahead and hired a car and driver for tonight and tomorrow. And one last thing. Can you wait until you get home to take a shower? They're waiting outside."

"Who?"

"You'll see. Here. I brought you your tweed coat. It's nattier than your ratty old denim."

She went out into the hall while he changed his clothes. Henry wondered what was up but was too fried to think clearly about anything. He rejoined her and they started down the stairs. There was a curious brightness below, as if a car were parked outside with its headlights aimed at the door. They stepped into the glare.

Two white lights mounted on tripods steamed in the aerosol drizzle. Below were a handful of video cameras, a few journalists, and forty or fifty fans. "Oh fuck," said Henry.

"There's the car," said Jessie. "Parked by the curb. The driver's name is Sasha. I'll wait for you there." And she hurried off, abandoning him to the jackals.

"What's this?" cried Henry in mock surprise. "My autograph? If you insist." He scribbled his name on one program, then another and another. These weren't anachronistic autograph hounds but "normal" people, regular theatergoers. He hadn't seen so many since the first week after they opened.

"Mr. Lewse?" a male reporter called out. "Is it true you've been cast as the lead in the movie of *Greville*?"

"I don't know if I'm supposed to say anything. But I've been approached." He continued to sign his name, pretending not to notice the cameras, feigning indifference to the large woolly object thrust in his face like an angora phallus.

"Are you giving up theater for the movies, Mr. Lewse?"

"Do I have to choose? I'd like to have it all. Wouldn't you?" He was pleased by how smooth he sounded, neither flippant nor earnest.

"How do you feel playing one of the most hated villains in popular fiction?"

"Dee-lighted."

And he was delighted. He was giddy, he was high. Everyone was smiling at him. Three million dollars was nothing compared to this public adulation. The money wasn't quite real. This wasn't real either, but it was more familiar, immediate, and fun.

"Thank you. Thank you so much," he called out as he backed toward the car. It wasn't a gaudy stretch limo, but large, tasteful, and black. He jumped inside and gave one last wave to the crowd as the car pulled off. He found himself happily breathless, like a younger man who'd just had a very nice quickie.

"How strange," he claimed. "But I didn't do too badly, did I?"

"Not at all," said Jessie with a laugh. "You take to this like a duck to water."

49

They were all on television: Allegra, Dwight, Henry Lewse, and Bette Midler. They were in a sitcom about a family of shadows left behind in a suburban house when the real family moved to Maine. A silly premise for a sitcom, but not surprising for the WB network.

Toby sat at home, watching the show with his parents. He was hurt that his friends were stars and he wasn't. Then he remembered that he was supposed to be on the show tonight, a guest star.

"Good grief. I'm late." And he ran out the door without explaining to Mom and Dad.

The show was filming in New York, of course, and his parents were in Milwaukee. But Milwaukee was now in New Jersey. If the bus came soon, he could get to the show in time.

The bus arrived, the door opened, Toby jumped on. "The WB and make it snappy," he told the driver and flung himself into a seat.

"Toby?" It was Caleb, and he was sitting by the window. "What are you doing here? Where have you been? I miss you."

Toby was overjoyed to see Caleb again but knew he shouldn't show it. "I've been busy with my career. I'm going to be in a TV show."

"That's wonderful. I am so happy for you."

"Are you? Really?"

Caleb was so pleased that he took Toby in his arms and kissed him, right there on the bus, a warm, deep kiss. The kiss was so strong that their clothes evaporated. The whole bus applauded the two nude bodies locked in tender embrace.

And Toby woke up. Alone in his dinky room in the apartment on West 104th Street. There was no bus, no Caleb, only his own dick sticking out of blue flannel pajama bottoms decorated with penguins.

It was sad to wake up alone after such a beautiful dream. Plus he needed to pee.

He tucked his rod back in and got out of bed, which was a baggy futon on the floor. He padded down the hall toward the toilet. They were doing the play here tomorrow, in this very space. He wondered if Henry would come; he wished it were Caleb. What a stupid, corny dream to dream the night before a show.

His erection had gone down enough for him to pee. He aimed at the side of the bowl so he wouldn't wake anyone. He didn't flush for the same reason, but he remembered to lower the seat for the girls.

Out in the hall he heard a hissing in Allegra and Boaz's room. It sounded like Boaz was arguing. He heard Allegra sobbing.

He lightly knocked on the door. "Are you guys all right?" he whispered.

Silence followed.

Then Allegra said, "We're fine, Toby. Go to bed. You didn't hear anything. You're just dreaming us. Good night."

"Right," he whispered. "Sorry. Good night. See you tomorrow."

50

An alarm began to beep and Jessie woke up.

It was her old travel clock with its hectoring, pulsing chime. Six o'clock. She lay wrapped in a sheet on a sofa. The big window in the next room was full of white sky and orange skyline. She was at Henry's apartment. She instantly remembered why.

She jumped up, went to his bedroom door, and knocked.

"Henry! Show time."

"Thank you!" he called out. He must have been awake already, lying in bed and gazing at the ceiling.

She went to the kitchen in her T-shirt and panties to start the coffee. They had a very full day ahead of them, a crazy day, which was why Jessie spent the night. They needed to be at the *ET* studio at eight, then *Rosie* at nine-thirty. Then lunch with Adam Rabb at the Royalton at noon—the men would eat alone, but Jessie needed to get Henry there—followed by a photo session and interview with Cameron Ditchley for the *Post*. Then a nap, because Henry still had *Tom and Gerry* to do tonight. And then the show and after the show Caleb's party. Jessie had not forgotten her brother's birthday party.

The shower sizzled in the bathroom. The coffeemaker gurgled like a scuba diver. Jessie poured herself a cup. The bathroom door popped open and out came Henry in flannel trousers and a linen deconstructed jacket, or whatever it was called. "The bath is all yours," he said and helped himself to the coffee.

You would think they were an old married couple.

Jessie didn't bother with a shower—nobody was going to notice her today. She pulled on pantyhose and a corporate-butch blue suit, and brushed her hair. She waited until she was sitting on the toilet, when her hands were free, to call Sasha on her cell phone.

"You're downstairs already? Great, Sasha. You're a gift."

She clicked off; she flushed.

She loved this. She was pure action today, pure activity, the octopus stage manager. It was only a part, of course, a role, but the role consumed everything. There was no time to think, no room to doubt or dither, no space for messy emotion.

They went out to the elevator and Jessie pushed the button.

"I had the most peculiar dream last night," said Henry. "An examination dream. I'm much too old for school dreams. But I was sitting in a classroom with a lot of young boys. And up on the blackboard was a maths formula. It looked simple enough at first, an x-plus-y-divided-by-x-squared sort of thing. But the longer I looked, the more complicated it became. Like it was growing. Into a maze of numbers. Just to read it was like crawling through a labyrinth. I knew it was only a dream but feared I'd be trapped in the dream, not allowed to wake up until I solved that awful equation."

The elevator arrived and they stepped on board.

"Are you nervous about these TV shows?" said Jessie. "You shouldn't be. You'll do great today. I know it."

"I'm not worried." He laughed. "And I'm not disturbed by the dream. As you see, I *did* wake up. But I do find it curious. I usually forget my dreams."

The elevator doors opened.

"After you," said Henry, and he followed her through the lobby to the front door. "What a lovely day."

The sun was out again, the rain finally over. It was after seven and Midtown was quiet, almost bucolic. Sunlight glittered on the braids of rainwater running in the gutters. A red cage of girders stood against blue sky over the construction site up the street. A sweet song poured from a dinky brown bird perched on the elbow of a yellow backhoe parked at the curb.

"A very lovely day," Henry repeated, looking at Sasha.

The driver stood by the car, a tall, big-boned, thirty-something

Russian with close-cropped hair. He jumped forward and opened the door. "Good morning," he announced, grinning at them both.

Jessie had already checked out Sasha when they met last night. She couldn't guess what team he played on. Nobody would call him beautiful, but his bony face was handsomely homely.

"We go to *ET*? I know already." He repeated the address of the studio, which was only a few blocks away.

"You *are* a gift, Sasha," Jessie repeated. It didn't hurt to kiss up to the help.

She and Henry slid in, slipping over the soft black leather.

Her cell phone twittered. Jessie answered. "Hello?"

"Good morning. Just wanted to see if you were up and out."

"Dolly? Good morning. Oh yes. We're on our way." It must be about noon in England now. "Would you like to speak to Henry?"

"If he's coherent."

Henry was watching Jessie, not frowning but not smiling either. He took the little phone and turned it, uncertain how to hold it.

"Good morning, darling," he finally said, much too loudly. "And how are we? I see. What? Yes. That's what we think too. But if Rabb has us trapped, it's a good kind of trapped, don't you think? Like those bodice rippers where women get raped by men they love. Of course. It is all *your* doing. And my own dumb luck. But then my finding you has always been wonderful dumb luck for me. Goodbye." He lowered the phone and studied it. "How do we shut this off?"

Jessie took it from him and clicked the button.

"The dear cow is pleased with how things are going. As well she should be. Fifteen percent of three mill is—well, a goodly pot of cash."

"So you're going to keep her as your agent?"

He screwed his eyebrows together. "When did I say I was going to give up Dolly?"

"You were talking to that Rizzo woman. Remember? At ICM."

"Oh. Her." He frowned. "I was only exploring. Sniffing around. I can't leave Dolly. We're much too close. Like brother and sister."

"*Entertainment Tonight!*" declared Sasha and pulled to the curb. He got out to open the door, although Henry had already tugged the handle and was climbing out.

"I don't know how long we'll be," Jessie told Sasha. "But be back in an hour. If it looks like it'll be later or earlier, I'll call."

Sasha nodded. "Our boss," he whispered. "He is a famous actor?"

"Oh yes. More famous in England than here. But he's done *Hamlet* and *Antony and Cleopatra*. Lots of Shakespeare. And Chekhov," she added.

Sasha nodded, looking impressed.

Jessie caught up with Henry in the lobby. The security desk called upstairs and sent them up in an elevator.

The shiny copper doors reflected him and her: a star and his handler. We look like we belong together, thought Jessie. Then the doors parted open on a sorority girl who was all teeth and hair.

"Mr. Lewse! What a thrill!" She shook Henry's hand with both hands. "Thank you for coming in on such short notice. I'm Louise Parker Davis. Associate producer here at *ET*. I'll be interviewing you. And this is your—?"

"Personal assistant," said Jessie. "Jessica Doyle."

The handshake changed in midshake from warmly effusive to dead-fish. "They want you in Makeup, Mr. Lewse. You look terrif, but these lights? *You* can wait in the greenroom, Jessica. There's coffee and maybe doughnuts. Now, Mr. Lewse—" She led him off.

And Jessie was left alone in a curved corridor whose walls and carpet were hoofprinted in *ET* logos. She walked along, peering into open doors until she found the greenroom, which was gray. She entered and poured herself another cup of coffee. She even took a doughnut before she sat down. They were Dunkin' Donuts.

The idiocy of it all amused her. It did. Was there anything for her in this glittering piffle? No. The success was *his* success, so it was only vicarious for her, pure voyeurism. Henry could toss her away as easily as he'd been ready to toss Dolly. Jessie knew not to trust him any more than she could trust the weather. But it was fun. It was exciting. She should enjoy it like a beautiful spring day.

Her phone twittered again. "Hello."

"I'm trying to reach Mr. Henry Lewse."

"He's not available at the moment. This is his assistant, Jessica Doyle." She wished she had another title. "May I ask who's calling?"

"Kenneth Prager. *New York Times*. I'm doing a profile of Mr. Lewse. I need to talk as soon as possible."

"Kenneth Prager?" said Jessie. "The critic?"

"Yes. A brief article. For the Week in Review on Sunday."

Ow, thought Jessie. Kenneth Prager. The man who killed my brother's play. And I have the power of saying yes or no?

"Mr. Lewse has a very full schedule today."

"There's no time this afternoon? I'd be happy to come to him."

"Oh no. His afternoon is packed."

"If I could just talk to him on the phone then?"

"Oh no. Mr. Lewse hates to be interviewed over the phone."

"Then could I talk with him after his show tonight?"

The *Times* must really want Henry. "He has a party after the show. But maybe he could give you a half hour in his dressing room," she offered. "After all, you are the *Times*."

"Yeees," said Prager in a mildly aggrieved drawl.

"The show ends at ten-twenty. If you come to the stage door, they'll let you in. I'll tell the stage manager to expect you."

He hesitated, then said curtly, "Fine. I'll be there."

"But he has this party," she repeated in a pesky, chiding tone. "He can't wait for you."

"I said I'll be there."

Jessie was enjoying this. She knew she shouldn't press her luck, but she couldn't help adding, "You're not writing reviews anymore, Mr. Prager? Have you been demoted?"

"Not at all," he grumbled. "I'm filling in. We need something quickly and I'm a *big fan*." He hit the words hard, sounding quite bitter. "I will be there at ten-twenty. Good-bye."

Jessie clicked off. She began to laugh, tumbling the phone around in her hand as if she were tumbling Prager himself.

The man had no sense of humor. He should've covered his butt by making a joke when she made fun of him. But the man was so proud, so vulnerable, so *New York* fucking self-important *Times*.

51

Kenneth hung up the phone feeling confused. A secretary gave him the runaround, then insulted him. Why? He loved her boss. His review last month had praised the man as the one great thing in a good enough show that happened to be the best new thing in town. He was going to stroke the man even more in a puff piece on Sunday. But the man's secretary mocked Kenneth, and it hurt. He was already in a very delicate mood this morning.

There was a knock on his open door.

Ted Bickle stood there in his red suspenders and bushy white beard, leaning on the cane that he'd used since heart surgery.

"Hello, Ted. Come in. Have a seat. What can I do for you?"

"I'm fine, Ken. Just dropped by to say sorry. For reducing you to a cub reporter. Jimmy Olson, huh?" He laughed. "But Week in Review said they need something on Lewse for Sunday or we're going to look foolish. And you're the best choice."

"I don't mind," said Kenneth. "Be fun. It's time I cross the fourth wall and talk to actors again. I miss it."

"You do?" said Ted.

"Oh yeah. I love talking to actors. The gossip, stories, and jokes."

"Good then. Good," said Ted uncertainly. "I guess I made the right choice. So. Have fun." And he limped away on his cane, looking mildly disappointed.

Damn Bick, thought Kenneth. This assignment is just his way of putting me back in my place. Kenneth had been a theater reporter years ago, writing up the half page of items that ran every Friday. In those days, people were delighted when he called. He was attention, he was notice, he was Michael Anthony from *The Millionaire,* the old TV show, changing lives with a certified check. Now he was just the second-string critic, the man who got blamed for everyone else's failures and unhappiness.

The interview was only filler. They could've sent any intern or assistant to talk to Lewse. But Ted gave the assignment to Kenneth. Because he thought Kenneth was getting too big for his britches. And because Ted was going to retire soon. And he would die, and Kenneth would still be alive, and maybe even writing for the *Times*.

52

Piece of cake," Henry cheerfully reported in the elevator. "Easy as pie. But all you have to do in this country is purr at people in a posh accent, and you have them eating out of your ass."

Jessie laughed appreciatively and Henry was glad again to have her here. So long as he could say such things to Jessie, there was less chance that he'd forget himself and say them on American television.

They came out on the street again. Their bulky, boxy Russian was waiting at the curb. Henry assumed Jessie found the fellow as attractive as he did.

"Thank you, Sasha." He climbed into the backseat and scooted over to make room for Jessie. "Who's next? Rosie O'Grady?"

"O'Donnell," she said. "She's very important. And popular. Even my mother watches her. She's kind of smart, but a smart-ass too. She acts like a tomboy from Queens, but used to be an actress. She'll josh with you, and you can josh back. You don't have to play any games with her about who you're seeing and why you're not married."

"I never do."

"And before I forget: Kenneth Prager called. He needs to interview you. I told him he could have fifteen minutes tonight. After the show. He's the guy who gave you the rave in the *Times*."

Henry took in everything with a roll of easy, regal nods. He suddenly stopped. "But Toby's play is tonight."

"So?" She thought a moment. "And after that is my brother's birthday party. You're still going?" Now she looked worried.

"I'd like to," he said. "Do you think we can do everything?"

"I don't know."

"Do we cancel the *Times*?"

She laughed. "No, we can't cancel the *Times*. Not in this town. But Toby's play is tonight? You can't see it some other night?"

"I don't know. I could ask. Would it be possible for me to use—" He pointed at her waist.

"Oh. Sure. Yeah. What's his number?"

He patted various pockets until he remembered he carried no phone numbers.

"I know where he lives," said Jessie. "I have their number." She took a plump little book from her purse, found the number, and entered it. She handed Henry the phone.

He felt like he was holding a pocket calculator against his ear. "It's ringing," he told her.

"Hello." The voice was thick and half-awake.

"Toby?"

"Henry? Oh. Hi. Hey."

Henry was delighted to hear his live voice. Since Wednesday he had spoken only with Toby's answering machine. He could almost smell warm bedclothes in the boy's sleepy, husky tone.

"Good morning, Toby. Sorry to call so early. You'll never guess where I am. In a hired car on my way to the *Rosie O'Grady*—I mean, *O'Donnell Show*." He grinned at Jessie and turned away into a corner, making a private nest. "A pity you didn't visit last night. There were paparazzi everywhere. Well, a few. But they would've photographed us together. You'd be known as my mysterious companion."

"Why were there photographers?"

"Oh, that's right. You haven't heard. I've been cast in a movie. *Greville*. Do you know it?"

"From the novel? The bestseller?" Now he sounded awake.

Henry was encouraged. "I'm the villain. They're paying me buckets of money." He almost confessed how much, but that would be bragging.

"You're not rich already?"

Henry laughed. "Oh no. Not me. Not yet anyway."

He was beginning to sound like one of those black rock stars crowing about his bitches and gold chains. To impress Toby?

He cleared his throat. "But I was calling to let you know that there's a chance I might not be able to get to the show tonight."

Silence. Then Toby's words came out in a rush. "But you got to come! You said you would. They're expecting you. My friends won't believe me ever again if you don't come."

"I'll do my best. I just wanted to warn you—"

"You gotta be there, Henry. It's a special performance. Just for you. And after the show, remember, we're going to Caleb Doyle's birthday party together."

"You and I?"

"Yes. He told me to bring you. I told you. Remember?"

Henry looked over his shoulder at Jessie. "Of course you did."

"And after that," said Toby, "I thought, well, we could go back to your place."

"My place?"

"If that's all right."

"Maybe." There was a lightness in Henry's chest that went first to his cock, then to his face. "I'd like that. Very much." He was hoping this was where things would end, but thought he would have to cajole and push to achieve it. This was much better. This was more promising. "All right then. I'll be there."

"You promise?"

"I promise."

"You're on *Rosie O'Donnell* today? Good, I'll try to watch."

"I hope you do. I'd love to hear what you think. American television. I do hope I don't make a fool of myself."

"You won't."

"That's so nice of you to say. Well then. Until tonight?"

"See you tonight, Henry."

Henry made a kissing sound at the device. He pressed the off button. He turned to pass the phone back to Jessie.

The car was stopped at a light. Jessie was watching him with a cool, sardonic, disapproving smirk. Sasha in the front seat was also looking at him: Henry saw an amused pair of Russian eyes in the rearview mirror.

"No," Henry told Jessie. "I cannot get out of going to this show tonight. Sorry." He began to chuckle under their scrutiny. "So we'll just go from one thing to the other, and if we're a little late, no problem. It's theater. Where people are always late."

Jessie irritably stuffed her cell phone back into her purse.

"Do you know this show?" Henry asked her.

"Oh yeah. It was directed by an ex-boyfriend."

"Oh?" So that's why she was unhappy. "You don't have to come, you know. You can go on to your brother's party and I'll meet you there."

"No. I'll come. I should see it. I'm curious. And I want to make sure you get to Caleb's party."

"Good. Yes. Excellent," said Henry. And Toby would "just happen" to be with them, so both Jessie and Toby would think that Henry was taking him or her to the party. Everyone would be happy.

Henry was quite happy himself right now. It was all falling into place. Everything was going well. Maybe sex would click for Toby tonight in a way it hadn't on Tuesday.

Leaning back in the soft leather upholstery, he found himself looking up through the rear windscreen at the sky. A tall white skyscraper slowly swung through a tempera blueness full of plump clouds. Then another skyscraper floated past, and another.

"Will you look at that sky," said Henry. "All those pretty clouds. Pure Constable. What a beautiful day. What a delicious day."

53

What a vile, stupid, shitty day.

The sun was out. The rain was over. There was no hope now that Caleb could cancel his party.

The buzzer buzzed shortly after ten. Elena, his housecleaner, usually came on Mondays, but Caleb had asked her to come today to help set up for the party.

"Good morning, Cow-lib. We get ready now your shindig?"

Elena was Romanian, a fiftyish schoolteacher from Bucharest, part of the Eastern Europe emigration that had filled New York since the fall of communism. Caleb had looked forward to discussions of poetry and politics with her, but Elena was finished with "that stuff" and only wanted to talk about American television.

"Go outside, Cow-lib, out of my way," she ordered.

He obeyed. He hated this party more than ever. He was surrendering his home, his privacy, his peace, and for what? So a pack of fairweather friends could eat his food and drink his wine and say, "Poor, poor Caleb."

He heard the buzzer buzz again inside. Elena answered. A few minutes later a stocky, middle-aged man came out on the patio. "Jack Arcalli," he said. "The caterer? I spoke to your agent, Irene Jacobs?" A very gruff, bass-voiced fellow with short gray hair, a chin beard, and a single hoop earring, he looked like an older, sadder Don Giovanni. He shook Caleb's hand. "May I tell you just how much I admire your work?" he said in grumbly, mournful tones.

"Uh, thanks," said Caleb, surprised and confused. After all, this was the caterer who'd wanted full payment up front.

Another man, skinny and younger with black curly hair, stood in the French door.

"My partner, Michael," said Arcalli. Caleb couldn't tell if he meant business partner or boyfriend or both. The two men seemed so serious, so caring, they were more like undertakers than caterers.

"If you will show us your layout," said Arcalli, "we can start."

Caleb took them through the rooms while Arcalli looked for the best spots to set up a table for food and another for the bar. There would be no waiters circulating with trays. People could serve themselves, which was not only cheaper but the apartment wasn't big enough for extra waiter bodies. Arcalli decided he would do the food outside—"I think the rain is over, don't you?"—and set up the drinks table indoors in front of the television.

Banished now from his patio, Caleb withdrew to his office. He sat at his desk, but not for long. His office would be open during the party, and he should make sure nothing revealing was left out. He inspected his shelves. He cleared his desk. He pulled open drawers. In the top right drawer was a badly printed booklet from the 1940s: a Kewpie-doll lady in garter belt and stockings ties up another Kewpie-doll lady with clothesline and spanks her. Claire Wade, his star, had given it to him on the opening night of *Venus in Furs.* Would Claire come tonight? Or would she abandon him too?

Only the bottom drawer had a lock, but Caleb had lost the key. He opened it and saw his spiral notebook on top. He took it out and flipped through it: his experiment, his exercise, his mental health doodle. Thirteen pages of pencil scrawl. Auden said that a man loves the sight of his handwriting as he loves the smell of his own farts, but Caleb hated those too. The pages looked like a play, but weren't. "Conversations with a Dead Boyfriend." That'd sure pack them in.

Caleb considered ripping the pages out, but couldn't. Not yet. Should he bring them to Dr. Chin? Or tell her about them? He tucked the notebook back in the drawer, set the spanking booklet on top, and covered it all with *Webster's Dictionary.* The sight of a dictionary would cause most people to close the drawer with a yawn.

The phone rang. Caleb answered.

It was Irene. "Good morning, doll. Just checking in. Jack there yet? Isn't he a trip? He used to be a journalist, then an actor, and is now a cook. Jack-of-all-trades, I call him. But he's good, believe me. I'm just calling to make sure you didn't cancel and send him home."

"Don't think I haven't thought about it."

"I know you have. But you should relax, dear. This is your birthday party. You'll have a good time."

"It's my party and I'll cry if I want to."

"There you go. Keep your sense of humor."

"You don't want to come over? I'm feeling a bit fragile right now. A little wired. It's like stage fright."

"What are you afraid of? It's a party. These are your friends."

"I don't know what I'm afraid of. It's just—I haven't seen anyone in days, you know."

"Then go take a walk. Have lunch with some friends. Or your sister. Or someone. Just to take the edge off."

"Are you free for lunch?"

"No. Sorry. But I'll be there this afternoon. Threeish. Can you hold out until then?"

"Sure." He took a deep breath. "You know, I didn't know how nutty I was feeling until we started talking."

"So don't talk about it. See you later. Bye."

Caleb hung up and sat there, taking deeper breaths, fighting his sudden surge of anxiety, wondering what was the matter. This really was like stage fright, wasn't it?

Out in the living room the TV came on. Elena often turned on the television for company while she worked. Caleb heard the others stop moving, as if all were pausing to watch.

54

"Henry Lewse. Wow. I can't believe I have you on my show."

"It's good to be here, Rosie."

"This man is a class act, folks. Henry is known as the Hamlet of his generation."

"Alas."

"That's not good?"

"Oh, I suppose it's better than being known as the Coriolanus of my generation."

When the audience only politely chuckled, Rosie laughed for them. "That's *minor* Shakespeare," she explained. "For those of you who, like me, think Shakespeare is just another one of Gwyneth Paltrow's boyfriends. Did you see *Shakespeare in Love?*"

"Oh yes. And enjoyed it thoroughly."

"So what brings you to our side of the herring pond? You're not doing Shakespeare here. You're in a very American musical."

"But it's all acting, Rosie. Whether you do the Bard or Broadway or soap commercials. Besides, I've done Romeo. I've done Hamlet. There's nobody else for me to play until I'm old enough to do Lear."

"Which is quite a few years yet, isn't it?"

"You're too kind."

"And that's your next big goal? To play King Lear?"

"Or Prospero. In *The Tempest*. We Shakespearean blokes are divided between those who hope one day to play a bitter old fool, and those who'd rather play a wise old man."

55

He smiled. He twinkled. He scratched his ear. He was so down-to-earth, not at all what she'd expected. He didn't even wear a tie.

Molly Doyle sat at home in Beacon watching *Rosie O'Donnell* as she did every weekday morning. It was a treat she allowed herself after indoor chores: to sit in front of the tube with a cup of instant gourmet coffee. She couldn't believe her ears when Rosie announced that her guest today would be Henry Lewse. Her daughter's boss. Who was going to her son's party. Small world, thought Molly. Small, small world.

"And you're a big villain, I hear?" said Rosie. "They've cast you as the evil Mr. Greville. In the movie of the bestselling book."

The audience ahhhed.

Henry chuckled—Molly couldn't help but think of him as "Henry" now. "Oh yes. I'll be the man you love to hate."

"But nobody can hate you, Henry."

"We'll see about that," he purred sinisterly.

"Ooooh," went Rosie, making her big-eyed chipmunk face as she waved her palms in the air. Then she announced a station break.

No, Henry Lewse was not the snotty, stuffy Englishman that Molly had pictured. He chatted about Shakespeare as if he were everybody's favorite writer. Rosie clearly liked him. But Rosie was smart herself, a little like Jessie. One of the things Molly loved about Rosie O'Donnell was how much she reminded her of her daughter, although Rosie was chubbier than Jessie, and happier.

The commercials ended, Rosie returned, but Henry was gone. Molly was sorry she wasn't going to Caleb's party tonight or she could meet Henry and tell him in person how good he'd looked on television.

"And that's all for today, folks," Rosie declared. "I want to thank my guests again. Oh, I almost forgot: you can see Henry in *Tom and Gerry* at the Booth Theatre. We'll be back Monday when our guests will be Mira Sorvino and her fabulous dad. Have a great weekend."

Molly turned off the TV and went into the kitchen to fix herself some lunch before she worked in her garden. Things should be dry enough outdoors after so many days of rain.

Small world, she told herself again as she opened a can of soup. She knew people who knew famous people. Her own children, in fact.

So why didn't she go to Caleb's birthday party? He invited her.

No, he didn't really want her there. He was just being polite.

But he and his sister had dared her to come. They said she was frightened of the city. Which was ridiculous. She wasn't scared of the city. She grew up in Queens. How could she be scared of New York?

She should go. It would knock her kiddos off their high horse. The train ride was only an hour and a half. She could zip down for a visit, see her son's new apartment, meet her daughter's famous boss, prove her love, and be back home by nine—or ten at the latest.

Do it, she told herself. But don't call them. Surprise them. That way, if she changed her mind, they wouldn't think she chickened out.

Molly finished eating and went upstairs to look for a nice dress, nothing too fancy, but not too casual either. This was another reason why she never got into the city. She didn't know what to wear anymore. Fashions changed so quickly.

But she refused to give up so easily. Here was a nice wool skirt that would go well with any blouse. And here was a blousy shirt that didn't look too dressy. And earrings. Good simple earrings would make her look nice without turning her into a dowdy old lady.

Piece by piece, she put herself together. She tried not to notice the flutters in her stomach, the coldness of her hands. It was a warm spring day, but her hands were freezing. She sat at her dressing table and brushed her hair. Good thing she'd been to the hairdresser this week or she'd use her gray hairs as an excuse. You are such a ninny, she told herself. What are you afraid of anyway?

Finally, she was ready. She went downstairs. And the flutters in her stomach became painful, like ice butterflies. She grabbed the car keys in the dish on the table, telling her body that this was no different from going to the supermarket. Her body should behave, dammit. It wasn't her head that was silly, it was her body. She clutched her black leather purse and thought a moment. She went back upstairs to her bedroom. She took what she wanted from the nightstand beside the bed. She felt foolish, yet calmer, safer, as if she were putting a lucky rabbit's foot in her purse, nothing more.

She drove straight to the station. She walked from the parking lot to the ticket window and out to the platform without pause or hesitation.

The day was lovely. Newburgh looked so green and pretty across the river. It was three o'clock already. She couldn't understand where the time had gone. The next southbound train arrived. She stepped aboard. It was only a train; it wasn't like flying.

She stopped being afraid, but the only thing she'd been afraid of, she decided, was being afraid, was going into a panic. Now she was fine.

The other passengers seemed safe. There was even a white lady Molly's age at the other end of the car, reading a book in hardcover. Molly wished she'd brought something to read. A murder mystery was even better than cigarettes for keeping one occupied. The river flickered and flashed in the windows. Mountains rose on the other side. The Hudson Valley really was beautiful, wasn't it?

Molly must have ridden this train a thousand times, but when was her last trip? A year ago? Ten years? All she could remember today were the Saturday trips when she took the kids into the city to shop for clothes. Her son was forty now, so that would have been *twenty-five* years ago? Surely she had been to the city since. But the trips with her kiddos were her favorite visits, her best memories. Rockefeller Center at Christmas, Fifth Avenue in the spring. They sometimes visited St. Patrick's Cathedral, but Molly had had too much religion in her childhood—know-it-all priests, fish on Friday, *Lives of the Saints*—and she wanted to spare her own children. She took them to the theater instead. They saw shows like *Hello Dolly!*, *No, No, Nanette*, *Follies*, and even *Grease*. Jessie might have been too young, but she was just as tickled by the singing and dancing as her mother and brother. They were all so happy together. Their father stayed home. Bobby hated New

York. The city had been his job for too long, and he knew only its dark side, the crime scenes and courtrooms. He said it was no longer the wonderful Oz across the river that they both knew as teenagers.

Molly grew up in Queens, in Sunnyside, a petty Irish village of snoops and snobs and too many aunts. She had dreamed of moving someday into the larger, freer world of Manhattan. Instead she married Bobby Doyle and escaped to the good life of the suburbs, first on Long Island, then north to Beacon. Only rich people could afford to live well in the city. But she could still visit, she could take her kiddos there.

Then one day she stopped. She couldn't remember why. Because it was too much trouble? Because her kids were old enough to go alone and didn't want her along? Or because of the stories on TV or in the newspaper or told by Bobby's cop buddies? Everything went to hell in the 1970s. New York was not safe for old ladies.

Which was ridiculous. She wasn't afraid of New York. She loved New York. She missed it. She just had no reason to visit it until today.

The train was passing through the Bronx. The projects began to appear, ugly brick boxes packed full of people. Nobody, black or white, deserved to live like that. Then older buildings, five and six stories tall, crowded around the train. There were the dead eyes of empty windows. A huge Technicolor face painted on a crumbling wall swung toward her. She expected to hear police sirens from the half-deserted streets below but heard nothing except the chuckle of wheels under her feet.

They plunged into a tunnel. Her heart was racing. Don't, she told herself. This is your hometown, this is where your children live. You have nothing to fear.

The lights flickered. Everything went dark. Then they came out into a dingy electric brightness. People quietly gathered their things. The train ground to a stop.

Molly slipped the strap of her purse snugly over her shoulder. She followed everyone out of the car and up the ramp.

And she entered the city of her childhood. Back in the days when everyone wore a hat, Grand Central was its gateway. The ceiling was still painted with an aquamarine sky full of constellations. Molly marched through the enormous room, feeling more confident, like she was young again and her whole life was ahead of her. Then she noticed the people talking to themselves.

They weren't the crazy black men of twenty years ago. They were white people, corporate men and women talking on those tiny new phones. The things looked like transistor radios or sometimes just a wire. And people talked at them. They talked, talked, talked, talked, talked. What could they possibly be talking about? Did they really have so much to say to each other?

Molly snorted at their foolery. And before she knew what she was doing, she stuck a finger in her own ear and said out loud: "Hello? I just got off the train. I'm in Grand Central Station. You wouldn't believe how crowded it is here. Why, it's a regular Grand Central Station."

Nobody noticed the crazy lady talking to her hand.

"What the heck were you afraid of?" she told her palm. "This city is a riot. This city is a hoot. And you, Molly Doyle, are a nut."

She dropped her hand and laughed. She stepped more briskly. She couldn't wait to see the faces of her smart-aleck son and daughter when their scaredy-cat mother showed up at their big-deal party.

56

Y ou love your wife and daughter, don't you?" said Dr. Chin.

Kenneth hesitated. "Well, yes."

"I didn't mean to suggest you don't," Chin gently added. "I'm just trying to establish what are the things you truly care about."

It was five o'clock on a Friday and Kenneth was back at West Tenth Street, sitting on the sofa, a pair of cold hands in his lap.

"I do love my family," he said. "I'm not always the best husband or father. But I try."

"You do things for them? You do things with them?"

"Absolutely. Yes, well, I'm not the chief breadwinner anymore. Gretchen's law work brings in a bit more than I make. And Rosalind is at an age where she no longer wants to do half the things we used to do together: go to movies or shoot hoops at the gym or even play chess. Her friends told her girls don't play chess." Yet he was never as good a father as he wanted to be. "But I'm hardly one of those art or theater types who has no other life. How does the Yeats poem go? 'Players and painted stage took all my love / And not those things that they were emblems of'? That's not me. No. I love the real things."

"William *Butler* Yeats?" said Chin. As if there might be another.

"Yes. From 'The Circus Animals' Desertion.' A major poem. It's the one with the line about 'the foul rag-and-bone shop of the heart.'"

Chin looked disturbed, puzzled, amused. Then she went back to her notes. "You and your wife have been married—fifteen years?"

"Yes. I love her, I trust her, I listen to her." He hoped Chin wouldn't ask about their sex life. "I mean, it was Gretchen who convinced me to continue seeing you when I wanted to stop."

Chin looked up. "You wanted to terminate our sessions?"

"Uh, yes." He hadn't intended to tell Chin that.

She appeared concerned.

"Because you said some things last week that made me feel you weren't the right therapist for me."

"Which were?"

He moistened his lips. "You said you hate theater. That you have a phobia about it."

"I can't believe I said 'phobia.' That's a clinical word, Kenneth. Not one I use lightly."

"You said you were embarrassed about seeing actors onstage."

"Oh that." She shrugged, as if it were perfectly natural.

"I'm sorry, Dr. Chin. But it struck me as a confession of weakness. It undermined your authority."

She lifted her eyebrows. "You see me as an authority figure?"

The question threw him. "You're my therapist," he said. "You must have *some* authority."

"You believe in authority figures, Kenneth."

"When it's earned. When it's deserved."

"You see yourself as an authority figure?"

"Not really," he claimed. What were they doing *here*?

"But you're an important critic."

"Only because I write for the *Times.* As I said last week. I'm nobody as an individual."

"That's like me saying that I'm nobody except for my certification as a psychiatrist."

He wondered what kind of certification she actually had.

"I'm an employee," he insisted. "Only an employee. Nothing more. Tonight, for example, I have to interview an actor. It'll be after dinner when I'd rather be at home with my wife and daughter. And I'm not a reporter, I'm a reviewer. But they give the commands and I obey. Like a good dog."

"And you resent that?"

"Not at all. I'm glad of it. Because it keeps me humble. It reminds me who I really am. It keeps me real."

Chin sat back, her mouth knotted in a skeptical rosebud. Had he said something particularly absurd?

"So?" she said. "Do you want us to continue? Or shall I recommend a new therapist?"

He was startled. "Because I feel your authority is compromised?"

She shrugged. "You'll feel that way about any therapist. Because you have authority issues. But if you want to try someone else, I don't mind."

Was she rejecting him? She wanted to get rid of him? Why?

"It's not about you," he insisted. "It's me. It's my problem." He laughed to signal he was making a joke. "I want you to be perfect."

"I'm not," she said.

She said it so flatly that he didn't know what to say for a moment. Then: "Maybe I should continue? For a little longer? We barely know each other, do we?"

She took her legal pad back into her lap and wrote something. "Good. I was hoping you'd stay. It *could* be a very interesting experience for us both."

She spoke as if keeping him were a challenge, a complication that she'd rather not have. Was he really so difficult?

"Let me toss out a few ideas regarding you and authority," she proposed. "You want to have power, but not be hated. You want to be king, but treated like an equal. You want to be loved but not loved too much."

Kenneth regretted that he hadn't taken the chance to escape.

"Have you ever considered quitting your job at the *Times*?"

The question took him completely by surprise. "What? And give up show business?" he said.

He waited for her to recognize the antique punch line of the ancient joke and laugh, but she gave it only a pained smile.

"You haven't mentioned your parents yet," she said. "Is your mother still alive?"

57

The sun burned low in the hazy sky over the billboards on the other side of Sheridan Square. It was only six-thirty. The party was not scheduled to start until seven, nobody would arrive before eight, but everything was ready. Jack and Michael had come and gone and come again. The undertaker/caterers were very proficient. A drinks table was set up in front of the television. On the terrace outside, under a square canvas umbrella, stood a trestle table covered in a pastel rainbow: green melon slices, orange cheeses, pink ham, and good brown bread. Plates of raw vegetables and bowls of dip were scattered around the rooms. The little kitchen was stuffed to the ceiling with backup food.

"And there we are," Jack declared when he finished showing it all to Caleb. "Except for the music. Is there anything in particular you wanted? For an outdoor party like this, I suggest a mix of Cole Porter and Gershwin."

"No music," said Caleb. "It just makes people loud. It makes them *think* they're having fun."

"You don't want that?" said Jack.

"No. If they want fun, let it be real fun. None of this fake fun."

And he laughed. He was not in the right mood to host a birthday party, was he?

The telephone rang: Irene. She was downstairs in a cab with the cake from Cupcake Cafe and needed help in bringing it up. Michael went down. He returned a few minutes later with Irene and a white box as big as a computer monitor. Inside was a cake covered like a gaudy Victorian dress in butter cream flowers.

"Makes my teeth hurt just to look at it," said Caleb.

"It's beautiful," said Irene. "Hmm. No room for candles."

"Thank God for that."

Michael carried the cake to the kitchen.

Irene circled the room, then stepped out to the patio. "Wow, Jack. You've outdone yourself. This looks great." She threw an arm around Jack's shoulders. "Didn't I tell you he was amazing?"

Jack hung his head in mock humility, then went back indoors.

"So beautiful up here," said Irene. "Aren't you glad you decided to go ahead with this party?" She looked at Caleb. "Is that what you're wearing?"

White dress shirt, blue jeans, moccasins, no socks.

"Awfully California," she said. "It needs a tan to work."

The buzzer softly buzzed.

"It's not even seven," Irene clucked at her watch. "There's always one. The person who didn't get the time right or who comes early to monopolize the host."

They went inside. Michael had already buzzed the guest up.

"So everything's set?" Irene continued. "You got your food, you got your drinks. All you need are your guests. Oh, and music. Hey, Jack! Put on some music."

"No music," Caleb repeated. "I don't want any music."

There was a knock at the door, which was already propped open. A small, middle-aged woman stood there, timidly peering in. She had wavy beige hair, no makeup, and a big purse. She looked like a retired schoolteacher. Then she said, "Hello, dear."

"Mom?"

She was smiling, but it was a confusing, contradictory, I-told-you-so/what-the-hell-am-I-doing-here smile.

Caleb was doubly startled: first that she came, second that he did not immediately recognize her.

"Mom!" he cried. "Oh my God." He threw his arms around her before he remembered that they weren't a huggy family. She felt remarkably small and light against him, like a bird. He promptly released her. "Wow. You came. Welcome. Wow."

"Oh yes. Your old mother came," she said, glancing around, not quite able to face him. She produced a snippet of laugh like a hiccup.

She looked as small as she had felt, which was stranger than it should have been. But Caleb had not seen her outside the home in years, not since he'd been a child. His mind's-eye mom was a larger, more timeless figure than this flesh-and-bone woman at his door.

"Mom. This is Irene Jacobs. My agent and manager and one of my best friends."

"Mrs. Doyle. So glad you could make it." Irene cut her eyes at Caleb in a satirical look of pity. She didn't understand that he was overjoyed to have his mother here.

Mom indifferently shook Irene's hand and looked around the room again. "Where's your sister?"

"She's coming," said Caleb. "She said she had to work late."

"I thought she'd be helping you with your party."

"Oh no. I've hired people for that."

She pulled a face like she'd never heard of such a thing. "What time do you think Jess'll get here?"

"Uh, later."

"Not too late, I hope. I need to catch the train back to Beacon."

But Jessie was bringing Henry, which meant she wouldn't come until after his show, which could be very late.

"I could give her a call and let her know you're here."

"No, no, no. I want to surprise her." She shrugged. "If she doesn't show, she doesn't show. But if she hears I came to see you but didn't wait for her—" She frowned. "Well, you know how your sister can be."

Yes, he knew. And Jessie was right. The mother-daughter bond was heavier and more tangled than the mother-son bond, even when the son was gay. I have it easy, thought Caleb. But he couldn't help feeling a little excluded, a little hurt.

He should call Jessie soon, on the sly, so she could visit the party before she picked up Henry and they could send Mom home.

"So this is your new apartment," said Mom. A wary, querulous tone took hold in her voice.

"Oh yes!" Caleb cheerfully declared. "Let me give you a tour before people start arriving."

"Your real home."

He said nothing for a moment, then, "As real as any home can get in New York."

He showed her the rooms: the kitchen—"Awfully small"—the bedroom—"Not much privacy with that window"—the bathroom—

"That old brass is hell to keep clean." Then he took her into the extra room that was his study. She said nothing for a moment while she stood in front of the wall where a dozen framed photos were hung.

"Where did you get this picture?"

"I can't remember," said Caleb. "You don't like it?"

She was frowning. "Not a good picture of me," she said. "Not at all. But very nice of your father."

"I think it's nice of you both."

They stood side by side at the beach, Cape May, New Jersey, 1959. Black-and-white, all teeth and tans, they looked so healthy and happy. It was a half-truth, like most family photos, or maybe only a quarter-truth. But a pretty truth, nevertheless.

A few inches over was another beach picture, this one in color: Fire Island, 1987. Two young men in baggies stood arm in arm, grinning. Another half-truth, although on some days Caleb thought this picture was a three-quarter truth.

"And that was Ben," she said.

"Yes," said Caleb. "Was."

He waited for her to say something else, that she missed Ben, or ask if Caleb missed him. Nothing special, just something more.

But she was already looking at the next photo, a color snapshot of a solemn seven-year-old boy sitting on a lawn with a baby in his lap, giving her a bottle. He held the bottle with surprising delicacy, too absorbed in his wide-eyed little sister to notice the camera.

"Oh yes," said Mom. "You used to adore your sister."

"I still love Jessie," he claimed.

She shook her head and sighed. "You would've made a wonderful father." She turned away, looked down at his desk and up at the window. "Nice room. It should be easy writing plays here."

"It should be," he said. He led her back out to the living room.

"Is there another floor?"

"Nope. This is it. And the terrace outside."

"This is the place you *bought*?" She sounded critical again.

"That's right."

They went up the two steps to the French doors.

"Ohhhh!"

Caleb thought she was appreciating the view, but no, she was looking at the table of food.

"I won't ask how much *that* cost."

She kept disappointing him, this mother he loved. She sounded trivial and shallow. But she was distracted today, her attention off.

He led her around the corner of the L-shaped terrace. The low skyline to the west was a jumble of billboards, old water tanks, and TV antennas. Pieces of sun were already flaring in a few windows of the flinty apartment building overhead.

"Noisy here. How do you sleep at night?"

"You stop hearing it."

She looked down. She stood a good three feet back from the parapet. "People," she said. "So many people."

He wanted to connect with her, but he didn't know how. She had come to him today and he was touched, moved, but he didn't know what to say to her.

"There you are!" a raspy male voice called out.

Caleb turned and saw a man come toward them: Daniel Broca.

"Happy birthday," he said in a harsh grumble that made it sound like a curse.

He was a short, proud, unhappy man in his fifties. He had failed as a playwright but succeeded as a college teacher. His students adored him, but Broca was prouder of his failure.

"Daniel. This is my mother. Mom. My friend Daniel Broca."

He brusquely nodded at her. "I see I'm the first one here." He thrust a gift-wrapped package at Caleb. "Take it. I know you told us not to bring presents but I brought one anyway."

"Oh, uh, thank you. I'll open it later?"

"Hmmm." Broca's mouth tightened, as if this were an insult but one he would try to overlook. "Nice penthouse."

"You haven't been here?"

"No. You never invited me to one of your parties."

"I've never given a party."

"Still. Nice place. You should enjoy it while it lasts. After that awful review in the *Times*."

"It *was* an awful review," his mother agreed.

"But just like the *Times*," Broca lectured her. "They make you a success, then turn around and ruin you."

"I'm not ruined," said Caleb.

In certain moods, Caleb actually enjoyed Broca's company. His general bleakness made Caleb feel sunny and good-humored. But not tonight, and not with his mother.

"They're just jealous," she said. "All those nobody critics."

"But the *Times* is the worst," Broca argued. "Because they're the most corrupt. And the most stupid. Kenneth Prager, the man who slammed *Chaos Theory,* is the worst of the worst."

Caleb needed to get his mother away from Broca, but he also needed to call Jess. If he could get Jessie here soon, then Mom could go home and he could stop worrying about her.

"Irene?" he called. "Could you come out here?" Irene knew how to jolly Broca. Caleb could turn the pair over to her.

"So where are all your other friends?" asked Mom. "What time does your party start?"

"Right now," said Broca. "Maybe they're not coming. Maybe they feel bad about not liking your play. Let me say again: I loved it. I think it's the best thing you ever wrote."

"I know, Daniel. Thanks." He turned to his mother. "People will come," he assured her. "It's early yet. Some don't like to go out in daylight. And others are in plays. It *is* a work night."

"Oh yeah," Broca agreed. "People will come. If not for your son, then for the free food and liquor."

Caleb smiled and turned around again. "Irene!"

58

Despite the canvas shades, the apartment was not entirely dark at eight o'clock. The amber twilight filled the living room with an audience of soft brown ghosts. The first performance of *2B* began.

Dwight blanked on the first line and Frank had to feed it to him. Boaz screwed up a song cue, so "Losing My Religion" played too soon and too loud. Melissa fell over a chair. Boaz missed another cue, and a mopey Moby song played too long, blasting the room while Chris and Melissa shouted their dialogue. None of the funny stuff seemed all that funny, and the biggest laugh came when Allegra jumped up on Dwight and he went down flat on his butt. Luckily he wasn't hurt. The march back to the bedroom created a traffic jam in the hall. Dwight and Allegra, naked for the first time with strangers, pulled on their clothes much too quickly and efficiently, killing the comedy. Only Toby's scenes passed without mishap.

It was like a classic dress rehearsal where everything goes wrong. Except this was a performance and the catastrophe had witnesses. The audience was all friends and fellow acting students, but Frank wanted their approval, not their pity. Watching it fail, and fail so publicly, he suffered more than he thought was possible. The show was only an hour long, but it felt like an eternity.

Finally it ended. There was applause, but it sounded like desperate charity. Most of the audience cleared out as quickly as possible. Only a few friends lingered to offer condolences, including Mrs. Anderson from P.S. 41.

He was embarrassed to see her here tonight, a wry old black lady with iron gray hair, thirty years older than anyone else in the room. But he was touched too. They had shared a lot on *Show Boat*.

"Sorry you had to see that," he told her.

"Oh no. I've seen worse. And not always from kids." A city public school teacher, Harriet Anderson was adept at finding silver linings. "I like how you use this apartment. The blond boy was nice to look at."

Frank laughed. "You want a date?"

She smiled and shook her head. "Seriously. He's got something. But the rest of it wasn't so bad. It'll get better."

"It can't get worse."

"Oh no, it could get worse," she assured him. "Much worse."

She left with the last of the witnesses. Only the criminals remained at the scene of the crime. There is nothing sadder than a stage after a bad performance, but this was also an apartment, a home. All joy had been sucked from these rooms. Frank gathered everyone for a post-mortem that wasn't entirely post. A second performance was scheduled at eleven.

"I'm not going to beat a dead horse," he began. "We all know this did not go well. There's little we can do before the next show except eat and rest. So let's think of this as an extra dress. We made lots of mistakes, but we know what our mistakes were and we'll learn from them. Okay? I have just a couple of notes, but you'll already know what they are."

His chief "suggestions" were that Allegra and Dwight get dressed more clumsily, and that Boaz lower the volume so the songs would not compete with the actors.

"Yeah, our show is about actors," said Allegra. "Not about your great taste in music."

Boaz remained by the stereo, on the stool where he had sat during the performance. "My music? My music?" He bared his teeth and gums at her. "This show stinks, so you blame *my* music?"

"Your music's great!" Frank said quickly. "But you created a very complicated set of cues for yourself. We need things simple. K-I-S-S," he said. "Keep it simple—" He left out the last *s* word.

"So it is my fault tonight is dud?" Anger flattened his English and sharpened his accent. "After all the things *you* did to *my* play."

"Your play?" said Allegra. "It's *our* play. All of us."

"No. I wrote it. And it was great. Before you and everyone else started fucking over my words. People hate this script. They would love mine."

"Your script," said Allegra, "was TV dog shit."

"Guys!" said Frank. "We're not going there. Nobody's blaming anybody. Okay?"

"Dog shit? Dog shit? I'll show you dog shit." Boaz got up and walked toward Allegra. *"You."* He pointed. "You and your cheating heart. Your dog shit lies. Your dog shit love."

"Bo-eeee?" Allegra leaned back in alarm. She shot a worried look around the room.

The others watched Boaz fearfully, all except Dwight, who watched Chris. Frank wondered what they knew that he didn't.

"You never loved me," Boaz sneered. "You used me. For sex and rent money and my script and my music. I am just a writer to you. Just a man. And you are a man-hating lesbo."

Allegra let out a gasp like a silent cough. She covered her eyes with one hand, then lowered the hand to her mouth.

"Fuck you with a spoon," said Boaz. "*Two* spoons. Anything but my meat. Because you're not going to use my meat again!" He stormed over to the door, threw it open, and charged out. His boots banged down the stairs.

Allegra dropped her hand from her mouth. "Wow," she said dryly. "Wow, wow, wow."

"Is anybody going to tell me what this is about?" said Frank.

"You don't want to know," Chris said sadly.

And Frank got it. "Oh shit."

"It's not like it sounds," said Chris. "It's not nothing, but it's not like it sounds."

"Hey. Thanks for the public declaration of love," said Allegra.

Chris faced her. "I told you. I'm sorry. But I don't feel about you the way you feel about me."

"You still don't trust me?"

"No! Because I still think you're straight."

"Didn't that prove anything?" Allegra pointed at the door.

"Yeah. It proves straight girls are trouble."

"Guys?" said Frank. "Guys? Can we finish this later? We still got another performance." But this was more interesting than their crummy little play. Frank wished they could drop the play and reenact the fight for the next show.

"Yes!" said Toby. "Henry Lewse is coming! Remember!" He was eager and enthusiastic, as if he hadn't noticed any disasters.

"Right, right, right," said Allegra. "I'm cool. First things first."

Henry Lewse was more important to her than either Boaz or Chris.

"I suppose Boaz won't be coming back," said Frank.

"I hope not," said Dwight.

"Okay then," Frank continued. "I'll do the music. Let me look over the CDs. Why don't the rest of you go get something to eat?"

He wanted to be alone; he needed to be alone. He sat on the stool by the stereo while the others drifted out.

Things could not get worse, he told himself. He wanted to believe in a Zen of failure, that once you hit bottom, things can only get better. But Harriet Anderson was right: anything can get worse.

"Frank? Frank? Do you like the stuff I added? Does it work?"

Toby, of course. He squatted down beside Frank like a farm boy, looking up at Frank, hopefully, needily.

"Works fine, Toby. If the rest of the show worked half as fine, we'd be in great shape." He continued to shuffle through the clatter of CD cases. Boaz had actually picked out some good songs. He just had too many of them.

Toby was nodding and thinking and nodding some more. "I just hope Henry likes it."

"If he doesn't," said Frank with a shrug, "I'm sure he'll understand. I bet he's done his share of turkeys."

"Henry Lewse? Oh no, not Henry." Toby thought a moment longer. "You think the show is a turkey?"

59

Applause erupted out front, solid and loud. Backstage in the dressing rooms, it sounded like a hailstorm. The phenomenon never ceased to amaze Jessie: it was weird like people but as natural as weather.

"I wonder if they like it?" she asked the *New York Times*.

"Hmp," went the *Times*.

They were in Henry's dressing room, Jessie and Kenneth Prager, the man himself. He sat there, gripping his little notebook, saying little. Jessie had seen him on TV and even in public—last week, in fact, at P.S. 41—but never this close. He was taller than she remembered, more physical, but also paler, drier. One might say he looked more like an accountant than a drama critic, but Jessie had a good friend who was an accountant, and *he* was smart and funny.

"Do you always wear a suit?" she asked.

"Of course not. I just didn't have a chance to change."

The simplest question seemed to make Prager squirm. She enjoyed needling him.

"So it's not mandatory? You could wear a Hawaiian shirt?"

"Excuse me, Miss—"

"Doyle. But you can call me Jessie."

"Miss Doyle." Her last name meant nothing to him. "You don't need to entertain me. I can wait for Mr. Lewse alone."

"No trouble. And I want to introduce you two."

It was hard to believe that this long, lean drone in gray was the maker and breaker of reputations, the Buzzard of Off-Broadway. Well, he did look kind of buzzardy.

They heard the actors coming, a growing noise, as if water were pouring backstage. Prager slowly stood up.

Henry swung into the doorway—and stopped.

"Kenneth Prager. *New York Times.*" He held out his hand. And a light snapped on in his eyes. It was a look of love: straight-guy love, a fan's love. Jessie remembered the same spark in her father's eyes whenever he spoke of a favorite baseball player or hero cop.

"If you say so," said Henry in his dry Hackensacker manner. He shook the hand as his own eyes blinked and darted around. He often came offstage looking like a man on amphetamines. "Jessie? Time?"

"Oh? Right. Ten-forty." The show had run a few minutes late.

He signaled her out. "You too, my friend," he told Prager. "We don't want this interview *too* intimate, do we? Family newspaper and all. Be with you shortly."

Prager joined Jessie in the hall, looking mildly hurt.

"Sorry," said Jessie. "We have another show to see tonight. And I should warn you: he can be real wired after performing. He's had a full day already. Talk shows and radio and stuff."

"I've had a full day myself," said Prager, pretending nothing was wrong. "I'd like to go home."

Princess Centimillia walked past, glancing at Prager. He gently turned away, as if afraid of being recognized.

The door snapped open and out charged Henry, already fully dressed in work shirt, jeans, and fancy linen jacket. He had not taken a shower but had sprinkled himself with cologne.

"Come along," he said. "You're the *Times* man? Sorry. We're late. I have another show to see. A friend's show. But you can interview me on the drive over, can't you? It won't be too out of your way."

They charged out the stage door into the alley. A thick pack of fans stepped forward.

"No!" Henry shouted. "Not tonight! Come back tomorrow. I'll give you everything you want tomorrow."

And amazingly enough, the fans backed away.

"I'm late, I'm late," cried Henry with a laugh, and he sprinted away. He'd make a wonderful White Rabbit, thought Jessie.

The limo was parked by the curb. Sasha stood by the open door, welcoming them home. They piled into the back: Jessie on the left,

Henry in the middle, Prager on the right. Jessie noticed *Hamlet* in paperback up front. Sasha must have bought it during the show.

"West 104th Street," said Henry. "And step on it, my good man. What time is it?"

"Quarter to eleven," said Jessie. "But they're not going to start without you."

"You think?"

Prager was playing with a black tape recorder the size of a cigarette pack. He aimed the pack at Henry.

"Mr. Lewse? Shall we?"

"Oh no. Call me Henry. Please. I'm turning more American every day. No more English formality."

"But he isn't America," said Jessie. "He's the *Times.* Where they mister and missus their own children."

"*Henry,*" said Prager, firmly and defiantly. "You're one of the most admired actors of our time. You've done everything from Shakespeare to Beckett. Now you're trying your hand at musical comedy. And there's talk of you playing a suave movie villain—"

"Buzz, buzz, buzz," said Henry. "We like to keep busy."

"So," Prager continued. "Do you see yourself as a highbrow visiting low culture out of financial necessity? Or do you actually enjoy trying as many different things as possible?"

A smart version of a tired question, thought Jessie, with a setup for a good answer. Prager might not be a total hack after all.

"Oh I want to try everything," said Henry. "High, low, middle. I'm a promiscuous slut. A happy hooker of the theater arts."

Prager looked uneasy. It wasn't quite a *Times* quote.

Henry sounded awfully giddy tonight, goofy. Jessie wondered if he'd snatched a few tokes in his dressing room.

"You don't see yourself primarily as a man of the theater?"

"Oh no. I see myself as— Excuse me. Jessie?" He turned to her. "You've seen this play? Does Toby speak or is it more a walk-on?"

"Oh no," Jessie assured him. "He has a sizable part."

"Good." He turned back to Prager. "Sorry. You were saying?"

Of course, thought Jessie. Henry was goofy over Toby. After a day of fame, Rosie O'Donnell, and big bucks, he was gaga over a large blond bunny. Which was sweet. Kind of.

The car hurtled up Broadway. Prager tried more questions. "Many of your peers from the Royal Shakespeare have gone on to careers that take them far from serious theater."

"Oh. Like dear old Alan Rickman?" Henry said indifferently. "But he did better work in *Die Hard* than anything else he's done."

"Do you see any common ground between playing a suave lover of little girls in *Greville*, and anyone you've played in Shakespeare?"

"Hmmm. Hamlet."

"Interesting. How is he like Hamlet?"

"Damned if I know. Except they're all like Hamlet, aren't they?"

The car turned a corner into a narrow side street. They came to a stop by an old building with a canvas awning.

"This is it?" said Henry. "Where's the theater?"

"There is no theater," said Jessie. "It's in an apartment."

"How creative. Let me out, please."

Jessie opened her door and got out.

"But we're not finished yet!" cried Prager.

"After the show," said Henry. "Come up and watch it with us. We'll finish afterward. I promise." He raced across the sidewalk to the front door without waiting to see if Prager followed.

Jessie bent down to speak to Prager through the door. "Hey. He's an artist. They're not like normal people."

Prager turned off his tape recorder and shoved it in an inside coat pocket. The *Times* was not like normal people either.

"I apologize. Really." And she was sorry. Not that she felt great sympathy for the Buzzard. She just didn't want to turn the *Times* against Henry. "He needed to see this play," she explained. "Well, not the play, but someone in it. If you know what I mean."

"I wish I'd known sooner," he grumbled. "Before I went out tonight on this wild-goose chase."

"Sorry," said Jessie. "You sure you don't want to come up and see the play? It's short. Only a half hour." Or something like that. She couldn't remember how long it was.

Prager remained in his corner of the backseat, stewing and thinking. "A half hour?"

"Or thereabouts." What would Frank think if she showed up with the *Times*? Would he forgive her or hate her more?

Prager shook his head. "I'll wait out here."

"You won't come up?"

"No. I'll wait in the car. I'm sorely tempted to catch a cab downtown and go straight home. But I won't, only because I don't have anything I can use yet."

"Oh good. Oh thanks. I really appreciate it," said Jessie. "Downtown? We're going downtown after this. We can drop you off."

"That won't be necessary."

"Just so you know. But see you in a few minutes? Sasha will take good care of you." She closed the door and tapped on Sasha's window. It whirred down. "Don't let him get away," she whispered.

60

A posterboard sign was taped to the plate glass of the door:

2B. Or whatever.
A New Play about Learning to Live with Your Craziness
by Boaz Grossman and the West End Players.
Suggested contribution: ten dollars.

Henry read the sign again, trying to figure out how to get in. Jessie
arrived behind him and pushed the door open.

"Oh? It was unlocked?"

He followed her up the stairs. He was very excited, very anxious,
which was silly. This was only a play, an amateur production featuring
an attractive boy whom he hadn't seen in two days. But it was fun to be
silly again.

They came to the second floor and an apartment with an open
door. A very pretty Spanish-looking girl glanced up. Her eyes nearly
popped out of her face.

"Henry Lewse! Oh my God. Good, good, good. You came. We
have a special seat for you. Hey, Jess."

"Hey, Allegra."

Jessie sounded mildly annoyed about something. Was it him?
Which of the many things that Henry had done wrong tonight irritated her?

Allegra led him to a big wooden chair with a calico cushion. None
of the other chairs had cushions.

"Oh, you'll want your ten dollars," said Henry. "All I have is a
twenty. Oh, but I'll get Jessie too. Yes. Here. Please. Take it. I insist."

Henry gave the pretty girl the money and sat down, fearing he'd have to chat with her. She was so overwhelmed, however, that she said only "Hope you like it" and fled.

He looked at the room: high ceiling, cracked plaster, old theater posters; it looked like an old drama student squat, very convincing. He read over his program. "Now I get it," he told Jessie. "To be or whatever. The apartment number is 2B? Very Tom Stoppard." But where was To Be Toby or Not to Be Toby? That was the question.

More people arrived, more seats were taken. There were two dozen chairs in three rows, like at an old-fashioned wake. There was no coffin, although Henry sensed people looking his way, as if *he* were the corpse.

"That's Frank," muttered Jessie, nodding at a slightly dumpy fellow fiddling with a stereo in back. "If he seems standoffish later, it's not about you, it's about me. We had a big fight."

"Oh? Oh. Of course." The fellow was not bad-looking, Henry decided, merely heterosexual with a receding hairline.

A song came on: "Love Thy Neighbor" sung by Bing Crosby. Lights were clicked off all over the apartment. The play was starting.

Henry folded his arms together. "What fun," he said.

A floor lamp came on directly in front of them. A large, stately black woman sat watching a silent television. There was the sound of keys in the front door—the apartment's real front door. The door opened. And there was Toby.

"Hey. Hi. What're you watching? Good show? I hope your day went better than mine. You wouldn't believe what I saw on the subway coming home."

He wore a loose necktie and carried a sports coat. He shifted his weight from one foot to the other. He did all the talking. This was one of those peculiar American acting exercises where an actor performs a dialogue with silence.

Henry had not seen Toby since Wednesday morning. He had hoped, or feared, his mind would say: Him? You've been pining away for Him? He's nobody special. But here he was again, and he was beautiful. He was sexy; he was warm, far warmer dressed than naked. He seemed doubly dressed playing a fictional role, so his warmth and sweetness were magnified.

Henry felt he could look at Toby for hours. He had forgotten about the privilege of just looking, the joy of voyeurism. Like most actors, he preferred exhibitionism, but looking was nice too.

The black woman turned off the floor lamp and the scene ended. Kitchen lights fluttered on—the kitchen was to the right—and here was the black woman again, chatting with a dinky white girl. Was that all this would be? A string of acting exercises? Henry didn't mind too much, so long as Toby returned.

The kitchen lights went off. Over to the left, a blue paper lantern came on. The curly-haired Spanish beauty, Allegra, sat on the sofa and talked with a large, androgynous teddy bear of a man.

There was a knock at the door.

The teddy bear looked nicely startled. Henry was impressed until Allegra said, "Now who could that be?" with a quoting inflection that suggested this was not in the script.

She got up and went to the door. She opened it.

Out in the hallway stood a tall, gaunt, male silhouette.

"Is that Boaz?" said a voice behind Henry.

It was light in the hall but dark in the living room. The figure could see Allegra but not the audience. The audience held its breath.

"Excuse me," he said. "Has the play started yet?"

"Oh yes," Allegra told him. "It started five minutes ago."

The man was Prager, the *Times* man. He looked in, squinting, still not seeing anything. "Where is the play?"

A few people began to titter.

"Here," said Allegra. "You're in it."

And the audience burst out laughing, Henry laughing as loud as the others. It must be the oldest theater joke in the world, the metaphysical joke of artifice tripping over reality, or however one described it. Henry never tired of it.

"Terribly sorry," said Prager, jumping back. "I'll go."

"No, no, no," said Allegra. "Just get in here." She waved him inside and he automatically obeyed. She closed the door.

He wildly looked around, needing a seat. Then he saw the sofa under the lantern. He raced over and sat beside the teddy bear actor.

The audience roared all over again.

"Pssst, pssst," went Jessie, standing up and patting her chair.

The teddy bear pointed her out to Prager. Prager jumped up, scuttled over, and seized her chair. Jessie sat on the floor.

"You were complaining about money," said Allegra, instantly picking up what they'd set down. "Better money worries than love worries. Love worries suck." They had put aside their make-believe for a minute, but it wasn't broken, it was intact, like an old hat.

Prager sat petrified beside Henry, audibly embarrassed, loudly catching his breath.

"I'm so glad you decided to join us," Henry whispered.

"I thought there was a theater up here," Prager hissed back. "I thought I could just come in and use the phone. I am so humiliated."

"All in good fun," Henry assured him. "We're all good friends."

"Sssssh," went someone behind them.

Henry made his voice lower. "And nobody knows who you are."

Allegra and the teddy bear continued to commiserate. They stood up. And she pounced. She jumped up on him, wrapped her legs around his waist, and buried her mouth in his. They bounced against the wall. They lurched across the floor and hit another wall. They bounced again and disappeared around the corner into a hallway.

The music came back on—"Love Thy Neighbor" again.

Jessie's friend, the director, Frank, came out and stood in front of everyone. Was the show already over? No, he held a finger to his lips and signaled the audience to follow him. People got up, one by one, and started down the hall.

"Very cool," Jessie told Henry. "Come on," she told Prager. "Don't you want to see what's back there?"

The audience trooped through, pausing to peek into a bathroom on the way, which made them chuckle. They crowded into a bedroom at the end. Henry hung back, not wanting to get caught in the crush, wondering what happened to Toby. He passed the bathroom.

A large, cream-colored figure stood at the sink: Toby, wearing nothing but red plaid boxer shorts. He looked at himself in the mirror with the saddest eyes imaginable.

Henry was the tail of the line. The people ahead were fixated on the bedroom, even Prager, who was craning his head over the pack. Henry slipped into the bathroom. "Hello," he said.

Toby did not look at him. "Please," he muttered behind his teeth. "Don't break my fourth wall."

This was even better than the Gaiety. Henry could just stand here, two feet away, and look and love without fear. Here were the nipples like plump freckles, the bare shoulders pebbled with goose bumps, the chewy upturned nose.

"You're very good," he said. "Quite good."

Two sets of thick blond eyelashes swept the air when Toby blinked. "You're enjoying the show then?"

"Oh yes. It's nice to watch you and your friends be yourselves."

There was laughter from the bedroom.

"You better go," Toby pleaded. "I got to get dressed so I can do my next scene."

"Of course. See you later. We'll see each other after, won't we?"

"Of course. We're going to that party."

"Oh good." Henry leaned over and lightly kissed his shoulder.

The boy didn't even flinch.

61

I t's working, thought Frank. It's finally working. Or more accurately,
it's not fucking up.

He stood in the back corner of the bedroom and watched as Allegra and Dwight picked up pieces of underwear, tried them on,
exchanged them, and tried again. This time it hit. It was like porno
Carol Burnett. The audience roared.

They finished the scene and Frank turned off the light. He
squeezed through the crowd, signaling everyone to follow him again.
The bathroom door was closed, but he could hear Toby in there pulling
his clothes back on. Allegra had been right: a little more skin didn't
hurt, especially Toby's skin. It hadn't spoiled the surprise of the post-
coital bodies. Frank returned to his post at the stereo and changed the
song. The music worked so much better when limited to three songs:
Bing Crosby, R.E.M., and Mozart.

K-I-S-S, he told himself. Keep it simple, stupid. He tried not to
think about Jessie out there; he refused to notice Henry Lewse. While
the audience stumbled back to their seats, he turned up the volume of
R.E.M. singing about being in the spotlight. He cut them off. The
actors resumed. And things still did not fuck up.

There *was* a Zen of failure. So much had gone wrong tonight until
everyone surrendered, let go, relaxed. They were so relaxed that the
latecomer, whoever he was, turned out to be a gift, a new joke that
Allegra could play like a pro. And Henry Lewse actually perked things
up, his presence tweaking the actors to sharper life. Frank had been
afraid they would overdo it, that Toby in particular would be thrown by
the presence of his boyfriend/one-night stand/star-fuckee, whatever the
Brit biggy was to him. But Toby was stronger than ever.

His final monologue began. It built naturally, then started to fly carefully out of control, like a runaway wagon rolling downhill toward the cliff.

"I am so on top of things. You wouldn't believe how much they want me for the new Sondheim. And Salomon Brothers too. I'm too multitalented for my own good. What would you do in my shoes? Business or theater? It's a hard choice. I walk into a room and people know. I'm not nothing. I'm someone important. Someone of value. And you know why they know that? Because I'm a positive person."

The audience laughed, but the laughter stuck in some throats. You could hear cringing little groans around the room as people recognized their own lies. Then when Chris stood up and Toby threw his arms around her in a panic, there were actual gasps.

This wasn't the last scene, but the audience now trusted the play enough to give it the benefit of the doubt. They entered the home stretch. Melissa and Chris threw dishes on the floor. People could see only a three-foot-wide slice of chaos through the kitchen door, but it was enough. Then the women broke up laughing over the idiocy of their fight. They began to clean up and Frank put on the Mozart, the slow movement of Piano Concerto no. 21, the *Elvira Madigan* theme. Dwight, Allegra, and Toby reappeared with mop, broom, and dustpan, and all pitched in. While the lyrical sunlit music softly puttered along, the friends cheerfully worked together to tidy up the mess of their lives. Or however people wanted to read it.

Even before the audience responded, Frank knew: it landed, it clicked. The applause was not much louder than the applause of the first show, yet it sounded different, more solid. The cast already knew. They grinned at the audience but smiled knowingly at one another, treating the applause as mere reinforcement for what they already understood.

They pointed at Frank and began to applaud him. He stood up, smiled, and bowed, accepting their praise as his due. Then he turned around, turned off Mozart, and it was over.

Allegra was instantly at his side. "We did it, Frank! We beat that sucker!"

"It didn't go too badly, did it?"

"Asshole," she said with a laugh. "We were fabulous. Wasn't I great with the jerk who came late? I thought I would choke, but I didn't. What did you think, Jessie?"

She stood behind Frank. She was smiling, blinking, thinking—he could almost hear her mind ticking—waiting for him to see her.

"It was good, Frank. Really. I don't know how you guys did it. But you made a silk purse out of a sow's ear. Well, not a sow's ear exactly, but you made something out of nothing."

"Exactly!" said Allegra. "Can you imagine what we could do with a *good* script?"

Frank looked at Jessie looking at him: wary, guilty, uncertain, amused. It was like looking into a mirror, and he wasn't absolutely sure which feelings were his and which were hers.

"Wait," said Allegra. "There's Henry Lewse talking to Toby. I got to ask him if he can give us a quote. Later." She raced off.

"So," Frank told Jessie. "So," he repeated. "I'm glad you liked it."

"I didn't just like it. I loved it. It's what I've always said, Frank. You got a gift for working up a big picture. You're great with actors."

"I don't do too bad for a loser, do I?"

She looked away, drawing a quick hit of air through her nose.

He regretted bringing up the other night, but she seemed so blithe, so bent on forgetting their ugly words. He was already feeling totally visceral standing next to her, as if they were still naked on the loft bed. The smell of her hair went straight to his stomach.

"We need to talk about those things we said," she admitted. "But later. Not tonight."

"Fine by me." Now that he'd mentioned them, he didn't want to talk about them at all.

"You want to come with us to Caleb's party?"

He jiggled his head as if he hadn't heard right. "Why?"

"I don't know. Be fun. Free food and drink. We can tell people about your show. You can keep me company."

"What? Henry isn't keeping you company?"

She gave him a heavy, humorous, fuck-you sigh. "Oh, Henry has a full platter tonight."

Frank wanted to say: Fuck you. He wanted to tell her: No more second fiddle for me. But there was a sad spaniel look in her eyes and his refusal came out softer. "I'd like to," he said. "But I promised the cast that we'd all go out together."

"So let's take them with us. They can come too. They deserve it. They were great. We can't all fit in our car. But they can take the subway. Hey, Allegra! Dwight!" She called them over, and before Frank could stop her, Jessie was inviting them downtown and giving them Caleb's address.

"Good, good, good," said Allegra. "We'll close up here and come right down. You coming too, Frank?"

"Yeah, but he's riding with us," said Jessie. She ran off to fetch Henry Lewse.

He had no choice now. He could not refuse without making a public stink. And the truth of the matter was he *wanted* to go. He was feeling good about the world and himself right now. He could hold his own at Caleb Doyle's party. And he did not want to let Jessie go roaring out of his life as abruptly as she'd roared back into it.

He saw her talking to Henry Lewse and the latecomer, the gaunt man in a gray suit. The man was trying to convince them of something. Henry Lewse, the big dog himself, didn't look so big or intimidating at eye level.

Toby joined them. Jessie and Henry Lewse gave their full attention to Toby. The latecomer noticed Frank. He came over.

"Excuse me. I apologize for crashing your show like that. But I enjoyed it. Very much. Is there a program I can take with me?"

"Oh sure," said Frank. He found one on the floor under the chairs, brushed off a bootprint, and gave it to the man.

"Thank you." The man folded it and slipped it into his coat before he followed Henry Lewse and Toby out the door.

"We'll see you there?" Allegra called to Frank from across the room. "Thanks for the invite, Jess. Now if only we can get your brother to see our show."

Frank started down the stairs with Jessie. "Who's the stiff with your boss? Some kind of agent?"

"No. It's Kenneth Prager."

"You're kidding."

"No. Really. He's trying to do a short profile of Henry, but Henry's not making it easy."

A large black four-door sedan was parked outside. Frank got in front with Jessie and the driver. The latecomer sat in back with Henry Lewse and Toby. Frank was still working to swallow the idea that that really was Kenneth Prager. Who had just seen their play. Who now carried a gritty copy of the program in his pocket.

They headed downtown, and Prager tried to resume his interview. Henry Lewse insisted on talking about something else.

"Charming. And funny. Warm and sloppy. But sloppy in a good way. A warm, sad comedy about a house full of unhappy people. Like Chekhov. The people are all wrong for Chekhov, of course. But who wants a bunch of noisy Russians with bad teeth?"

Yes, that was Henry Lewse, the famous Henry Lewse, Jessie's boss, Frank's rival—sort of. And he was nattering away about Frank's play. Well, it was Toby's play too, and Frank presumed half his praise was for Toby's sake, like putting salt on a pretty bird's tail. But the other half sounded genuine. The man was not what Frank had expected. Lewse was up to his tits in self-conceit but seemed oddly innocent, without arrogance or malice, like an enormous baby.

"And you're the director. I keep forgetting *you're* here."

A friendly hand squeezed Frank's shoulder.

"Well done, sir. Very well done."

Jessie smiled at Frank, as if she had just proved something.

Already they were racing through Times Square. Neon zebra stripes slid over the shiny black hood of the car. Giant ads for Kodak, Microsoft, and Tommy Hilfiger dwarfed the handful of theater marquees.

"My mirror scene in the bathroom?" said Toby. "Did that feel right to you or was there too much pathos?"

"Henry," said Prager. "Do you think you'll continue to work in theater after going Hollywood?"

It's a four-door madhouse, thought Frank. He expected Jessie to roll her eyes and laugh about it, but she grew oddly quiet as they approached Downtown, as if becoming guilty or anxious or uncertain.

They came to Sheridan Square and the car turned left. They eased past the late-night crowds lining Seventh Avenue.

"Sasha?" Jessie told the driver. "Over there."

The car pulled up beside an iron-fenced triangle of garden.

"Just drop us off, then park the car and you can join us. The party's up there." She pointed through the windshield.

"What, what? We're there already?" said Henry. "But I haven't given you what you need," he told Prager. "I am so sorry. Why don't you come upstairs with me, we can each get a drink, find a nice quiet corner, and finish this properly."

Prager looked up at the high stone walls, windows, and rooftops that surrounded the triangular bay of streets. "Whose party is this?"

"Just a birthday thing for my assistant's brother. Nothing fancy. But I promised I'd drop by."

"Henry, look!" said Toby. "That's you."

They all turned and saw a billboard. The art deco cartoon for *Tom and Gerry* stood on the opposite side of Seventh Avenue.

"Fool's names and fool's faces," said Henry. "Only it's not my face, is it?"

Jessie walked on ahead, without waiting for the others. Frank saw her go toward her brother's building. He followed her.

He could hear no party sounds from the building, no music, nothing. He wondered if the party were already over. Then the rumble of traffic paused, there was silence, and Frank heard a loud bubble and coo overhead, like a mob of pigeons massing on a rooftop.

62

Irene was right. Most people never arrive at a New York party before eight. As the sun sank behind the roofs and water tanks to the west, and a crescent moon grew brighter in the deep blue sky to the east—a thin fingernail clipping of moon—other guests began to appear.

The first was Kathleen Chalfant, the actress from *Angels in America* and *Wit,* a handsome mix of Virginia Woolf and Annie Oakley, with the throaty voice of a melodious raven. "What a *lovely* place," she sang, lifting her hands palms out on either side of her face, a gesture that mocked itself even as it expressed real pleasure. With her was her husband, Henry, a soft-spoken man in glasses who made documentaries about street gangs, graffiti art, and salsa music. "Hello, Caleb," he shyly murmured.

Caleb introduced them to Daniel Broca—"You're brilliant," Broca blurted at Kathy, then shriveled up in embarrassment—and his mother. "You live nearby?" said Molly, stunned that two people in their fifties actually lived in the Village. Caleb turned her over to the Chalfants, who were perfect company for anybody's mother.

Next came Tom Steffano and Matt O'Brian, two whey-faced waifs like anorexic choirboys who had more weight in their stage identities, Leopold and Lois.

Caleb was suprised to see them. "The show still running?"

"Oh yeah," said Matt, or maybe it was Tom—Caleb couldn't tell them apart out of drag. "This is our night off. That shit review in the *Times* was a kick in the nuts, but we'll survive."

They were joined by Michael Feingold, the theater reviewer of the *Voice* often confused with a singing piano player with a similar name. Critics aren't supposed to fraternize, but Feingold was always up front in his reviews about whose food he'd eaten, and it never seemed to affect his opinions. He always praised the actors and damned the playwright. Nobody mentioned his review of *Chaos Theory* when he greeted Caleb.

Here was Cameron Ditchley of the *New York Post* in his deliberately absurd ascot and seersucker, admiring the view and asking Caleb if he could see into his neighbors' windows. Then came Craig Chester, the actor, followed by John Benjamin Hickey, another actor. Soon there were too many guests for Caleb to greet each new arrival; he lost track of who was here. He remained on the terrace, in the prowlike corner with his back to the sunset, noticing now and then the change of light as the stucco wall turned pink, then rose, then blue. The lights inside grew brighter. The party became a sea of bodies with an occasional familiar face bobbing to the surface.

"What did I tell you?" said Irene, bringing him another soda. "You do have friends."

"Or people who have nothing better to do on Friday night." But he was happily surprised by how many peers and acquaintances were here. He was not anathema after all. "Is my mother still with the Chalfants?"

The Chalfants had left, but Irene thought she'd seen Molly helping Jack in the kitchen.

"Well, so long as she's happy." He had tried calling Jessie, but her cell phone was off, and he left a message asking her to get here as soon as possible. "If worse comes to worse, I suppose I could ask Mom to spend the night."

Then another wave of guests was upon him and he stopped thinking about his mother. There were more actresses now—it was after dark. He was pleased to see Cherry Jones and her lover, the lesbian architect, and Welker White, who had quit acting to have a baby, and Hope Davis, who was back from Los Angeles with lots of jokes about the Land of the Lotus Eaters. No, the people in his world of theater did not abandon him. What was he thinking? They too had known failure as well as success, and they weren't going to avoid him like a fellow thief hanging from a gallows at the crossroad.

The next time Caleb looked at his watch, it was ten o'clock. He was drinking Diet Coke, so it wasn't alcohol that was making the time fly but party adrenaline.

The terrace was filled like the deck of a pleasure boat. There was a steady milling of bodies around the food table outside the French doors. This was a West Village party, which meant people were fairly laid-back. They were here to see and be seen, of course, but mostly they were here to talk. This was New York, and it was uncool to stare at celebrities. There were no real celebrities anyway, until Claire Wade, star of *Venus in Furs,* arrived.

"Caleb? Where's my pal Caleb?" a honeyed soprano called out. The crowd parted and Claire Wade emerged. Her semiclassical face, like a Garbo with freckles, came forward. "Oh, sweetie. How are you?" She gripped each of his hands and gazed deep into his eyes. "Happy birthday, my love. Happy, *happy* birthday."

She spoke in her best Joan Crawford manner, a bit grand despite the casualness of her short hair and khaki slacks. Caleb didn't care. He was delighted she'd come. He could feel the whole party watching them.

"So how are you?" he asked. "Doing any movies?"

"I'm waiting for them to make *our* movie. But—I probably shouldn't tell you this—" She lowered her voice. "I'm in the running with Sarandon. For the mother in *Greville.* Do you know the book?"

"Uh, yes." He considered telling her that Greville himself was supposed to come tonight, but decided against it. Claire would want to stay and meet him. He didn't know if his good spirits could survive the spectacle of *his* star rubbing like a cat up against *that* star.

Irene came over. "Oh hi," she told Claire. She felt no awe for movie faces. "Caleb. It's getting late. Shouldn't we cut the cake?"

"Sure. Go ahead."

"But we have to toast you and sing 'Happy Birthday.' Or something. How do you want to do this?"

"Can't we just serve the cake and forget about me?"

"It's a *birthday* party. Come on, Caleb, dear. Do you want me to make a toast? Or I could get your mother."

"Oh God, no. Not my mother."

"What about me?" Claire offered.

"You don't have to do that," said Caleb.

"But I want to," Claire insisted. "It'd be an honor. A privilege. And then I really must go. I have a very early day tomorrow."

Irene led them indoors, into the surprisingly bright lights of the living room. Jack was already setting the rose-choked cake on the drinks table, with a stack of clear plastic plates on the side.

"Where's my mother?" Caleb asked him.

"She went into the bedroom to lie down for a minute."

"Is she ill?"

Jack shook his head. "She just wanted to rest. Very nice lady, your mother. And funny."

"Oh yeah," said Caleb. "She can be very funny around strangers. I better go get her."

He felt terrible for abandoning her, for forgetting her. She had come all the way into town, a major undertaking, but the caterer had seen more of her than Caleb had. He went to his bedroom. He lightly rapped on the door. No answer. He pushed the door open.

She lay on his bed, flat on her back, her left arm over her eyes, her mouth wide open. She was sound asleep, and snoring. Her feet stuck off the end of the bed. One loafer still hung on her toes, the other had dropped to the floor. She seemed both young and old, like a college girl passed out at a mixer, and a grandmother exhausted by a day at the zoo. Caleb felt guiltier than ever. And full of love. He decided to let her sleep. He would wake her when Jessie got here.

He turned off the light. Her snores sounded louder in the dark. He gently pulled the door shut and rejoined the party.

"Attention, please!" called out Claire, tapping a glass with a knife. "The time has come. The time is here."

All around the room, people stopped talking or chewing or drinking. They faced the table with the gaudy cake and movie star.

"Friends?" Claire began. "Friends. We are gathered this evening to mark a very special . . ."

Caleb stood beside her with the conventional bashful smile, looked out at the room, and felt a strange, deep, sudden sadness.

The party had been going well. It turned out so much better than he had anticipated. But now, hearing himself toasted by a friendly stranger, surrounded by friendly strangers, he felt terribly alone. Nobody absolutely necessary to him was here tonight. Except Irene. But Irene was different. Irene was as much business as friendship. His mother was here, but she was asleep. Where was his sister? And where was—?

But there was nobody else, was there? That's why this hurt so much. That's why he had dreaded tonight. Throwing himself a party was like rubbing his nose in his failure to connect with people.

"And so, my dear," Claire concluded, "your friends and I wish you all the happiness in the world. On this, your birthday." She lifted her glass, and everyone applauded.

"Thank you," he mumbled. "Thank you." And he bowed and wiggled his shoulders, as if too overwhelmed for words. Thank God, there were no candles for him to blow out.

He stepped back and let Jack carve the cake. He wished he could step outside and be alone with his sadness, but this was his party and he was trapped here. As people came forward to wish him happy birthday again, he envied actors their false selves, their public faces and handy dishonesties. But he was not a true theater person. He never was and never would be.

Claire kissed him good-bye on the cheek. Then there were kisses from John Hickey, and Edward Hibbert, and Roz and Charlotte, and a host of other people he hadn't even known were here. The party emptied out a little.

When he looked at his watch again, it was after midnight.

He went back out on the terrace to get a breath of air. It was so much cooler outside, less crowded too.

"Here," said Jack. "You never got a piece of your cake." He held out a fat yellow slice with a delicate cross-section of a blue rose.

"Thank you," said Caleb. He took the plate and took a bite. The butter cream rose tasted wonderful, a smooth, sweet, comforting thing. He looked up at Jack and smiled. Leave it to a food man to know what a body needed.

But before Caleb could discuss it, before he could ask Jack what *his* life was like, he looked past Jack's big hoop earring into the living room and saw his sister enter.

Here was Jessie, at long last, coming through the door with a remarkably motley pack of men.

63

The elevator arrived and Jessie lead her posse up the single flight of stairs to Caleb's open door. Here I am, she thought proudly, but she was also having second thoughts. Because she brought not just Henry, and Toby too, but Kenneth Prager. It was mischief rather than malice, and not deliberate but accidental—well, accidentally on purpose. She hadn't realized until they were halfway downtown that she'd be infecting the party with the very man who had killed her brother's play.

Caleb's apartment was totally unrecognizable with a celebration inside. The sofa was pushed against the wall, a bar set in front of the TV, and there were people everywhere. Jessie spotted Michael Feingold—or was it Feinstein?—sitting in an armchair, holding forth on German expressionist drama. The party was still at full boil. It should be easy enough to slip in and disperse without Caleb knowing who had arrived with whom.

"Oh my," said Henry, surveying the people in the room. "I see that the sixties are back. And the fifties. *And* the seventies."

Jessie did not catch sight of her brother anywhere.

"Look, there's a terrace," Henry told Prager. "We can go outside to finish our interview. Let me get us something to drink. What will you have?"

"Nothing for me," said Prager, then whispered, "I need to find a lavatory. I'll join you outside." He hurried away.

Jessie saw her chance. "Henry, wait. Don't go yet. I want to introduce you to my brother."

"No, me," Toby insisted. "I was going to introduce them."

"You?" said Jessie. "But why? You're his ex."

"We're still friends. And I can prove it by introducing Henry."

Which was too weird, but Jessie recognized that she was just as weird. They each needed to prove something, didn't they?

"May I introduce myself?" said Henry. "Is that acceptable?"

Jessie noticed Frank standing by. She had brought him, but why? Did she need him here as her conscience?

Then she saw Caleb across the room, framed in the double doors to the terrace. He stood beside a fat neo-punk waiter, looking a bit like a waiter himself in his white dress shirt and Elvis Costello glasses. She could not get used to those glasses or his little soul beard. They still looked like a disguise.

He saw her. He saw *them*. He stepped inside. He stepped down into the slightly sunken living room, looking at her, looking at the two men with her. No, three. She kept forgetting about Frank, but Caleb wouldn't care about Frank.

"Happy birthday!" she sang when Caleb stood in front of her. She gave him a kiss on the cheek. It came out sloppier, wetter than intended. "Sorry we're late. But better late than never, huh?"

64

Caleb stared at the three faces. Or no, four faces, but Frank Earp was not part of this equation. Frank stood back, frowning, waiting, looking chilly. The others—Jessie and Toby and the famous Henry Lewse—were all grinning at Caleb like a pack of shit-eating dogs.

"You must be Caleb Doyle," declared Lewse.

He held out his hand, and Caleb took it without thinking. The hand felt dryer and tougher than Caleb expected.

"So good to meet you at last," said Lewse. "When I've heard so much about you."

Which could not help sounding loaded when he stood between Caleb's sister and Caleb's ex-boyfriend. What had they told him? Not that it mattered. The man was only an actor. Caleb had known too many actors. With no role to play tonight, no character, Lewse was an absence, but an oddly precise absence, his long face suggesting a footprint in the sand.

"Hello, Caleb," said Frank. "Happy birthday."

"Thanks, Frank. Good to see you." He suspected Frank disliked him, although he wasn't sure why. But Caleb respected Frank. Frank wanted nothing from Caleb.

"Caleb? Caleb?" said Toby. "Happy birthday, right?"

"Yeah. Hi, Toby. So glad you could make it. And that you brought your new friend."

Toby grinned and nodded, oblivious to sarcasm. "Henry saw our play tonight. He thinks it's good. Don't you, Henry?"

"Quite good. We were all delighted by how good it is." Lewse spoke in round, plummy, flirtatious tones, still smiling, never dreaming that his host might despise him.

"It is good," said Jessie. "Really. You got to see it, Caleb."

"Anyone want something to drink?" said Frank. "I sure do." And he left without waiting to hear from the others.

Toby continued to gaze at Caleb, all big-eyed and expectant, like a giant puppy hoping to be petted. He wanted Caleb to be jealous. He was so transparent that it was laughable. So why wasn't Caleb laughing? He'd known Toby and Lewse were coming. He had assumed he wouldn't feel a thing. But he couldn't look at Toby now for fear he'd picture him running his tongue over that public English face.

Lewse was watching Caleb with a mild, thoughtful, curious expression. Did he really expect Caleb to be friendly?

Jessie looked pained and apologetic—as well she should. Caleb was furious with her for shoving this pair at him.

He ignored the men and faced Jessie. "You'll never guess who came tonight. Not in a million years," he said. "Mom."

Her head jerked as if the building had hit a bump. "*Our* mom?"

"Uh-huh. Don't you ever check your voice mail?"

"You're kidding. She came into the city for your party?"

"Yeap. But she wanted to see you too."

"She went home already?"

"Oh no. She's still here."

"Oh my God. Where?" Jessie wildly looked around.

"Your mom's here?" said Toby. "Neat. I've never met her."

The intrusive sound of that slightly froggy voice angered Caleb beyond reason. He turned to Toby and Lewse.

"You two must be hungry. There's food out on the terrace. Why don't you go help yourselves."

"No, I'm fine," said Toby. "I'll get something later."

"Toby." Caleb kept his temper, but just barely. "Please. Could you and Mr. Lewse allow me and my sister to finish our talk in private? It's a family matter."

Toby stared and winced, squinting as if Caleb had just said something vicious.

"Come along, Toby," said Henry. "Let's go put on the feed bag."

"Right," said Toby. "I'm coming." His temper raised his voice. "Because I'm hungry. Real hungry. And I'm not gonna be hungry another minute just so other people might think I care about them more than I care about my stomach."

He wheeled around and stomped away.

"Ah, youth," said Henry. He nodded good-bye and followed.

Caleb watched him go. He was still angry but was free to express it now, and it all fell on his sister. "Jesus, Jessie. You had to bring your whole damn entourage tonight?"

"My what? Oh no. Only Henry and Toby." She nervously looked around, as if other unwanted bodies may have followed her. "Is Mom really here? Or did you make that up?"

"No, she's here. She lay down to take a nap in my bedroom. She *was* asleep."

"But she's so phobic about the city. I wonder why she came?"

"Out of love for me," he said with a perfect deadpan. "And for you too," he admitted. "She said she couldn't go home until you got here. Because you'd be all pissed and out of shape."

"I wouldn't be pissed. A little miffed, maybe." She chewed on the idea a moment. "She didn't really say that?"

"Why don't you go ask her? We can go wake her up."

"That's okay. Let's let sleeping moms lie."

A few minutes ago, Caleb had felt criminally alone at his own birthday party. Now Jessie was here, and he felt less alone, not wrapped in love but tangled up in meaningful aggravation.

"So that's the great Henry Lewse," he said.

"What? Oh right." She stopped fretting about Mom. "But see? He's not such a bad guy."

"I guess. For somebody who's fucking my ex-boyfriend."

She made a little pout, looking surprised by the idea, then decided not to play dumb. "But I thought you were finished with Toby. You having second thoughts?"

"Not at all. Especially when he shows up with your boss, hoping to make me jealous."

"Yeah, I was picking up those signals too. But if he can have Henry Lewse, an actor, why would he still want you, a writer?" She smiled. It was a joke, sort of.

"And now he's going to be a movie star," said Caleb. "Greville."

"You don't need to sneer. Have you read the novel?"

.

"No. Have you?"

"No. But I read the script. Yesterday."

"And?"

She was smiling again. Her smile broke apart in a laugh. "It's a *Lolita* rip-off. Only this time Lolita is legal—eighteen—and she and her mother team up and kill Humbert Humbert. So it's a feel-good *Lolita*. Where mothers can bond with their daughters."

Caleb laughed with her. No matter how angry he might be with Jessie, he respected her intelligence and enjoyed her humor. So why couldn't she get her shit together?

"Are they really fucking?" he suddenly said.

"What?"

The question had broken into his brain and he had to ask it. "Or does Toby just want me to *think* they're fucking?"

"I—uh—er—um—" Jessie was thrown, not by the question but by the look on his face, the tone of his voice.

"Tell me! That's why you brought them here!" he charged. "You want to put me in my place! Let me know my life is as big a mess as yours! You must know if they're fucking or not!"

"*Caleb.*" She held her ground, she did not flee. She lowered her head but looked straight at him. "Yeah, I think they're fucking," she said calmly. "But it's got nothing to do with us."

"Sorry," he said. "Sorry. I don't know where that came from."

But he knew exactly where it came from: his sister loved him, but her unconscious hated him. For various sibling reasons. And his own unconscious understood that and had struck out at her. He understood *her* unconscious better than he understood his own. Maybe. Yet what does one do with such knowledge? Now was hardly the time to exhume old grudges and built-in sib antipathies.

"Want some cake?" he asked.

65

So *that's* Caleb Doyle, thought Henry as he followed Toby out to the terrace. Not quite what he'd expected. He was scrawnier, less American, more bookwormy than Henry had imagined—but he *was* a playwright. Nevertheless, there was something appealing about him, a mysterious familiarity, although that may simply have been the fact that Henry saw the man's sister every day. He'd been circling Doyle for the past week, ever since he brought him to orgasm over the telephone. And now they finally met. But there had been no spark, no electric recognition. They had gazed upon each other with as little mutual sympathy as a dog and a cat stranded on an ice floe.

"Damn him," said Toby. "Did you see the way he looked at me? Like I wasn't even there. And then he told me to beat it. Get lost."

"And how did you hope he would look?"

"Like he was sorry, like he still loved me."

"Like he was jealous, you mean. Which was why you wanted *me* here." Henry spoke matter-of-factly, without resentment.

They were standing beside a table loaded with food, neither of them taking a thing. Toby suddenly turned and walked away.

Henry hesitated, then followed. Toby stomped past knots of people, head down, shoulders hunched. He disappeared around a corner. Henry found him facing a stucco wall. He wondered if he were going to bang his head against it. But no, Toby planted a foot on a rung of ladder there and hoisted himself upward.

"Where are you going?" Henry grabbed the boy's belt.

Toby looked over his shoulder. "Up on the roof. To escape this stupid party."

"May I come along?"

Toby produced a dull sigh. "I guess."

Henry followed the heavy hams in khaki as they flexed and swung their way up the ladder. There was a roof above the roof, a tar-paper flatness over the terrace, somewhat shabby but startlingly dark as soon as you stepped back from the edge.

"This is my spot," said Toby. "From when I stayed here and needed to be alone." He crawled around the darkness and sat down.

Henry remained standing. The people below were too deep in the gargle of conversation to look up and see him. The terrace suggested the crowded rampart of a castle, a Ludwiggy thing perched on an improbable aerie in a ravine of taller buildings. The windowed mountains stood all around, most of the windows dark—it was after midnight—but a few flickered with telly lights. The ravine narrowed in front of the castle, closing over a pitch-dark garden, then opened wide again on a bright, noisy valley: a street corner full of tiny pedestrians. VILLAGE CIGARS, announced a big red sign. Over the sign were two billboards, one of them that jaunty ad for *Tom and Gerry*.

"This party," sneered Toby. "These people. Do you see any real artists down there? No. Just a bunch of jerks on the make."

"My boy," said Henry patiently. "We're all on the make. It's as natural as breathing. Frivolous to get righteous about it."

But Toby didn't hear. He was talking about something else anyway. "He won't come see our show. He looked right through me. Like I meant nothing to him."

Henry carefully folded his legs together and sat down beside Toby. They were not sitting on tar paper but on fibrous plastic mats, like floor mats from a car. "Yes, I imagine how that must hurt," said Henry, still playing Mr. Nice Guy. "But at least you have me."

He was surprised that he could enjoy being used by this young, self-centered romantic. He supposed he was in love with Toby, but it was an oddly platonic, amused kind of love. The boy was nice to look at. Henry didn't need to touch him. Or no. That wasn't entirely true. But looking was sweet as his eyes adjusted to the light.

"Why can't he love me anymore? He did once. I'm sure of it. But gay men are like that. Shallow. They can love for only so long. He couldn't even feel jealous. It's too deep an emotion for him."

Henry was losing patience with Toby's single-mindedness. Here was the boy, sitting on a roof with a man who was not just a major Shakespearean, or so the critics said, but soon to be a major movie star. And all he could talk about was that scrawny-arsed playwright down below.

"Here's an idea," Henry proposed. "Do you know what'd make our friend truly jealous tonight?"

Toby thought a moment. Then he snorted and shook his head. "Forget it. And you don't really want to make him jealous. You just want us to have sex."

"You are so wise, Toby. So perceptive."

"I thought we were just going to be friends."

"Nothing could be friendlier."

"You just want to use me."

"As you've been using me. Not that I mind," he quickly added. "I'm amused. Even flattered. But I must confess"—he decided to say it all—"that I do find the spectacle of you getting up on your moral high horse *extraordinary*. I've been fair to you. I've always treated you as an equal. But it's been a one-way street. I mean, take the other night. I did everything I could for you, obeyed every request, touching you here, there, pumping away until I was blue in the face. But did you do anything for me? Not a damn thing!" But that wasn't the point, that was not what he needed to address here. "Oh but we love the young," he explained. "They have energy, beauty, hope. They are all future tense. All light and air. But your sense of entitlement, Toby, your apparent belief that your youth and good looks put you *above* a successful veteran of the theater is *beginning* to annoy me."

"What are you saying, Henry? You're pissed because I didn't— reciprocate the other night?" He couldn't even name it.

"No! It's not about blow jobs. It's more than blow jobs. It's what a blow job represents."

Toby was silent for a moment. "I *can* be selfish," he confessed. "I'm sorry, Henry. But that proves how much I love him, doesn't it? That it can make me mean to other people."

Henry irritably crossed his arms together, so he wouldn't slap him. "It's not that you're mean. I'd just like to be appreciated more."

"All right. I'll make it up to you. Why don't you lie back?"

"I beg your pardon?"

"I want to appreciate you, Henry. I want to reciprocate."

Before Henry could argue, before he could explain that he was not just talking about sex, Toby leaned forward on all fours and kissed him on the mouth.

It was a warm, slow, friendly kiss. It was a wonderful kiss, like a first kiss, no hands but lots of tongue, like when you're fifteen and you start snogging backstage with your best friend, the Artful Dodger, not knowing how far a kiss can go, where it will take you.

Toby broke off the kiss. "Yes? Okay? Please." He was unzipping Henry's zipper. "It'll make *me* feel better." He brought a plump prick out into the night air. "Lie down. Make yourself comfortable."

Henry leaned back with his head toward the ladder. He could clearly hear the party below. He'd have to twist his neck around if he heard someone climbing the ladder. He propped himself on his elbows to watch Toby.

It did not look like an act of love. It looked more like penance. Henry was not fully aroused. And Toby was not very good. He did it timidly, as if it were unclean, keeping his mouth wide open. There were occasional ticklish snorts into Henry's fly. But it didn't have to be good sex. It was only symbolic sex.

Henry remembered the windows all around, where people may or may not be looking down on them. Not a very flattering picture of a beloved Broadway star, he thought.

66

When Jessie came out to the terrace, she found Frank standing at the table under the beach umbrella, loading a plate with wedges of cheese, ham, and melon.

"I just realized," he said, "I haven't eaten all day."

"Me neither." But she had no appetite. Just looking at the picked-over rainbow of food was enough to fill her.

"Your brother didn't seem very happy to see us."

"Who knows what the fuck Caleb wants anymore?"

Frank gave her a forlorn, miffed, knowing look. "What did you hope to prove by bringing everyone down here?"

"I wasn't out to prove anything. I just wanted to have fun. I thought it'd be fun. Can't anybody have fun anymore? The rest of you people are so damned serious."

"Uh, Jessica?" It was Kenneth Prager. "Have you seen Mr. Lewse? He told me to meet him out here to finish the interview."

Jessie peered through the French doors, then up and down the terrace, looking for Henry, but also for her brother. Not that Caleb would be freaked to find Prager here. He'd probably find *that* funny. And if he didn't, screw him.

"Sorry, Kenneth. Don't know. Did you check the john?"

"I was just there myself." He sounded indignant that she hadn't kept track of his whereabouts. "I'll check inside again," he said with a grave sigh. "And then I'm going home."

Frank watched him depart. "It wasn't just fun," he told Jessie. "You brought us here to make a big ruckus and get attention."

"That's a good one," she said. "A real ripsnorter. Caleb says I did it to put him in *his* place. To prove his life is as shitty as mine."

"But you have a good life. Both of you have good lives. Although that won't mean much coming from me, the loser."

"You're never going to let me forget I said that, will you?"

"No. Because it hurts each time I remember it. But especially now when you're working for a big winner."

"Look. Henry's the winner. I'm still a loser."

He studied her a moment, then shook his head. "Excuse me. I got to go get something to drink. To wash down this crap." He lifted his overloaded plate to show that he was being literal as well as metaphorical, and went back inside.

Jesus, thought Jessie. When did tonight suddenly become Shit on Jessica Night? And she hadn't even talked with Mom yet.

There was a commotion inside as more guests arrived, which was a surprise at this hour. But it was the *2B* cast—Allegra, Dwight, Chris, and Melissa—who had come downtown by subway. Allegra came out on the terrace with Dwight, still yammering about the play.

"Whatever happens was meant to happen," she was saying. "I fell in love with Chris not because I'm queer but because I needed to fight with Boaz. Because once Boaz walked and Frank took over, the play began to work. Hey, Jess! Nice party. Where's Henry? I need to ask Henry if he could add just *one* more tiny thing to his quote."

Caleb appeared behind Allegra, waiting to ask Jessie something.

Then a new disturbance indoors made everyone turn around and look.

67

Kenneth stayed in the bathroom longer than he intended, sitting on the lowered toilet lid with the tape recorder pressed to his ear, listening to what he had and trying to come up with one last good question for Henry Lewse. He'd hoped to beat Bick by turning his punitive assignment into a nice little article, but circumstance and Lewse himself worked together to reduce the night to a wild Lewse goose chase. The show uptown had been a nice surprise, but Kenneth needed to focus now. He would try one more question—Is there a single actor or actress you hope to work with before you die?—and then he could go home.

He came out of the bathroom and looked for Lewse. A swell party, he thought. He wondered whose party. A swell apartment too. He and Gretchen could never afford such a place.

He found the assistant out on the terrace, but she hadn't seen Lewse and did not seem terribly interested in finding him. He went back inside and checked the kitchen, then an office full of the strangest assortment of books: artist biographies and books about math. He tried the bedroom next, lightly knocking on the door, which was already open, so he pushed it. A fan of light spread over a bed with an old lady stretched out on the covers.

"Excuse me! Sorry!" he exclaimed and pulled the door shut.

He hurried back out to the living room. He asked the bartender if he'd seen Henry Lewse depart.

"Henry Lewse? The actor? He's here? Are you sure?"

"Of course I'm sure. I arrived with him."

The bartender excitedly looked around the room. "Wow. Hey, I'll keep my eyes peeled."

Kenneth went back out to the terrace.

"No luck?" said the assistant.

He shook his head and hurried past her, wondering if she were hoaxing him. Were they *all* hoaxing him? They would soon claim that Lewse was never here and Kenneth must be crazy. It would be their revenge for all the awful things the *Times* had done to actors.

Kenneth headed toward the far corner of the terrace, which was darker. All he could see were the silhouettes of guests standing in front of the orange-tinted cityscape.

"Henry?" he said. "Henry? Has anyone here seen Henry?"

"Not me," said a young man. "Unless your name is Henry?" he asked his companion.

"No. Is *your* name Henry?"

"I don't think so," the first man replied. "My brother used to call me Thomasina. But it's not the same thing, is it?" He turned back to Kenneth. "Sorry. No Henrys here."

Kenneth came up beside the pair of the silhouettes. They were two skinny young men in jeans and black T-shirts leaning against the parapet. He sensed that they were gay, maybe even a couple.

"Hen-reeee! Henry Aldrich!" cried out the first man. Or maybe it was the second. They were like an East Village Tweedledum and Tweedledee.

"Hey," said his friend, closing one eye and studying Kenneth with the other. He was slightly drunk. "You're Kenneth Prager."

This often happened at public gatherings. There was nothing to do but accept it. "Guilty," he joked. "Glad to meet you." He held out his hand, which was all most people needed.

But neither of them took his hand.

"I wouldn't stand too close to the edge if I were you," said the second man. "Not while you're talking to us."

And Kenneth laughed, as if it were a joke, although he suspected it wasn't. "I'm sorry. Do I know you?"

"No. You don't know us at all," said the first man.

"You might think you know our alter egos," said the second. "But you don't know them either."

"Does the name Leopold ring a bell?" said the first man.

"Does the name Lois?" said the other.

"*Oh?*" said Kenneth, squinting, trying to see two shabby nightclub performers in the scrubbed blandness of these two boys, even as he took a healthy step back from the parapet.

"Murderers?" said the first man.

"More in need of therapy than a review?" said the second.

Actors took their notices much too seriously. Directors and writers could be grown-ups about criticism, but actors were children. A bad review was like telling them there was no Santa Claus.

Kenneth drew himself up to his full height. "Sorry. I call them as I see them. Your audience seemed to enjoy you well enough."

"And that's why you hated us, old man?" said the first one.

"Damn but you're old," said the other. "Couldn't they have sent someone our age? Someone who was alive enough to get it!"

Being called "old" didn't hurt. Of course these brats would see him as old. But their desire to hurt him? *That* hurt.

"You're upset," he told them. "Which is natural. But you did your job, and I did mine—"

"Our job is to make art and yours is to destroy it?"

"I'm sorry we can't be more mature about this. But it was nice meeting you. Good night." He nodded to each, then turned and walked away, very calmly, he thought, very adultly.

His heart was pounding like a drum. He remained in control of his body even as it braced itself for a blow to the back of the head or kick in the seat of his pants. But nothing happened. Leopold and Lois didn't even shout a last insult.

He went straight to the bartender inside. "Gin and tonic." That's all he needed, a quick drink before he took a last look for Lewse, and then he'd go home. He wouldn't be fleeing. It was late. "Thank you," he told the bartender and gripped the cold glass. The first sip brought him back to himself. He decided to take his time with the drink and enjoy it.

Glancing around the room, he saw a middle-aged lady perched alone on a sofa. She sat with a purse in her lap, drinking something clear, looking faintly lost. With a suburban hairdo and old-fashioned lipstick and earrings, she did not look like a theater person, but like somebody's mother: safe and sane. Kenneth wanted to sit down anyway, and she looked like good, grown-up company.

68

Molly was at the zoo. The animals were having cocktails: martinis and highballs and manhattans and sidecars.

A sudden banging drove the animals away. And a door opened, letting in an angry bright light. "Excuse me! Sorry!" said a man. He instantly pulled the door shut.

Molly lay in the dark, wide awake now. She'd been dreaming. Of course. She had fallen asleep. But where was she? There seemed to be a party in the next room, not animals but people. This was not home. Was she still dreaming? Was she drunk? There was a mild ache in her head, but she did not feel tipsy.

She slowly sat up. A big window hung over the bed. Outside the window hung an enormous building full of more windows, most of them dark. And she remembered: she was in Manhattan, visiting her son Caleb for his birthday party.

What a night. What a pack of chatterboxes. She felt like she'd been talking to people ever since she arrived. She rubbed her jaw to make sure it was still there. Well, they did the talking. All she had to do was listen.

She was reluctant to go back outside, but her daughter should be here by now. Once she said hello to Jessie, she could say good-bye and go home. She hoped it wasn't too late.

She opened the door and peeked out. The party still sputtered and fussed. She slipped around the corner into the bathroom, where she splashed cold water on her face and freshened her lipstick, so she wouldn't look like an old souse. She was confused by the heaviness of her purse until she remembered why. She felt silly for keeping the purse with her, as if someone would steal it. But you never knew who might show up at a New York City party. Not that she didn't trust Caleb's friends, but what about friends of friends?

She came back out to the living room. There were no familiar faces left, except for Jack, the bartender with pirate earrings.

"Molly. Where have you been?"

"Hello, Jack. Just needed to rest my eyes. I was going to help clean up before I went home, but this thing isn't over yet, is it?"

"Oh no, it's going to go for a while. Irene left two hours ago."

"Two hours ago?" Molly said worriedly. "What time is it?"

"After one."

"Oh for pete's sake."

"We're not in Kansas anymore," teased Jack. "This'll probably go on until four or five."

Caleb came over. "Mom. Hi. You feel better after your nap?"

"Do you know what time it is?" she scolded. "Why did you let me sleep? Why didn't you wake me? I got to get home."

"It's too late to go home. You can spend the night. It won't kill you," he pleaded. "Oh, Jessie's finally here."

"Jessie?"

"My sister. Your daughter."

"I know who she is! Don't be a smart-aleck. I'm still half asleep." That's right. She needed to see Jessie. To prove to her daughter that she loved her as much as she loved Caleb. Or some such nonsense. So now she was trapped for the night in this godforsaken city.

"I'll go get her," said Caleb. "Right back."

"Would you like something to drink?" asked Jack.

"I'd love something, Jack. But I better not. My daughter'll think I'm a lush. Just give me some seltzer."

Jack poured her a glass of cold, bubbling soda water. Molly took it to the sofa and sat down. It was silly to worry that Jessie might think she was drunk. She couldn't understand why she feared her children's judgments. Was she such a terrible mother? Just because she never came into town to see her kids?

She impatiently waited for Caleb to return with his sister. Was Jessie refusing to come? What had Molly done wrong now?

"Excuse me? Do you mind if I sit here?"

A tall scarecrow of a man in a trim gray suit stood over her.

"It's a free country," she said.

But as soon as he sat she wished she'd said no. She did not need to have her ear talked off by another damn actor. And she should be saving the seat for Jessie.

"Nice party," said the scarecrow.

"Very," she replied.

And he said nothing more. Which was a wonderful change from all the other chatterboxes. She looked around for Caleb and Jessie.

A heavy, hairy fellow stood in front of the scarecrow. "Prager?" he said. "Kenneth Prager. You don't remember me? Michael Feingold. The *Voice*? We keep meeting at previews."

"Oh yes. Hi," the man mumbled.

"I can't believe *you're* here. After you trashed Doyle's play."

"Doyle? What Doyle?"

"Caleb Doyle. Who wrote *Chaos Theory*." He broke into a hearty laugh. "You didn't know where you were? That's a good one! Well, don't worry. I won't tell him." He walked away, still chortling.

And the scarecrow just sat there, screwing his eyebrows together like a man trying to thread a needle, only there was no needle and thread in his hands.

Molly stared. It was him. The critic. The know-it-all critic who had destroyed her son's show. Who had made Caleb so unhappy.

"You?" she said. "You write for the *Times*?"

He slowly faced her. "Kenneth Prager," he said wearily. "Pleased to meet you." He wore a small, pinched smile. He didn't bother to hold out his hand or even ask her name.

"You," she repeated. "You—!" Words tumbled from her brain to her tongue, so many words that she couldn't begin to speak. She had to open her mouth wide just to make room. "What gives you the right to say a show is bad or a show is awful? Who voted you God?"

He lifted his chin and lowered two tired eyelids at her, as if she were an insect telling off an exterminator.

"You think *Chaos Theory* was awful? I know people who loved it. And I should know, because my son wrote it."

"You're the playwright's mother?"

"Yes!" she said proudly. Now he would have to show some shame or guilt.

But his weary smile widened into a grin. He squeezed his eyes shut, then snapped them back open, as if he couldn't believe this. The grin became a chuckle. He thought she was just a harmless old lady.

She opened her purse and reached inside. She would show him the service revolver that she'd tossed in there with her Kleenex and lipstick on her way out the door this afternoon. Just show it to him. That's all. It would be enough to let him know she wasn't harmless. Nobody in the world is harmless. You must always behave well and speak well in this life, because you never know who might be armed.

69

When the playwright's mother pulled a gun from her purse, Kenneth assumed she was joking. It was just another absurdity on top of the first absurdity that this *was* the playwright's mother. It must be a toy or a stage prop or maybe even licorice. It was black like licorice. Would a white woman even carry a gun? She waved it at him as if it were nothing worse than a steam iron.

The first time the gun went off, Molly nearly jumped out of her skin. And then it went off *again,* which was damn embarrassing.

The first shot sounded no worse than a cap pistol to Kenneth's untrained ear. Then he saw the woman's face. She looked frightened, as if the gun were suddenly alive and out of her control. She seemed to grab for it, even though the gun never left her hand.

It went off again and something bit Kenneth's arm: his right arm, the underside, between the wrist and the elbow.

Was he shot? Was that possible?

His arm stung, but not much worse than a bad insect bite or a cigarette burn. In fact, his coat sleeve bore a tiny rip like a cigarette burn. The worst physical pain Kenneth had ever experienced was a toothache. This wasn't nearly as bad.

Not at first. But it grew, a white pain that became whiter, stronger. Kenneth decided to be a man and bear it in silence. But the pain became white hot. Until there was no possible response except to shout or cry something. And the first words to come to mind were: "Oh my God, I've been shot!"

And someone laughed. Kenneth actually heard some son of a bitch laughing.

Then another voice shouted, "Oh shit, he's bleeding!"

Caleb was out on the terrace waiting to speak to Jessie and bring her inside when he heard the odd noises. Popping ballons? Firecrackers? He turned around and saw people facing the sofa, where his mother sat. He stepped through the door. He saw Molly sitting like a statue on the sofa with—Kenneth Prager? He recognized the long, lean critic from photos and television. *What is* he *doing at my birthday party?* He was clutching his right arm, which seemed to be bleeding. And Caleb's mother held a small black revolver.

"Mom?"

He hurried over and knelt beside her. Without time to think it through, he heard himself say, "Mom? Just give me the gun. Please? Everything's fine. Just give me the gun."

She looked at him as if he were nuts talking to her in such an insipid tone. "Here. Take it. Please."

He recognized their father's old snub-nosed .38 from home. She handed it to him with the barrel pointed at the floor.

"Careful," said Jessie, standing directly behind him. "You'll get your fingerprints on it."

"What? And get charged with murder instead of Mom?" Only this wasn't murder, not yet. But Caleb didn't know what to do with the gun. He kept it pointed at the floor, clicked the safety on, then snapped the cylinder out and began to pry out bullets.

Toby rushed into the room. "Oh my God! Oh my God! He's been shot? Somebody. Quick. Dial 911."

"I'm dialing it already!" Jessie snarled as she punched the beeping numbers of her cell phone.

"Here, let me look," said Toby. "Good grief, you're bleeding. You're bleeding bad. Lie down. I know first aid. Lie down on the floor. Keep your arm up."

Prager didn't move. He stared at his coat sleeve, which was now wet and black, then he looked up and saw the audience.

People stood scattered around the room, watching, wondering, worrying, not knowing what to do.

Caleb handed the revolver and bullets to Jessie and came forward to help Toby ease Prager down to the floor.

"I don't think it's an artery," said Toby. "So we don't need a tourniquet. Direct pressure'll do. We need some towels or cloths."

He sounded a bit too sure of himself, falsely confident, like an actor overdoing a part, which worried Caleb. But Toby knew the part and nobody else did, so he let Toby take charge.

"Towels in the bathroom!" Caleb shouted. "Bring some towels."

Frank Earp ran off to fetch towels.

Henry Lewse appeared. He sat on the sofa arm, leaned down, and set a hand on Molly's shoulder. "There, there," he told her. "There, there." His trousers were marked up with black chalk or soot. He too seemed to be playing a part in a scene, and playing it well.

"They're on their way," said Jessie, closing up her cell phone. "They're sending an ambulance from St. Vincent's, but the cops'll be here first. So what do we tell them?"

Caleb looked up again, first at Jessie, then at their mother.

Molly sat perfectly still, as calm as stone, watching the men at her feet. Her hands were locked in her lap, her left hand gripping her guilty right hand.

There was a blink of bright light, a camera flash. Cameron Ditchley stood across the room with a pocket-size digital camera.

Toby laid the man on his back. He pulled off the man's jacket and passed it to Caleb. The man wore a white shirt. Suddenly his blood was bright red like paint. Toby took a deep breath—he was sure he would faint—but the swoony nausea passed. The moment took over, the action continued. He applied pressure to the flat of the arm with both hands, one on top of the other, like they'd taught him in the Boy Scouts in Milwaukee. The blood felt hot on his hands, then sticky. Then he was using towels, white terry cloth, and the blood became squishy.

"You'll be okay," he told the man. "You'll be fine."

The man had turned away, unable to look at his own blood. His face was candle-wax white. His five o'clock shadow looked like black pepper on his white skin. His head was raised. Caleb had rolled up the man's jacket and set it under his neck.

Toby didn't know if he was helping the man or hurting him. Maybe the wound was minor and would stop bleeding on its own. Or the man would bleed to death anyway. Toby didn't know, yet there was nothing else for him to do but continue. He could only go through the motions and hope they were the right motions.

Here was Caleb beside him. What did Caleb think? But he was not doing this for Caleb. No. Caleb no longer counted. And here was Henry too, but Henry didn't count either. His dick in Toby's mouth was nothing compared to a gunshot wound. No, Toby was taking action solely for the sake of this poor man, this stranger. And for the experience. Toby was able to hold himself together, keep his panic under control by thinking, Remember this. Every sensory memory, thought, and emotion. You can use them all one day.

70

Nobody fled the party, but people knew to get out of the way. Half of the guests were on the terrace watching through the French doors when the police and paramedics arrived.

The two paramedics went straight to Prager and knelt beside him. A cop with a dense mustache stood over them, talking to Caleb.

"It was an accident," Caleb told the cop. "My mother was showing this man her gun and—"

"She shot me!" cried Prager from the floor. "I gave him a bad review and his mother shot me!" The critic had not said a word since the "accident," and his anger startled everyone. He was furious, but he sounded panicked too, his voice breaking. There was more fear than righteousness in his bugged-out eyes.

"Chill, buddy," said a medic. "Relax."

Molly still sat on the sofa, Jessie beside her, holding her mother's hand. "I don't know how it happened," said Molly. "I was just talking to the man and the next thing I knew I was waving my gun to make a point."

"Where is the gun?" said the cop.

Jessie passed him the large sandwich Baggie in which she had put the revolver and loose bullets.

The cop examined it. "Why's a nice lady like you carrying?"

Toby remained with the medics, watching them, studying their movements, gently whispering to Prager, "You're gonna be fine, you're gonna be fine."

The bloody shirtsleeve was torn away, the forearm swaddled in a blue bandage, the arm locked in a clear plastic tube. A third paramedic appeared with a stretcher. Toby helped them lift Prager onto it. They strapped him in. He grew calmer, hugged by the straps, but he was still angry.

"Is there anyone we should call?" asked Caleb. "So we can tell them where you are?"

"Your mother shot me and you want to be nice?"

"Sir," said Henry. "She was following her instincts. Like a mama lion." He spoke with only the faintest hint of a smirk.

Prager looked left and right in a panic when the medics lifted the stretcher. They swung him out the door and down the stairs to the elevator. Toby went with them, carrying Prager's jacket.

A detective arrived, a thirtyish fellow named Plecha. He had two-toned bleached hair, which looked odd on a cop, and a gym body, which looked odder still. Even cops changed with the times. He conferred with the patrolman, then spoke to Molly, then Caleb. He spoke to Henry too, but only because Henry radiated a certain authority. "I know you from somewhere. Like TV or movies."

"It's possible," said Henry. "I *am* an actor."

But Plecha didn't pursue it. He addressed the room. "That's all, folks. You don't have to stay. You can go home. Just don't walk through the blood on your way out, okay?"

People began to leave. A few spoke to Caleb as they passed, saying such things as "Good luck" or "Sorry" or "If you need help, call." Nobody said anything clever or sarcastic, which surprised Caleb. But people prefer to be kind, even theater people. They saved the smart, cool jokes—and there must be jokes—for later.

Plecha put the Baggie with the gun and bullets into a black rubber evidence bag and began to take down addresses and phone numbers.

"So our mom's not under arrest?" said Caleb.

"Of course she's under arrest. There's firearms involved." He looked down at Molly. "I hereby inform you that you have the right to remain silent. Until you are with counsel of your own choosing or assigned by the state."

Molly nodded and offered him her wrists.

"Please," said Plecha. "What kind of asshole do you think I am?"

"You're a reasonable man," purred Henry in his most English accent. "This is a good woman. She's old enough to be a grandmother. You can't possibly arrest her for what was clearly an accident?"

"Sorry, pal. That's for a judge to decide. I'd book my own granny under these circumstances." He helped Molly to her feet.

Molly straightened her dress and picked up her purse. She seemed terribly reasonable herself, disturbingly reasonable, like a robot. "*This* is why I don't like to come into the city," she declared.

"I'll talk to Irene," Caleb told her. "We'll get a lawyer tonight. You won't be there long."

"I'll go with you," said Jessie. "I'm going too," she told Plecha.

"Sorry, miss. You can't ride with us. Procedure. You can meet us there. We're taking her to the Sixth Precinct. Over on Tenth Street."

The cop with the mustache pulled Henry aside. "You're not just any actor. You're the star of *Tom and Gerry.*" The mustache brushed Henry's ear. "How can I get tickets?" he whispered. "My wife'd love me forever if I got us into that show."

Henry told him he'd see what he could do.

The cop rejoined Plecha, and they escorted Molly down the stairs to the elevator. The others followed.

"I'll meet you over there," Jessie called out.

"I'll be there too," said Caleb. "With the lawyer."

Their mother looked so strange stepping into an elevator between a detective and a uniformed cop. She tried to smile at her son and daughter, but the smile looked broken, almost psychotic. Then the elevator door closed and she was gone.

Everyone else started down the stairs. Caleb ran back up to the apartment. "We have to go to the police station," he told Jack. "You can lock up after you finish, can't you?"

"Sure thing, friend. What a night. What can I say? Hey." And his caterer gave him a warm, brotherly hug.

Caleb did not use the elevator but walked down the five flights, worrying about his mother, wondering about Prager, finding the unreality of tonight so, well, unreal. But if a flesh wound isn't real, what is?

Outside there were no police cars or ambulance, no sign that anything extraordinary had happened. It was a soft, mild spring night with herds of people still strolling the street.

The others were waiting for him, not just Jessie, but Frank and Henry.

"Does anyone know what happened to Toby?" said Henry.

Caleb had forgotten about Toby.

"My guess is he went to St. Vincent's with the ambulance," said Frank. "The police station's over this way." He pointed toward Seventh Avenue, and they all started walking.

Caleb saw no point in everyone's going, but they had already started, so he said nothing. He needed other people right now, no matter how superfluous. He felt terribly superfluous himself.

The apartment upstairs was nearly empty. There was nobody on the terrace. A light breeze fluttered the canvas umbrella and blew empty plastic cups off the table, one by one.

Inside the only people left were the two caterers, Jack and Michael, and the cast of *2B*.

"Crazy party," said Dwight. "Psycho party."

"Poor guy," said Jack. "Even if he is a critic. Poor Molly too."

They all knew one another. Dwight, Chris, and Allegra sometimes worked for Jack as cater waiters. Chris and Dwight now helped clean up. Allegra sat cross-legged on a table, eating a piece of Caleb's cake.

"Wow, wow, wow," she said. "Kenneth Prager was at *our* show. And Caleb's mom shot him? He's not gonna think well of tonight."

"Oh well," said Jack. "Maybe next time."

"Just when the fun was starting," sang Chris in a low sweet contralto. "Comes the time for parting."

Jack laughed and sang with her:

Oh well.
We'll catch up
Some other time.

"What do we do about this blood on the carpet?" said Dwight. "Do the police want us to save it? Should we put salt on it?"

"That works only for wine," said Michael. "Look at this. Yuck." He held up the bloody shirtsleeve the paramedics had torn off.

"Bring me the arm of the Buzzard of Off-Broadway," said Allegra. "Maybe we can sell it on eBay."

Meanwhile Jack and Chris continued with the song from *On the Town*, a wry, sad, sweet number with a slippery, difficult tune:

This day was just a token.
Too many words are still unspoken.
Oh well,
We'll catch up
Some other time.

SATURDAY

71

Three-thirteen. The clock on the precinct station wall was like the plain white wall clocks of elementary school. The whole station reminded Jessie of elementary school: bulletin boards, plate-glass partitions, yellow cinder-block walls, fluorescent lights.

She sat with the others in the plastic scoop chairs along the wall, Frank and Henry on her left, Caleb on her right.

"I see," said Caleb. "And what time will that be? You're kidding? You mean nothing could happen until morning?"

He was using Jessie's cell phone to talk to Irene.

"Yes. I know it's Friday night. Or Saturday morning or whatever you want to name it. But don't you think—?"

The station on West Tenth Street was nothing like the police stations their father described in his war stories. A regular Friday Night Fight Club, he told his golf buddies, and the Saturday Night Knife and Gun Club was even wilder. But that was the Bronx in the 1970s. Here cops wandered in and out, and there were occasional arrests—an angry black drag queen, a drunk white college kid with a bloody nose—but things seemed relatively quiet. Jessie couldn't tell if it was just the neighborhood that was different or the decade.

"Right back," she told the others and walked over to the desk sergeant. "Our mother's still here, right? They wouldn't load her into a paddy wagon and send her downtown without telling us, right?"

The sergeant assured her their mother was still here. Jessie returned to her seat.

It'd be different if they could see Mom, but she was out of sight, tucked away in an office down the hall or maybe in a cell.

Jessie's common sense continued to argue with her imagination of disaster. Kenneth Prager couldn't die. Her mother couldn't be charged with murder. But he could sue. Or Mom could be charged with attempted murder. Or carrying a gun without a permit. Or something that would mean they'd spend the rest of their lives in court. There were so many awful things to imagine.

But more confusing was that Molly Doyle had done such a thing in the first place. She pulled out a gun and shot a man. Maybe not deliberately, but the emotion was real, the anger. Jessie was frightened not only *for* her, but *by* her. Who was this lady?

Around the corner, an older man called out, "Molly? Molly Doyle? What in blazes are you doing here?"

Jessie leaned to the left but could see nothing down the hall.

"Jimmy Murtagh," the voice declared. "I used to work with Bobby, rest his soul. So what's this I hear about you and . . ."

The voice disappeared as a door was closed.

Jessie looked at Caleb. He had heard the man too. He paused for a moment, then resumed his talk with Irene.

"I know you're an entertainment lawyer. But if you can't reach that guy, you'll come, right? You promise? Thank you."

He snapped the phone shut and passed it back to Jessie.

"She knows a good defense attorney," he said. "Who she'll try to wake up and get here. If she can't get him, she'll come herself. But we can't expect anyone before six."

Jessie let out a groan. "I can't leave while Mom's still here. I'm afraid they'll move her. Send her elsewhere and then we'll never find her again. I know it's neurotic, but it's how I feel."

Caleb nodded. "I feel the same. But no point in us all waiting. Maybe I should walk over to St. Vincent's and see how Prager is."

Jessie screwed up her eyes at him.

"I won't try to talk him out of pressing charges or anything like that," he told her. "I'd just like to know how he's doing."

"I'll go with you," said Henry.

Caleb frowned. "That won't be necessary."

"But I'd enjoy the walk. And I might be able to reason with Mr. Prager. Better than you. After all, he admires *me*."

Caleb looked at his sister, wondering if she could explain Henry's motive.

She didn't have a clue. "Go ahead," she said. "I'll be fine. I've got Frank here. You'll stay, won't you, Frank?"

He nodded. "Definitely."

Frank seemed pleased that she needed him, and she was glad to have him here. But things were not entirely right between them, were they?

"Fear not," Henry assured her. "All will be fine." And he followed Caleb out the door.

72

It's nothing like the movies, thought Henry. After the big ado—the gunshots, blood, and cops—time stood still the way it does in hospitals. The police station was dull and awful like a hospital. So when Caleb Doyle announced that he was going to visit Prager, Henry seized the chance. "I'll go with you."

Out on the street it was still dark, pleasantly dark after the glare of tube lights. The air was cool and faintly damp like a summer night on Hampstead Heath. The narrow street was lined with scrappy trees like bottle brushes. Henry walked alongside Caleb in silence, content to maintain a stoic, manly peace, for a few minutes anyway.

"Extraordinary," he finally said. "Utterly. And I have to say it: my mother never shot a critic for me."

Caleb grimaced.

Henry quickly added, "She seems like a tough cookie. She can hold her own in there."

"Maybe," muttered Caleb, not looking at Henry.

Henry knew he should probably shut up, but he wanted to talk, he needed to talk. "So, Mr. Doyle. We finally meet. I've heard so much about you. First from your sister. Then from our, uh, friend, Toby."

Caleb shot him a look, then faced forward again. "You can't believe anything you hear from Toby."

"Oh? Because he's still in love with you?"

Caleb grimaced again. "No. He only thinks he's in love with me."

Henry laughed. "Isn't that the same thing? But no. I know exactly what you mean. Often it's just love they love, or something else entirely, and we're caught in the middle."

Caleb looked at him now more kindly, almost friendly. "I don't want to talk about Toby. Why does everyone always want to talk about Toby? What's so special about him?"

Henry thought a moment. "He has a beautiful bottom."

Caleb scowled, as if that were a crude insult. But then he sighed and said, "Yes. He has a beautiful bottom. And he's a good actor. And there's no malice in him. No meanness."

"He's a very good actor. You should see him in this show."

Caleb didn't seem to hear. "But there's no there there with Toby. No core identity. No understanding of the difference between self and others."

Henry smiled, recognizing the traits, pleased to have Caleb talking. "He thinks you can't love him back because you're still in love with a deceased partner."

Caleb's face shut down again. "He told you that, huh? What else did he tell you?"

"Very little. Except that he's in love with you. Which seems to cancel out every other particular." Henry almost asked Caleb if Toby had talked about *him,* but he already knew the answer. "Don't you remember what first love is like? As solid and certain as rock. As stupid as rock too." He laughed lightly. "I must say, I'm disappointed to learn you feel so little for him. I was hoping I'd get to play the Marschallin here and step aside for young love."

Caleb shook his head. "I wanted to fall in love with him. But I couldn't. I didn't. So it was mostly sex. Which was nice. Except he wanted more. And I wanted more. Real conversation. Grown-up talk. Interest in something *besides* us."

"Forgive me for asking, but— Did you find. That Toby. *Liked.* Sex." The question was tougher to ask than he thought it'd be.

Caleb looked startled, confused, amused.

"I see," said Henry. "I suppose it's all me then."

"No, I didn't mean—" said Caleb. "I just— I'm surprised. By your honesty."

But Henry noticed a pleased look on his face, a relieved look. The playwright was human enough to enjoy hearing that his ex wasn't spraying the walls in bliss with another man. Henry didn't need to tell him about the purely symbolic blow job on his roof.

"He liked sex well enough," Caleb finally said. "But in a dutiful, deliberate manner. Like he was a little afraid of it. Maybe he was just afraid of me not loving him back." He made a face. "I'm not still in love with Ben. The dead boyfriend. Toby has no reason to think that. Except that I don't love him but I did love Ben."

"Grief and love are not exclusive," Henry agreed.

Caleb looked over, surprised he understood. "Except this isn't grief grief," he explained. "Ben died six years ago. I don't *violently* miss him. But I miss missing him. Do you understand? Especially now. I wrote a new play and it bombed. Which hurt. It always hurts. But afterward I began to think more about Ben. Like I needed real hurt, real pain, to put the silly pain of bad reviews and a closed show into perspective." He snorted at himself. "But Toby doesn't get it. He thinks it means I'm in love with Ben. But it's more like I'm in love with my loss. Just temporarily. Just for now."

"What was Ben like?" asked Henry. "Was he in theater?"

"No. Which was one of his best traits." He laughed. It was a willed laugh, but he clearly enjoyed talking about Ben. "He taught math in high school, a private school here in New York . . ."

And he described a man who dropped out of grad school to teach kids, who was eight years older than Caleb, who was with Caleb for ten years, who was hardly a saint: he liked to fool around and sometimes used it against Caleb. But these few facts did not mean as much to Henry as the way Caleb spoke about the dead, with warmth but no sugarcoating, an affectionate realism.

Caleb was still talking about Ben when they came out of the side street into a wide, empty boulevard: Seventh Avenue. A solitary bread truck hummed past. The bars and cafés were closed. The only place open was a fruit and vegetable market on the corner. A tall Korean in a chef's hat made of paper stood in the spill of light out front with a golf club, practicing his putt. The night sky in the east was paling into a pretty powder blue.

Caleb pointed to the left and they turned up Seventh. "He was sick for three years," he said. "In and out of hospitals."

"You were his caregiver the whole time?"

Caleb nodded.

"Isn't it a bitch?"

Caleb looked over at Henry.

"I lost Nigel *ten* years ago," said Henry. "I was *his* wet nurse. His doctor, cook, and bum wiper."

He smiled at Caleb, then faced forward again.

"Hard to believe, isn't it? Moonbeam that I am." He shook his head. "I don't like to talk about it. People look at you funny. They treat you as special. Not good or evil, but as damaged, different. I can tell *you* because you've been through it too. You already know. How exhausting it is. How boring. How helpless you feel." The old choke of anger came back into his voice. "So when Nigel finally died—and he was younger than I, fifteen years younger. But when Nigel died, I told myself: That's it. I'm done with being unhappy. I've paid my dues. I will not suffer unnecessarily. Not for love. Not for art. I will suffer no more than is absolutely necessary for my acting." He smiled again, almost sneering, daring Caleb not to believe him.

"You've had no lovers since Nigel?"

"Many lovers, no boyfriends. Young fellows like Toby. Who are wonderful company for a few months. Before they move on. They always move on. And when they do, my heart isn't broken. I don't have the emotion for it. All emotion goes into my work. Actors need low-maintenance boyfriends anyway. Which might explain why I turned in so many bad performances during Nigel's illness."

Henry had wanted to walk with Caleb so that he might know Caleb better. But no, it seemed that he wanted Caleb to know *him*.

"But I'm not entirely certain what I want anymore," he continued. "As implied previously, sex with Toby was not totally successful. But here's what's strange. I didn't care. I still enjoyed being with him. Sometimes. I don't know if it's age or him or hormones. But it's more than that. Part of me wants to find another way to express love besides fucking."

He noticed the confused, cold twist of Caleb's mouth.

"Listen to me," he scoffed. "Your mother just shot a man, and all I can talk about is my changing libido."

"Not at all," said Caleb. "I was just thinking about *my* life. And about Toby. He should be having fun at his age. Not wasting his time pining after an old coot like me."

"Like us, you mean," said Henry. "I agree. When I think of how I wasted *my* twenties. London in the seventies. I went to the parties, but

I didn't partake. I was always working. I was so damned earnest. A gloomy sort of boy. I wasn't terribly out, either. I've been trying to make up for it ever since. Too late. Is this it?"

They were approaching a huge redbrick structure with rounded corners, an enormous building out of scale with the row houses across the street.

"Over here," said Caleb, who clearly knew the place.

He led them past an ambulance loading dock into a waiting area for the emergency room. A plate-glass window faced the street. Inside were molded chairs similar to the chairs in the police station. They had walked from the metaphor of a hospital to a real hospital. A dozen people sat in the chairs; most of them were black, but a few were white, and one was Toby.

He didn't see them come in. He was too busy talking to the man sitting beside him, a handsomely thuggish white man with a crew cut. Henry did not recognize the man until he stood up.

"Mr. Loooz. You are here. Good." It was Sasha, his driver. "I get late to the party. I hear what happened. So I come here. I find Toby. We talk." He twisted around to grin at his new friend.

"Hello," said Toby. He remained seated, looking very solemn, very grave. He gave no special notice to the fact that Henry and Caleb were together. "They're treating his wound. I think he's okay, but they won't let us in. They let his wife in, but not us."

Sasha set a hand on Toby's shoulder. "This is some man. He is a hero, I think." He jostled his shoulder. "A big hero."

He was obviously taken with Toby. And why not? They were roughly the same age. They shared the same beefy blond pinkness, two muscular cherubs, though Sasha was more muscular. His arms were like leg-of-mutton sleeves. Henry couldn't guess what Toby thought of Sasha, but he'd have to be a fool not to be interested.

Caleb was warily eyeing the Russian.

"Sasha, my driver," said Henry. "Caleb Doyle."

"Your mother shot the man!" He eagerly shook Caleb's hand. "Very sad story! So sad!"

Caleb glanced at Henry, as if to ask if Henry suspected what Caleb suspected, and why did they suspect it? Only then did Henry feel it: a tiny stab of jealousy, like a splinter in his pride.

"We should find Prager," Henry declared and hurried over to the receiving window. "We're here to see Kenneth Prager."

"Are you family?"

"In a manner of speaking." He smiled his wittiest smile. "We're in theater and he's a critic. He gave me a rave notice and my friend here a bad one. You could say we're bound as close as any family."

The nurse was not convinced. She said they could fill out a message card, however, and she'd take it in to him. "Or you can speak to his wife. That's her coming out now."

A confused-looking woman in a man's windbreaker slipped through the swinging door.

"Mrs. Prager?" said Henry. "We're friends of your husband. We came down to see if there was anything we could do."

She looked up, squinty and red-eyed. "Yes? Who? Sorry. I absolutely need a cigarette right now. Can you talk to me outside?"

They followed her out to the sidewalk. She didn't seem to know who Henry was, which was just as well. She lit up a cigarette, filled her lungs with smoke, and gratefully exhaled.

"How is he?" asked Caleb. "I can't tell you how sorry I am about what happened. Really."

"He's fine. He was scared out of his wits, but he's fine now." She sounded remarkably calm. "I'm surprised it didn't happen sooner. That it doesn't happen all the time." She shook her head. "It shows how civilized the world really is."

"There is nothing like being shot at to make one appreciate the rest of one's life," Henry offered.

She automatically nodded. "So who was this crazy lady anyway? An insulted actress? A failed writer?"

"Uh, no. She's my mother," said Caleb. "I'm the failed writer."

Gretchen Prager stared at him. "Your mother. Your *mother*?" And she burst out laughing. She bent forward and it spilled out, hard little cackles of mirth.

Henry and Caleb looked on in disbelief, Caleb openmouthed like a fish.

She abruptly recovered. "Sorry," she said. "Not funny. No." She straightened up, blinking and gasping, trying to catch her breath. "I know it's not funny." She faced Caleb again. "But your *mother*?"

73

The police station remained quiet. It somehow felt both eerie and drab, like a spook house with fluorescent lights. Jessie looked back at the clock. It was just after five.

"Want something to eat or drink?" said Frank. "I could go out and look for an open deli."

"No. But if you want to go get something for yourself, go ahead," said Jessie. "Or you can go home if you like. I'm fine. Really."

"No, I'll stay. I'm fine too." He leaned back and folded his arms.

"I really liked your play tonight," said Jessie. "I liked it a lot."

"Thanks," said Frank, but in a dry, automatic manner.

"I'm not just making small talk," she said. "I *do* like it."

He looked at her more closely. "Thank you very much then." It didn't sound terribly different from his first thank-you.

"Frank? Why're we still angry with each other? We have so much in common. We should be real close. Especially now."

His sleepy eyes opened a little wider in his round face. His face looked rounder than usual, the muscles slack with fatigue.

"This should be a lesson to us all," he said, sounding lightly sarcastic. "There's no telling when someone's gonna pull out a gun and start shooting. So don't sweat the small stuff."

Jessie narrowed her eyes at him. "We're not small stuff."

"Not us." The sarcasm vanished. "Our pride. Our egos."

"Yours or mine?"

"I was thinking of mine. But you're not innocent either."

Jessie drew a deep breath, tempted to argue. Then she said, "No. I'm not. But you need some pride to get along in life. Some ego."

"But our egos have gotten all tangled up in our affection." He looked away for a moment. "We feel we don't deserve to be loved unless we're successful."

"I told you back at the party. I'm a loser too. Remember?"

"You don't really believe that."

She hesitated. "No. Not really. I'm having a great time playing Octopus Lady. And I'm good at it. But I have no illusions about Henry needing me or keeping me. No, when he finishes here and heads off to Capri or wherever, he's going to forget about all of us. Which is fine." Was it? She hoped so. "Working for him will make a good story. But it'll be small potatoes compared to this one."

Frank was looking at her, surprised, concerned. "We said some really vicious things to each other the other night."

"I know. And I'm sorry."

"I'm sorry too." His *sorry* sounded almost as dry as his *thank you.* He frowned. "But I *am* in love with you."

"You love me like a pig loves mud," she told him.

"Yes," he said flatly. It wasn't a pretty phrase. "Which leaves me naked. I have a harder time forgiving you than you must have forgiving me. Because you're *not* in love."

"No," she admitted. "Not like you."

He did not look hurt. He wasn't being manipulative, merely factual.

"But I don't want to lose you," she told him. "I don't want us to have to be all or nothing."

"Me neither. But I might have no choice. It's hard to be friends with an unrequited love. It can make you crazy. It can make you act like a real shit."

"It's no picnic for the beloved either," she argued. "Feeling guilty all the time. Getting sick of seeing puppy-dog eyes."

They looked at each other, frowning, squinting, swallowing. They were nothing like puppy dogs now.

"Jessikins!" a gruff male voice called out. "My God. Will you look at you. Little Jessikins ain't so little anymore."

A stocky red-faced man in his sixties strode into the room, holding out his hand, necktie flapping against his belly.

"Remember your Uncle Jimmy? I'm Captain Murtagh now."

"Oh my," said Jessie. She jumped up and shook his hand. She did not remember him—he must be one of the cops who regularly visited them in Beacon when she was a toddler—but she played along. "I can't believe you're not retired yet."

"Not dead, you mean. You and me both, sister. Good thing I was here tonight, though. No telling what might have happened to your dear old . . ."

Jessie saw her behind the captain: Mom, walking very slowly, uncertainly, looking somewhat *miffed*. There was no other word for her expression. The face was pinched and proud, like that of someone who was embarrassed but refusing to show it. Jessie was confused. She had been so full of fear for her mother that she didn't know what to think when she saw Mom looking so, well, like Mom. Nothing was changed. Her blouse and skirt were clean, her beige hair neatly waved, her purse still at her side.

"Now, Molly," Captain Murtagh was saying. "You have to be at court on Monday. Like with a traffic violation. Except here there's hell to pay if you don't show. As of now you're charged only with illegal possession and reckless endangerment. But a judge in a bad mood could change it all to attempted murder. So you better be nice."

"Thank you. You've been a big help, Jimmy," said Mom in a surprisingly perfunctory manner.

"I'm just glad I was here to pull a few strings. It's the least I could do for Mrs. Bobby Doyle."

Mom gave him a nod and a pained smile and hurried outside.

The captain turned to Jessie. "Don't worry. She's a cop's widow. No judge in his right mind will throw the book at her. But right now she needs sleep. That's why she's a little wacky. Take her to your brother's place and put her to bed. Oh, and don't forget this." He gave Jessie an official form, the summons or citation, like a doctor handing over a prescription for an elderly patient.

Jessie joined her mother outside. She stood on the sidewalk with Frank.

"Did you want me to get you a cab, Mrs. Doyle?"

"Not at all. I can walk," she said crisply. "Where're we going?" She stared at Frank. "*Who* are you?"

"This is Frank," said Jessie. "My boyfriend." It just slipped out, but nobody seemed to notice. "We can go back to Caleb's and you can get some sleep. Before you go home to Beacon. You want to walk?"

"Yes, I'd like that. I need the air." She started walking, Jessie and Frank joining her on either side.

The sun was not yet up, but the street was full of light, a soft wash of color. The birds were singing, always a nice surprise in the city. The sweetness of the sound made Jessie feel sadder, more tender. She took her mother's arm.

"Don't be silly." Mom tugged her arm back. "I'm fine. Perfectly fine. You don't have to fuss over me. I just thank my lucky stars I don't live here and nobody knows me. Because God knows what they'd think seeing me being let out of jail at the crack of dawn."

Frank gave Jessie a worried look, as if this were strange behavior, but Mom was only being herself.

Sooner than expected, they were crossing Seventh Avenue to Sheridan Square. Caleb's building was closer to the police station in daylight than it had been at night. Jessie used her keys to get in the front door. There was no answer upstairs when she knocked. She went ahead and opened the door, dreading the mess inside.

But the apartment was neat and orderly, the rooms full of early-morning shadow, nothing more. You would never know there had been a party here last night, much less a shooting.

"Mom? Why don't you go lie down in Caleb's room. Get a little sleep. You'll feel better."

Her cell phone rang. It was Caleb at the hospital. Frank walked Mom over to the bedroom while Jessie talked to Caleb.

"Only a flesh wound," he reported. "Prager's fine. The shot ripped his arm like a knife, but nothing was permanently damaged."

Jessie told him *her* good news.

"You're kidding. They just let her out? No bail or nothing? Jimmy Murtagh? I remember him. He was Dad's partner in Pelham Bay, a bachelor cop who lived with his mother. All right, I better call Irene and tell her we won't need a lawyer today. I'll be home in an hour or so. Henry? Oh yeah, he's still here. See you shortly. Bye."

Frank returned from the bedroom and she relayed the news.

"Good," he said. "One less thing to worry about."

"I should tell Mom too, before she falls asleep."

But she found Mom just sitting on the bed, feet on the floor, hands balled in her lap. "I can't sleep in a strange bed," she said. "And I don't have any pajamas."

"Oh, Mom. It's Caleb's bed. A family bed. Here. I'll find you something to sleep in." She knelt at his dresser and began to open drawers. "That was Caleb on the phone. He said Prager is fine. The bullet wound is no worse than a nasty cut."

"Thank God for that." She remained seated upright on the bed, as rigid as an Egyptian statue.

"Mom? Are you okay? How are you feeling?" Jessie sat beside her. She took her hand. The skin was cold but the pulse clear.

"I'm fine!" Again she pulled away, yanking her hand back. "Why shouldn't I be fine? It was an accident, for chrissake. Everybody carries on like I did it deliberately. Which is ridiculous. Which is such malarkey when nobody—"

She twisted around and seized Jessie's shoulders with both hands. She buried her face in Jessie's neck.

"I almost killed him!" she cried. "I could have killed him!"

Jessie was too stunned to speak or move. A hot, wet oven of tears pressed against her collar.

"I can't do anything right! I either love you too much or love you too little! You and your brother get so unhappy. I'm a terrible mother. There's nothing I can do to show my love except try to protect you. So I almost killed a man!"

Jessie timidly lifted a hand. She petted her mother's shoulder, she stroked her mother's hair.

"This city scares me. But I'm the one who's scary. I'm dangerous. I'm crazy. I should be terrified of *me*, not the city."

"You're not crazy," whispered Jessie. She felt tears prick her eyes, then fill her eyes and spill down her cheeks. She wrapped both arms around her mother and held her tight. "You're not crazy," she repeated. She wanted to say something wise and tender in response to her mother's need. But all she could offer was, "You're not crazy."

When her sobbing passed, Jessie released her. And she saw Molly's face, wet and twisted. She was terrified that her mother would be furious with her for seeing her like this. But if your daughter can't see you in pain, who can?

"Here," said Jessie. "You can wear this." She handed her the T-shirt she'd found in the drawer and had held in her lap all this time, a shirt from *Venus in Furs* with the cartoon Claire Wade face/logo.

"Thank you," said Molly, spreading the shirt on the bed. "Very much." She pretended to thank her for the shirt, but Jessie understood she was thanking her for not making too much of her confusion and panic and tears.

Jessie wiped away her own tears with the heel of her hand. She got up and drew the calico curtain over the casement window. "So you can sleep," she said. "We'll all feel better after a little sleep."

Molly nodded and Jessie gave her mother a motherly kiss on the cheek. A wet glaze remained on both their faces.

Frank was not in the living room. Jessie was grateful that he'd kept away when she was with Mom, but now she was afraid he'd gone home.

She found him in the office, stretched on the daybed under the bookcase, looking at Caleb's copy of *Chaos* by James Gleick.

"Do you understand that science crap?" she said.

"No. But the pictures are pretty." He held open the book on a computer-generated photo of manic paisley patterns, like a gorgeous mess of clockwork gears. "Here," he said and put the book down and scooted over to make room for her.

"Sure," she said and kicked off her shoes and lay beside him.

"How is she?" he asked.

"Wigged out. I can't guess half of what she's feeling right now. But I wonder if she knows everything she's feeling." Jessie idly tugged at one of Frank's fingers. "Poor Mom. I'm always afraid I need her more than she needs me. But now? She needs me more."

She lifted Frank's arm so she could snuggle into his armpit and get more room on the narrow bed. She liked having him beside her, a solid weight like half a hug.

"Or not more," she corrected herself. "As much. She needs me as much. Maybe."

74

The sun rose and the birds sang louder. There was a riot of birdsong. One would never guess so many birds lived down here, hidden in the trees behind the cafés and stores and tenement buildings.

An early Saturday morning in New York can be so beautiful, especially when you know that a man wasn't killed and your mother won't be going to jail—not this week anyway. Caleb strolled down Seventh Avenue with Henry. They had been together long enough, and liked each other well enough, that they could be companionably silent. They were the only pedestrians in sight, except for a young woman walking a fat white bulldog wheezing like an asthmatic pig. An isolated handful of cars and trucks roared down the wide avenue.

"What a night," said Henry. "What a drama. 'We have heard the chimes at midnight, Master Shallow.' "

"Were you ever fat enough to play Falstaff?"

"No. But it'd be lovely, wouldn't it? To forget about exercise for a few months? Get fat in the name of art? Which way is uptown? I should be going home."

"You can catch a cab here and it'll turn around," said Caleb.

But the avenue was deserted at the moment.

"How remarkable," said Henry. "I can't remember the last time I witnessed daybreak sober. When I wasn't stumbling out of a club with some pretty piece of tail. But here I am with a clear head, going home alone. It makes one feel very virtuous. Or very old."

"Too bad I have a full house," said Caleb. "Or I might invite you home with me."

Henry stared at Caleb. "Oh. I see. You're kidding."

"I am and I'm not." Caleb *was* kidding until he saw that Henry took him seriously. And suddenly Caleb was interested. He shrugged. "We've shared everything else," he admitted.

"We certainly have." He looked Caleb up and down, brazen and satirical, yet Caleb felt a sexual shiver, as if goosed. "Too bad I have a matinee today."

"And I have a full house," Caleb repeated.

"And I don't think we're each other's type."

"We'd probably just lie in bed and talk."

Henry produced a sly grin. "We *could* ask Toby to join us."

Caleb froze. Then he burst out laughing. "Uh-uh. Sorry. That's way too sophisticated for me."

"Oh well," said Henry sweetly. "Just an idea. But thank you for asking. It's always nice to be asked. Oh look. Here comes a taxi."

He stepped off the curb and waved. A block away, a lone cab saw him and swung toward their side of the street.

Henry turned to Caleb. "This has been an adventure. I'm glad we were able to share it." And he stepped back up on the curb with one foot, lifting his face into Caleb's face, and kissed him, hard.

It was a deep kiss in broad daylight, full of tongue and teeth.

The cab stood by, waiting.

Henry released him and dropped back down to the gutter, grinning. Then he jumped into the cab and drove away.

Caleb remained at the curb, catching his breath, then laughing. Did Henry's kiss say "Let's fuck" or simply "Fuck it"? Probably the latter, which was fine with Caleb. He resumed his walk home.

He liked Henry. He liked him very much. Jessie was right. Henry was not a bad fellow. But like all actors, the successful ones anyway, he *was* a people pleaser. So much so that Caleb wondered if he should trust his liking of him. Henry meant to win Caleb over, and Caleb was won. It had been fun to flirt. Caleb did not regret flirting. But he was relieved that he and Hamlet would not be seeing each other naked anytime soon.

Caleb entered his elevator, the door closed, and he remembered everything else. He had no business being happy. Nothing was settled yet. So much was left unresolved. God only knows what Dr. Chin would say when he saw her on Monday. And she thought that he was done with Kenneth Prager.

The elevator arrived. He dreaded what he'd find: the mess of the party, his mother and sister fighting, something awful. He trudged up the flight of stairs, unlocked his door, and—

The place was spotless. It was cleaner than it was *before* the party. It was quiet, so quiet that it felt haunted. But not haunted by ghosts. He heard people sleeping.

He stepped gently over the floor, afraid to disturb the peace. Snores came from the other side of the living room, not his bedroom but his office. If all the animals were asleep, then he could go to sleep too. He could wait until later to deal with the messes.

He heard a kitchen drawer grind shut. He turned the corner.

She stood in the kitchen, his mother. She was not startled; she'd heard him come in. "I couldn't sleep," she said. "I was looking for warm milk or beer or something to help me doze off."

Her face looked vague and colorless without its lipstick. She was wearing his robe, which swam on her. She shyly wrapped it tighter around her waist. Under the robe was a ratty T-shirt with a picture of Claire Wade.

"I could make some chamomile tea," he said. "I could use some myself." He went over to the sink and began to fill the kettle.

They had so much to say to each other. He didn't know where to begin. So he said, "Who's snoring? Is that Jessie's friend Frank?"

"No. It's Jessie. You didn't know your sister snores?"

"She's just full of surprises, isn't she?"

"Don't make fun of your sister."

"I didn't mean anything bad. She's surprising in a good way. We don't have to stand. Let's sit while we wait for the water to boil."

They went out to the living room. The sofa was back in its place facing the television. They settled into opposite corners.

"How're you doing?" he asked. "You okay?"

"You don't have to worry about me. Your sister got an earful of *that*. A pity party for myself. But I was exhausted. I feel better now. I'm more myself again. Even though I'm having the damnedest time falling asleep in a strange bed."

Caleb wondered what Jessie had heard. They knew two very different sides of Mom. If she got under Jessie's skin more than she got under his, Jessie was also closer to their mother than Caleb. He envied her the knowledge if not the aggravation.

He noticed something lodged in the wood by his shoe, like a misplaced nail. It was a bullet. It burrowed in the varnished wood, as if trying to hide. It was ludicrous to pretend nothing extraordinary had happened here. But where to begin?

"I know things got out of hand last night," said Caleb. "But I can't help feeling touched by what you did. I never knew my work meant so much to you." It was not really about his "work," but he didn't know how else to say it.

She made a face at him, a skeptical grimace. "It was very stupid of me. Very foolish."

"I know. But nobody got killed. So it was a beautiful gesture."

"Yes. It'll make a very funny story," she bitterly declared. "One that you'll be telling your friends for years and years."

"Why not? I like funny stories. So do you."

"Not when I'm in them!"

The kettle whistled. Caleb jumped up and escaped to the kitchen. He busied himself with the tea: setting bags in the mugs, pouring the hot water, letting the bags steep.

He didn't know what else to say to her. He didn't know yet what needed to be said. It would take hours spread out over weeks and months. All he really wanted to tell her this morning was: Thank you, I love you, Are you okay?

He thought that he'd said those things already.

75

Toby woke up in his room on West 104th Street. Sunlight spilled through the blinds, painting yellow stripes over the floor and futon and the sheet that covered the large nude body sprawled beside him: Sasha, the Russian. He lay on his back with the sheet pulled up to his belly button, an arm thrown over his crew cut, the cup of his armpit fizzy with blond fur. His red lips were drawn back from his big teeth in a joyful smile. It took Toby a moment to realize that Sasha was still asleep.

Most of the men that Toby slept with looked better dressed than naked. Not Sasha. He was beautiful naked. Usually Toby couldn't wait to get out of bed the next morning, take a shower, and be "good" again. But not today. Sasha looked so humpy. Toby barely knew him—he didn't even know his last name—but sex last night had been perfect, as hot and mutual and easy as the sex in dreams.

Toby wanted to stay in bed forever, but he needed to pee. He got up and pulled a pair of gym shorts over his cumbersome erection. His clothes were happily strewn over the floor with Sasha's. They both wore Old Navy jeans and 2(x)ist briefs.

Out in the hall Toby saw nobody, but he heard the TV in the living room: a boring Sunday-morning news show. It still felt funny that their home was also their stage. They had given another performance last night, and it went well again, even after the craziness on Friday. But the gunshot wound and ambulance ride felt like weeks ago. It felt like weeks since he'd met Sasha too, but both events were only thirty-six hours old. There had been a reporter in the audience last night, but it wasn't half as exciting as seeing Sasha in the front row. He had come to see Toby. Standing over the toilet, Toby couldn't help sniffing his own shoulder and smelling another man's brand of soap there.

He hurried back to his room, whipped off the shorts, and hopped under the sheet. He crawled against Sasha, laying an arm across his chest, a leg over his middle. He wanted to be here when Sasha woke up. He was amazed by how happy he felt, how joyful.

He heard the front door open and close. There were voices in the living room. Feet stamped over the floor.

A fist knocked on Toby's door and the door flew open.

Allegra charged in, followed by Dwight and Melissa. "Look, look!" They shook a fat tabloid newspaper at him, the Sunday *Post*. "Do you believe this? Do you fucking believe this?"

They all crouched around the futon, paying no attention to the other body.

Across the middle of the front page was a washed-out color photo of a young man on his knees beside an old man on his back. They weren't doing anything dirty. Toby couldn't figure it out until he read the headline—"Everybody's a Critic"—and the caption—"Actor gives first aid to gunned theater reviewer."

"You're famous!" cried Melissa.

"They talk about you!" said Allegra. "They talk about us!"

"We're all gonna be famous!" said Dwight.

Toby propped himself up on an elbow and opened the paper. Inside was a story, two full pages with black-and-white photos: an old picture of Caleb looking stuffy; a police mug shot of Caleb's mom, front view only, looking drunk; a fancy-dress photo of Kenneth Prager, the wounded man—he was theater reviewer for the *Times?*—and finally, Toby himself, an ugly old head shot—where did they find that?— of a skinny dork with a shaggy *Brady Bunch* haircut. There was no picture of Henry, which surprised Toby and pleased him.

He felt Sasha waking behind him, rolling over, and seeing the people around them. Sasha didn't care. He scooted up behind Toby and embraced him from the back, locking both arms around Toby's chest. "That is you?" he murmured at Toby's shoulder.

Toby turned back to the front page.

"Look at the byline," said Dwight. "Cameron Ditchley. He must have been the guy who took the picture."

"See!" said Allegra. "They mention the play. They give the title and the address. We're gonna go through the roof tonight."

"It's still a showcase," said Melissa. "We can charge only fifteen bucks, right?"

"Oh fuck Equity," said Allegra. "We're not legal anyway. People are gonna pay through the nose to see our celebrity here. And that's just the beginning. Everybody's gonna talk about this for *weeks*."

But Toby stopped listening. He lay among admiring friends, naked under his sheet, snug in the muscular life jacket of Sasha's arms, Sasha's boner nuzzled against his bottom—he was hard too—while he gazed at himself on the front page of the *New York Post*.

Could the world get any sweeter?

AUTHOR'S NOTE

This novel was written with the generous help of a fellowship from the Guggenheim Foundation.

I was also helped by friends who remain my sharpest, toughest readers: Victor Bumbalo, Mary Gentile, Damien Jack, Paul Russell, Ed Sikov, and Brenda Wineapple. My agent, Edward Hibbert, shared both his literary expertise and his experience in his other profession, acting. Neil Olson and Jesse Dorris provided important support and advice. I owe special thanks to my editor, Meaghan Dowling, her assistant, Rome Quezada, and my copyeditor, Shelly Perron.

Even more than on previous books, Draper Shreeve gave me so much here, not just his intelligence, humor, and sanity but also his first-hand knowledge of the world of circus animals. He brought me into that world. I could not have written this novel without him.

 Perennial

Books by Christopher Bram:

LIVES OF THE CIRCUS ANIMALS: *A Novel*
ISBN 0-06-054254-3 (paperback)
A *NEW YORK TIMES* NOTABLE BOOK

Leaping from one life to another, one day to the next, *Lives of the Circus Animals* throws playwrights, theater critics, actors, and their personal assistants together in a serious comedy about love, work, and make-believe. A look at theater people who are just like everyone else, only more so, it's a comic celebration of how we all strive to stay sane while living in the shadow of those two impostors, success and failure.

"A biting comedy of manners. . . .Lively, useful, whip-smart." —*Entertainment Weekly*

"[A] sexy, witty novel." —*Detroit Free Press*

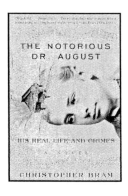

THE NOTORIOUS DR. AUGUST
His Real Life and Crimes
ISBN 0-06-093497-2 (paperback)

A sweeping chronicle of the sixty years from the Civil War to the early 1920s. Augustus Fitz William Boyd (alias Dr. August), an improvisational pianist, is in love with Isaac Kemp, an ex-slave who sometimes returns his affections. Isaac Kemp is also involved with prim white governess Alice Pangborn. Locked in the strange and painful love triangle, the three travel the world until a tragedy forces them to examine their choices and upsets their relationships in ways that could not be foreseen.

"Wonderful. . . . Impressive. . . . The novel is about what it means to be a human being in a complicated world." —*New York Times Book Review*

"A true epic . . . examining love, sex, race, and the meaning of art in spectacularly entertaining detail." —*Washington Post Book World*

.